She _must_ resist the rogue's allure . . .
and a passion that tells her to submit.

A

*He'd just settled in when he heard
a movement near the door.*

And there she stood again, poised in the doorway, her hair the color of fire and autumn leaves with those few silvery strands glinting like moonlight. He met her gaze and felt his heart speed a few beats faster.

For my own sanity, I ought to dismiss her, he thought, wishing he felt nothing but calm disinterest in her presence.

But exactly as she'd promised, she'd seen to the efficient management of his household, which was humming along as smoothly as it ever had under Mrs. Beatty's reign. She was performing her job, and he had no legitimate cause to terminate her employment. No reason, that is, other than his own unwanted desire for her.

No, he admonished himself, *I am a man, not a beast, and I will govern my needs—even if it may kill me.*

By Tracy Anne Warren

THE BED AND THE BACHELOR
WICKED DELIGHTS OF A BRIDAL BED
AT THE DUKE'S PLEASURE
SEDUCED BY HIS TOUCH
TEMPTED BY HIS KISS

TRACY ANNE WARREN

The Bed and the Bachelor

AVON

An Imprint of HarperCollinsPublishers

This is a work of fiction. Names, characters, places, and incidents are products of the author's imagination or are used fictitiously and are not to be construed as real. Any resemblance to actual events, locales, organizations, or persons, living or dead, is entirely coincidental.

AVON BOOKS
An Imprint of HarperCollins*Publishers*
10 East 53rd Street
New York, New York 10022-5299

First Avon Books mass market printing: August 2011

*Each story is a labor of perseverance,
imagination and love.*

*To my wonderful fans,
who come along for the ride.*

Acknowledgments

My sincere gratitude to—
My editor, Lucia Macro,
and my agent, Helen Breitwieser.
Emmanuelle Jappont for her invaluable assistance
with French expressions and translations.
Merci beaucoup, Manue!
My kitty cats—
Christofur, Violetta and Georgianna—
who always keep me company while I write.
And last, but never least,
to Leslie.
I couldn't do it without you, sis.

The Bed and the
Bachelor

Byron Family Tree

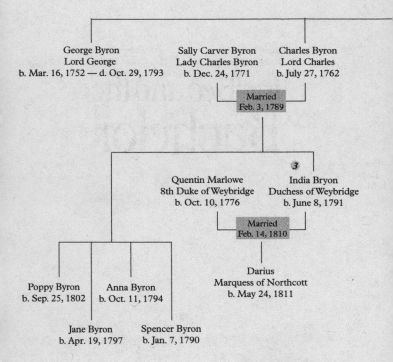

George Byron
Lord George
b. Mar. 16, 1752 — d. Oct. 29, 1793

Sally Carver Byron
Lady Charles Byron
b. Dec. 24, 1771

Charles Byron
Lord Charles
b. July 27, 1762

Married
Feb. 3, 1789

3

Quentin Marlowe
8th Duke of Weybridge
b. Oct. 10, 1776

India Bryon
Duchess of Weybridge
b. June 8, 1791

Married
Feb. 14, 1810

Darius
Marquess of Northcott
b. May 24, 1811

Poppy Byron
b. Sep. 25, 1802

Anna Byron
b. Oct. 11, 1794

Jane Byron
b. Apr. 19, 1797

Spencer Byron
b. Jan. 7, 1790

1 *Tempted By His Kiss*
2 *Seduced By His Touch*
3 *Four Dukes and a Devil*
4 *At the Duke's Pleasure*
5 *Wicked Delights of a Bridal Bed*

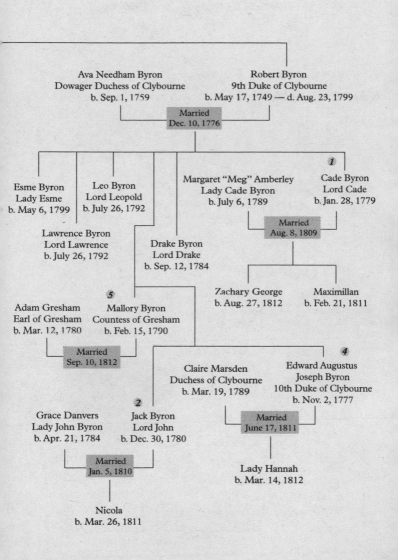

The Bed and the
Bachelor

Chapter 1

London, England
April 1813

*L*ord Drake Byron strode briskly into his study, wiping chalk dust off his hands onto a white silk handkerchief. He'd come directly from his workshop, where he'd been deeply immersed in formulating his newest mathematical theorem. But as his butler had interrupted to bluntly remind him, his appointment was waiting—and had been waiting for the good part of the past hour.

He cast a quick glance at the back of the bonnet-clad woman seated before his desk, noting the correct set of her shoulders inside her serviceable dark blue gown. He supposed she had every right to be irritated by the delay. Then again, waiting was a servant's lot in life, was it not?

If he decided to hire her for the housekeeping job, she would simply have to get used to his erratic and unpredictable habits. She would also need to have a strong constitution, enough so that the occasional unintentional explosion from one of his experiments didn't send her into a paroxysm of nervous terror. He'd lost more than one housemaid that way, girls too delicate to abide the bangs, booms and acrid smells that emanated through the town house from time to time.

His mother still worried that he might blow himself up, but over the years she and the rest of his family had come to accept his interests and eccentricities and given up any attempts at changing him. At present, however, she had no cause for concern since he was once again indulging his love of theoretical mathematics rather than his fascination for scientific invention.

Still, he hadn't meant to be late for today's interview. Though come to think, he never *meant* to be late for anything. He just got so involved sometimes, he completely forgot the hour.

"My apologies for keeping you waiting," he said as he rounded his desk and took a seat. "I was working and could not break away." Without looking up, he rifled through the papers scattered in tall stacks across the polished walnut surface, thumbing through several before pulling a page free.

"The—um—employment service sent over your credentials, Mrs.—Greenway." He perused the page, still not glancing up. "I haven't had time yet to review your background in depth, so why do you not just tell me about yourself. I assume you brought references?"

"Yes, your lordship," she answered in a gentle, silvery voice that put him in mind of birdsong, summer breezes and, strangely enough, warm sheets tangled after a lusty tumble. "I have them right here."

A shiver slid like the tip of a hot finger down his spine. Looking up, he stared.

He'd expected a middle-aged woman, someone plump perhaps, and motherly, like his previous housekeeper. But this woman was neither plump nor middle-aged, and she didn't put him at all in mind of his mother. Nor any mother with whom he'd ever been acquainted, come to that. Quite the opposite, in fact, he thought as he took in her slender figure and youthful countenance.

How the deuced young is she? he wondered, studying her features.

Glancing down again, he gave the character in his hand a quick skim.

Name: *Mrs. Anne Greenway*
Marital Status: *Widow*
Age: *29*

Nine-and-twenty? How could this young woman seated across from him be a full year older than he? If he hadn't just read her credentials, he wouldn't have believed it possible for her to be more than a handful of years out of the schoolroom. Then again, he supposed determining a person's actual age was an inexact science. As were looks, for though she wasn't pretty in the classical sense, there was something undeniably appealing about her. She was . . . vibrant, her ivory complexion and high, smooth cheeks dusted the delicate hue of just-picked apricots. Her face was heart-shaped with long-lashed, whiskey gold eyes, a long, straight nose and full, rosy lips that looked as if they'd been formed for the express purpose of being kissed.

But it was her hair, which she'd braided and ruthlessly pinned into a bun beneath her bonnet, that surprised him the most. From what he could discern, the strands were a lush array of autumnal colors ranging from deepest brown to warm red and pale gold. Yet threaded among them were a surprising number of silvery strands that gleamed like the precious metal itself.

She is going grey, he mused.

Maybe she really was nine-and-twenty, after all.

"I believe you'll find everything in order," she ventured in that lyrical voice of hers. Leaning forward, she held out a piece of fine cream-colored vellum, her hand small inside a dark blue glove.

Frowning, he paused for a moment before accepting the character. Opening the page, he began to read.

"You appear to come highly recommended," he said. "You last worked for the Donald family in Armadale, Scotland, I see. I'm not familiar with the town. Where is it located?"

"In the far north on the Isle of Skye."

"Ah, and why did you leave?"

A faint scowl briefly marred her features. "The . . . family decided to emigrate to America, as so many of the Scots have done in recent years. I had no wish to follow them."

"You're not Scottish yourself," he said, his words a statement rather than a question. "From your accent, you sound English. The Lake District, if I'm not mistaken."

Actually, she sounded amazingly cultured as well, he decided. Had he not known better, he would have taken her for a member of the gentry at least. But then, upper servants often worked at erasing the broad vowels and dropped consonants of their birth in an effort to improve themselves and their opportunities.

She raised an eyebrow in surprise. "Yes, that is correct."

"And Scotland? How did you come to be employed at such a distance from your home?"

Her gaze lowered to her hands. "The Donalds advertised, much as you have done, my lord. After my husband died, I found myself in need of a situation. Prior to my marriage, I'd worked in service, first as a housemaid, then as a lady's maid. Employment as a housekeeper seemed a much better prospect."

He nodded, glancing again at her credentials. "You have no children, correct?"

"No, none."

"And you believe London will be to your liking? It's very different from a village in the north." Briefly, he paused. "There is also the fact that I am an unmarried man with a household that is not at all similar to the one to which I expect you are accustomed. With no wife, nor any wish to obtain one, I tend to come and go as I please with no regular routine. I may spend one week locked inside my workroom and the next decide to throw an impromptu gathering for friends. Should you find yourself in my employ, you will perforce need to adjust to a continually changing environment."

A curiously wry expression crossed her face. "I believe you will discover that I am quite adaptable to any situation, my lord. As for the running of your household, I expect one domicile is very like another at its heart, so I see no difficulty in its management, however unpredictable your schedule may be."

She drew a breath before continuing. "As for London, city life suits me perfectly at present. I am looking forward to the excitement and change of new things."

"Hmmph," he said, the sound an indecisive exhale beneath his breath.

That is precisely what troubles me, he thought, *new things and the potential excitement and change of having her in my house.*

She was far too attractive, and despite her stated age, much too young-looking for comfort. Were he interested in taking a new mistress, well, that would be a different story entirely. He'd have her installed in her own neat little town house in a trice. But she wasn't there to warm his bed, and he wasn't the sort of man who took advantage of his maidservants—or his housekeeper. Then again, he'd never had cause before to be so sorely tempted by a member of his domestic staff, even a prospective one.

If only his former housekeeper, Mrs. Beatty, hadn't decided to quit so abruptly last month. Entirely without warning, she'd given her notice and announced with a nervous urgency that belied her usually steadfast nature, that she was leaving for the seaside. "My health isn't what it used to be," she told him, "and my doctor suggests a milder clime."

She'd always appeared in the peak of health as far as Drake could see, but how was he to argue? And so, with little more than a week's notice, she'd packed her bags and taken a hired coach out of the city as fast as it could go.

Glancing down again, he studied the papers in his hand.

Mrs. Greenway seemed exceptionally well qualified to be sure, and heaven knows he had no interest in being put to the bother of interviewing more candidates, and yet . . .

Laying her credentials aside, he met her lovely golden gaze and prepared to do what he ought.

If only she weren't so dashed appealing.

He's not going to hire me, Sebastianne Dumont realized, her nails flexing deep into the brown cotton twill of the reticule on her lap. Her heart beat like a trapped bird in her chest, alarm squeezing painfully beneath her ribs.

But he has to hire me. Anything else is unthinkable.

The interview had seemed to be going so well at first, the answers she'd practiced with such determined concentration rolling easily off her tongue. She'd thought he seemed impressed, but then he'd grown quiet, contemplative. Her fingers clenched tighter as she mentally reviewed his questions and her responses.

Did I make a mistake?

Has he figured out that nearly every word I've told him is a lie?

But how could he know she was lying when her script had been so well researched, so carefully prepared by those who made a profession of deceiving others?

She knew Napoleon's men had gone to great lengths to arrange this position for her so she could gain entry into Lord Drake Byron's house. They'd made sure his former housekeeper left her longtime situation—using cash and threats to pave the way.

She knew they'd made sure she, Sebastianne Dumont, would be the one sent by the employment service for this interview.

She knew they expected her not only to obtain the housekeeping position but to retrieve the information they wanted as well.

There could be no failure. For if she did not succeed, the price would be beyond redemption and cost her everything she most loved in this world.

As for her prospective employer, he wasn't at all how she'd imagined him.

Over the years, she'd heard her mathematician father mention Lord Drake as one of today's brightest lights in the fields of science, theoretical physics, and mathematics. A prodigy who'd earned advanced degrees from Cambridge and Oxford before his twentieth birthday, he'd won a number of prestigious awards, including the Copley Medal.

Had there not been a war raging in her homeland of France and elsewhere across Europe, she was sure he would have been welcomed on the Continent with open arms. As it was, certain parties coveted his work, particularly the secret work he was presently undertaking for the British government in the realm of cryptography and mathematical ciphers.

Work she'd been sent here to acquire.

Knowing his background, she'd assumed he would be

older, more of a contemporary of her father's, with thinning hair, lined features, and a belly that had gone as round and soft as bread dough.

But there was nothing doughy or lined about Lord Drake.

Quite the reverse since he was young, handsome, and extremely fit. Tall and leanly muscled, he sported solid shoulders, a broad chest, and a flat stomach that belied any notion of his ever developing a paunch.

As for his features, he would catch any female's eye whatever her age. From his head of thick chestnut brown hair to his aristocratic nose, sculpted lips and square chin, he was everything that was pleasing to behold.

Still, it was the intelligence and light of good humor shining in his translucent green eyes that appealed to her the most—eyes she had best be careful never to gaze into too closely for fear of being unmasked. For above all else, she must keep him from realizing who she really was and the wrong she planned to commit against him.

But first, she had to convince him to hire her, or all the rest would make no difference at all.

"I am a hard worker, your lordship," she told him before he had a chance to speak the words that would end their interview. "You will not find better, I promise."

His brows gathered close. "I am sure that is true, Mrs. Greenway, still I am not entirely positive that—"

"I understand from something I heard mentioned at the employment agency that your former housekeeper was with you for a good many years," she interrupted.

He nodded. "Since I first acquired the house here on Audley Street."

"Then I am sure her departure has been most disruptive to your routine, even one as admittedly irregular as your own."

"It has been, yes," he said, his mouth curving up at the corners.

"Then allow me to put it to rights. Hire me for the position, and I shall have your household running again as smoothly and easily as it ever did. More so, I dare say."

"More so, hmm?" he mused in a mellow baritone that seeped through her like a draught of warmed brandy.

"You don't lack for confidence, I'll say that." He paused, silence settling between them, as the frown returned to his brow. "You are clearly qualified and yet—"

Her chest squeezed painfully, fingers curled against her reticule to hide their trembling. Without thinking, she leaned forward in her chair. "*Please*, your lordship, I need this position. Travel from Scotland is not without expense, and my severance will only last me so long. Let me prove to you what an asset I can be. You won't regret it, I swear."

At least not right away, that is, she added silently.

Her mouth grew dry, pulse thudding dully in her veins as she waited for his answer. He simply had to say yes. Otherwise, she would have to resort to other measures, desperate ones that frightened her to even consider.

Slowly, he lifted his gaze to hers, those clear green eyes of his burning into her own. Holding steady, she forced herself not to look away, not to flinch or in any manner reveal her duplicity.

Abruptly, he nodded. "Very well, Mrs. Greenway, you've convinced me. Starting tomorrow, you are my new housekeeper."

Chapter 2

"... And this is your bedchamber," the upper house-maid, Parker, announced the next day as she led Sebastianne into one of the third-floor attic rooms inside Lord Drake Byron's town house.

Glancing around, Sebastianne set her black leather portmanteau on the floor beside the plain pine bed with its clean but simple counterpane of faded blue chintz. As she did, she took note of the freshly whitewashed walls, narrow oak wardrobe and washstand with its blue china washbowl and pitcher arranged on top. A small painting of a shepherd tending his flock hung on the wall. Despite the room's admittedly spare decoration, it seemed comfortable and tidy, any aspect of closeness held at bay by the surprisingly good quantity of summer light flooding in through a pair of dormer windows.

Nevertheless, her chest contracted with a wistful pang as she thought of her room at home, with its pretty buttercup yellow walls, flowered curtains and rosewood writing table. Since the war, the little cottage near Montsoreau had grown shabby. Yet she'd done everything in her power to keep it cheerful and bright, cherishing the few luxuries still left, as well as the memories of happier times.

She'd learned to make do these last few years, learned to accept hardship and struggle, and she would do so again now. She would do whatever was necessary to secure her family's safety and be back with them once more in their *petite maison* near the Loire.

If all went well, she told herself, that reunion would not be long in coming. A couple of weeks—a month at most—and she would have the information she needed to satisfy her handlers. Then Anne Greenway, housekeeper, would cease to exist, and Sebastianne Dumont would be able to be her true self again. Until then, she had a part to play, one the young maidservant across from her needed to believe without question.

Sebastianne had already caught the look of curious speculation in the other woman's dark eyes despite her outward show of friendliness. She knew she was going to be watched, measured and tested by her fellow servants every bit as much or more than by the master himself. If she had any hope of success, Sebastianne knew she would need to be on guard every moment of the day—and even, she feared, at night.

"You're to 'ave the room all to yerself, of course, you bein' the housekeeper an' everything," Parker offered, as if echoing Sebastianne's musings about her nocturnal circumstances. "Me an' Edith—Cobbs, that is—share a room just down the hall," the maidservant continued, hands clasped behind her short, slightly rounded frame. "Finnegan and Polk—they're the kitchen maid and scullion—they share the room beneath the eaves. Last room belongs to Mrs. Tremble—she's the cook and has been with his lordship from the first day he owned this house."

"And how long has that been?" Sebastianne inquired with polite interest.

Parker scrunched up her mahogany eyebrows in thought. "Well now, going on eight year, I think. Mrs. Beatty was with him all that time too afore she gave her notice. She were the housekeeper here prior to yerself, ye see."

"Yes, so I am given to understand," Sebastianne stated, straightening her shoulders at the sudden unspoken challenge in the housemaid's voice and eyes.

Despite the fact that she and the other young woman were likely a similar age—two-and-twenty in Sebastianne's case—she couldn't allow herself to be intimidated. Forcing herself to hold firm, she met the housemaid's gaze with implacable determination.

A few seconds later, Parker looked away.

Clearing her throat, the housemaid shuffled her feet beneath her starched black uniform skirts and crisp white apron. "Here now, I'd best be getting along else Mr. Stowe thinks I'm turning lazy. He said I were to see you settled and invite you to join everyone belowstairs soon as yer ready. He'll assemble the staff then fer a proper introduction."

Sebastianne nodded. "Thank you. Please inform Mr. Stowe that I shall be with him directly. I am eager to review the household since I am sure there is a great deal of work to be done."

"Oh there's always plenty of that," Parker agreed, "even if his lordship hardly pokes his head out of his workroom most days. He's a deep one, he is, but fair. And sharp. He may seem dreamy-like sometimes, lost in his figuring and inventions and such, but still, he don't miss a trick. Always knows what's what, his lordship does."

Sebastianne swallowed against the fresh knot in her throat, wondering if the maidservant's words had been spoken out of innocent observation or rather as a veiled warning instead? Either way, she decided, by the time this was over, she'd likely have enough knots tied in her insides to impress a bosun's mate on His Majesty's finest frigate.

Assuming I haven't been unmasked as a spy by then and am locked in the hold of a prison hulk awaiting execution.

But that wasn't going to happen, she assured herself. Her British accent was as flawless as a native's, and she'd studied everything about housekeeping she could possibly need to know. There was no reason for anyone to suspect her of being someone other than the person she claimed to be.

Except for her youth, of course, since most housekeepers were in their forties or fifties or even older. Then too there was the fact that she'd never worked a day in her life as a servant. But those were minor details that could be overcome. She'd already faced the toughest challenge before her—getting hired. The rest would fall into place.

She hoped.

"Well, thank you for showing me to my room, Parker," Sebastianne stated in a pleasant tone that also served as a clear indication of dismissal.

The maid stared for a moment before lowering her gaze. "Yes, ma'am. As I said, lots to do."

"I am sure."

She was also sure that Parker's first stop would be the servants' hall to gossip about her impressions of the new housekeeper, Sebastianne judged, as she watched the maid curtsey, then close the door behind her.

Only after the girl's footsteps faded away did she release the breath she'd been holding and sink with trembling limbs onto the bed.

Mon Dieu, *I am so alone, so afraid. May the good Lord watch over and keep me from harm.*

Forcing herself to stand again after a minute, she opened her portmanteau and began to unpack her meager array of belongings.

* * *

In another part of the house, Drake came awake with a start, blinking in confusion for a moment before realizing he was in his workroom. Obviously he'd fallen asleep at his desk again, dozing off sometime in the small hours of the night as he'd been mulling over his latest theorem.

Sitting up, he stretched his arms over his head to ease some of the stiffness from his muscles before running a set of fingers through his disheveled hair. He glanced at a gilt mantel clock to check the time, its hands mirroring those of the other half dozen, gently ticking timepieces perched in various locations around the room—all of them accurately calibrated to within a half second of each other.

At present, they all read twenty-one past nine in the morning.

He supposed he ought to make his way upstairs for a bath, shave and change of clothes, particularly since he was expected at Clybourne House later that day. His sister-in-law, Claire, was hosting her first nuncheon party of the Season, and his mother had given him strict instructions that he was to attend.

"Too much work will only make you dull," Ava Byron had declared last week when the subject arose after a family dinner. "You're forever wrapped up in one puzzlement or another, and a break will do you good."

He'd sent her an indulgent smile. "But I like being 'wrapped up' in puzzlements, as well you know, Mama. Not to worry though. I shall be here for Claire's fête since you ladies have both worked so hard on it."

He only prayed Claire and his mother hadn't invited a gaggle of dewy-eyed ingénues to the party as well, each one looking to snare a husband during her first London Season. He had no interest in young misses just out of the school-room and even less in marriage.

At least the visit would give him a chance to talk to his eldest brother, Ned, about a few refinements he was making to the cipher he'd developed in secret for the British government. Edward, the Duke of Clybourne—or Ned as he was known to the family—was highly placed in the War Office, the duke's involvement known only to a select handful at the top.

Because of Drake's talents as a mathematician, Ned had approached him a couple of years ago about doing code work for the government. Intrigued, he'd agreed, finding the endeavor not only challenging but worthwhile since he was as committed as the rest of his family to seeing Britain prevail in her fight against Napoleon.

So far, his forays into the world of espionage were proving an excellent complement to his other intellectual pursuits. Plus, the Crown paid a surprisingly excellent stipend, remuneration that a younger son—even the fourth son of a duke—wasn't at all loath to receive.

Without warning, his stomach gave an irritable rumble that brought him back to the immediate matter at hand, however mundane it might seem. Reaching out, he straightened the notes scattered across the scarred and stained oak surface of his desk, then returned the crystal stopper to its bottle of ink. He left a variety of pens, pencils and nubs of chalk where they lay, not far from a dish full of bolts, a coil of thin copper wire, an open penknife and a hammer.

He stood, then walked from the room.

Located as it was on the ground floor in the rear of the town house, his workshop was closer to the servants' back staircase than to the main stairs. Often he found it far more convenient to use the servants' stairs to make a quick jog up to his suite of rooms on the second floor than to go around to the front.

Opening the concealed door in the wall, he started up.

He was just rounding the landing leading up to the final flight of steps when a swish of dark skirts and a pair of small, leather-clad shoes appeared directly above him.

"Oh!" cried a woman, her voice skimming over him like a silken hand.

He stopped just in time to avoid colliding with her, the two of them crowded bare inches from each other on the narrow staircase. "Mrs. Greenway, is that you?"

Her gaze met his, her golden eyes bright as a pair of copper pennies. "M-my pardon, your lordship, for not seeing you there."

He brushed her apology aside. "No, no. Entirely my fault for taking the servants' stairs." He paused, tipping his head back for a better view.

And what a view it was, he decided, finding Anne Greenway even more attractive than he remembered, with her graceful figure, winsome mouth and creamy complexion. A faint dusting of color spread across her cheeks, a pale pink that reminded him of the delicate inside of a seashell.

"So, you've arrived?" he said, the remark sounding foolish even to his own ears.

"Yes," she agreed, her hands clasped at her trim waist. "Only this hour past."

He crossed his arms, then lowered them again when he noticed that it only brought him closer to her. "Are you finding everything to your liking so far? Your room? Is it acceptable?"

A tiny V appeared between her eyebrows, her expression clearly indicating her surprise at the inquiry. Completely valid, he supposed, considering that most employers wouldn't have bothered to ask at all.

"Yes," she said. "More than acceptable. Thank you, your lordship."

He rocked back on one heel. "And the house? Have you had a chance to look around?"

The frown and the look of surprise made a second appearance. "No, not yet. I was just making my way belowstairs in order to meet the staff and acquaint myself with the premises. I am most eager to begin my duties."

A pleasing enough statement for a housekeeper, he judged, one any employer should be glad to hear. So why did he have the impression she wasn't nearly as eager as she said but rather nervous instead? Then again, why shouldn't she be nervous? After all, this was her first day of employment in a new city, in a new house with a new master and a houseful of servants who were strangers to her. Under those circumstances, he would likely be nervous too.

"You'll do fine," he said, surprising them both this time. "First days are always difficult."

She paused, an arrested expression in her eyes. "They are indeed. Thank you for your confidence in me, your lordship."

Her lashes lowered in a graceful sweep before she bent her head forward. As she did, a brilliant shaft of sunlight rained down from the window above, shining onto her neatly pinned hair. She wore no bonnet this time, her richly hued tresses creating a glorious riot of autumnal color—lush browns, gleaming reds and vibrant golds that ranged from pale ash to the deepest topaz. And entwined among them like rare strands of silver were those few grey hairs that ought to have once again reassured him of the appropriate advancement of her age.

Then he studied her face, finding her profile lovely and young.

Too young.

Too pretty.

Why did I hire her again? he wondered.

Because you're an idiot, that's why, came the answer.

Shifting his stance, he became uncomfortably aware of blood rushing to parts of his anatomy that he'd rather not think about at the moment and had no business feeling.

"Well, I suppose I ought let you be on your way," he said, taking a step back so that she might move past him. "Should you have any questions or concerns, pray address them to me without hesitation."

She nodded, then started forward. A second later, she stopped. "Actually, I do have a question."

He pressed himself back against the wall of the staircase, fighting the impulse to step forward instead so he could press *her* against the wall and kiss her. His pulse sped faster, imagining the taste and sensation of her lips moving under his own. Instinctively, he knew she would taste delicious.

"Yes?" he encouraged, half-hoping she was going to make his fantasy come true and ask him to do exactly what he'd been imagining.

"Do you wish to be consulted regarding the dinner menus?" she inquired with quiet interest.

He gave her a blank stare, managing only by force of will not to betray his disappointment—or his desire.

Take charge of yourself, man, he thought, giving himself a firm mental slap. *She's the new housekeeper, and for her good and your own, you'd best remember that fact.*

"Ordinarily I would discuss such matters with the lady of the house," she continued, clearly unaware of his inner turmoil, "but since this is a bachelor's establishment, I thought perhaps you would like to be personally consulted about the menus instead."

He drew a slow, steadying breath. "There's no need. So long as you don't have Cook feed me fried liver or quail's eggs, you have my leave to arrange the menus however you like."

"No liver or quail's eggs," she repeated, a tiny smile curving over her mouth. "I believe I can remember that."

He glanced away, her mouth far too tempting. "You'll find that Mrs. Tremble has a deft hand at arranging such matters. You may put your trust in her judgment."

"And so I shall. Thank you again, your lordship."

"Mrs. Greenway."

Moving back another inch, he let her slip past him, her low-heeled shoes clicking softly against the wooden treads of the stairs. Only when she'd gone did he heave out an exasperated sigh.

He'd been working too long and too hard, he decided, and been neglecting his physical needs. Had he been less preoccupied with work of late, he surely wouldn't have found himself so instantly and powerfully attracted to Anne Greenway.

It isn't her per se, he assured himself. *I'm just in need of a woman, that's all.* Maybe he would pay a call on Vanessa this evening. A lusty night spent in the arms of his mistress could only do him good. Besides, he hadn't seen Vanessa in nearly a fortnight, and he always enjoyed her company, both in bed and out.

Feeling reassured by the idea, he turned and went up the last flight of stairs. But as he strode down the hallway to his bedchamber, it wasn't Vanessa who was still on his mind.

Chapter 3

Sebastianne hurried down the stairs, her lungs straining for air although not from the physical exertion.

Mince alors, she exclaimed under her breath. *For just a moment I thought Lord Drake was going to kiss me.* He'd certainly had a glint in those beautiful green eyes of his that spoke more of passionate affairs than mundane household ones.

Of course, she must have imagined it. He was her employer, after all, and from everything she knew of him, a true gentleman as well. Certainly there had been no hint of impropriety in either his voice or manner. He'd behaved exactly as an English aristocrat should. Had he wanted her, he would surely have made his desires known, leaving her to find a way to fend him off.

Assuming she would have wanted to fend him off.

She stopped, gripping the stair railing as she considered the matter. What would she have done if Drake Byron had tried to kiss her? Would she have pushed him away or invited him closer?

A shiver ran through her at the idea.

Thankfully, she hadn't needed to make the choice, more disturbed by the question and her likely response than she cared to admit.

But such musings mattered not. After all, anything she might or might not feel in regard to Lord Drake was irrelevant. She was here to retrieve the cipher, make her way back to France and use it to secure the safety of her family.

Nothing more, nothing less.

Developing feelings for anyone in Drake Byron's household would be a mistake, most particularly developing feelings for the master himself. Only trouble could come of it, and she'd already known more than her fair share of unhappiness and loss. There was no point in inviting more by coming to care for the people here, the servants or their master. If all went well with her plan, she would barely have time to know them anyway, her memory of them as transient and insubstantial as the clouds that sailed past in the sky.

Deciding she'd spent far too much time mulling over her situation, she forced all such thoughts from her head, then continued down the last flights of steps, which led into the basement.

A homely combination of scents—burning tallow, woodsmoke, boiling beef and lye soap—greeted her arrival, voices drifting to her ears from a nearby room. Making her way along the surprisingly well lit hall, she pushed open the door and walked into the kitchen.

The space was both warm and inviting, wide and refreshingly open, with a large worktable that dominated the center. On its clean-scrubbed wooden surface lay a pile of fresh vegetables waiting for peeling and chopping. The green tops of a bunch of carrots were tucked beside a mound of earthy brown-skinned potatoes and yellow onions that were nearly as big as fists. Several feet away, tendrils of steam rose from a number of cast-iron pots and pans that were set onto a very modern-looking stove, a heavy wooden spoon protruding from the largest one.

A thin woman with a hawkish nose and wiry red hair turned at her entrance, studying her out of a pair of watery blue eyes. All talking subsided in the room as the others noticed her as well, two young women and a man with a blackened polish rag in his hand. He halted his work to regard her, the silver table knife he was cleaning momentarily forgotten in his grasp.

"Well then, ye must be the new housekeeper," the redhaired woman remarked from where she stood at the stove. "I'm Mrs. Tremble, the cook. Mr. Stowe should be along any moment to show you around. Here there, Lyles," she ordered with a wave of one callused hand, "go tell Stowe that Mrs.—Greenway, is it?" she questioned with another assessing glance at Sebastianne, "that she's down and ready for her tour."

The young man, who Sebastianne now noticed was dressed in a reserved dark blue and brown livery, set his rag and knife aside and got to his feet, obediently leaving the kitchen.

"And you there, miss," Mrs. Tremble said, turning her back on Sebastianne to point at one of the young women. "You've got potatoes need peeling. If I were you, I'd start on those sharp-like, else we'll have nothing to eat for the midday meal."

"Yes, ma'am." Casting another curious peek at Sebastianne from under her stubby dark lashes, the kitchen maid hurried forward, took up a paring knife and set to work. The other young serving maid, clearly having no wish to receive a similar scolding, picked up a tray of pans and dishes and crossed to a deep metal sink located across the room.

"Polk, is it?" Sebastianne said, quietly addressing the girl. "Or are you Finnegan?"

The servant froze, a potato gripped tightly in one hand. "Finnegan, ma'am. How'd ye know?"

"Parker obviously," Mrs. Tremble pronounced, tsking under her breath as she moved to bustle around the stove. "That girl uses her tongue far too freely if you've a mind to ask me. A hard worker she is, though, and make no mistake about it. Cobbs as well."

Angling her gaze, the cook sent a speaking glance toward her kitchen helper, who had once more paused in her task and was listening with avid interest. Ducking her head, Finnegan reapplied herself to her vegetable peeling.

"You'll find I run my kitchen with a fair but demanding hand, as I've been doing for nigh on a decade now," Mrs. Tremble stated. "So there won't be any need for the reorganizing of things."

Sebastianne met her gaze, having noticed the cook's unmistakable emphasis on the word "my" as well as the challenge behind her words. Although she could have, Sebastianne had no intention of meddling with a housekeeping system that clearly functioned to the liking of all parties involved. However, she wasn't about to let the other woman know that or allow her to lay down rules, even if she didn't plan to be in the house long enough for it to really matter.

"Reorganization, I have found," Sebastianne said smoothly, "is only useful where there is an honest need for improvement. So long as I find no such need, then there shall be no adjustments. I have every hope that shall prove the case."

The cook narrowed her pale blue eyes to study Sebastianne afresh. Then she huffed out a breath and turned back to the stove. "Sit and I'll pour ye some tea. Unless you'd rather have the making of it yerself, that duty rightly belonging to ye as housekeeper."

Sebastianne supposed she ought to press the point of her

new authority, but since the other woman had unbent enough to make the offer, she decided to accept. "Tea would be most welcome. Time enough after I'm settled to take up the task."

Waving Sebastianne toward a small table and chair in the corner, Mrs. Tremble went to prepare the brew.

Sebastianne crossed to take a seat, pausing for a moment to straighten her serviceable dark blue skirts before settling in. She wondered how much longer Mr. Stowe would be, deciding that perhaps his delay stemmed in part from a desire to first give her a few minutes to become acquainted with Mrs. Tremble. Clearly, the older woman held a great deal of authority in the house and a great deal more seniority than Sebastianne would ever achieve.

Mrs. Tremble bustled up, plunking down a mug and saucer on the table. "Kettle's nearly at a boil. It'll just be another tick. So yer a widow, are ye?"

Sebastianne's shoulders drew tight, not prepared for the question—although she ought to have known the subject would arise eventually. "Yes, that's right."

The cook folded her arms at her aproned waist, plainly waiting to hear further details.

Sebastianne didn't offer any.

But Mrs. Tremble clearly wasn't the sort to let a bit of judicious silence deter her. "Lost him in the war, did ye?" she pressed. "Soldier, was he?"

Reaching out, Sebastianne played a fingertip over the handle of her mug, remembering the man she once had loved. Still loved, come to that, despite the more than three years that had elapsed since his death.

"Yes, he was a soldier."

A cavalry officer actually, who'd looked so dashing in his dark green uniform with its crimson facings, silver epaulettes and shako helmet with a high red plume. She decided not to mention the fact that Thierry had fought for the

French side rather than the British. She didn't think Mrs. Tremble would approve.

"He took a saber to the chest and died almost instantly," she continued. "At least that is what I was told, and I prefer to think he didn't suffer overmuch."

The older woman's face softened. "Ye've my condolences on yer loss. War's a terrible, senseless thing, if ye ask me. All those brave lads fighting and dying. I'll be glad when it's finally done."

Yes, Sebastianne thought, *I can think of nothing I would like more,* imagining the relief she would feel when the day finally arrived and the war was over at last. When she could lead her life again without fear or threat or deprivation.

Without Sebastianne quite realizing it, Mrs. Tremble moved to the stove and back, returning with a teapot in hand. Deftly she poured Sebastianne a cup, then set down the pot. Steam wafted in tiny spirals from the russet-hued surface of the beverage, leaving Sebastianne to wait until it cooled enough to drink.

"If ye don't mind me asking, Mrs. Greenway," the cook said, laying a fist at her hip, "what's yer age? Frankly, ye don't look as if you have enough years on you to be a housekeeper."

Sebastianne cocked her head and locked gazes with the other woman, her heart beating strongly in her chest. If she was to succeed, she knew she must rise to each challenge, every test. This one clearly could not be ignored.

"And if you don't mind *my* saying," Sebastianne told her, "you don't look as if you have enough fat on you to be a cook."

For a long moment Mrs. Tremble stared, her faded blue eyes turning wide. Then she shook her head and barked out a laugh, displaying a set of crooked teeth. "You an' me, we jest might get on after all."

Sebastianne returned her smile but made no effort to answer the other woman's question.

After a moment, the cook turned and made her way back to the stove. "Not fat enough! Ha, ha," Mrs. Tremble repeated under her breath, plainly amused.

As for Finnegan, the kitchen maid was staring again—openmouthed this time—a half-peeled carrot dangling from her fingers. Polk looked astonished as well, the pan she held dripping soapy water. Taking note of Sebastianne's inquiring gaze, the two young women returned quickly to their tasks.

Sebastianne had just taken a first sip of tea when the kitchen door opened, and the butler, Mr. Stowe, strode inside. He was lean and moderately tall with greying black hair and eyes that put her in mind of a wise grandfather. Prior to that day, he was the only person in the house whom she had met—excepting his lordship, of course. Even so, she knew him very little, having only exchanged a few brief words with him at the time of her interview. But he had been kind and polite to her on that occasion—qualities she admired, actions she would not soon forget.

"Pardon me for keeping you waiting so long," he said, looking dapper in a neat black suit, a pair of square spectacles perched on his nose. "If you're ready now, Mrs. Greenway, it would be my pleasure to show you the rest of the house and to give you a proper introduction to the staff."

Setting down her cup, she stood. "Thank you, Mr. Stowe. That would be most welcome."

"I presume you and Mrs. Tremble have had an opportunity to become acquainted?" he began.

"We surely 'ave, Mr. Stowe," the cook piped up from where she stood, stirring something in one of the pots for a moment before slamming a lid on top. "Mrs. Greenway and I 'ave been having a right coze here at my table before ye came to find her."

A faint look of surprise lighted the butler's brown eyes as if he hadn't expected Mrs. Tremble and the new housekeeper to get along. Words had quite likely been said among the staff prior to her arrival, along with expressions of unswerving loyalty for the former housekeeper, Mrs. Beatty— as well as promises not to easily accept Sebastianne as the other woman's replacement.

"Says I'm too skinny to be a cook, she does, Mr. Stowe. Have ye ever heard the like of that?"

One thin eyebrow lifted at the remark. "You are very slender, which is a curiosity I suppose considering your pleasure in sampling your own fare. A paradox, if ever there was one."

"*A parawhatox?*" The cook snorted and waved a dismissive hand. "All I know is you can't tell if a meal's fit to be served unless you take a taste or two of it first."

Stowe nodded as if this were a familiar conversation, then turned back to introducing Sebastianne. "These two young women are Finnegan and Polk," he said, indicating the others. "Please stop what you're doing for a minute and come forward."

Wiping their hands on their aprons, the two kitchen maids did as they were told. Standing together, they politely bobbed their heads and curtseyed.

"Lyles is the underfootman whom I believe you have also met, albeit briefly," the butler continued. "Ah, here he comes now, back to finish polishing the plate."

The liveried footman she had encountered earlier came through the doorway, along with a dark, curly-haired man a few years his senior. Realizing that introductions were being made, the pair fell into line as did another two women who'd followed the men into the room.

Parker, the upper housemaid, Sebastianne already knew, but the plump blond girl with her was a stranger. She assumed this must be the much-discussed Cobbs.

With the staff lined up in a neat row, the introductions continued. The curly-haired man's name proved to be Jasper, and he was the upper footman. His affable smile and open, cheerful demeanor put her instantly at ease. She'd already met the kitchen maid and scullion, of course—Polk and Finnegan returning to their tasks as soon as they were formally made known to her by Mr. Stowe. Parker, the upper housemaid, gave her a friendly nod while the other housemaid, who was indeed the elusive Cobbs, squeaked out a quiet greeting before executing a respectful dip of her knees.

Mr. Stowe informed Sebastianne that Lord Drake also employed a coachman, Mr. Morton, and two grooms, Jem and Harvey.

"You'll meet them at mealtimes," he said, "since otherwise they stay in the mews, occupied with the horses and carriages."

And last was his lordship's valet, Waxman, who not surprisingly kept his own schedule and took orders from no one but Lord Drake himself. As if mention of his name had summoned him, Waxman abruptly appeared, walking quickly into the kitchen.

At first glance he reminded her of a rule-bound gendarme—tall, proud and full of arrogant self-assurance. His dress was immaculate, as it should be, she supposed, given the custom of valets receiving their masters' cast-off clothing. His light brown hair was brushed into a sleek wave that he combed high in an obvious attempt to hide the bald spot forming on the back of his head. His features were even, pleasant in a bland sort of way, but not his eyes—his gaze an exacting steely grey that was critically observant of all it surveyed.

I'll have to be careful not to unduly attract his notice, Sebastianne thought, instinctively realizing she would need to take pains to avoid Waxman when she conducted her search of the house.

"His lordship requires breakfast," the valet announced in an imperious voice. "Eggs, toast and coffee. I should like the tray made ready in no more than ten minutes."

Mrs. Tremble shot him an annoyed look. "Ye'll have it in fifteen and be glad of it. Takes nearly that long to grind the beans and set the brew to steep."

Before the valet had time to offer a rejoinder, Sebastianne stepped forward. "I would be happy to prepare the coffee for his lordship. Are the beans and mill kept in the stillroom?"

"Aye, and thank ye kindly," Mrs. Tremble said, appearing grateful for the offer. Clearly focused on the meal she was about to prepare, the cook hooked a wicker basket over one arm and disappeared into the larder.

"Name's Waxman," the valet said, suddenly addressing Sebastianne. "And you must be the new housekeeper."

Sebastianne met his gaze. "Yes, I'm Mrs. Greenway. How do you do?"

"Busy."

She paused. "Ah, but then aren't we all?"

Waxman pursed his lips, casting a sideways glance at the housemaids and footmen who loitered listening, and who he clearly thought should be engaged in some more active task.

Before he could make a further remark, Mr. Stowe rejoined the conversation. "I still need to show you around, Mrs. Greenway," the butler said. "But it can wait a few minutes more while you see to Lord Drake's breakfast. Pray join me in my room whenever you are ready."

"Yes, I shall, thank you, Mr. Stowe."

She frowned as she watched him leave, hoping she hadn't offended him. But then why should she worry how smoothly she fit into the household? She wouldn't be there long enough for it to matter.

Remembering the promised coffee, she hurried toward the stillroom.

Chapter 4

"Drake, you came!" Claire, Duchess of Clybourne said, gliding toward him only moments after he entered the elegant Clybourne House drawing room.

"Well, of course, I did," he replied, leaning down to brush a friendly kiss over his sister-in-law's soft cheek. "Mama would have my head if I failed to turned up for your party, nor have I the least wish to disappoint you. So? How are you?"

Pausing, he cast an appraising glance at the rounded curve of her belly, which to his untutored eye seemed to grow bigger every time he saw her. "Still glad you braved the journey to London rather than remaining at Braebourne this spring?" he asked.

"I'm barely seven months along and have plenty of energy," she defended, as if she'd heard the same before—quite likely from Ned. "Anyway, I couldn't very well let the fact that I'm with child keep me from being in Town for my own sister's come-out."

"Your mother could have handled it surely."

Claire made a face and lowered her voice to a careful sotto voce. "Yes, but could poor Ella?"

He barked out a laugh that drew glances from several guests, who studied him briefly before turning away again.

"And what of you, Drake?" Claire inquired. "How have you been in the week since last we met? Have you located a new solar system or something of an equally amazing nature? You're always dug deep into one endeavor or another that we mere mortals can barely hope to comprehend."

He raised an amused eyebrow at her teasing. "I believe you comprehend just fine, dear sister, even if your interests don't lie among the stars."

"Oh, I like the stars just fine—star*gazing* that is. I simply don't care to know the best method for calculating their orbits."

"Ah," he mused aloud, deciding to indulge in his own bit of teasing. "Then I suppose I won't engage you in a discussion about Kepler's Laws and why they apply to planets but not stars. Nor point out that the sun is really an extremely large star, which means that when you look into the sky on a sunny day, you're actually stargazing then too."

Seeing her arrested, faintly slack-jawed expression, he realized he'd gone as far as he ought. "But enough talk of astronomy." He paused, changing the subject. "You asked how I've been. Truth be told, my time of late has been spent in rather ordinary pursuits. I've hired a new housekeeper, who started only this morning."

As soon as the words were out, he wished he could recall them, his thoughts abruptly filled with images of Anne Greenway—her bewitching features, her lyrical voice, the luminous intensity of her golden eyes and the kissable shape of her full, ripe, ruby lips.

He swallowed, his throat suddenly dry.

"Might you care for a refreshment?" he asked, glancing

around in hopes of finding a footman circulating close by with a tray of beverages. He could down two or three, he felt sure.

Luckily, Claire didn't seem to notice his abrupt discomfort. "A lemonade would be most welcome," she said. "And I am relieved to hear that you have found a replacement for Mrs. Beatty. I know her abrupt departure caused a great deal of unnecessary strife, but now you'll be able to relax again."

Drake fought the urge to admit that, for him at least, his new housekeeper was anything but relaxing.

"Come and let us have that refreshment," she told him with a smile. "Then I suppose I should do my duty and mingle. As should you. No retreating to a convenient corner with pencil and paper in hand so you can scribble away the afternoon."

"But that's my favorite occupation at parties. You're heartless to deny me."

Chuckling at his mock outrage, she tucked her arm through his and led him forward.

As they walked, he took note of a great many people with whom he was acquainted, as well as many members of his family, including aunts, uncles and the usual assortment of cousins. He caught Edward's gaze and exchanged a slight nod, unable to help but notice the expression of annoyance on his brother's face as he stood conversing with the prime minister, Mr. Liverpool. As a confirmed Whig, Ned's opinions were rarely in accord with the Tory leader's.

Moving on, he saw his brother Cade, Cade's wife, Meg, his younger sister Mallory and her new husband, Adam, Earl of Gresham—an old friend of the family's whom he'd known since they were both very young men.

Mallory laughed just then and smiled up at Adam, her eyes shining with undisguised love. Adam smiled back, his own adoration—that frankly bordered on the besotted—

clear for all to see. Drake was glad Mallory was so happy, particularly after the heartache she'd suffered not so long ago.

Honestly, though, he mused, he was beginning to feel a bit outnumbered, what with all of his older siblings and one of his little sisters falling in love and getting married. Even Jack, the wildest, most rakish Byron brother of them all— assuming one discounted the twins, Leo and Lawrence, who at twenty were working hard to outstrip Jack's well-earned reputation—had traded in his freedom for a ring and vows of true love.

In fact, Jack wasn't in London at all right now, having opted to skip the Season to be with his wife, Grace, their daughter Nicola and new baby, Virginia "Ginny," at their home in Kent. Based on the last letter he'd had from Jack, his brother seemed to prefer the quiet, rural existence he shared with his new family. Apparently the raucous, fast-paced city life he used to enjoy with such exuberant excess was now little more than a vague, unmourned memory.

Certainly Drake wished all his married siblings the best and liked his sisters-in-law and brother-in-law very much. Yet he couldn't help but fear it was giving his mother ideas concerning him. If he wasn't careful, he'd soon find himself wed as well.

Not if I have a say in the matter, he thought, stopping to procure a lemonade for Claire and a glass of wine for himself.

He'd just taken a drink when his mother appeared at his elbow, Claire drifting away with a friendly waggle of her fingers.

"Drake, you came!" exclaimed Ava Byron, in an echo of her daughter-in-law's earlier remark. Her clear green eyes, that were very much like his own, sparkled with youthful exuberance and delight. Truthfully, if she wasn't the mother of eight children—only one of whom was still young enough to be in the schoolroom—no one would believe she had passed her fiftieth year. With barely a few strands of grey in her light brown hair and scarcely a line on her face, she was still one of the most beautiful women in the room.

"I told you I'd be here," he said, leaning over to press a kiss her cheek. "You and Claire ought to have more faith."

"We have plenty of faith, but we both know you well enough to realize how . . ." She paused, clearly in search of a word that wouldn't offend. " . . . *preoccupied* you sometimes become with your work."

"Forgetful, you mean. Well, not today. Otherwise, you told me that I was in danger of becoming dull."

Ava smiled. "You could never be *dull*. You're a Byron! But you do seem to spend a very great deal of time locked inside that workshop of yours. You need to be out among people. You need to mingle more."

He sent her a penetrating look, a prickle of warning running down his back. "As hostesses, it's your and Claire's job to mingle. I'm just here to eat and drink, speak to a select few people, then go home."

"And I know just the people with whom you should speak."

"*Mama,*" he said, the prickle sending up a definite alarm this time. "What are you up to? You're not trying to match-make, are you?"

Ava looked offended. "Of course not. And I'm not *up* to anything. You know me better than that."

He nodded, relaxing slightly.

"But an old acquaintance of mine, Lord Saxon, does happen to be here. He's a widower, and he has brought his daughter with him. It's her very first Season, and she's a rather shy girl, in spite of her pretty face."

"*Mother—*" He scowled.

"—You don't have to pay court to her. Just engage her in a little conversation, perhaps offer to escort her into nuncheon."

"I'm not *escorting* her anywhere, and nuncheon is out of the question."

"Just make her acquaintance then. And be nice."

"I'm always nice," he said on a rumbling growl.

Ava sent him another look. "Nicer than that."

He swallowed a sigh of resignation. "Fine. I'll be good. Lead on, and don't blame me afterward if she wishes we'd never met."

Sebastianne collapsed into the wide chair in the housekeeper's room—*her* room she supposed now that she had officially assumed her new duties. The chamber was small, yet tidy, an interesting combination of office and sitting area that was located in the basement. Here she could prepare marketing lists of goods and foodstuffs, reconcile the household accounts and speak to any staff who needed a word in private. The room was also the place where the senior staff—Mr. Stowe, Mrs. Tremble and Mr. Waxman—should he decide to join them—removed each day to enjoy their dessert, coffee and a glass of sherry once the servants' dinner was finished.

After her tour with Mr. Stowe, she'd assumed she might be able to sneak in a few minutes here and there to search for the cipher. With Lord Drake out of the house for the afternoon and evening, it seemed an excellent opportunity. But to her great frustration, she couldn't find a moment to spare amid the myriad tasks that settled upon her shoulders. First, there were Parker and Cobbs to be satisfied, the housemaids hovering with clear expectation that she would want to inspect their work. Aware that this task was indeed part of her job, she walked through each room, checking for cleanliness and order. All the rooms, that is, except Lord Drake's workroom.

"We're not to go in there without his lordship's express permission and never when he's out of the house," Parker volunteered in a confidential tone. "Says we disarrange things even though they're all a jumble to start. But he has a system, he says, and it's not to be meddled with."

Cobbs nodded her agreement with solemn assurance.

"Yelled at me something frightful one time when I first started," Parker continued. "All's I did was straighten a pile of his papers, and you'd think I'd tossed 'em all on the hot grate the way he carried on. Says I cost him an entire week's work, but I don't see as how I could have."

Sebastianne did, though, thinking of her father's seemingly hap-dash way of organizing his own space. He too had a system that was incomprehensible to everyone—everyone but her. Over the years, when she hadn't been busy taking care of the family household, she'd served as his assistant. As such, she'd learned mathematics from him even though females were traditionally discouraged from studying such a masculine discipline. But Papa had always been proud, encouraging her to learn in spite of her mother's gentle admonitions that such knowledge would only lead to trouble.

Ironic that her mother had been right though not for the reasons either of them had imagined at the time. Fateful that Mama, who died when Sebastianne was only fifteen, had unwittingly provided her with the other essential skill she needed in order to perpetrate her current charade. For if her mother had not been British, Sebastianne would never have known how to speak English so flawlessly that everyone would assume she was a native born and bred.

Half–born and bred, she corrected, thinking of her dual heritage and her resulting affinity for languages. In addition to French and English, she was fluent in Spanish and Italian, with enough German and Russian to make do. But she had a pretense to maintain, she reminded herself, aware that she must remember to appear as British as possible at all times.

Linking her hands behind her back, she forced her memories aside, struggling as she did to quiet the churning in her stomach over knowing herself a cheat. For no matter what choices she made now, she was destined to hurt and betray someone. Better those for whom she did not care, she reasoned, than those she loved.

Without warning, Drake Byron's face popped into her mind. Her pulse sped faster as she thought of his angular features and clear green eyes, which were so honest and insightful, so captivating and breathlessly male. It would be easy for a woman to lose herself in eyes like those. Easy to forget herself and her true purpose.

Bah! she told herself, coming back to the present.

With an imperceptible shake of her head, she sternly banished the image, calling herself a ridiculous widgeon.

"If we are not to enter his lordship's workroom," Sebastianne said, returning to the discussion at hand, "then how is the chamber ever cleaned?"

"Oh, he lets us in every so often to do a dusting and polish," Parker volunteered. "So long as we don't move anything, he's fine enough. Mrs. Beatty used to wait until he went out, then sneak in and clean."

But despite her own wish that she could "sneak in," Sebastianne found her afternoon far too busy to play spy. Instead, after her inspection of the housemaid's work, she went to the linen cupboard to sort and arrange the contents—removing a few sheets that needed mending.

Returning belowstairs, she'd been greeted by Mrs. Tremble, who pointed out that there were deliveries from the butcher's boy and the greengrocer that required checking to make sure they were of good quality and the right weight and measure.

"Ye never know when one of the tradesmen will turn cheat," the cook advised with a sage nod. Having dealt with her own share of unscrupulous merchants in her time, Sebastianne could only agree.

At supper, in spite of being given a reprieve on overseeing the arrangement of Lord Drake's meal at table, she'd still been expected to carve the roast joint of beef for the servants. It had proven a daunting experience that had made her hands shake. Apparently, she did well enough, however, quiet with relief as she ate her first evening meal among the staff.

Afterward, she hoped she could retire for the day, but more work awaited. Since she was responsible for the management of the larder and stillroom, it was her job to grind the spices, sift and measure out the sugar, and stone the fruits and raisins, among other tasks. And to her silent dismay, once she had finished with that, there was a large basketful of clothes and linens in need of mending—the fine sewing also her duty to perform.

Leaning her head back as she sat in the housekeeper's room, she wondered if she had the strength to walk up the four flights of stairs to her bedchamber. Closing her eyes, she let the long, tiring day wash over her, her mind as exhausted as her body.

She came awake with a start some while later, unsure of the time. Peering at the clock on her desk, she saw that it was a few minutes past two in the morning.

She cupped a hand over an eye-watering yawn and she tried to shake off her drowsiness. Unless she wanted to spend the rest of the night in this chair and risk waking up stiff in the morning, she supposed she had best go to her bedroom. A scant few hours remained before she would have to begin a new day and start her duties all over again.

Still, with everyone else slumbering, maybe this would be the perfect time to do a bit of searching?

Dare I try?

Taking up a candle, she made her way silently from the room.

"G'night, milord," Morton called quietly from where he sat perched atop the coachbox.

Lifting a hand, Drake gave a friendly wave, then started up the steps to the front door. He listened to the fading clip-clop of the horses' hooves on the dark, silent street as he slipped his fingers inside his waistcoat. Digging briefly inside its silk-lined pocket, he located the house key he carried for just such occasions and applied it to the lock.

He knew the servants would all be abed since he'd long ago dispensed with the practice of keeping a footman stationed at the door until his arrival. What was the point in making one of them stay up half the night when even he didn't know what time he would return?

Even Waxman, who was dedicated to a fault, had stopped waiting up for him years ago. Instead, he'd adopted the habit of laying out fresh towels, Drake's robe and setting a tin of water on the hearth to stay warm for Drake's use whenever he came in for the evening.

Smothering a yawn, he went inside, then turned to lock the door behind him. The pleasant quiet wrapped around him like a coverlet, cool and dark, the house peaceful in its stillness.

It was just what he wanted after the hot, bright gleam of Vanessa's town house, with its red silk walls, crystal chandeliers and profusion of gilded mirrors. Then there were the large, ornate cages she kept throughout the house, filled with a variety of chirping yellow canaries and the jewel-toned songbirds that she adored with unabashed affection.

Not that he didn't enjoy her lush abode, with its comfortable sofas, perfumed sheets and soft feather mattress. Even so, when it came to sleeping, he preferred to do so in his own bed.

"Are you sure you won't stay the night?" Vanessa had murmured from where she lay against the rumpled bedclothes, her creamy white arms stretched above her head in a way that emphasized the ripe curve of her full, pink-tipped breasts.

He shook his head and reached for the shirt he'd tossed to the floor in a passionate haze not long after his arrival. "It's late and time I went home."

"If you prefer." She stretched like a cat, allowing one of her rounded thighs to shift so that he could easily see everything he was passing up. "Then again, it's not as if you've a wife waiting for you at home. If you let me, I promise I'll make you glad you stayed."

He'd laughed and pressed a languid kiss to her palm. "I'm sure you would, since you've already made me *glad* several times tonight. But I have work."

"Yes, your work," she said in an understanding tone. "I know how important it is to you."

"You're right. It is." He stepped into his trousers, fastening them before taking up his discarded cravat.

Long moments passed in silence, Vanessa reaching to pull the sheet over herself before she reclined once more against the pillows. "You know, Drake, I wonder if there will ever be a woman who is more important to you than your work?"

"Do you?" He raised a considering brow.

"Hmm, yes," she continued. "I just wonder if the woman exists who could drag you away from all the notions and numbers that dance around in that brilliant head of yours? Someone so special she would have the power to make you forget everything and everyone but her?"

He paused, studying her, aware the question must be an academic one since Vanessa had told him on more than one occasion that she had no interest in a permanent relationship and none whatsoever in marriage. As a wealthy widow, she enjoyed her freedom, in bed and out. It was why the two of them fit together so well. No ties. No strings. Just pleasure and easy, undemanding friendship.

Now she wanted to amuse herself by speculating about some hypothetical great love who would mean the world to him, mean even more to him than his family or his work.

Absurd.

Suddenly, Anne Greenway leapt into his mind. Her shapely figure, gentle smile and rich autumn-hued tresses that looked as if they'd been dusted with gleaming faerie silver beckoned within his imagination.

How curious that he would think of her. How impossible when there could be nothing between them.

Ever.

Giving himself an inward shake, he banished her from his thoughts.

Setting a last knot into his neckcloth, he came back to the bed and leaned over. "Speaking as a mathematician, I would have to say that the odds of my ever being hopelessly in love are slim to none, particularly since I'm not much given to romantic fancy." Smiling, he kissed her. "Besides, why would I need a woman like that when I have you?"

Clearly appeased, she'd laughed again and flung off the sheet. A few kisses later, she persuaded him to stay just a little while longer after all.

But he was glad to be home again now, glad to know he would be sleeping well sated in his own comfortable, solitary bed. Smothering another yawn, he started toward the staircase.

Just then, he noticed a narrow pool of light gleaming at

the end of the hallway and stopped. Who could be awake at this hour? he wondered.

"Hallo?" he called softly. "Who's there?"

A soft gasp broke the quiet, the candlelight flickering wildly.

Peering through the shadows, he pondered the subtle exclamation. "Mrs. Greenway? Is that you?"

A long pause descended before the brush-brush of leather soles came whispering against the polished floorboards and over the long Aubusson hall runner. Slowly, her figure grew more distinct as she drew nearer, light from the candle she held revealing the rapid rise and fall of her chest. "M-my lord? I d-didn't realize you had arrived home. You startled me."

"Then we share the same dilemma since you surprised me as well. What on earth are you doing wandering around the house at this hour?"

An expression that looked curiously like guilt spread over her features before she smoothed it away. "I . . . I . . ."

"Yes?" he drawled, even more intrigued now to hear her answer.

Her eyes gleamed faintly in the mellow light. "I hope you won't think badly of me, but I fell asleep in the housekeeper's room downstairs. I only just awakened and was on my way to bed."

Whatever suspicions had been forming in his head vanished, fresh surprise moving to replace them. "Has your first day been so tiring then? I trust your duties aren't of such an onerous nature that you cannot find time to retire for the evening?"

"N-no, not at all. The tasks, they are just a bit unfamiliar, you see and . . ." Her voice trailed off, a tiny frown settling across her russet colored brow. "That is to say I am merely learning the rhythm of the house and had much to do. There is no need for concern. I am managing quite ably."

"I am sure you are, but there is no point in wearing yourself out. In future, you are to retire at a far more reasonable hour since it won't do having you exhaust yourself. Whatever work remains at day's end can wait until the morrow, I am certain."

He smiled, hoping to put her at ease, but her frown deepened.

"As you wish, my lord," she murmured.

He tucked a hand into one pocket. "And the staff? How are you finding them?"

"Very friendly and hardworking. Everyone is most agreeable."

"Even Mrs. Tremble?" he asked, wondering how his sometimes-irascible cook was taking to his choice of housekeeper.

Her lips twitched, a good-humored light dancing in her golden gaze. "Especially Mrs. Tremble. She has been of great assistance, just as you said she would be."

"I am glad to hear it," he replied.

Silence descended, the darkness enfolding them in a way that made him suddenly aware of just how alone they were and exactly how advanced the hour.

As if aware too, a pink flush warmed his new housekeeper's cheeks, turning her skin to burnished cream, her eyes shining like twin coins as her mouth beckoned with the softness of rose petals.

Drake stared, unable to look away as he leaned imperceptibly closer.

When he'd arrived home, he'd been sleepy, but now he was wide-awake again.

When he'd stepped out of the coach, his only thought had been to climb into bed and slip into the world of dreams.

But suddenly what he really wished he could slip into was *her*.

To his complete consternation, he grew abruptly aroused, his body ready and randy again in spite of the satisfying hours he'd spent in Vanessa's bed. Tonight's visit to his mistress was supposed to have rid him of this inexplicable desire he felt for Anne Greenway. It was supposed to have calmed all his lustful needs and put him once again in control, so they would be master and servant and nothing more.

Instead, here he stood, wanting her again with a longing that made him ache, that left him wishing he could set aside the candle she held and sweep her into his arms. Kissing her all the while, he would carry her upstairs to his bed, then proceed to pleasure them both for what remained of the night.

Force of will alone kept him from reaching for her, his hands flexing in frustration at his sides. Abruptly, he took a step away. "It's late," he stated in a hard tone, "and we both need our rest. I shall bid you good night."

She stared before giving a nod, exhaling a soft breath that nearly made him change his mind. "G-Good night, my lord," she said. "Rest well."

Hah! he thought. *I doubt I'll rest at all.*

But he would try, just as he would strive to conquer this unwanted desire he felt for a woman he barely knew and dare not let himself have.

For some men it would have been easy. She was only a servant, after all. She lived in his house and was under his authority, which for many equated to the right to do with her as he liked. But to him, such behavior was unacceptable. Only a brute took advantage of his employees—particularly sexual advantage. And so he would find the means to end this longing, to snuff out his craving with the finality of extinguishing a candle flame.

With a nod he hoped wasn't too curt, he resumed his original course to the stairs, forcing himself not to look back as he ascended the steps to his bedchamber.

Sebastianne laid a hand against her breasts and blew out a pent-up breath, relieved that the encounter was over. For an instant at the very start, she'd thought she was caught, worried he knew precisely what she'd been doing in the darkened hallway. Thank heavens she hadn't had time to actually go into his workroom and start searching, or there wouldn't have been any doubt. Only imagine if he'd found her rifling through his belongings on her very first night in residence! She'd been lucky, she realized, and would need to take special care in the future so that she wasn't seen doing anything of an unusual or suspicious nature.

With a sigh, she decided she ought to follow Lord Drake's example and continue upstairs to bed. Unfortunately, she wasn't the least bit tired anymore. The shock of happening upon him had sent an electric jolt through her system that had apparently driven away her weariness. It had also caused her heart to gallop with the speed of a Thoroughbred—a reaction not the least bit improved by the intimate proximity in which they'd stood conversing together in the quiet and the dark.

For whether she cared to admit it or not, Lord Drake was an undeniably attractive man, and she was far from immune to him or the sexuality he seemed to exude like the bouquet of a fine, robust wine. She didn't even think he was aware of his appeal, his thoughts much too inwardly focused to pay heed to such personal conceits as his own looks or charm.

Indeed, he'd appeared rather disheveled, his hair framing his face in a careless disarray of silky caramel waves, his clothing properly buttoned and tucked, yet lacking the crisp elegance of a well-turned-out aristocrat. And for a few brief moments, she believed she'd caught a hint of musk and gardenias that clung to him like a pair of lover's arms.

Was he with a woman tonight?

Her fingers tightened reflexively around the brass candlestick she held before she forced them to relax again. Then, with a rueful shake of her head and a Gallic shrug worthy of her paternal ancestors, she brushed the reaction aside.

Why should I care if he keeps a mistress? she reasoned. Truly it would be odd if he did not. After all, what man of his station and circumstances would choose not to avail himself of feminine companionship, particularly a man as innately virile as Lord Drake? He might be an intellectual, who often lost himself in his work, but that didn't mean he lacked the usual male drives and needs. Even on so short an acquaintance as theirs, she sensed the deep vein of passion that ran in his blood and suspected he brought the same level of focus and intensity to his lovemaking as he did to his work.

Shivery warmth tingled low in her belly at the thought of Lord Drake in bed, making her aware just how long it had been since she'd been with a man. How many years had passed since she'd even thought of one in such a way.

She'd been a virgin when she'd married Thierry, and there had been no one since. After his death, she'd been too wrapped up in her grief and in the day-to-day demands of simple survival to give a moment's thought to such matters—particularly given the selection of men still living in the village. They were either too young or too old, all the ones fit for service having gone to war.

Yet in no more than a day, she found herself reacting with awakened interest to a man who was little more than a stranger, wondering what it would be like to be held in Drake Byron's arms. To be kissed. To be loved.

Bah! C'est ridicule!

She was lonely and missing home, that was all. Why else would she be having such insane thoughts and inappropriate imaginings?

Sleep—that's what she needed. Several deep, dreamless hours in which she could forget all about Lord Drake and her unexpected attraction to him. When she awakened in the morning, her awareness of her new employer would be gone, nothing more than a vague fantasy that was quickly and easily forgotten.

And if it was not?

Then she would do her utmost to avoid him, keeping to her duties and her mission, hoping she would locate the cipher soon so she could be on her way.

Covering a sudden yawn with a palm, she walked toward the stairs and started up to her bedchamber.

Chapter 5

The next week passed quickly, although not in the way Sebastianne had hoped. Despite the modest size of the household, there was nothing modest about her duties, which kept her steadily occupied from morning to night. Given such constraints on her energy and time, she had scant opportunity to search the town house for the cipher. On the rare occasion when she did find herself alone during the day, she took the opportunity to sort through a drawer here and there and inspect a few likely-looking volumes on the library shelves. So far, though, her efforts had proven fruitless.

As she had from the beginning, she strongly suspected that the code was being kept in one of two locations—Lord Drake's workroom or his bedchamber—neither of which was easily searched, particularly with Waxman, Parker and Cobbs never more than a quick shout away.

Then there was Lord Drake himself, who came and went with no reliable pattern, exactly as he'd informed her was his habit. One day he'd leave the house early in the morning, then spend the evening at home, while the next he'd shut himself into his workroom for the afternoon, then depart for a late evening out. From what she'd observed and a few comments made by the staff, Lord Drake required very little sleep, seeming to exist quite satisfactorily on four or five hours a night.

After almost getting caught by him on her first evening in residence, she'd been afraid to sneak around at odd hours, worried he might appear unexpectedly and find her out. So instead she concentrated on learning her new job—no small feat—and settling more solidly into the household.

She also did her best to limit the amount of time she spent around Lord Drake—an arrangement that seemed to suit him as much as it did her. She ought to have been glad he made it so easy to forget the heightened tension of that first night. Forgetting was what she wanted, after all. Wasn't it? Still, she couldn't help but wonder at his polite, yet distant reaction to her of late.

Had he also been affected by their encounters and thought it best to avoid further fraternization? Then again, mayhap those moments on the servants' staircase and later in the night-darkened hallway had meant nothing to him, and he was merely behaving with the careless indifference with which most employers treated their servants.

Domestic servants, after all, were supposed to be all but invisible, quietly doing the work of the household before fading back into its shadows. Her greatest problem, she guessed, was that she didn't think of herself as a servant.

She hadn't grown up believing in the inherent right of a wealthy, privileged few to rule the masses. Her father was the dispossessed, impoverished son of a French gentleman and had lost everything in the Revolution. Rather than rely on the faded glory of his birthright, he'd made his own way in the world as a mathematician, as one of the intellectual elite. She was proud of his achievements, and had always regarded him as being every inch as worthy as anyone—even a king!

Although she couldn't accuse Lord Drake of being a snob, he was nevertheless the son of a duke and a member of the aristocracy. To the English way of thinking, with its rigidly entrenched class system, he was her superior in all ways—breeding, intellect, manners, privileges and rights.

Which meant that for the present, she needed to take particular care to appear mindful of her supposed "proper place," especially around the other servants, who would notice any irregularities in her attitudes and opinions. Remaining aware of that essential point was proving every bit as difficult as pretending to be a knowledgeable housekeeper—as much at times as fulfilling her mission as a spy.

"Is his lordship's tea ready?" Sebastianne asked Mrs. Tremble that afternoon as the two of them stood on opposite sides of the big wooden table in the kitchen.

"Nearly done," the cook declared as she picked up a gleamingly sharp knife and cut the crust off a few slices of bread with a practiced hand.

In less time than Sebastianne would have imagined, the sandwiches were made and on a plate. With deft efficiency, Mrs. Tremble filled another plate with biscuits and sweetmeats, then added a dish of blackberries that had come fresh from the market that morning—the fruit one of his lordship's favorites, Sebastianne had been told.

"There ye are," Mrs. Tremble stated, as she spooned thick, clotted cream into a shallow china dish alongside one she'd already filled with golden-sweet honey. "Want me to ring for Parker?"

"No," Sebastianne said, arranging the plates and dishes on a silver tray in a way that left room for the teapot that Mrs. Tremble was now in the process of filling with boiling water. "I'll take it up myself today."

She could have let Parker carry the tray upstairs to Lord Drake, but since she'd had no opportunity yet to get inside his workroom—where he'd been closeted since early morning—this seemed an excellent chance to gain entry.

"As ye like." Mrs. Tremble set the heavy china pot onto the tray, then, duty done, returned to her dinner preparations.

Lifting the tray, Sebastianne walked out of the kitchen and a short way down the hall to the dumbwaiter that was fitted into the wall.

The small elevator, which worked on a system of weights and pulleys, was nothing less than a godsend for the staff, who used it to transport a wide variety of items between floors. It saved substantial time and energy and was just one of the many interesting and highly useful mechanical improvements Lord Drake had installed in the house. Among them were: outdoor gas lamps that illuminated the front entry and the rear garden; a pump that brought fresh water into the kitchen and laundry; and, most astonishing of all, a modern bathing chamber in his lordship's suite of rooms that contained an immense tub, a tall, boxlike stall called a "shower" and a copper water reservoir with a coal-fired heating clement that Lord Drake had engineered himself.

For the present, however, she was grateful for the more ordinary marvel of the dumbwaiter. Honestly, she wasn't sure she would have been able to carry the heavy meal upstairs on her own—at least not without overbalancing the china and sloshing hot tea across the linen-covered silver tray.

After working the pulleys and securing the box on the ground floor, she went upstairs to collect its contents. With Lord Drake's workroom close by, it was a quick walk to his door. Balancing the tray, she gave a knock. A long silence followed, so she knocked again.

"Come," he called after another lengthy pause, his tone clearly distracted.

She opened the door and moved into the room. "Good afternoon, your lordship," she said cheerfully. "I'm here with your tea and a bite to eat."

He didn't look up from where he sat hunched over a wide wooden desk, the pencil he held moving swiftly across a sheaf of paper. More notes and several books lay scattered haphazardly around him, his chestnut hair tumbled into careless disarray as if he'd spent the better part of the last hour or more running his fingers through it. Very likely he had done just that, she decided, as she watched him work, the rhythmic ticking of the various clocks scattered around the room providing the only intrusion.

Finally, his pencil ceased, and he raised his head to cast her a sideways glance. His shoulders seemed to tighten for a moment before relaxing again. "Mrs. Greenway, good day. Where is Parker?"

Since Mrs. Beatty's departure, Parker had taken to bringing Lord Drake his tea. This was only the second time since Sebastianne had become housekeeper that he had been home in the afternoon long enough to require that tea be served.

"Parker is occupied with other duties," she said, "so I am seeing to your repast myself. Where would you like to dine?" With the tray seeming to grow heavier by the moment, she cast about for a place to set it, but every surface was covered.

Piles of papers and periodicals rose in small hills and valleys across every surface and spare seat. Books—some open, others closed—towered in stacks and lined an entire wall of bookcases. A long workbench, the wood grooved and scarred by age and use, stretched the length of another wall, every surface covered in tools and wire and other mechanical paraphernalia, a great deal of which she couldn't hope to identify. A row of glass bottles stood on a shelf filled with liquids of various colors and potency, their level of hazard unclear. Not far from his desk stood a large, modern-looking globe of the world and a huge slate set into a move-able wooden frame. Advanced mathematical calculations were written across the black slate in broad strokes of white chalk—calculations that had nothing whatsoever to do with the code, she saw, but which were fascinating nonetheless. She did her best not to study them too closely but to concentrate instead on finding a place to set the tray.

There wasn't one.

Apparently realizing her dilemma, Lord Drake stood and crossed to a nearby table. Gathering up two stacks of news-papers and a pair of heavy leather-bound books, he shifted them aside. "There," he stated. "Put the tray here."

Gratefully, she did as he suggested. Straightening, she took another moment to glance around the room, linking her hands at her waist as she did. Then she remembered that, in her role as housekeeper, she ought to be pouring his tea.

In a rush, she reached out.

He chose that instant to do the same, their hands accidentally brushing together in midair over the teapot.

A charge like a spark of electricity ran through her, tingling as it traveled across her skin and through her body as though she were a human lightning rod. From the hum radiating along her nerves, she wondered if that might actually be the case.

Their gazes locked, his eyes a pure, translucent green that shone with the vibrancy of a new spring forest. In them burned a wealth of emotions that sent her heart pounding and her lungs searching desperately for air.

Then he blinked, and the look was gone.

So was his hand as he pulled away.

She did the same, withdrawing as quickly as he. Glancing down, she stared at her sturdy black leather boots and fought to steady her emotions. The entire episode had lasted no more than a few seconds, perhaps he hadn't even noticed.

Drawing breath, she forced her gaze upward again. "Shall I—that is would you like me to pour?"

His eyebrows drew tight. "No. Leave the tea. I'll see to it myself."

She nodded. "As you wish, my lord."

Dipping a quick curtsey, she took a step back to leave. As she did though, she remembered her real purpose for wanting inside this room—the cipher she'd made no progress so far in retrieving. This brief visit today had revealed nothing of use, not even a hint as to which of the many papers might hold the information she sought. She needed to be able to come in and out of the room at will without anyone questioning her presence—most especially Lord Drake!

But how?

In a sudden flash of insight, she had the answer—assuming she could convince Lord Drake that is. Drawing herself up, she met his gaze. "Your lordship, there is one more thing before I depart."

His brows arched this time. "Oh?"

"I couldn't help but notice the state of the room."

His scowl returned.

"That is to say you must be aware it could do with a good cleaning and polishing."

He crossed his arms over his chest. "Perhaps, but I like it the way it is. As I'm sure you've heard already, I don't allow anyone to touch the things in my workspace."

"Of course not, and I would treat your possessions with the utmost respect and the care they deserve. But even you must admit that every room requires a deep cleaning every now and again, even this one."

"I let Parker sweep and run a cloth over the bare spots on

occasion," he grumbled, shifting his stance from one foot to the other. "That's sufficient."

"I beg pardon, but I must disagree, my lord, given the dust I can see on the books and many of the shelves as well. And from the smudges on the windows, they look as if they haven't been washed in several months."

His jaw tightened. "Be that as it may, I can't have the maids in here buzzing around disturbing me, not to mention disturbing my things."

"Then I shall arrange for a time when you are not present."

He shook his head. "I used to have similar discussions with Mrs. Beatty, and we agreed that the servants could clean every room in the house. Every one *except* this one."

"Correct me if I am wrong," she persisted, "but I am given to understand that you did let Mrs. Beatty inside to tidy up every now and again."

"She took care not to rearrange my papers and such," he admitted begrudgingly.

"As would I," she said, her heart beating out a hopeful tattoo. "Why do we not have the same agreement as you did with Mrs. Beatty? I shall do the cleaning myself, and should you discover anything missing or out of place, you may reprimand me and dock my pay."

"Or sack you," he mumbled under his breath as if he had already contemplated such a thing.

She made no effort to pretend she had not heard. "You may do that as well should you find yourself displeased."

And then wouldn't I be in the broth, she thought, her chest suddenly tight with fear. *Tossed out of the house without the cipher.* But she sensed this was her best chance, and if she didn't find a way now, getting back into the room to search would be nearly impossible and doubly dangerous.

He studied her for a long moment, his brows furrowed over his penetrating eyes. "You're to leave the books and papers exactly as you find them. You're not to straighten or organize or rearrange in any manner whatsoever. You're not to clean or polish any of the tools or fiddle with the bottles since some of them contain potentially harmful substances."

Fitting her hands at her waist, she suppressed a smile.

"And you are never—and I mean never—to smudge, wipe or erase anything you may find written on the slate board. Some of those calculations are months, if not years, of work and you will be dismissed if they are tampered with."

"I shall give the slate a wide and reverent berth," she promised, forcing the inner elation from her voice.

A long moment of silence fell before he spoke. "Very well. You have my leave to clean and polish when it does not disturb me. See to it I have no cause to regret my decision."

"You won't, my lord, I promise. Now, I will leave you to your repast before your tea grows cold. Should you require anything further, you have only to ring."

One corner of his mouth curved up. "Thank you, Mrs. Greenway. I shall be sure to keep that in mind."

Giving a polite nod, Sebastianne turned on her heel to leave. As she did, a sharp rap of knuckles sounded at the door, and a tall, well-dressed man strode confidently over the threshold. Seconds later, he appeared to stride in again—or rather a duplicate of him did—the second man a seemingly exact copy of the first.

Twins! she realized, blinking at the unexpected sight. And not just any twins but a pair who bore a striking familial resemblance to Lord Drake. Young, handsome and strongly built, they were leanly broad-shouldered, with wavy golden brown hair and irreverent smiles. A devilish light glinted in their arresting green-gold eyes, their identical expressions giving her a disconcerting sense of seeing double. Which actually, she supposed, she was.

"Hallo, Drake," one of the young men drawled in a pleasant baritone. "Hope you don't mind us dropping in."

"We were taking a turn in the neighborhood—" the other began in his equally deep, melodious voice.

"—And decided to see if you were home," finished the first.

They smiled, their eyes turning toward her. The young men, who looked as if they were of university age, gave her a keen, head-to-foot perusal.

She straightened her shoulders and sent them a stern look for their boldness.

Rather than their being fazed, however, their smiles only widened. The one on the right even had the nerve to wink. "And who might this lovely specimen of womanhood be?" he inquired, before making her an elegant bow.

"Yes, do tell," the other said, following his brother's lead. "Had we known you had such a charming visitor, Drake, we would have called on you earlier."

Drake snorted under his breath and stepped forward. "She is not a visitor, she is my housekeeper, and I'll thank you two not to work your nonsense on her."

The winker laid a hand on his chest. "What nonsense? We're merely overwhelmed with admiration."

"Quite overcome," his twin agreed. "You leave us breathless, ma'am."

She couldn't but laugh, unsure whether to be offended or flattered.

Lord Drake, on the other hand, growled low his throat. "Well, I'm sure Mrs. Greenway has no need to listen to your guile." Standing now at her side, he met her gaze. "You are to pay no heed to my raffish younger brothers. Flirtation is their favor pastime."

"Second favorite," the winker said with an impish humor dancing in his eyes, which she suddenly noticed had slightly more green than his twin's. "I'll leave you to guess the first."

She glanced down so they wouldn't see her smile, looking up again only when she had control over her emotions. "Well, it is a pleasure to make your acquaintance, my lords—"

"Leo," the winker said before gesturing toward his twin. "And this is Lawrence."

"Lord Leo. Lord Lawrence," she greeted. "I was just on my way to the kitchen. Might I bring you some refreshment?"

"Yes," they chimed together.

"No," Lord Drake said at the same moment. "That is to say, you may send one of the footmen up with another pot of tea. I'm sure you have other matters to which you need attend."

"Indeed I do. However, I believe I can find a moment to ask Mrs. Tremble to prepare a few more sandwiches along with the tea," she ventured.

"Capital! You're as kind as you are gracious, dear ma'am," Lord Lawrence said, making her an elegant bow before stepping forward to help himself to one of the biscuits on the tray. "In the meantime, Leo and I will have to content ourselves with sampling Drake's portion. Tell Cook I look forward to more of her delectable fare." Smiling, he bit into the snack.

"Pray extend my regards as well," Lord Leo said, sending her another roguish smile.

Drake shot his brothers a dark look before returning his gaze to her. "You may go, Mrs. Greenway," Lord Drake told her. "Thank you for the tea."

"Your lordship." With a respectful smile, she turned and walked from the room.

Chapter 6

"Always knew you were deep as the Baikal Sea," Leo remarked the moment Mrs. Greenway's footsteps faded away, "but this goes beyond even my expectations. Be honest, is she *really* your housekeeper?"

Drake's jaw tightened. "Of course she is. Have I not just said so?"

Leo exchanged a quick glance with his twin, whose face wore an expression of equal amazement. "Well, I must say I can't fault your taste," he continued. "She's nothing like Mrs. Beatty."

"As I recall," Drake said, "you always liked Mrs. Beatty."

"Oh, I did. Lawrence too. Didn't you, Lawrence?"

"Most definitely," his twin agreed. "She was an excellent woman."

"Sweet as our own grandmother were she still alive," Leo went on. "But I never had the least interest in admiring Mrs. Beatty. The moment I saw your new housekeeper, it was as if I'd wandered into a garden and accidentally discovered a lush, fragrant rose in full and glorious bloom."

Lawrence gave an appreciative smile. "Exactly."

Drake's brows shot skyward. *Full and glorious bloom, my eye! What rubbish!*

The twins might be young men of twenty and continually on the prowl for any attractive females that passed their way, but he would simply have to impress upon them that dallying with Anne Greenway was forbidden.

Strictly forbidden!

Without conscious awareness, Drake's hands curved into fists at his sides. How dare they discuss Anne in such a bold fashion. Leo and Lawrence had no right to think of her like that, let alone flirt with her. Just because he himself had desired her from the first didn't mean the twins had leave to do the same.

"Mrs. Greenway isn't a rose, and you won't be admiring her in any way, shape or form, is that understood?" Drake stated in a chill tone. "She is in my employ, and you will treat her with the respect her position deserves. Besides, she is a mature woman, far too old for puppies like you."

Lawrence shrugged.

As for Leo, he just grinned, undaunted by the setdown. "Oh, a little difference in age doesn't bother me. I rather fancy older women, don't you know."

Drake tossed up his hands, then stalked to the tea tray, turning his back on them as he fought to regain his usual even-tempered, logical composure. Honestly, he didn't know why he was having such a strong reaction to his brothers' overt appreciation of Anne Greenway. Ordinarily, the twins amused him with their irreverent, devil-may-care antics, and he wasn't the jealous type. He couldn't remember ever losing his good humor over a woman before. Yet there was just something about her that brought out the most unexpected emotions in him.

The most puzzling emotions.

The blasted woman had even managed to wheedle a promise out of him to let her clean up his workroom when he'd had no intention of permitting any such thing.

Sighing inwardly, he lifted the teapot and poured himself a cup, cursing when a few drops splashed on his hand. Without bothering to offer his siblings a libation, he took a careful swallow of the hot brew in his cup, then reached for a sandwich. Maybe some food would regulate his mind, particularly since he'd only had a slice of toast and a cup of coffee for breakfast.

Turning around, he regarded his brothers. "What are you two doing here, by the way? Aren't you supposed to be up at Oxford finishing up your term?"

Lawrence sauntered forward and appropriated another handful of biscuits. "Ordinarily, yes," he said before taking a bite, "but we made special arrangements this year."

Drake arched a brow. "What *special* arrangements? Blister it, you didn't get tossed out, did you? Ned will have an apoplexy."

"Of course not," Leo declared with some affront. Stepping forward, he helped himself to a stack of sandwiches. "Term's nearly over, and we wanted to come down for the Season, so we convinced the dean to let us sit for exams early."

"Oh? And how did you manage that miraculous feat?"

The twins paused, exchanging a highly charged look.

Leo, who had always tended to be the chief spokesman for the two, continued the story. "Seems Dean Whittlesby owed us something of a favor."

Intrigued in spite of his better judgment, Drake waited to hear the rest.

"Whittlesby's son, Bertie, is in our year, you know," Leo said. "A wild sort, who likes his drink rather more than he ought."

"Likes bullying people, too, especially the first-termers, whom he delights in cheating out of their spare funds," Lawrence volunteered. "Mind you, he's an idiot, who doesn't have the sense God gave a jackstraw. If he weren't one of the dean's sons, he'd have gotten the boot ages ago."

Leo nodded. "Well said, brother. Anyway, we happened to be walking past an alley one evening not long ago—"

On their way to or from a pub, Drake surmised, though he said nothing.

"—when we noticed ol' Bertie getting the supper beaten out of him by a trio of none-too-pleasant-looking local journeymen. Seems he'd been trying to dupe them at cards and made a hash of the matter.

"Normally we'd have left him to enjoy the fruits of his labor as it were, but he looked in a bad way and was moaning like he was fit to die. Lawrence and I don't countenance murder, so galling as it seemed at the time, we stepped in."

Drake shook his head. "Did you never think to call the constabulary? What if those men had had help from more of their friends?"

"Oh, they did," Leo said, calmly munching his sandwiches. "Turned into a vicious brawl, two against one. But we knew how to handle ourselves. We didn't grow up with four older brothers, who were all handy with their fives, for nothing."

Lawrence grinned.

Leo grinned back, the pair of them clearly having enjoyed the encounter.

Drake lowered himself into a chair and stretched out his legs. "So you stopped the beating and took your . . . well, I won't say friend—"

"Classmate," Leo suggested.

"—Classmate back to his rooms?"

The twins exchanged another look. "Not exactly. That's

when the constabulary did show up. We convinced them not to take the three of us down to the gaol but instead over to Dean Whittlesby. Besides, anyone could see that Bertie needed a doctor, and the authorities weren't too keen on risking the life of an Oxford dean's son, nor arresting the brothers of a peer. So off we went."

"And?" Drake encouraged, taking a drink of his now-lukewarm tea.

"And the dean was grateful. Thanked us for saving ol' Bertie's life and for keeping the school from facing a potentially embarrassing scandal. He seemed rather anxious not to be in our debt and offered us a reward for our—how did he put it?"

"—'Brave actions and gentlemanly discretion,'" Lawrence quoted.

Leo snapped his fingers. "That's it. I think he meant to pay us off, but instead we said we could do with a couple of favors."

"The early exams, obviously," Drake supplied. "What else?"

"We didn't think it right to leave Bertie free to continue his reign of terror there at school, so we asked Dean Whittlesby to put the pinch on him and make him stop bullying the first-years.

"He seemed genuinely shocked at that piece of information and said he'd be pleased to do precisely that. The old man was furious over it, I'll tell you. So I don't think Bertie will have such an easy time of it next term, even after his broken ribs, fractured jaw and head-to-foot bruises heal. So here we are in Town and looking forward to a bit of fair weather sport."

"Well, welcome to the city," Drake said with a wry smile. "Have you stopped at Clybourne House yet, or am I the first to receive a call?"

Leo ran his fingers over his gold watch fob. "Actually about that—"

Just then a knock sounded at the door, and Lyles entered with the second pot of tea, cups and more sandwiches. Once he'd gone and another good share of the food had been plated and consumed, Drake continued the discussion. "You were saying?" he encouraged.

The twins exchanged sideways glances.

Lawrence set his plate aside and wiped his mouth with his napkin. "We were thinking of taking up bachelor's quarters."

"We're coming on one-and-twenty soon," Leo stated, "and what with Ned and Claire adding to their nursery—

"—not to mention she and Mama busy with Ella's come-out—" Lawrence inserted.

"—We thought it might be a good time to strike out on our own," Leo continued, as the two of them began talking back and forth in tandem as they had since they were small boys.

"—The only problem is the funds—" Lawrence said.

"—Which we'll have with next quarter's allowance, but that's not until June—"

"—And we don't want to wait."

"—Or ask Ned, I presume," Drake concluded aloud.

They both met his gaze, then shook their heads. "No."

Drake steepled his fingers and let them wait in suspense a minute more. "Find something reasonable, and I'll give you what you need for the rent," Drake told them, wondering if he'd been this adventurous and full of fire at their age. Then he realized he'd been too obsessed with his studies back then to worry over mundane matters such as independent living quarters and how to extract the most fun from the Season.

He was still rather too obsessed with his work, he admitted to himself. But he loved what he did and wouldn't want his life any other way.

His gaze fell on the tea tray, his thoughts drifting again to Anne Greenway and how quickly and effortlessly she'd fit into his household. As for the way she fit into his life . . . well she'd stirred that up from the instant she'd arrived. And if his response to her earlier was any example, he feared she would continue to do so.

Before he had time to ruminate further, Leo and Lawrence hurried forward and shook his hand. Wearing identical white-toothed grins, they thanked him profusely for his generous assistance.

He waved off their gratitude. "Just see to it you stay out of trouble—" At their sudden looks of concern, he amended his statement, "Life-threatening trouble anyway. Nothing illegal or needlessly dangerous."

"I believe we can promise that," Leo stated.

"Yes, you have our word," Lawrence agreed solemnly.

"Good. Now, I have work to do, which you and Mrs. Greenway have each succeeded in disrupting. So drink the last of that tea and be off with you."

The twins did exactly as they were told, and bid him a friendly good-bye. Eating one last tiny sandwich that had escaped his brothers' notice—a delicious ham and pear chutney—he returned to his desk.

He'd just settled in when he heard a movement near the door.

And there she stood again, Anne Greenway, poised in the doorway, her hair the color of fire and October leaves with those few silvery strands glinting like moonlight. He met her gaze and felt his heart speed a few beats faster.

For my own sanity, I ought to dismiss her, he thought, wishing he felt nothing but calm disinterest in her presence.

But exactly as she'd promised, she'd seen to the efficient management of his household, which was humming along as smoothly as it ever had under Mrs. Beatty's reign. She was performing her job, and he had no legitimate cause to terminate her employment. No reason, that is, other than his own unwanted desire for her.

Even his brothers were attracted to her. Then again, the twins liked anything female that was warm and had a pulse, so they weren't really much of a gauge of Anne's true allure.

No, he admonished himself, *I am a man, not a beast, and I will govern my needs—even if it may kill me.*

"Yes?" he asked in as pleasantly disinterested a tone as he could manage. "Is there something you require?"

She took a step inside the room, her hands clasped against her skirts. "I stopped to inquire whether I should lay extra places at the dinner table tonight for your brothers. Are they planning to return?"

He shook his head, gripping a fountain pen tightly between his fingers. "No, not this evening, though I'm sure they'll visit again when the mood strikes." He paused. "They wanted an advance in order to acquire their own residence. Seems they're anxious to assert their independence."

His fingers stilled against the pen, wondering why he'd shared that bit of information with her.

She smiled and walked a little farther into the room. "Boys are like that, or should I say young men in their lordships' case."

"Yes, boys like to stretch their wings, and young men as well." He studied her for a moment. "Do you speak from personal experience? I never thought to ask if you have siblings. Sisters? Brothers?"

"No sisters . . . but I have brothers," she said, lines suddenly appearing on her forehead. "Two brothers."

Why did she look so uncomfortable? Surely discussing one's family wasn't cause for upset. Then again, not all people were as lucky with their families as he was with his own.

"Well, I have five brothers and two younger sisters," he continued as if he hadn't noticed anything untoward about her reaction. "Makes for quite a crowd when everyone is together."

"Y-yes, I am sure it does." She twisted her fingers against her skirts and glanced away. "If there are no special arrangements for tonight, then, I shall leave you once again to your work. I have disturbed you quite enough for one afternoon."

Yes, he thought, *you have,* warmth curling in his belly. "By the way, I shall take my dinner in here tonight."

"As you wish, my lord. I will inform Mrs. Tremble." Coming forward, she picked up the tea tray, with its now-empty plates and cups, then turned and departed.

More than a minute passed before Drake was able to focus enough to return to his calculations and equations.

Whatever is the matter with me? Sebastianne thought as she slid the tea tray into the dumbwaiter. *Why did I tell him I have brothers!* she asked herself, walking a few steps before pausing near the door to the servants' staircase.

Hadn't she been warned countless times against this very possibility? Hadn't the operative who'd trained her given her a list of strict instructions from which she was not to deviate?

Always stick to your cover identity and don't lose sight of your objective.

Never forget that Byron is a mark, and your reaction to him is irrelevant.

Work to gain the trust of the household, especially Byron, so you can locate and copy the cipher, then return to France.

And above all else, never reveal the details of your real life.

But France—and her real life—already seemed so far

away, like a dream that might never come again. Her brothers, Luc and Julien . . . she ached for missing them. Papa, too. How much she wished she could be back with them all. And yet she was doing this for them, she reminded herself. She must, since there was no other way.

So why was it so difficult to harden her feelings toward Lord Drake? Why did her defenses weaken in his presence and make her forget they were enemies instead of two people sharing an enjoyable conversation? He'd told her about his family and without considering, she'd told him about hers, revealing details she never should have shared.

Then there was the awareness that hummed between them like a gathering storm, a silent connection that had nothing to do with plots or plans, but of genuine rapport instead. Genuine attraction too, fierce and fiery such as she'd never before experienced, not even with her darling Thierry.

But her love for her husband had been real, while her emotions for Lord Drake were . . . well, she didn't know what they were other than dangerous.

And forbidden.

Temptingly, tantalizingly forbidden.

A tremor raced through her, her mouth growing dry. Then she scowled, the lines on her forehead becoming so tight the skin actually hurt. Abruptly aware of the discomfort, she forced the frown to ease.

Remember your instructions, she reminded herself.

Remember that any feelings you might have for Drake Byron are immaterial.

Protecting my family is all that matters.

Accomplishing my mission is the only goal—even if it was an objective not of her choosing but rather something that had been forced upon her by means of fear and threat of retribution.

She sighed, so tired of this war, so weary of the strife

that had plagued what ought to have been good years, joyous times if only Thierry and Maman were still alive. But they were gone, and she had her duty, however repugnant it might be.

Straightening her spine, she resolved to do what she must. At least she'd made progress and gained permission to enter Lord Drake's workroom. Surely the code was hidden someplace in that scattered mess of papers and projects, books and notes and gadgets. If it was there, she would find it.

She could afford to do no less.

The servants' door swung open on well-greased hinges, Lyles walking through. "Mrs. Greenway," he said by way of greeting. "I came up to clear away his lordship's tray."

"Already done," she said. "However, please inform Mr. Stowe that Lord Drake will be dining in this evening. I shall do the same for Mrs. Tremble."

"Right, ma'am. I'll go find 'im now."

"I believe Mr. Stowe is in the front drawing room replenishing supplies."

Lyles smiled. "Maybe he can use some help."

She watched as he disappeared up the long hallway. Only when she knew she was alone did she let a bit of the starch ease out of her shoulders. She had accounts to see to and fine pastry to make for his lordship's dessert, so she'd best be getting on with it.

Rallying again, she started downstairs.

Chapter 7

Over the next three days, Lord Drake remained in his workroom, coming and going from the chamber at erratic, thoroughly unpredictable hours of the day and night. This gave Sebastianne absolutely no opportunity to set her plan in motion to clean the room—and search it. Instead, she was forced to bide her time and concentrate on her duties as housekeeper.

In fact, the only time she actually saw Lord Drake was when she brought his tea or a meal to him. He was unfailingly pleasant on these occasions, but distracted, his thoughts clearly somewhere besides the confines of his house on Audley Street. The few brief glimpses she was able to get of his work led her to suspect he was postulating theories regarding the solar system. Her assumption was further reinforced by the large, finely made orrery she caught operating a time or two, the tiny model planets circling impressively on their wire-suspended, clockwork-driven orbits.

When she was a child, her father had owned one of the wondrous machines; she could remember watching it in fascination as he told her about the stars, moons and planets and how each one revolved around the sun.

But her father's orrery was long gone, destroyed in a house fire in Paris the year before her mother died, together with a number of priceless family mementos and many cherished volumes from her father's once-extensive book collection. She wondered if Lord Drake owned any of those same works and wished she had the luxury of exploring his library in depth.

But she resisted, confining herself to her duties instead. After all, it wouldn't do for Lord Drake or the staff to discover her poring over his beautiful leather-bound books—particularly the ones related to science and mathematics. Not to mention the fact that a fair number of them were written in languages other than English, including her own native French.

While on her daily rounds inspecting the rooms for dust and general cleanliness, she'd noticed that he maintained volumes in more than a dozen languages, including Greek, Latin, French, Arabic, Russian and Italian. She could read all those except the Arabic. As for the rest, she could only hazard an educated guess about their origin and contents.

What about Lord Drake? Was he able to read all those languages? She rather suspected he could and perhaps a few more as well.

Now, early on the fourth morning, Lord Drake finally emerged from his self-imposed hibernation. She was crossing the hallway with an armful of neatly pressed linens when he opened the door and stepped out of his workroom, pausing for a moment to stretch his arms above his head in a most appealing manner. His clothing and hair were rumpled, she saw, his cheeks shadowed with at least two days' growth of whiskers. Despite his disheveled appearance, though, he looked delectable.

She tightened her arms around the sheets and schooled her features so they revealed nothing of her inner thoughts. "Good morning, your lordship," she said with polite deference.

He smothered a yawn, one that failed to erase the smile that played around his mouth. "And to you, Mrs. Greenway. A brilliant day, is it not?"

Considering the thick, dark storm clouds lumbering menacingly on the horizon, she wasn't sure "brilliant" was an apt description. But who was she to gainsay Lord Drake's clearly buoyant good humor? He must have made substantial progress in his calculations, she surmised. Papa always celebrated like a little boy who'd found an extra franc in the street when he finished one of his equations. Apparently Lord Drake took after him in that regard.

"Well, the garden does need watering," she observed.

His grin widened, clearly approving her optimism. "Exactly." Another yawn caught him just then, his eyes tearing slightly in a way that made his translucent green eyes sparkle like gems. Still smiling, he wiped the moisture away with the edge of his fingers.

I wonder if he slept at all last night? Assuming his latest mathematical proof was indeed finished, he could afford to get some rest—and take a morning meal.

"Shall I have breakfast sent up to your bedchamber?" she asked. "Or would you prefer to dine in the morning room?"

He sent her a brief contemplative look, rubbing a large palm over his stomach. "I am famished, now that you mention it. Tell Mrs. Tremble I'll be wanting the full board this morning, including some of her excellent beef-and-kidney pie, if she has any in the larder."

Sebastianne smiled. "I believe she prepared one fresh only yesterday."

"And eggs. Be sure to fry them so the yolks are warm and runny."

"Warm and runny they shall be."

"Good." He paused, his gaze roaming slowly over her face for a contemplative moment before glancing away. "Well, I'd best be on my way upstairs."

So should I, she thought, but she wasn't about to follow after him. The linens could remain here on the ground floor while she went to consult with the cook. Clutching the sheets more tightly against her chest, she waited for him to precede her.

He turned and started for the staircase, then stopped. "Oh, one more thing. I shall be going out this evening, so please inform Mrs. Tremble that I will not require dinner."

So he will be gone tonight, will he? she thought. If she arranged matters right, she would have a chance to search his workroom. Swallowing against a sudden pang of nerves, she nodded her understanding.

For a moment he looked as if he might say more. Instead, he turned on his heel once again and leapt up the stairs with far more energy and agility than a man who'd lost a night's sleep ought to have.

Sighing, she too went on her way.

Rather than wait until Lord Drake left the house that evening, Sebastianne decided to start cleaning his workroom while it was still light outside—or at least as light as the rainy day would allow. After all, he'd given her permission to proceed at a time when he was not using the room, and what better occasion than a day when he was sound asleep upstairs?

She'd learned this helpful bit of information from Waxman, who had appeared in the servants' hall to inform the staff in a deadly serious tone that his lordship was resting and was not to be disturbed. He shot a very pointed look at Parker and Cobbs, who'd been gossiping together over a midday cup of tea. They grew instantly silent and assured the valet that they would tread on cat's feet should their duties take them anywhere near the master's rooms.

The moment Waxman departed, the two young women had rolled their eyes at each other, placed a single finger each against their lips and mimed a humorless "Shh." Whereupon they both began to giggle.

Tremble shushed them for being "pert" and "full of unbecoming nonsense," but Sebastianne knew the two maids were only teasing and that they would rather walk over broken glass in their bare feet than cause Lord Drake a moment's displeasure.

The entire staff felt that way, everyone treating his lordship with a warm respect that bordered on adoration. For in spite of his eccentricities, Lord Drake was generous and kind and always treated his servants with consideration and respect.

"Best master I've ever had the privilege to serve," Mr. Stowe had told Sebastianne once, and even in the brief time she'd worked there, she had to agree.

Which left her stomach twisting and her hands damp when she went into his workroom that afternoon, knowing she was about to betray him—or at least make an earnest attempt to do so.

But it has to be done, she told herself as she pushed aside her qualms.

Having already informed the staff that she—and she alone—would be cleaning Lord Drake's workroom, she entered the chamber and closed the door behind her.

Nearly three hours later, she'd rid the room of a great deal of dust, hidden grime, and small items clearly destined for the rubbish bin—broken pen nibs, bits of chalk, spent ink blotters, wadded-up scraps of paper and assorted other useless ephemera that he'd obviously never quite managed to throw away. She'd taken special care not to disturb any of his books and papers, as she'd flipped methodically through each one in search of scribbled notes and equations related to the cipher.

The rain stopped as she cleaned, the sun peeking out from behind the clouds to spread a cheerful illumination through the room. In spite of extra light, however, her efforts proved futile, at least when it came to uncovering the cipher.

Tired and irritated, she wiped the back of one arm across the light sheen of perspiration beading her forehead and despaired of ever locating the secret code.

He must have hidden it, she realized.

But where?

Perhaps it was in a locked cabinet or even a money chest? But she saw no evidence of a metal safe or vault, and as for the cabinets, she'd already checked inside those and found nothing out of the ordinary.

She was just about to begin her search again with an eye to finding a concealed strongbox, when she heard a footfall that made her turn and look up.

Lord Drake stood on the threshold—freshly bathed and shaved, his close-trimmed chestnut hair brushed neatly away from his face. As for his attire, he looked utterly resplendent in a black evening coat and breeches with fine white linen, a Marcella waistcoat and polished black leather dress shoes.

For a moment, she couldn't tear her gaze from him, captivated by his sheer masculine splendor. To say he was handsome was a gross understatement. Looking as he did, she was sure he could stop any woman in her tracks and make her pant with hopeful lust for his time and attention.

At the thought of time and lust, she wondered where he was going this evening. Was he planning to pay a visit to his mistress, perhaps?

Her hands clenched at her sides at the idea before she

shook off the reaction. Whatever his plans, she scolded herself, they didn't matter to her. The only thing of importance was finding the blasted cipher and the place where he'd hidden it.

She didn't move or speak as he glanced around the room, one of his eyebrows arching upward in obvious recognition of her housekeeping efforts.

"Am I going to have to sack you, after all, Mrs. Greenway?" he drawled, as he continued to survey the room. "Considering your promise not to disturb any of my things, this room appears rather too shipshape for comfort."

Her stiff posture unfroze, annoyance over his accusation warming her muscles. Perhaps her primary goal had been to search for the cipher, but she'd done an excellent job cleaning and sorting through his mess while she was at it. The least he could do was show some appreciation!

"Everything is still here and where you can easily locate it," she countered. "As for the room being 'too shipshape,' that's because I took a dust cloth, a broom, and a rubbish bin to the problem. In future, you oughtn't let the stray bits collect so long. I mean, honestly, would it hurt you to toss out broken pen quills and bits of used-up chalk every now and then?"

"Ah," he said, "but that's why I employ a full complement of staff. So they can toss out the stray bits for me."

"When you let them," she replied. "Mrs. Beatty must have had her hands full."

Suddenly she stopped, realizing she sounded more like a young woman who'd grown up speaking her own mind than the respectful, deferential servant she was supposed to be. What if Lord Drake took offense and actually did dismiss her? Then where would she be?

Waiting quietly, she listened to her heart pound out a frantic tattoo in her chest.

A long moment passed before a begrudging smile curved his lips—much to her profound relief.

"And now it seems the reverse is true," he remarked.

As she contemplated his meaning, he strolled farther into the room.

Does he mean he has his hands full with me?

Before she could form a retort she knew she oughtn't make, he began flipping through various books and papers, making little "umms" and "hmms" low in his throat as he conducted a kind of audit.

"You'll find everything in order," she stated when he offered no actual words of criticisms.

"It all *seems* to still be here."

"Just as I assured you it would." Spine straight, she folded her hands at her waist.

He ambled toward the large, movable slate board and stopped to peruse the chalk-written calculations that crowded the surface.

"Your astronomical equations are completely intact," she said. "I didn't touch so much as the chalk dust on the frame."

He swung sharply around and pinned her with a look, his eyes suddenly narrowed. For long seconds, he stared. "How did you know that proof deals with astronomy? For that matter, how is it you're even familiar with astronomy? It's not a commonplace discipline."

A sick lump dropped to the bottom of her stomach.

Oh, my accursed tongue, she fretted. *I really ought to have cut it out long ago. Now look what I've done.* And if she hoped to salvage the situation, she knew she'd better think and think fast.

"Well," she said slowly, giving herself as much time as possible to form a reply. "You've got dozens of books and notes strewn from one end of the room to the other, all dealing with planets and stars and moons. I couldn't help but read a few words here and there. Not to mention the o—"

She clamped her lips closed, cutting herself off this time before she had the chance to say the word "orrery."

I really do seem determined to destroy myself today, don't I?

"—The . . . um . . ." she waved at hand toward his orrery, "the m-machine there that makes all the little balls twirl around. Which is why I just assumed that the bit of mathematical scribbling up on your slate must be related as well."

She drew a breath before continuing. "As for knowing what astronomy is, I am literate and enjoy reading when I have the opportunity. My education is broad enough that I've heard of astronomy even if I don't understand any of the specifics of the subject. After all, a visitor to a museum can recognize a piece of artwork without knowing how to create it. So you see, my comment was nothing more than a logical guess. Assuming I'm right?"

Heart thundering in her ears, her throat dry as a windswept street, she waited to see if he believed her tale. Or had she pushed her explanation too far?

He met her gaze for another long moment, his own eyes still narrowed with lingering suspicion. Then, abruptly, he relaxed. "Yes, you are exactly right. And familiar with the subject or not, you have more native understanding than most university-educated men. Half of them don't even know that the earth actually revolves around the sun and not the other way 'round."

"Does it?" she quipped with deliberately feigned ignorance.

He smiled. "It does."

Unable to help herself, she smiled back.

After a moment, he glanced away. "I have an engagement this evening as I advised you earlier, so if you have finished with your cleaning, I would appreciate a measure of privacy."

"Of course, your lordship. I was just polishing a few last odds and ends when you came in. I'll collect my supplies and leave you to your work."

Giving a nod of thanks, he strode behind his desk and busied himself with some of the documents stacked on its surface.

Gathering her rags and broom and buckets, she carried all of them into the hall, drawing the door closed behind her. She was relieved to find the corridor empty since a fine tremor chased over her skin the moment she was clear of the room.

Leaning back against the wall, she gave an inaudible sigh.

A minute passed as she steadied her nerves.

Then another.

She was about to collect the cleaning implements and make her way belowstairs when she noticed that the work-room door—which she thought she'd firmly latched—had drifted ajar. It stood open the faintest sliver of an inch, providing a narrow view into the room. As she reached out to close it, she stopped, her gaze riveted on Lord Drake.

No longer seated behind his desk, he'd crossed to the far end of the room so that he stood in profile. Clearly unaware that she was watching, he reached up and lifted a rather unremarkable landscape painting from the wall. She'd dismissed it entirely when she'd been searching the room.

Now she realized what a grave mistake that had been. For behind the painting, engineered into the very wall boards themselves, lay a safe.

Why had she not thought of it before? *He has a hidden safe!*

But even as she began contemplating ways to get inside, she saw that it wouldn't be easy. The safe appeared to be of a sophisticated design, similar to one of several her contact had shown her as part of her training for this task. If Lord Drake's safe was the same as that other one, then it used a special key to unlock a system of internal iron bolts that ran the length of the door. Nearly impossible to penetrate, she knew she didn't have the skill to even attempt opening it—not even with the smattering of lock-picking skills her contact had also done his best to teach her.

No, she would need the key to get inside, just as Lord Drake did.

Watching, she waited to see where he kept that key, waiting for him to take it out of his pocket or from a drawer inside his desk—a lock she might have a chance of picking open.

Instead, her mouth opened in silent amazement as she saw him insert a pair of fingers into his elegantly tied neckcloth and begin extracting what appeared to be a fine gold chain.

Up and up it came, the chain lengthening until at last he pulled free a gleaming brass key.

Why of all the infallible precautions!

Even if she had somehow discovered the safe on her own, she knew she would have gone mad trying to locate the key. After all, who would imagine he wore the blighted thing around his own neck!

Unable to look away, she watched him insert the key into the lock and open the metal door. Inside were stacks of pound notes and a few leather pouches she assumed contained coins. She also saw the thick, dark outline of bundled papers that could only be extremely important documents. Among them must surely be the cipher. She would stake her life on it.

A man like Lord Drake wouldn't take such elaborate precautions just to protect money and ordinary papers. No, he was protecting something of far greater worth.

He was protecting secrets.

Secrets she finally knew where to find.

Heart beating wildly between her ears, she backed stealthily away from the door, knowing she dare not so much as touch it lest Lord Drake turn and catch her spying.

Leaving the cleaning supplies where they sat for fear she would make a noise, she tiptoed away; she would send one of the maids up in a little while to collect the items.

In the meantime, she had a great deal to contemplate.

She now knew where to find the cipher. But *mon Dieu,* how was she ever going to get the key, since Lord Drake wore it around his own neck?

Chapter 8

With a bag of gold guineas in hand, Drake counted out what he thought would be sufficient for his evening on the Town, then slipped them inside the interior pocket of his coat. Pulling the strings closed on the leather pouch, he reached to place it back inside the safe when a long, unlikely creak sounded in the hallway. He paused and looked around, noticing as he did that the door to his workroom stood open a couple of inches, wide enough for anyone walking past to glance in and see exactly what he was doing.

Striding across, he opened the door, half-expecting to find one of the servants in the hallway. But the corridor stood empty—or at least empty of human beings—only the broom, bucket and dust cloths Mrs. Greenway had used for her cleaning expedition taking up space where they had been propped against the wall.

Curious she hadn't taken them with her, he mused. But then, he supposed that was one of the upstairs maids' jobs, his housekeeper only troubling herself to clean his workroom today because he wouldn't let anyone of the others inside.

He'd lost a week's work the last time one of them had touched his things. Another man would have dismissed Cobbs for the error, but she'd cried and said she was ever so sorry and it would never happen again. Knowing Cobbs was a well-meaning sort and generally performed her duties with skill, he hadn't had the heart to do anything but give her a reprimand and send her on her way, vowing never to let any of them clean his domain again.

Until today.

Until Mrs. Greenway, who, he begrudgingly admitted, seemed to have managed the task without causing any damage. Everything was basically where he'd left it—only a little neater now—and more importantly, intact. The room smelled sweet too, the floors and woodwork tidy and gleaming with a fresh coat of lemon polish, the window glass sparkling and clearer than he could recall its being in ages.

Odd how she'd guessed that his mathematical proof dealt with astronomy. Then again, as she'd said, her conclusion was only logical, he supposed, considering all the books and papers on the subject that he kept strewn around the room. Reasonable, as well, that the noise he'd heard was nothing more than that—a noise. Old houses creaked and squeaked and groaned sometimes—his own being no exception.

Giving a shrug, he shut the door, making sure the lock clicked tightly this time. Returning to the safe, he tucked the money pouch back inside. As he did, he shifted some of the contents around inside. Among them, within a leather sheath, was the secret code he'd developed for the War Office. And just recently he'd improved the code, adding a number of even more complex equations to the mix.

The War Office had a copy for safekeeping, as did his brother Edward, but he preferred to keep the originals in his own hands. In his own safe, which he'd taken great pains to make sure was the best and strongest available. He knew the

French would love to get their hands on the code since apparently even their finest minds couldn't replicate his work, or so Edward had heard it secretly rumored.

Of course there had been the attempted burglary here at the town house last fall, but he'd put excellent precautions in place and wasn't concerned. His staff had keen eyes as well and were unfailingly attentive and loyal, which they'd amply proven on that occasion.

On the evening in question, Morton and Harvey had been up late caring for a sick horse when they'd seen a faint light in the house and noticed the window to Drake's workroom braced open. Aware that Drake was away at Braebourne, Edward's principal estate in Gloucestershire, they knew something was amiss. They investigated and discovered a strange man going through their master's belongings. With surprise on their sides, they'd subdued the intruder with only a minor scuffle, then called in the authorities.

Nothing had been taken, it was found, and the man had none of Drake's possessions concealed on his person even though he claimed he'd broken in to steal valuables. But why, Drake had wondered afterward, had the thief chosen his town house when there were others nearby with items of far greater worth to steal? And why pick this particular room, when any burglar with sense would have gone straight for the dining and drawing rooms in search of the silver? Drake had no proof, but he was convinced the man had been there searching for the code.

Well, if they tried again, they would be just as unsuccessful. Not only had he installed the sophisticated wall safe that lay behind the landscape painting, but he'd taken to wearing the key that opened it. No one but he and his valet knew he wore the key around his neck, and he had complete faith in Waxman, who'd served in the Army before he'd been mustered out with a bad knee and gone into service.

There was Vanessa, he conceded, but she had no curiosity about such things and even less interest in his work. They never spoke of the key, and he never mentioned either the code or the reason he'd taken to wearing the key. In deference to her wishes, he usually removed it while they were in bed together, but it was always back around his neck again when he dressed to leave.

Speaking of which, he thought, as he closed the safe door and locked it, he supposed he ought to pay her a visit. She'd sent him a note a couple of days ago—instantly identifiable by its pink stationery and gardenia fragrance—which urged him to put aside his work and pay her a call. Instead, he'd put the note aside, far too immersed in his theoretical constructs to be interested in conducting any midnight trysts. But with his work concluded, for the time being at least, he was free to do as he liked. Yet even as he considered the idea of spending the night in his mistress's bed, he rejected it.

For one, he was scheduled to attend the theater tonight with the family and would likely find himself invited for a late supper afterward at Clybourne House. He could always excuse himself, he was sure, but strangely enough he wasn't certain he wished to be excused. Part of him would much rather watch the play, talk and relax with his family, then return home.

Then again, if Anne Greenway were the one waiting for him . . . ruefully he knew he'd dash off his excuses for both the theater and the supper and unhesitatingly spend those hours in bed with her.

Ignoring the arousal that was suddenly plaguing him, he lifted the painting from where it sat on the floor and hung it back in its place. Taking his time making certain the canvas was straight, he focused on ridding his mind of thoughts of his housekeeper and how lovely he imagined she would look lying naked against his sheets, her magnificent hair flowing around her like scattered autumn leaves.

And here he'd spent the past week assuring himself he was doing better on the wanting-Anne-Greenway front. *So much for effective self-delusion.*

Well, the inclination to bed her would pass soon enough, and what better way to put her out of his mind than to surround himself with family. Within the hour, she'd be the last person in his thoughts.

Drake traced his pencil over a page in the small notepad he always kept tucked in his coat pocket. Usually he used it to jot down ideas and random equations. Instead, as he sat in the Clybourne box, waiting for the curtain to rise on a performance of *Macbeth,* it wasn't mathematics on his mind.

"Who is that?" murmured the dulcet voice of his sister, Mallory, from the seat to his right.

Imperceptibly, he jumped, having failed to notice her as she'd slipped into the seat a few moments ago. Her husband, Adam, was still across the small aisle talking to Cade and Meg about harvesting methods of all things.

"She's no one," he lied.

Putting a halt to his sketching, he flipped the leather cover closed over the drawing he'd been doing of Anne Greenway, then slid the notepad into the inner silk-lined pocket of his evening coat.

Mallory angled her head and gave him a clearly disbelieving look. "For *no one,* she's awfully pretty. Someone you're pursuing? And don't worry, now that I'm married I can admit to knowing all about the amorous liaisons in which men engage. Adam tells me such tales of things he hears at the club. You wouldn't believe the half of them." She paused. "Then again, maybe you would, especially if you ever set foot in the club."

"I visit on occasion, and clearly Adam should keep his mouth shut," Drake grumbled.

Mallory let out a chortling laugh. "I'll have to tell him you said so."

He frowned, casting a quick glance toward the man in question and his other relations to make sure his conversation with Mallory was going unnoticed. Assured it was, he relaxed—slightly.

Only imagine, Drake thought, *if I told her the truth—that I was drawing my housekeeper!*

A good thing Mallory rarely paid visits to his town house, or she would realize instantly the identity of the mystery woman. But he preferred to leave Mrs. Greenway exactly that—a mystery—along with his interest in her.

"Let us speak of other things," he said, wanting done with the topic. "I hear felicitations are in order and that I'm to be an uncle again. When is the little one due?"

Mallory flushed in a way that made her cheek glow with happiness and contentment, her curiosity clearly diverted at mention of her impending motherhood.

"It's probably a tad too soon to be absolutely positive, and Adam wasn't supposed to tell anyone, but December, I think. Assuming I truly am with child—"

"—Which you obviously believe you are," he said.

Cheeks glowing brighter, she nodded. "Mama is already encouraging Adam and me to stay at Braebourne for my lying-in. But I'd like to have the baby at home, at Gresham Park. I just have a feeling it's going to be a boy, and I want him born in the place that will one day be his."

"Well, so long as you're both healthy afterward, that's all that matters."

Smiling, Mallory leaned forward and brushed a kiss across his cheek. "He's lucky to have an uncle like you."

Drake gave a quiet snort. "He'll have loads of uncles.

And cousins. Good Lord, if the lot of you keep producing offspring at the rate you are, we'll have a cricket team in no time."

"Apparently Jack has already made mention of the idea. He says his girls should be allowed to play since he knows they'll beat any of the boys. Knowing Jack—and Grace—I rather suspect he's right."

This time, they both grinned.

Not long after, the cackling pronouncements of witches began the play, Adam sliding into his seat on the other side of Mallory. From the corner of his eye, Drake saw them join hands.

Forcing his attention to the players on the stage, he watched the story unfold. By the time the interval arrived, however, he was more than ready to stretch his legs. Offering his excuses, he made his way into the hall, hoping if he went quickly enough, he could make it downstairs to the refreshment tables before he was stopped by an acquaintance wanting to talk. He hadn't gone ten feet before his hopes disappeared.

"Lord Drake. We were just coming to pay our respects to you and your family," Richard Manning, Viscount Saxon, said as he extended a gloved hand.

Possessed of a tall, robust frame, the viscount had thick dark hair that was greying heavily along the temples. It gave him a rather distinguished look that complemented his square jaw and long Roman nose. Despite being in his early fifties, the viscount exuded a confident charm that Drake guessed still had the power to attract the ladies.

When they'd been introduced a couple of weeks before at Ava and Claire's afternoon fête, Drake had learned that Lord Saxon owned a prosperous, well-run estate in Devonshire; that he was a widower, who had lost his wife seven years earlier; and that he was very protective of his only child, Verity, who at nineteen, was making her come-out this Season and her very first trip to London.

Drake had made Miss Manning's acquaintance at Ava and Claire's fête as well, finding her a pretty, well-mannered, yet shy young lady. Having been forewarned by his mother that he was already in the offing as a possible suitor for her hand, he'd done his best at the time to be polite and attentive without giving the least bit of encouragement on that score to either Verity Manning or her father.

To his exasperation, however, he could see that his efforts had failed to take hold and that they were both still under the mistaken impression that he might be brought up to scratch. Although why Saxon thought he'd make a good husband for his daughter, Drake didn't know.

Mama, no doubt, had been singing his praises to the man, leaving out certain bits of information, such as Drake's complete lack of interest in being leg-shackled.

In general, Mama wasn't the sort to interfere in her children's lives, especially when it came to playing matchmaker. But perhaps all the recent marriages in the family had been putting unfortunate ideas in her head. One would think, since she had eight children, that she could let one of them remain unwed—namely himself. He knew she only wanted him—and all his siblings—to be happy, but he wished she would accept the fact that he liked his bachelor state and leave it at that.

He also wished in future that she would refrain from setting him in the path of the eligible young daughters of her acquaintances and friends. Although to be fair, he supposed that happening upon Lord Saxon and his daughter tonight in the theater corridor couldn't be laid at Mama's feet—or at least not directly.

Wishing once more that he'd quite literally been faster out of the box, he mustered a pleasant smile and reached out to shake the other man's hand. Like the time before, he found Saxon's grip as firm and forthright as the viscount was himself.

"How do you do, my lord? Miss Manning?" Drake began. "I trust both of you are enjoying tonight's performance?"

"Very much," Lord Saxon stated. "I think Verity in particular is relishing the experience. This is her first time seeing Shakespeare performed in a real theater."

Drake turned his gaze toward Miss Manning. "Then how fortunate that the players are so skilled this evening. Bad acting can ruin even the Bard's illustrious work."

"Oh, I cannot imagine that," Verity Manning stated with enough enthusiasm that her sweep of blond curls danced around her head. "To my mind, Shakespeare is always grand, no matter who may recite his words."

"Perhaps you are correct, Miss Manning," Drake said with a polite inclination of his head, "and it is I who underestimate the power of the realm's, if not the world's, finest playwright. But come, you mentioned a wish to renew your acquaintance with my family. They are just along here in the Clybourne box. Let me show you both the way."

Drake turned and led their small party forward, taking care not to offer his arm to Verity Manning lest the gesture be seen as courtly encouragement.

"The duchess is here tonight, I hope," Saxon asked after a moment. "The dowager, your mama, I mean."

"Yes, Mama is here. She rarely misses an opportunity to attend the theater when she is in Town. It is one of her favorite kinds of entertainment."

Lord Saxon smiled. "Ava was always partial to theatricals when she was a girl, so I am not surprised to hear she still loves them." At Drake's inquiring look, Saxon continued. "We knew each other many years ago, you see."

"So Mama mentioned," Drake said, studying the other

man and suddenly wondering at the connection. "She said you were old friends. However, I hadn't realized you'd known each other for so many years."

A rather wistful expression appeared on Saxon's face. "We lost track of each other until recently, when I brought Verity to Town. But yes, your mama and I are very old friends. Very old friends indeed."

As Drake digested that sliver of information, the three of them arrived at the entrance to the Clybourne box. Mallory, Adam, Meg and Cade were gone, having apparently decided to stretch their legs. He realized they must have walked in the opposite direction since he hadn't happened upon them in the hallway. Edward, Claire, Claire's younger sister, Ella, and Mama remained inside, however, along with a trio of young gentlemen who were clearly vying for Ella's attention.

Perhaps one of Ella's beaux might take a fancy to Miss Manning, Drake thought with a hopeful turn of mind as they went inside.

Over the next several minutes, however, Drake found himself chatting with Verity Manning and to his dismay ended up being compelled to ask her to go driving with him the following afternoon. The invitation had stuck in his throat, but with everyone in the box looking on, he could do nothing but speak the words. To do otherwise would give offense, and even though he had no interest in pursuing Verity Manning romantically, he didn't want to hurt or embarrass her. She was a nice young woman and merely needed to find her way in Society. Perhaps a drive in the park with him would lend her a small bit of cachet—although it would be small indeed, since as a younger son he was far from a prime catch. But he would be kind, as his mother had asked him to be once before, and hope that Miss Manning met someone else soon and forgot all about wanting him as a suitor.

Relieved when the interval finally drew to a close, he resumed his seat. Taking out his notepad as the action began once more on the stage, he thumbed through the pages, slowing when he came upon the one of Anne Greenway. Studying her features, he found himself wishing he hadn't come out after all.

Paying barely any attention to the play, he waited to go home.

Chapter 9

ot long after sunrise the following morning, Sebastianne strolled along the rows of fruit, vegetable and flower stalls that lined the streets of Covent Garden. In the air drifted a symphony of fragrances ranging from sharp to sweet. Tangy cucumbers and earthy potatoes, exotic pineapples and bright-skinned lemons, heavenly bunches of dried lavender and the delicate perfume of lilies of the valley mingled with the less harmonious odors of dirt, refuse and human sweat.

But such was the case in cramped thoroughfares like these, the area crowded elbow to ankle with merchants, tradesmen and tinkers, all come to market in hopes of selling their wares to the throngs of interested customers there to browse.

Curiously, she'd learned from the staff that another variety of commerce took place along these same streets after the market closed for the day. In the afternoons and evenings, the denizens of a different type of society emerged, the area a notorious haven for prostitutes, press-gangs and unscrupulous sorts of all kinds. But at this early hour of the morning, the whores, pimps and thugs that roamed the darkened streets were fast asleep in their beds and of no threat to her.

Nevertheless, Jem had accompanied her on her shopping excursion, the stable lad driving them in a well-sprung dog cart that was at her disposal for such errands.

Generally, Mrs. Tremble made the once-a-week trip to the market, which she undertook in addition to the daily deliveries of meat and produce that were brought to the town house's kitchen door early each morning.

"It's good, sensible practice," the older woman said, declaring that a savvy cook needed to get out periodically and inspect the goods with her own two eyes—and to verify what the market prices were as well.

In some households, the outside marketing was the job of the housekeeper rather than the cook, but Sebastianne had been content to let the old arrangement stand. Yesterday, however, Mrs. Tremble told her that she needed to visit her sister, who had just been brought to childbed, and would Sebastianne be willing to do the weekly shopping? Eager for a chance to see more of London, she had agreed with alacrity.

After arriving in the market square, Jem left her to shop while he went to buy some leather and a few tools for repairing reins, saddles and the like. She also suspected, based on a comment she'd overheard him make to Harvey before they left, that he planned stop off in one of the numerous taverns that lined the streets near the Piazza and indulge in a dark, frothy pint of ale.

"I'll find ye," he promised upon seeing her doubtful look when she learned they were to split up. "And don't worry none over loading any of the heavy items," he said. "Let the merchants hold 'em and I'll be along to do the lifting."

Mostly reassured, she let him go on his way.

Turning, a wide wicker basket held over one arm, she went to inspect the market. She couldn't help but be curious to see how it compared with the wonderful *marchés volants* in Paris, the ones she and Maman used to visit when she'd been a young teenager.

After a few minutes, she found herself marveling at the variety and freshness of the items for sale—a veritable cornucopia of produce all to be had for the price of a few coins. But she was shopping for Lord Drake and his household, she reminded herself, careful to confine her purchases to items she and Mrs. Tremble had agreed upon prior to the cook's departure.

After buying several bunches of herbs tied together with bits of string, she paused in front of a fruit stand and inspected a crate nearly overflowing with plump, brilliantly hued strawberries—the very first of the season.

"Free samples to ye, miss," the seller offered, clearly aware that she must be employed in a good home and capable of bringing him profitable custom. "Ye'll find none sweeter," he promised, his encouraging smile as wide as the big, calloused hands he held pressed against his round, apron-covered belly.

Tempted by the beautiful red color, decorative green tops and a sweet fragrance she could detect even from where she stood, she accepted his offer. The berry burst in her mouth like candy, juicy and sweet against her appreciative tongue.

He was right. The berries were excellent.

Swallowing the last of the fruit with a smile, she met the grocer's confident gaze. "They are delicious indeed. How much for a pound?"

She haggled with the skill of a seasoned Frenchwoman, getting a price both she and the merchant knew to be fair. With a promise from the grocer to hold the berries until Jem came by with the dog cart, Sebastianne continued on her way in search of a variety of delicate lettuces and the best beets and carrots she could find.

She rounded the corner of one set of stalls and was moving toward the next a couple minutes later when a male hand curved over her elbow.

"Could I interest you in some oranges, madam?" asked a low, throaty voice.

"No, I'm sorry, thank you," she said automatically, trying to pull away.

But the hand only tightened, his fingers pushing into her tender skin and muscle in a way that was just short of painful. She looked up and stared into the long, leathery face and close-set black eyes of a man she'd hoped never to see again. Her heart pumped out a thick, heavy beat. "Vacheau," she whispered.

He didn't react by so much as blinking. "I believe you have me confused with someone else. My name is Jones. But come, the items I have to show you are just around the corner, along that lane."

The lane—more of an alley really—was dark and narrow, with only a pair of stalls near the entrance. The sellers, she noticed, were conveniently absent. She couldn't tell what lay beyond the opening, but it looked dank and unwholesome, the sort of place murderers—and spies— liked to haunt.

For a second she considered pulling away and breaking into a run, but she knew it would only attract unwanted attention and do nothing to change her circumstances. Still, she couldn't help but cast one last glance around, searching for Jem.

"If you're looking for your companion, he's still having a drink," the cold voice said in faultless English. "Come, while we have time. I won't keep you long."

Sebastianne fought down the need to tremble, knowing she had no choice but to obey. Her footsteps leaden, she walked toward the lane.

The man she knew as Vacheau followed at a leisurely pace.

The alleyway proved as dark and foul as she'd expected, the paving stones littered with refuse and other unmentionables that cast up a dreadful stink. Taking a clean handkerchief out of her pocket, she held it to her nose and mouth.

"It is unpleasant, I agree," he said at her gesture, "but we are less likely to be disturbed here."

She knew he must be right, for who would want to dwell in such a place?

They came to a spot where a patch of watery sunlight managed to slip past steeply pitched roofs that were so close they nearly closed out the sky. She stopped, muffling a cry when a rat scurried suddenly along the wall near her feet and disappeared into a crack at the base of the foundation.

She shuddered, a flash of anger burning in her stomach as she lowered the handkerchief away from her face. "I am here, Vacheau. Say what it is you have to say and be quick. I don't care to make up explanations when I am missed."

His mouth curved into an unpleasant smile that showed his surprisingly straight white teeth. "I told you, my name is Jones. Do not forget."

"Very well, *Monsieur Jones*. Proceed."

"It is you who needs to proceed. Have you found the cipher?"

Her chest tightened. "Yes."

His black eyes lit with interest. "And is it in your possession?"

She hesitated, her stomach churning again, only this time on a queasy wave. "No."

He scowled. "Why 'no'? If you are aware of its location, then what is the cause of the delay?"

"He keeps it locked in a safe and has the key in his possession. I'm trying to figure out a way to obtain it without his knowledge."

And how I am going to do that, I still have no idea, she thought on a note of desperation.

"If it weren't for the trouble it would cause, I could just kill him and take the key," Vacheau suggested aloud. "But I am afraid my superiors would not approve."

Sebastianne stifled a gasp, gooseflesh forming on her arms at the thought of any violence coming to Lord Drake. "I shall get the cipher," she said, somehow managing to speak in an even tone. "Do not be concerned. It is merely a matter of conceiving of a workable plan."

Vacheau's eyes narrowed, hard as flint. "See to it you *conceive* that plan soon. Time is growing short, and the war does not go as well as we had hoped. We need that information."

She nodded. "A few more weeks, and I'll have it copied and in my possession. To hurry now will only alert his lordship and his servants to my true purpose for being in the house."

"You have exactly one month and no more. After that, I may be able to persuade the others of the wisdom in choosing an alternate plan."

Harming Lord Drake, he means.

Assuming he could get to him.

Based on her short acquaintance with her employer, she'd come to realize that he was no vapid lord, who quaked in his polished dress pumps at the mere mention of violence. In spite of his cerebral nature, Lord Drake seemed more than capable of taking care of himself in a fight—even a dirty, bare-knuckle street brawl. But any man could be murdered if the assassin was skilled enough—and had the element of surprise on his side. From what she knew of Vacheau, he was capable of both.

"It will be done, you may rest assured," she said.

An icy smile curved over his lips. "If it isn't, remember the consequences. The Army is badly in need of soldiers these days, and your brothers are of an excellent age to serve."

"They are only ten and twelve, you immoral bastard!" she said, unable to contain the outburst.

"*Ah, ah!* Such language," he reprimanded with a back-and-forth wag of one finger. "One loathes to employ such measures as conscripting boys, but the war must be waged, after all."

Yes, appalling as it might be, she knew, such innocents were used as fodder and decoys: boys too young and too afraid to know how to protect themselves from English guns and bayonets. She'd even heard rumors that such children were preyed upon by their fellow troops, exploited because of their weakness and vulnerability, robbed of food, clothing—and worse.

"As for your papa," Vacheau continued in a matter-of-fact voice, "I am surprised they haven't sent him to prison for his continued incompetence. Even now, he refuses to aid us, claiming he is unable to comprehend this code of Byron's. But I think he comprehends far more than he says, and were it not for the few friends he has left in the government, he would be made to put that brain of his to better use."

"He is an old man and not able to work the way he used to," she defended, in spite of knowing that her father was as clear-minded as ever when it came to his mathematical endeavors.

Still, while it was true that her father had no great love for the Emperor or his war, she felt sure he would have replicated Lord Drake's work by now if he could. Given the threats and hardships their family had endured over the past couple of years, he would have done nearly anything to see her and her brothers freed from the schemes and coercions of vile *cochons* like Raoul Vacheau.

It was the only time she'd ever lied to her father, knowing he would be adamantly opposed to her coming to England to steal the cipher. But she'd been unable to see any other way out of their dilemma. If she didn't comply, Luc and Julien would be sent to fight and likely die on some forlorn battle-field, while their father would be thrown into prison. A long bout with pneumonia last winter had already weakened his lungs, and she knew incarceration would be tantamount to a death sentence.

And so she'd concocted a story about a sick cousin in Paris who desperately needed her aid. She'd worried her father would see through her ruse, but worn down with lingering grief over her mother's death and the stresses of the war, he'd accepted her tale with few questions asked. Her brothers had taken a bit more convincing, particularly Julien, who understood far more than he ought for a boy of twelve, but in the end they'd accepted her story and waved her on her way with promises to return as soon as may be.

As for herself . . . well, she didn't want to imagine what men like Vacheau might do to her should she find herself alone in the world. Prison, she suspected, would be far preferable to the degradation they had in store.

She couldn't suppress a shudder at the idea.

"You wouldn't want your papa sent away, now would you?" Vacheau taunted softly. "Or your dear *petits frères* either."

"No," she whispered in a strangled tone. Forcing her chin high, she met his soulless black gaze. "Are we finished now? I will be missed for certain if I delay much longer."

Displaying his teeth in a cruel smile, he gestured with an

arm toward the entrance to the alleyway. "You are right, you ought to run along. Don't forget. One month and no more."

One month.

So little time to save everything she held dear.

She walked back the way she'd come, willing herself not to break into a run for fear she might fall and draw Vacheau's mocking laughter. At the edge of the lane, she paused and glanced back, expecting him still to be watching. But he was gone, vanished like the wisps of smoke that curled from the coal fires used all over the city. Even so, she knew she had not escaped his notice. She wondered if she ever would again?

Emerging into the sunlight and crowds of milling passersby, she breathed more easily. She walked several feet and turned a corner, stopping in front of a stall filled with a selection of fresh blooms. She lifted a bouquet of violets to her nose, relishing their supple petals and sweet fragrance.

"There ye are," Jem declared, appearing suddenly beside her.

Sebastianne jumped and nearly dropped the flowers. "Jem, I didn't see you."

"Did I startle ye? It's right sorry I am, missus. Do you have everything ye need? I've got the cart just there."

Glancing sideways, she noticed the dog cart, the horse who pulled it waiting with patient unconcern. "Yes, my shopping is nearly concluded."

Forcing her mind to recollect exactly what she'd purchased before Vacheau had shown up, she told the stable hand the items, including the strawberries, that he needed to retrieve. With a nod, he hurried off, promising to find her again in five or ten minutes.

"Ye want those, miss?" the flower-seller asked, nodding at the violets she'd forgotten she still held. For a moment she hesitated, thinking to refuse and lay them back among their fellows. But after the dreadful stench of the alleyway, the innocent aroma of the purple blooms seemed exactly what she needed.

"Yes," she said. "And I'll take another bunch with me as well."

Chapter 10

*D*rake relaxed into one of the pair of comfortable brown leather chairs in the Clybourne House study—the elegant, yet masculine room a favorite retreat for several generations of Clybourne dukes.

His brother Edward, the tenth—and current—man to hold the title, had done little to change the room since their father's time, Drake noted. In the past few years, Edward had updated a few items of furniture, such as installing the chair in which he now sat, and replacing a worn rug from Charles II's era with a new Aubusson carpet woven in shades of brown and blue. Otherwise, everything was basically the same—a large desk, a wall of ceiling-to-floor shelves lined with leather-bound books, and a few substantial pieces of furniture collected from different ancestors in varying epochs. The room always put Drake in mind of their father and how he'd sat behind the desk with the authority of a god—his edicts sometimes stern but more often benevolent.

There was one prominent addition, however, that Edward had hung with exquisite care above the mantel—a beautifully rendered portrait of his new duchess and their young daughter, Hannah. Mother and child sat close together on the settee in the family drawing room, their heads bent, lips smiling as if they were both privy to some secret bit of humor. But it wasn't just humor that shone in their luminous eyes, it was happiness and the unmistakable glow of love and contentment. Their world was exactly as they wanted it, and it showed.

What must it be like to love and be loved that way? Drake mused.

He'd never given the question much consideration before, his work had always been his first—and some might say—only love. He was well aware that relationships—good ones anyway—took care and nurturing, and he couldn't imagine a woman in the world who would put up with his erratic way of life. Nor could he think of a woman he'd want to put up with on a daily basis, imagining the never-ending list of demands and recriminations she'd likely dole out over his absentminded preoccupation and frequent need for quiet contemplation and solitude.

Only this morning, he'd awakened early and gone into his workroom, shutting himself inside while he got down as much as he could on the slate. Later, on the way to see Edward, he'd thought of a few refinements and sat in the carriage outside Clybourne House for ten minutes while he made additional notes.

As he'd finished, he'd come across the pencil sketch he'd done of Anne Greenway the other evening.

I really ought to tear the deuced thing out and give it a toss, he'd thought. But even as his fingers moved to obey, they stilled again, brushing across the page. With a sigh, he'd closed the cover and tucked the pad, drawing and all, back into his coat pocket.

"Brandy?" Edward asked, pulling Drake's attention back to the present.

Drake's brows drew together. "Seems a bit early, don't you think?"

Edward stopped in front of the finely crafted satinwood cabinet where he kept the liquor. "Considering your recent outing to the Park, I thought perhaps you could use something rather more robust."

"Don't remind me," Drake groaned. "The tabbies' tongues are wagging all over Town. If only I hadn't decided to do the decent thing and take Miss Manning driving."

Edward reached for the brandy, pouring shallow draughts into two snifters. "She seems a pleasant enough girl from what I've observed."

"She is, but that doesn't mean I have any interest in courting her. I did the polite thing, that's all. You should have seen the reaction in the park, matrons' eyes round as gibbous moons with speculation. If I'm not careful, the matchmakers and gossip dealers will have us married before the Season is out."

"Would that be so very dreadful?" Edward asked in a quiet voice.

Drake's jaw dropped, his chin so low it added a new crease to his neatly tied neckcloth. "Good God, not you too! I suppose Mama has been working on you. And Claire, for all I know. Why are women always after men to get married?"

"I believe they think it will make them happy," Edward said with an amused smile.

"Well, I *am* happy, exactly as I am." Drake reached out a hand. "Now give me that drink. Seems I can use it, after all." He swallowed half in a single gulp, glad for the burning slide of the alcohol down his throat. "But look, that's not why I came 'round here today. I have other things to discuss."

Serious once again, Edward lowered himself into the chair opposite. "What things?"

Drake swirled the amber liquid in his glass. "I'm not certain, mind you, but I think the house is being watched."

His brother grew still. "Your town house, you mean?"

Drake gave a nod. "Ordinarily, I wouldn't have noticed, but there's been a dustman along the street several days in a row."

"And what makes you think he's not what he appears?" Edward asked, before taking a slow drink from his glass.

"Have you ever seen a dustman wearing polished boots? This one's gleam like he takes blacking to them every night. And his clothes—"

"Yes?"

"They're shabby and worn, rather filthy actually, but they don't look old. There's something about the fellow's clothes that reminds me of an actor dressed for a role, as if he's treading the boards at Drury Lane."

"Hmm? Well, I always believe in abiding by one's instincts," Edward mused aloud. "If your hackles are up, then you ought to pay attention."

Drake met his brother's astute blue gaze. "Precisely the reason I decided to mention it to you. I thought perhaps you could put a man or two on surveillance."

"I know just the ones." Edward agreed. "Consider it done."

Drake cradled his brandy glass inside his palm and gave the alcohol another slow swirl. "Can't say I like the idea of men watching the house, even if they're your men. Then again, there is the cipher to protect."

"Are you sure you don't want to move the original here to Clybourne House, or even to Braebourne? The French would never manage to get their hands on it there."

"They haven't gotten their hands on it in Audley Street, nor will they," Drake countered before giving a resolute shake of his head. "No, it's secure enough where it is. They may be watching the house, but they'll never get into my safe."

I'd be able to get into that safe if I could only figure out a way to secure the key. But how, when Lord Drake wears the deuced thing around his neck! Sebastianne suppressed a grumble of frustration as she leaned back in the chair in her office, the list of accounts she was supposed to be reconciling forgotten beneath her unmoving quill pen.

Nearly a week had elapsed since her troubling meeting with Vacheau, yet she was no closer to a solution than she had been that morning at the market. After all, she couldn't very well walk up to Lord Drake and ask if she could borrow the key. And trying to steal it from him while he was sleeping—tempting as that notion might be—was nothing short of absurd. Even if he was an unusually heavy sleeper—which she doubted—she was sure he would wake up if she tried to slip the key from around his neck one night.

Of course, if all she cared about was stealing the key, she supposed she could knock him out with some heavy object, take the cipher, and run. But as much as she needed that key and the code, she would no more resort to violence against Lord Drake than she would against one of her brothers. In truth, Vacheau's threats against Lord Drake had shaken her, leaving her dreams plagued with nightmares in which he was set upon and left beaten and bleeding and worse.

On more than one occasion, she'd awakened trembling and afraid, gasping into the warm summer darkness as she came awake only to find herself alone in her attic room in the town house, the sheets tangled around her. Yet in spite of the lies and thievery she was sworn to commit, it would be best for everyone, particularly Lord Drake, if she found a way to infiltrate his safe, copy the cipher, and leave. Only then would he and his household be safe. Only then might she rest easy knowing she'd kept Vacheau from their door.

But she could do none of these things, not without that key!

Tapping her quill absently against the ledger again, she racked her brain for a solution.

She was still deep in thought some while later when a light knock sounded at her door. Glancing up, she straightened in her chair and carefully laid down her pen. "Come," she called.

The door opened, and Polk, the scullery maid, stepped inside. She halted less than a foot inside the room, her work-roughened hands twisted into her apron. Her cheeks were usually fair and florid, but today they were as pale as the chalk in Lord Drake's workroom. "S-sorry to disturb you, ma'am," the girl said in quiet tones, "but I'm feeling ever so peaked. Mrs. Tremble said what I could come and ask ye fer a cure."

Sebastianne rose quickly to her feet. "Well, of course. Come and sit—" She gestured toward a very comfortable, upholstered armchair set at an angle near the empty fireplace grate. "You truly do look most unwell."

"I c-couldn't sit *there*, ma'am," the girl protested at the suggestion. "It's much too fancy fer me."

Sebastianne made a tsking sound beneath her breath and came forward to lead the maid toward the chair. "Don't be silly. Of course you must sit. Now tell me what ails you?"

A tear leaked down Polk's plump young cheek as she sank against the cushions. "It's me head. Hurts something fierce. I gets like this sometimes, but I never know when or why they come on."

"Megrims. My Maman—I mean, Mama—used to have them," she said, hoping the girl was too unwell to have caught her unintentional slip. "I know how dreadfully she always felt," Sebastianne hurried on. "Would you like some laudanum?"

"Oh no," the maid refused. "I can't take it 'cause it always turns me sick and gives me the heaves. I were wondering . . . that is . . . Mrs. Beatty used to stir up a powder that puts me straight to sleep. Do you think you could give me something like that?"

"A sleeping draught?" Pausing, she cast her mind over the array of recipes and remedies she'd learned while studying to be a housekeeper. A good housekeeper, after all, was knowledgeable about more than the preparation of foodstuffs and cleaning aids, she could also concoct cosmetics, perfumes, and a wide variety of medicaments designed to alleviate a broad host of ailments.

"Yes," she told the young maid, "I believe I know something that should help the pain and allow you to rest. You go on upstairs to your room, and I'll send someone along with the remedy shortly."

On a tremulous sigh, the girl stood and walked slowly into the hall, then up the staircase, clutching tightly to the railing as she went.

Sebastianne, her mind already filled with potential ingredients, made her way to the stillroom. Once there, she inspected the various bottles and canisters that contained herbs, roots, tinctures and extracts. After a long minute's thought, she decided on white willow bark, feverfew and linden for the pain with valerian, passionflower and a pinch of catnip added to aid with sleep.

Putting the herbs into a pestle, she began preparing a compound that could be steeped into a tea. She was applying her strength to grinding when the answer to the problem of the key abruptly appeared.

A sleeping draught! Of course, why didn't I think of that earlier?

Difficulties would still remain, she knew, since she would have to enlist the help of a far-more-skilled herbalist than herself. She had neither the expertise nor the assortment of ingredients required to fashion a sleeping serum strong enough to knock out a man as large and vital as Lord Drake. The herbalist would need to take particular care as well that their formula caused no lasting harm nor resulted in deleterious aftereffects.

Locating such a person would doubtless take some time and effort, but surely in a city as vast as London, a reliable chemist could be found. Loath though she was even to think of resorting to such means, she would contact Vacheau if need be. Before she'd come to Lord Drake's residence, she'd been provided a communications point where she could leave a message. So far, she hadn't used it and wouldn't unless she had no other choice. For now, however, she would see what she could come up with on her own.

With a plan finally in place, she made herself focus on completing the headache powder for Polk. Rolling it into a small square of brown paper, she went to the kitchen to turn it into tea.

Chapter 11

"His lordship will be taking dinner at home tonight," Waxman informed the staff as the valet strolled into the kitchen several afternoons later. "Lord Drake informed me that he is embarking on an important new experiment and prefers not to be unduly disturbed."

At the news, Sebastianne's fingers tightened against the handle of her teacup. She was seated at the small kitchen table, where she'd been having a chat with Mrs. Tremble and sampling her fresh-from-the-oven Banbury cakes. Casting down her gaze, she worked to regulate her features in case they revealed the sudden leap of nerves that made her heart pound like one of the cook's best wooden mallets.

"Humph," Mrs. Tremble grumbled under her breath. "It's us ought to worry over being *unduly disturbed* if he's up to those experiments of his again. Near gave me a paroxysm of the heart last time he started in with all that noise and such. And that little housemaid . . . what was her name—" Breaking off, she waved a flour-covered hand in the air, clearly struggling to remember.

"Mae," Finnegan offered from where she stood stirring a pot of deliciously scented chicken-and-barley soup that would be served at the servants' table in a couple of hours.

"Mae! Exactly so," the cook chimed in with a satisfied nod. "Poor girl wasn't here above three days when his lordship scared her so much she quit without even finding time to ask for a new character."

"What did he do?" Sebastianne inquired blandly, taking a drink of tea to cover her own bout of anxiety—thoughts that had nothing to do with the present conversation running wild inside her head.

Is tonight the night? she wondered, thinking of the powerful sedative locked even now inside the lowest drawer of her desk inside the housekeeper's room.

As she'd assumed, obtaining the draught had been far from easy. First she'd had to locate an herbalist who could produce the type of medicament she required. Then she had to make sure, for a rather large sum of money, that the person would agree to conveniently forget she had ever paid his establishment a visit.

Luckily, Sebastianne hadn't needed to contact Vacheau. Instead, as providence would have it, another visit to Covent Garden market had elicited the names of three possible chemists. She'd chosen the one farthest away from Audley Street and in the least refined neighborhood, visiting only yesterday on her afternoon off. And now, Waxman had just announced that Lord Drake would be dining at home this evening.

Do I dare try for the key tonight?

But she already knew the answer. Nearly two weeks of her allotted month had passed already, and she would be incredibly foolish to squander such an opportunity. Even more, with the aristocratic Season at its height, Lord Drake often went out in the evening, attending dinner parties, balls and the theater.

And four days ago, quite without warning, he'd informed her that he was having a group of gentleman to the house for dinner and libations and to ready the house for their arrival. She'd had no time to think of sleeping draughts and ciphers that evening, every servant in the house, including herself busy managing the entertainment.

No, she would have to make a try tonight and hope it succeeded.

"—with a bang fit to wake the dead and a smell so horrible it were as if a couple of 'em were laid out inside the house," Sebastianne heard Mrs. Tremble say as her attention returned to the cook's story.

"Poor Mae had been sweeping the hall floor outside his lordship's workroom when the explosion went off. Girl came running in, shaking so I thought she'd fall ter pieces. Up and quit on the spot, she did. Said she wouldn't work in a madhouse." Taking up a long-handled whisk, Mrs. Tremble began beating the eggs she'd cracked into a bowl. "Guess the rest of us are made of sterner stuff."

Sebastianne sipped her tea again and hoped such an emotion proved to be the case tonight. She would need to be made of very stern stuff indeed if her plan was to prove successful.

Inside his workroom, Drake sat at the long wooden bench built against the east wall. On its top he had arranged a grouping of glass Leyden jars that he was using to create what was known as a voltaic pile—or as the American Benjamin Franklin had termed it in his day—a battery. Using copper and zinc rods and solutions made separately of potassium and sodium, he planned to create a viable electrical charge that would produce enough power to create light inside another attached glass tube.

"Only imagine the way the world might work if people

weren't forced to rely on candles, wood, and coal to light and heat their homes," he mused aloud.

For the present, however, even he was still confined to such antique methods of illumination, his workroom lighted by the mellow glow of two branches of fragrant beeswax candles. While he'd been working, night had fallen, warm early-summer sunlight fading gradually from the sky without his notice—at least until the room had grown too dark to see, and he'd been forced to pause and use a flint to light the candles.

Glancing at one of the myriad, quietly ticking clocks positioned around the room—every hand pointing toward the hour of fifteen minutes to nine, he stretched his arms over his head and wondered how much more work he could squeeze in before dinner arrived.

Engrossed in his efforts, he'd forgotten all about the meal by the time a gentle tap sounded at the door. "Come," he called absently, applying a wrench to a particularly stubborn nut and bolt he was tightening.

"Good evening, your lordship," said a melodious feminine voice.

The wrench slipped off the nut, coming within a millimeter of hitting one of the Leyden jars.

Bloody hell, he swore under his breath, thankful it hadn't broken. What a colossal mess that would have been. From the way he acted, you'd think he was some green youth in the throes of his first infatuation. He gave a low, derisive snort. And here he'd been once again assuring himself that he had finally conquered his lustful tendencies where his pretty housekeeper was concerned.

"Good evening," he replied, careful to reveal none of his inner musings. Keeping his back turned, he busied himself with the housing for one of the voltaic cells.

"I've brought your dinner," she continued, carrying in a heavily laden tray.

He gave a slight nod. "Set it on the desk. I'll eat there."

"S-should you like to wash up first?"

Aware of the grime and various chemical solutions lingering on his hands, he supposed he ought to do so or else risk poisoning himself. "Yes," he agreed, laying down the wrench. "I shall be back directly."

Striding out the door, he walked down the hall to the small ground-floor commode that always held a pitcher and bowl with a supply of freshwater and towels.

The instant he was gone, Sebastianne hurried to the desk and set down her burden. Pouring wine into a waiting goblet, she stoppered the crystal decanter, then reached quickly into her pocket for the small vial of finely ground powder inside.

She'd been assured it was tasteless, or nearly so, hoping any slight bitterness would be disguised by the heavy port wine. She'd chosen the vintage herself for exactly that reason, relieved Mr. Stowe was away from the house this evening since procuring wines and spirits was part of his usual list of duties.

But luck seemed to be on her side. She only prayed it held long enough for Lord Drake to fall asleep so that she could make an impression of the key. She'd taken the precaution of preparing a small, two-sided plate, rather like a visiting card case, into which she'd poured an especially soft kind of wax. Once the impression of the key was secured, she would be able to take it to a locksmith, who could use it to fashion a new key solely for her use. With a duplicate at her disposal, she would be able to open the safe when she knew Lord Drake was away from the house. That way, she could copy the cipher, return the original to its hiding place, and leave her actions virtually undetectable.

First, however, she had to actually get her hands on the key.

Knowing time was growing short, she tapped just over half of the sleeping powder into his wine, then used a spoon from his tray to give it a good stir.

She'd just dried off the utensil on a handkerchief and set it back down—the vial containing the sleeping draught secure once more inside her pocket—when Lord Drake walked back into the room. Removing the covers as if she'd been busy arranging the tray all the while, she revealed a delicious-looking and succulent-smelling supper of roast guinea hen, honeyed parsnips, new green peas and an herbed bread dressing. Brandied pears and a pudding made of caramel and almonds rounded out the meal. She wondered how much of the repast he would manage to enjoy before the sleeping draught took over.

Pushing aside the knot of guilt clenched like a band around her middle, she finished arranging the tray, then stepped aside to let him pass. "If there is anything else, your lordship, you have only to ring."

He shot her an enigmatic glance before seating himself behind his desk. "From the looks of this, I'm sure I shall be well provisioned." Leaning forward, he picked up the glass of port.

She nearly called out for him to stop as she watched him lift the goblet to his lips. But he had to drink the wine, and she had to let him, however wretched she felt about the prospect.

With her fingers twisted against her skirts, she kept her silence, wondering how many minutes it would take for the drug to take hold. The herbalist had explained that the efficacy of the sleeping draught depended strongly on the individual who consumed it. Given Lord Drake's size and constitution, Sebastianne suspected it would be a while.

"Thank you, Mrs. Greenway," he said, returning the goblet to its place before reaching for his napkin. Shaking it out, he laid it across his lap. "That will be all."

Realizing she was hovering, she came back to herself. "Enjoy your meal, my lord." With a curtsey, she let herself out of the room.

Once in the hall, she took a moment to regulate her breathing, her heart thudding like a blacksmith's hammer. She would check on him in twenty minutes or so. She only knew that those few minutes would seem like an eternity.

Drake waited until he heard the door close behind Anne Greenway; only then did he relax in his chair. Despite her absence, however, he couldn't shake his awareness of her, the subtle fragrance of the violet water she wore lingering in the air. Closing his eyes, he drew in a deep breath, letting the scent tease his senses.

Moments later his eyes snapped open again, his brows furrowed. *Honestly, I either need to put her out of my mind or bed her.* Unfortunately, neither option seemed likely at present, which left him exactly where he'd been since the day she walked into his life.

With an exasperated sigh, he reached again for the wine, quaffing a pair of deep swallows. Grimacing, he set it down again and picked up his fork. *The wine seems off,* he thought, as he inserted the tines into the crispy, golden skin of the roast guinea hen and the tender flesh beneath. *I'll have to talk to Stowe when he returns and see if there's a problem in the cellar.*

In silence he ate, the gentle ticking of the multitude of clocks providing a soothing rhythmic accompaniment. As was his habit when he dined alone, he opened a book and began to read, focusing his attention between bites.

About halfway through the meal, he started to yawn, a curious weariness stealing over him. Too many late nights and early mornings, he supposed, although generally he didn't require a great deal of sleep. Usually, he felt fit with

no more than a catnap here and there, and five or six uninter-
rupted hours at night—or morning depending on when he
decided to take to his bed. He could rest for a while now, he
supposed, but the evening was still early yet, and he had a
great deal more work he wished to complete.

Finishing the poultry, dressing, and most of the vegetables, he downed his dessert in a few quick bites before
shoving the tray aside. He tossed back the last of the wine,
smacking his lips against the off flavor before setting down
the glass with a careful thump.

*Perhaps some coffee would help shake off this lan-
guor,* he thought, determined to return to his experiment.
Hands braced on the edge of the desk, he shoved to his
feet and crossed the room to the bell pull. He gave the
cloth a sharp tug, then strode across to his workbench and
dropped into his seat. Forcing his eyes wide, he reached
for the wrench.

He startled slightly when a knock sounded at the door a
few minutes later, and his housekeeper entered the room.

She's back, he thought, catching another whiff of violets
as she walked farther into the room.

"Coffee," he said after affording her no more than a cur-
sory glance. "Black, no sugar." The more robust the brew, he
decided, the more good it would do him.

But instead of leaving to do his biding, she stood motionless for a long moment, her auburn brows gathered into a
frown. "C-Coffee, my lord?"

He scowled back. "Yes. And you may take the tray. I'm
finished with dinner."

Still, she hesitated. "Are you . . . that is . . . are you sure
you're feeling all right?"

"Of course," he lied, fighting off another wave of exhaustion. "Why wouldn't I?"

A faintly startled expression crossed her face before it

cleared as abruptly as it had come. "No reason. I–I shall get your coffee."

Retrieving the tray, she left the room.

A savage yawn took hold the moment she departed, moisture gathering in the corners of his eyes as he pressed a fist to his open mouth.

Plague take it, I'm tired, he thought, as another yawn followed the first.

Maybe if he put his head down on the workbench and closed his eyes for a few minutes, he would feel refreshed. But somehow he sensed a nap wouldn't help this time. He needed his bed and sleep, not work and coffee.

Still, he forced himself to concentrate on his work for a couple of minutes more. Finally, though, with everything but the need to sleep forgotten, he lurched to his feet and went to the door.

Coffee! Sebastianne murmured under her breath as she walked downstairs and along the servants' hall to the kitchen. *Zut alors,* but he ought to have been passed out by now! Instead, she walked in to find him working, of all things, and looking far too alert for comfort. He might have seemed a tiny bit sleepy but not enough for her to proceed with her plan.

Resisting the urge to fidget, she set down the tray on the kitchen table and told Finnegan to put the kettle on to boil while she went to grind the coffee in the stillroom.

Had she given him enough of the sleeping powder, she wondered? She'd been relieved to see that he'd drunk all the wine, yet he seemed little changed. Perhaps he needed a higher dose? Then again, she didn't want to give him too much. The idea was to mimic a deep, heavy sleep, not put him into a stupor so intense it would be obvious he'd been drugged.

She'd counted on his passing out at his desk, which would look to any of the other servants as if he'd decided to sleep again in his workroom.

Instead, he wanted coffee!

By the time the beans were ground and steeping in a pot of boiling water, she decided to add the other half of the sleeping powder to his coffee. Surely he wouldn't drink more than his body would tolerate before he lost consciousness, she assured herself. And once he did, she would be able to put the rest of her plan into action.

Arranging the coffee service on a fresh tray, she carried it to the dumbwaiter and set to working the pulleys.

When she reached his workroom soon after, she lifted her hand to knock. As she did, she noticed the door standing ajar. Pushing it wider, she stared at the empty interior.

Lord Drake was gone.

Chapter 12

"His lordship has retired for the evening," Waxman told Sebastianne nearly an hour later, as the two of them stood in the corridor not far from Lord Drake's bedchamber. "I have seldom seen him so weary. Clearly his work has left him exhausted."

If only Waxman knew that *work* had nothing to do with what had exhausted Lord Drake. But the valet was better off believing what he would instead of the truth.

As it had turned out, an additional dose of the sleeping draught hadn't been necessary, the drugged coffee growing cold in its pot. Once she'd realized that Lord Drake had gone upstairs to bed, she'd carried the coffee service back downstairs. Rather than risk one of the staff rewarming it to drink, she'd tossed the brew down the wastewater drain and rinsed out the pot. She'd waited several minutes, then gone up to check on Lord Drake.

Yet as relieved as she was over the fact that the sleeping powder had produced the desired effect, she found herself in a quandary over how to proceed. In all the scenarios she'd run through her imagination, she'd never thought Lord

Drake might take the draught, then walk upstairs to his bed!

Bon Dieu! Now what was she going to do?

Well, she decided with a sigh, as she made her way up to her own room on the fourth floor, there was nothing for it. She would have to slip into his bedchamber later and slip out again, completely unnoticed.

After a great deal of inner debate, she decided to bathe and change into her night attire as she always did in the evening. If luck should fail her, and she happened upon one of the other servants on her way to or from Lord Drake's room, she would simply tell them she'd been unable to sleep and was headed to the kitchen for a cup of warm milk.

Once she'd finished her ablutions, donned her nightgown and robe and brushed her long hair, tying it at her nape with a plain blue ribbon, she stretched out on her bed to wait. With only a few minutes remaining until midnight, she knew it was still too early to sneak downstairs. Jasper and Lyles always made a last check of the house around this time, securing the windows and doors before seeking their own slumber.

Closing her eyes, she relaxed.

She came awake on a gasp, her gaze darting to the watch she'd laid on her side table. Peering at the hands by means of the single lighted candle in its holder, she saw that it was half past one in the morning.

Everyone should be abed and fast asleep by now.

Swallowing against a sudden lump lodged at the base of her throat, she tucked her bare feet into her slippers, picked up the candle, and made her way quietly from the room. Careful to make no noise, she closed the door at her back.

The house was dark and silent, save for the soft ticking of the tall, mahogany casement clock in the second-floor hallway, as she made her way across the Aubusson hall runner that led to Lord Drake's suite of rooms. She shivered, not from cold but nerves, the wax-filled case, with which she would make an imprint of the key, heavy as an iron bar inside her robe pocket.

Thankfully, Waxman didn't sleep anywhere near his master. The valet's room was one floor below and at the back of the house, which meant that she wouldn't have to worry about waking him and being discovered as she carried out her plan.

And then she was at Lord Drake's door, the candle flame flickering slightly inside her quavering fingers. Aware she dare not delay, she turned the knob and stole inside.

The room was dark, the curtains pulled tightly against any light from the street outside. At first she didn't see Lord Drake, his long form swathed in shadows. Then she walked forward, the candlelight pouring in a gentle wash of illumination over his recumbent form, where he lay beneath the sheets in a huge, cherrywood tester bed.

Deeply asleep, he showed no signs that he was the least bit aware of her presence. He lay on his back, one arm flung outward across the sheets, while the other rested against his chest.

His very *naked* chest.

It was broad and firmly muscled, a veritable work of art, with dark golden curls scattered over its taut plane and downward in a narrow line that ran over his flat stomach before disappearing enticingly beneath the sheet.

Unaware of her actions, she stepped nearer and raised the candle higher in order to get a better look. As she did, she vaguely registered the slender gold chain and brass key nestled among those tantalizing curls. But she paid it little heed, too entranced with the sight of Lord Drake to think of aught else.

Then he inhaled, his chest rising and falling on a swift breath.

She jumped, her gaze flying to his face to see if he had awakened. But he slept on, oblivious to everything but his own dreams. Studying him, she couldn't help but notice the light stubble that shadowed his strong cheeks and jaw, nor the almost boyish quality to his features, relaxed now from their usual musings and preoccupations.

Forcing her gaze away from his handsome visage, she reminded herself why she'd come to his room—and it wasn't to admire Lord Drake, no matter how deliciously appealing he might be. Besides, she cautioned herself, she didn't know how long the sleeping draught would keep him in its hold, so she had no time to squander while she proceeded with her mission.

Relying on stealth and a huge measure of caution, she set down her candle on his night table, then turned to inch as close as she could to the bed. Taking care not to jostle the mattress, she pressed even closer and leaned over Lord Drake.

Her heart thundered violently in her ears, so loud she feared the pounding would bring him awake. When it didn't, she drew a soundless breath and willed her hands not to tremble, perspiration bedewing her skin in a light, slippery sheen.

Bending closer still, she slid her fingers over the clasp on the chain around his neck—thankful the fastener had slipped forward so it wasn't located behind his neck.

Then she unfastened it.

Ever so slowly she eased the chain and its precious cargo away from his chest, lifting both key and chain free in a single, graceful move. Clutching them to her own chest, where her heart beat like wings, she waited to see if Lord Drake would awaken.

But he slept on, mercifully oblivious, courtesy of the powerful sedative effects of the sleeping draught.

Stepping carefully back, she reached again for the candle, then crept across the room toward a small table-and-chair arrangement, where it appeared he sometimes read. Setting down the candle again, she found a flat bit of space, then dug inside her robe pocket for the leather case.

Making an imprint of both sides of the key proved far quicker and easier than she'd dreamed, the wax she'd prepared just right for the task.

Expelling a quiet breath, she patted her forehead dry with the handkerchief she also kept inside her pocket, then folded the cloth in half and wiped the key clean on the other side. The brass gleamed in the candlelight, winking as if it were in on the plot.

She suppressed a renewed wave of guilt that made her stomach as sour as a freshly squeezed lemon and returned the key to the chain. Placing the handkerchief and the leather-bound case with its precious imprint back in her pocket, she took up the candle once more. Turning, she gazed across the room at Lord Drake's recumbent form.

Nearly done, she assured herself as she studied him sleeping in the dark. *Just get this chain fastened around his neck again, make it safely back to my bedroom, and no one but me will be the wiser.*

Buoyed by her success, she padded soundlessly across the carpeted floor and set about reversing the process she'd done a brief time before.

Her fingers were steady and dry, her heartbeat working at a more moderate pace as she bent over Lord Drake and slid the chain cautiously back around his neck. The key nestled lightly against his chest as if returning to its home. The fastener clicked closed, and she was just drawing away, when he moved, his hand flashing up to catch hold of her wrist.

She glanced up and stared—straight into his open, grass green eyes. A silent gasp burned inside her lungs, her pulse leaping like a rabbit trapped inside in a snare, her mouth as dry as a desert.

Bon Dieu, how long has he been awake? More importantly, how much does he know?

She waited for his accusations to begin, fearful of the questions he would ask and the answers he would force her to tell.

But he said nothing; he just stared.

Only then did she notice the odd glittery sheen to his gaze, his eyes curiously unfocused and confused. Incredible as it might seem, she began to wonder if he was truly awake at all.

Deciding to test the theory, she gave a slight tug at her wrist, hoping he would let go. But his grip tightened, not painfully, but enough that she realized it was unbreakable— for the moment at least.

He stared at her, his gaze sweeping her face as if trying to make sense of her presence. "It's you," he murmured, his words thick and raspy.

A shiver ran through her, an unwanted awareness mingling with her anxiety. "No, it's not," she said nonsensically. "So why don't you release me and go back to sleep?" she told him in a soothing whisper, the sort she'd often used to calm her young brothers when they'd awakened from a bad dream.

His brows drew tight, clearly puzzling over what she'd said.

Her pulse knocked hard in her captured wrist, her thoughts racing. *Why isn't the sleeping draught working anymore? And what in heavens am I going to do to extract myself?*

She needed to convince him this was nothing more than an illusion, she decided hurriedly, and that he needed to forget she was even there.

More than anything, he needs to forget I'm here!

"You're dreaming, my lord," she murmured, modulating her tone. "I am nothing but a figment of your imagination. Relax now and drift off to other worlds and other women besides me."

But rather than closing his eyes and sinking back to sleep, a slow, devilish smile moved over his lips. Without warning, he tugged her closer so that she half lay across his warm, bare chest. "But I don't want other women," he said huskily. "I only want you. I've had this dream before, of you lying here in my arms, in my bed. So come and let us share another night of passion, my beautiful, bounteous, Anne."

He's dreamed of me?

Before she had time to react to that amazing revelation, he cupped a wide palm behind her head and took her lips. She gasped, trembling beneath his possession as he plundered her mouth with long, rapacious kisses that sent her senses spinning.

She couldn't think, the pleasure he'd promised cascading over her in a deluge of delicious sensation. Odd as it might seem, it was as if they were lovers already, as though there was no touch too intimate, no need too great.

In the weeks since she'd first met him, she'd wondered what it would be like to kiss Lord Drake, to touch him with ardor rather than having to show the indifferent restraint of a servant. But never in her wildest imaginings had she expected anything like this. He'd done nothing more than kiss her, yet she ached all the way to her toes. His touch was pure bliss, more tempting and powerful than any she'd ever known.

Not even Thierry, whom she'd loved to distraction, had made her feel so much. With him she'd known tenderness and delight, but never such deep, yearning need. She'd known desire beneath his sweet caresses, but never this instantaneous abandon that made her long to forget everything but the man in whose arms she lay. Lord Drake was nothing like her husband, yet she felt more in this moment with him than she had in the whole of her life.

The startling realization made her blink as some spark of caution flashed back to life inside her brain. *Bonté divine, what am I doing?* she thought dazedly. *I have to stop now before I let this go too far.*

With a gasp, she wrenched her mouth from his, viscerally aware of the damp throb of her lips and the wet heat pooling between her thighs, both sensations urging her to put aside her qualms and let matters proceed.

But she couldn't, she told herself. She had to make herself remember the reason she'd come to his bedchamber. And it wasn't to make love!

Drake, however, didn't seem concerned by her withdrawal. Instead, he tugged her higher against his body while simultaneously sliding one of his large palms down her back. A shiver traced over her skin as he paused to caress the dip at the base of her spine, heat boiling like fire over her as he began gathering the thin material of her robe and nightgown between his fingers, so that both inched slowly up her legs.

She squirmed against him, then froze, abruptly realizing that her actions had simply made matters worse by settling her more firmly atop his erection. Of its impressive size she had no doubt, not with his flesh and her own separated by nothing more substantial than a thin silk sheet and the cotton lawn of her nightclothes.

"My lord, you must stop," she said on a breathless pant.

"Why?" he drawled, his eyelids heavy with undisguised passion. Angling his head, he pressed an openmouthed kiss against the exposed side of her neck. Then, as if that weren't devastating enough, he licked her, the tip of his tongue swirling like satin against her skin before roving onward.

She shuddered, her eyelids fluttering downward on a pleasured slide.

Yes, why? she puzzled, her mind growing misty again. It was as though she were the one who'd been drugged tonight, she thought, fighting to shake off the strange pliancy creeping through her limbs.

Remember, she ordered herself.

Remember what?

Without warning, he rolled her to her back, stringing kisses along her throat and collarbone as he lay above her. In that moment, the key swung around his neck, glinting briefly in the low amber glow of the candlelight.

Sebastianne stared at the metal.

The key. Of course, the key.

She had to get out of his bed, out of his room, immediately! But how, with Lord Drake so clearly determined to keep her in it? What she needed, she decided, was a diversion.

Reaching up, she stroked a palm across his cheek and drew his attention. "W-why don't you give me a minute to freshen up?" she suggested in a purring tone. "I promise I'll be right back."

The hand gliding upward along her bare thigh stopped, his forehead wrinkling over her statement. "Freshen up?"

"Yes, to splash a bit of water, you know. I'll just slip out, then slip back. You'll hardly know I've been away."

And once she was away and safely inside her room again, he would with any luck have grown tired enough in his waiting to forget about her and fall back to sleep.

"I'll come with you," he said, moving as if to climb out of the bed.

"No!" she said, curving a hand around one of his bare upper arms. "You stay right here. I'll return in mere moments."

He studied her with glazed green eyes for several long seconds, then leaned away to let her slip off the bed. Puffing out a quiet breath of relief, she made good her escape.

Hands trembling, she lifted the candle she'd earlier set on his night table, then walked on alarmingly unsteady feet across the large room to the door of his bathing chamber.

He was watching her as she paused with her fingers on the knob, making her aware that she had no choice except to enter. But that wouldn't be a problem, she knew, since the room had two doors, the second one that led out into his dressing room. She would go in one door, then out through the other and disappear through his sitting room on the far side.

Inside the bathing chamber, she found herself far too distracted to truly admire the modern chamber, with its clean white tiles, shining brass fixtures and huge porcelain bathtub. After locking the door behind her, she crossed to the sink and picked up the yellow-and-white Sèvres pitcher, already filled with water. Pouring a cool, wet inch into the basin, she splashed for a few seconds so that it would sound as though she really were washing up.

Once finished, she decided that she ought to dispose of the evidence since she didn't want to leave clues that might lead Lord Drake to wonder if her presence in his bedroom had been more than a dream. Draining the water into the bathtub, she returned the basin to the precise spot where it had been, then carefully dried her hands on a nearby towel so no marks would show. Then, convinced she'd waited long enough, she padded on hushed feet toward the dressing-room door.

A strangled gasp rose in her throat at the sight of the tall shadow waiting on the other side. With her heart beating in painful strokes, she pressed a fist to her chest, while the flame from the candle she held wavered in a crazy dance.

"All freshened up?" Lord Drake asked. He swayed slightly where he stood, one hand braced against the wall. Even in the low light it was plain that he was naked—the rest of his body every inch as magnificent as his chest.

She couldn't help but look, her gaze roving over his narrow hips, long thighs corded with muscle, and the powerful erection rising up between them. Her mouth grew moist at the sight, even as her throat grew dry.

"What are you doing out of bed?" she said on a high-pitched squeak.

For that matter, *how* was he out of bed, considering the sleeping draught she'd given him? Now she wished she'd used the entire dose in his wine rather than dividing it in half. Obviously, he had the constitution of an ox. *Or a bull,* she thought, unable to keep from glancing again at his substantial arousal.

"The other door was locked, so I came around here," he said in answer to her question, his tone implying a kind of irrefutable logic. "So, are you ready?"

Ready?

She swallowed convulsively, her traitorous body throbbing in her most secret places. "M-my lord, I think perhaps we—"

"—should go back to bed," he finished. Pushing himself away from the wall, he moved close, his hands reaching for her gown. "But first, let's get you out of these."

"I-I think I should keep them on." She took two steps back, eluding him.

But he followed. "I don't. I want to see you, and this is my dream, after all."

Dream? Did he still believe he was asleep and this interlude between them was nothing more than a fantasy? Mayhap she could still find a way out of her predicament, she mused, if she managed things right. Worrying her lower lip between her teeth, she wondered once again exactly how to do that.

Then he took the candle out of her hand and set it aside, the low light flickering around them in a way that cast seductive shadows against the walls. Reaching for her again, he grasped the tie at the waist of her robe and pulled it loose.

"My lord," she said, trying to forestall him as he pushed the robe from her shoulders.

"Drake," he told her, edging her slowly backward. "You always call me by my name in my dreams."

"Dr-Drake, then. I still need a bit of time. Why don't you return to bed, and I'll follow."

He shook his head. "But you'll slip away."

He was right. She would.

Without warning, she bumped into a smooth panel of wood that rose upward behind her. The door—the one she'd locked when she'd first entered the room. Reaching back, she fumbled for the key, trying to turn it and reopen the door.

As she struggled to work the mechanism, Lord Drake stepped closer. Her pulse leapt wildly in her chest at having him so near.

So naked.

But instead of trying to unfasten the buttons on her thin cotton nightgown as she expected, he laid both of his wide, capable palms over her breasts and cupped them with a bold, knowing possession. Squeezing her flesh with the lightest of touches, he began caressing her with his thumbs.

And mercy on high, did he caress her, her nipples beading into tight, aching peaks that made her spine arch of its own accord. Her fingers stilled against the key, wrists growing lax as he began using slow, circling touches in a way that literally made her whole body throb. Her eyelids slid closed, a sigh of pure bliss whispering from her lips.

Before she had time to collect herself and her wayward

thoughts, he was kissing her, taking her mouth with a heady intensity that undid her even more. His tongue slipped inside to play with her own, giving her the kind of openmouthed kiss good women were warned was sinful.

But how could anything so wonderful be a sin? And why did she no longer seem to care what might pass between them tonight?

Behind her, the key dropped to the floor.

She barely heard its metallic ping, pressing herself against Drake as she threaded her fingers into the thick chestnut silk of his hair. A whisper of air brushed against her body as he unfastened the buttons on her nightgown, the thin plackets parting as they hung open to her waist. Then his hands slipped inside to stroke her, flesh to heated flesh.

How much time passed, she had no idea, her judgment lost beneath a tide of desire. He surprised her again though when he broke their kiss and leaned fractionally away. Weaving ever so slightly, he gazed into her eyes. "Come," he said, his words as much a request as a command.

She swayed a little herself, breathless and unsteady, her senses spiraling madly around her.

Come? Come where?

But where else could he mean but to his bed?

He waited, clearly wanting her consent when another man would only have demanded.

This was her chance, she realized, her opportunity to refuse and flee from him at last.

She looked again at his open hand, his wide, waiting palm.

Without giving herself another instant to think, she laid her own hand within.

Chapter 13

The room spun around Drake as he and Anne Greenway sank together onto the feathery softness of his bed.

In the near darkness, he'd stripped her of her clothes, the curiously sensible cotton garments falling in a soft heap onto the carpeted floor. Odd, he'd thought fleetingly, considering she'd always been clothed in something filmy and flimsy in his other dreams—some thin scrap of material that fell away at his slightest touch.

But this was like no dream he'd ever had. There was a strangely realistic quality to it that left him puzzled, as if something wasn't quite right. One minute, everything seemed to be swimming hazily around him, dreamlike and muddled, while in the next, events seemed as clear as daylight, as though the experiences he was having were actually happening.

Were they?

Or were they not?

He honestly wasn't sure. If he hadn't known better, he would think he was drunk. But that made no sense since he rarely overindulged when it came to spirits. Besides, he was sure he'd been soundly asleep when he'd found her bending over him in his bed. And why in heaven's name would Anne Greenway, his housekeeper, be in his bedroom, leaning over him while he lay naked and sleeping, unless it really was a dream?

Has to be a fantasy, he told himself, as he slid his hands over the rich silk of her skin and hair. But then again the sensations were so vivid and compellingly real. He could even smell her, each new breath filling his head with the delicate fragrance of rain-washed violets and the intoxicating spice of sultry feminine heat.

Dream or reality, he really didn't care at the moment. The only thing that mattered was the fact that Anne—beautiful, desirable, forbidden Anne—was lying in his arms, her body warm, naked and wanting, exactly like his own.

Taking her lips, he kissed her with a dark urgency, craving her the same way he did life's most vital necessities. But neither food, nor air, nor water could compare to the simple beauty of her slightest touch, the quiet majesty of her body entwined with his own.

In faith, he couldn't remember the last time he'd hungered for a woman so strongly— or if he ever had at all. The intensity of his passion left him ravenous, his body shaking with the need to join himself to her, to lodge his flesh so deep and true it really would seem as if they were one.

With that goal in mind, he pleasured her with his lips and hands, her answering moan a symphony to his ears. Her hands moved over him as well, small feminine palms that made him ache and arch, his muscles tightening with a savage need that made him shudder.

Dappling kisses along her throat, he roved lower, exploring each new span of flesh as though it were a territory he was set on conquering. Cupping one round, supple breast in his hand, he rolled her nipple between his thumb and fore-finger, applying just enough pressure to make her squirm beneath him. Her legs moved restlessly against the sheets, her short fingernails raking lightly over his back.

In that moment, he knew he had to taste her. Bending, he drew the tautened nub into his mouth, laving it with his tongue the way he would an especially delicious morsel of candy.

How sweet she is, he thought, *better than sugared fruits and summer rose petals.*

She whimpered and thrust her fingers into his hair, as she had done earlier, clearly determined to hold him in place. Only too happy to oblige, he suckled eagerly, closing his eyes as he drew upon her with increasing ardor.

He gasped a few moments later when she began playing her fingers in and along the dip at the base of his spine. His shaft hardened more, if that was possible, blood draining out of his head to pulse in thick, violent beats. Unconsciously, he thrust against her hip, then raked her plump breast with the edges of his teeth.

A throaty cry soughed from her lips, her fingers clench-ing briefly in his hair while the other hand wandered in random paths up and down his body.

With a shiver, he skimmed his mouth lower, scattering kisses over her belly and hips and thighs. When he reached the triangle of soft curls between her legs, he paused, trying to decide whether he wanted to touch her or taste her—or both.

But this was his dream, after all, and he could do as he liked. And what he liked was her—everything about her.

Without further consideration, he parted her thighs with his hands, feeling her legs tremble beneath his grasp.

And then he lowered his head.

* * *

Sebastianne's eyes popped wide, a strangled gasp sticking in her throat.

Mince alors, what is he doing? Surely he isn't kissing me where I think he's kissing me!

But from the slick, wet glide of sensation in her most intimate of parts, she was forced to accept the fact that he was.

Instinctively, she wanted to push him away, then curl in on herself and hide with shame. Yet even as she gathered herself to refuse him, her body had other ideas, arching toward him rather than away, wanting more rather than less.

Ah, Dieu, she thought, as her quavering fingers twisted helplessly into the sheets. Never had she known such exquisite pleasure, such mindless delight. It was as though he'd found the very heart of her and was making it come alive from the inside out. Making *her* come alive from the inside out.

In rapid pants, shallow breaths rasped from between her lips, her senses overwhelmed by a wealth of uncontrollable needs and barely tapped emotions. Yearning rose within her like a maelstrom, turning her half-mad and nearly wild.

Then suddenly, and without the least bit of warning, the storm broke, ripples of astonishing pleasure breaking over her in heavy, crashing waves. She shuddered and writhed, wondering how she would possibly survive.

Somehow she did, though, her heart continuing to beat fiercely inside her chest, as the world spun dazedly around her.

She'd just started to recover when Drake began again, using his fingers as well as his mouth this time, so that she was left nearly incoherent by the time he'd finished.

Limbs quivering, body aglow, she lay completely pliant as he slowly eased his way up her body again, kissing and touching her in delectable intervals as he went.

Holding himself above her, he crushed her mouth to his

for a long, hungry, possessive kiss that demanded both her surrender and her participation. Finding her strength again, she kissed him back, matching his every touch with an equally enthusiastic one of her own.

Below, she let him part her legs with his knees and settle himself between.

"If this really is a dream," he said on a hoarse rumble, "it's by far the best one I've ever had." Then he thrust inside her, filling her completely.

She clung, shivering at his deep, heavy penetration. It had been years since she'd been with a man, and even then, her days as a wife had been so brief she'd been left little more than a maiden.

Part of her wasn't ready for this, for Drake. He was so forceful, so masculine. But another part of her knew this claiming was long past due and that she was glad it was him.

Being with any other man would have been unthinkable since being with another man wouldn't have included love.

She gave a quiet gasp at the realization, as the truth spread slowly inside her.

Ah, no, how could I have allowed this to happen?

But she had.

Without the least intention on her part, she'd fallen in love with Drake Byron.

Then he began to move, and her body came powerfully to life even as her mind went blank with ecstasy.

Jesu, she's so tight, Drake thought as he worked himself within her. Her body fit him like a sleek, hot, velvety sheath. Just the sensation was enough to drive him right to the edge. Somehow, he held back, wanting to know she'd taken her pleasure again before he gave himself permission to claim his own. Besides, their coupling would be better; couplings always were when the woman enjoyed herself as much as he did.

Yet she isn't just any woman, he knew, relishing the feel of her slender arms wrapped around his back, her shapely legs twined around his waist.

This is Anne. And finally, at last, she is mine.

Needing her, all of her, he captured her mouth in a fervid kiss, tangling his tongue with her own as he established a demanding rhythm that she was compelled to match. He drank in the sweet scent of her skin, his own skin growing hot and slick with a light sheen of perspiration. His pulse thundered out a crazy tattoo between his ears, his blood pumping in thick, sultry beats through his veins.

Gliding his fingers over her pliant flesh, he stroked the tender peaks of her breasts before roving lower, then lower still to tangle between their merged bodies.

A long, keening moan issued from her throat as he touched her most sensitive places, her hips thrusting upward to meet his own as her body bowed with unmistakable rapture and shuddering, gasping completion.

Then he too gave himself over, stripping off the last of his restraints as he thrust with a raw, almost primitive need inside her. Bliss poured through him as he climaxed, his entire body shaking from the devastating force of his release.

The world spun around him for several long moments before he rolled to his back and cradled her against his heaving chest. Closing his eyes, he wondered again how she could be anything but real. Stoking a hand over the length of her tousled tresses, he let himself dream.

Sebastianne lay stunned, returning slowly to herself as she listened to the reassuring rhythm of Drake's heart beating beneath her ear. She knew she should leave, memory of the imprint of the key returning to her like a ghoulish specter. Still, she didn't have the strength to move; Drake had wrung every ounce of energy from her body with the heady beauty of his lovemaking.

Never in her life had she known such bliss. Never before had she been so content. She wished this moment would never end.

But it will, whispered a cruel voice. *It must.*

For now, though, she would steal a few moments more. She needed him, needed this in a way she wouldn't have imagined possible even a few hours ago.

He was asleep again, his breathing slow and measured once more. With the sleeping draught still pumping through his system, would he even remember any of this come morning? For her sake, she knew it would be better if he did not; yet she couldn't help but wish otherwise.

Snuggling closer, she let herself drift, praying for tomorrow never to arrive.

Some while later, she awakened with a start, blinking into the grey darkness that warned of the approaching dawn. *Zut alors!* she cursed, remembering everything, aware that she must leave Drake and the warm comfort of his arms while there was still time.

Ever so carefully, she extracted herself from his embrace, relieved when he didn't move but instead slumbered on. Aware she dare not light a candle, she felt her way carefully across the room, searching with her toes for the soft cotton of her nightgown and robe puddled in a heap on the floor.

Luck helped her find them, and remained on her side while she pulled on the garments with shaking hands—the wax case with the imprint lying like an accusation in her pocket. She located her slippers as well, tucking her feet silently inside.

Listening a few last moments to Drake's quiet breathing

where he lay in bed, she put aside the ache in her chest and forced herself to turn away. With a soundless turn of the latch, she let herself out.

She reached her room without incident, meeting no one on the stairs. Falling onto the bed, she huddled with her knees drawn into a ball, knowing she would have to get up again soon. She was painfully aware she would need to pretend that she'd passed an easy, uneventful night, and that nothing at all had changed.

As for Drake?

What if he remembered? What if he did not?

Either way, his reaction would do nothing to cure her already broken heart, for she could never stay with him. Nor could she ever let him know of her love.

Squeezing her eyes shut, she let the tears flow.

Drake squinted against the sunlight filtering beneath the heavy bronze damask curtains in his bedroom. Rolling over, he buried his face against the pillows and willed himself to go back to sleep.

Although considering what time he'd retired to bed last night, he ought to have had plenty of rest by now. Thinking back, he recalled that he'd eaten dinner and drunk a glass of port, then he'd grown so tired that he'd come up to bed and fallen straight to sleep. Flashes of memory chased through his mind, scenes and sensations rising from the depths of his nocturnal oblivion.

What an amazing dream I had, he thought. In truth, it had been the most extraordinarily sexual dream he'd ever had, not even the randy longings of his teenage years could compare. The memory alone was enough to make his body tighten with remembered pleasure and a shiveringly intense level of satisfaction.

If he hadn't known better, he would have thought Anne

Greenway really had been in his bed. If he hadn't been aware it was only a dream, he would have believed that her soft arms actually had been curved around his shoulders, her legs locked at his back as he thrust deeply into her warm, feminine depths. And that he'd kissed her, over and over again, her mouth as warm and rich as sweet cream, the intoxicating fragrance of her skin playing erotic games with his head.

Even now he could smell her—fresh violets in a cool, early-morning field.

Delicate violets.

Turning his head, he breathed deeply into the crisp linen case covering the pillow beneath his cheek, smelling the scent of flowers more strongly than before. Real flowers that had nothing to do with dreams, and a genuine, entrancing feminine scent that lingered on the fabric.

A scent that smelled exactly like . . . Anne Greenway.

His eyes popped open, and he sat upright, the sheets pooling around his bare waist.

By God, that was no dream. I really did sleep with her last night.

Chapter 14

I *should run while I still have the chance,* Sebastianne thought the next morning as she forced herself to go about her usual duties. Seated at her office desk, she dipped a pen into an open bottle of black ink, then began copying out next week's menu in her best copperplate hand.

If I time it right, she mused, as the quill scratched over the vellum, *I could stuff a few of my belongings into a pillowcase, since my suitcase would be far too noticeable, then sneak out the back servants' door before anyone realizes I'm gone.*

But running wasn't an option, she concluded with an inward sigh. At least not without the cipher—and in order to get her hands on that, she needed the key.

An image of the small case with its wax imprint came to mind, along with the place beneath her mattress where she'd hidden it. As soon as may be, she planned to take the imprint to the locksmith and have him fashion a duplicate key. Until then, she would simply have to brazen it out and pray that Drake didn't realize what she'd done.

Lord Drake, she corrected herself sternly. It wouldn't do to let herself start thinking of him in casual terms, regardless of the fact that she'd lain naked in his arms last night, as intimate as a woman could possibly be with a man. Breathtakingly, heart-stoppingly, soul-shatteringly intimate in a way she knew she would never forget, not even if she lived to be so old she could barely recall her own name.

Laying down the quill, she pressed a fist against the sudden ache in her chest. *How could I have let myself fall in love with him?*

Hadn't she sworn when she'd come to this house that she would keep her emotions inviolate? Hadn't she assured herself she would complete her mission and leave with no ties or regrets?

So how had it all gone so horribly wrong?

Not only had she come to like and admire the other servants with whom she worked—a realization that made her feel guiltier by the day for deceiving them—but now she'd done the very worst of all by tumbling head over ears for their master!

Bon Dieu, how was she going to carry on? And what if Drake caught her?

She trembled at the idea, fearing his retribution nearly as much as the inevitable heartache she must face at losing him.

He was a proud man. And smart, too smart to forgive being duped and manipulated. Should he realize . . .

Fingers trembling, she wiped them against her skirt as she pushed the thoughts away—or tried to, her nerves frayed to the point of exhaustion. Of course a nearly sleepless night hadn't helped. She wished she could sneak away and take a nap. Even if her duties permitted it, however—which they didn't—she knew she wouldn't be able to fall asleep. She wondered if she would sleep even tonight, despite her weariness.

Smothering a yawn against the back of one hand, she picked her pen up again.

She'd just begun to concentrate once more on the menu when a soft tap came at the door. Pausing, she called her permission to enter.

"Beg pardon, missus," Jasper said, smiling a friendly greeting where he stood tall and lanky just inside the door. "Came to tell you that his lordship is wanting his breakfast."

Her pulse jumped at mention of Drake.

So he's awake, is he?

Glancing at the clock, she saw the time was a few minutes past ten. Ordinarily, Drake was an early riser, but considering the night just past, she wasn't surprised he'd slept late. She would have enjoyed sleeping late herself. Speculating, she wondered at his mood. And more to the point, how much of last night did he recall?

Making sure none of her thoughts showed on her face, she gave a nod. "Very good. Please inform Cook to prepare a tray and have it taken up."

"I already stopped in the kitchen. Mrs. Tremble is toasting bread and poaching eggs right now. His lordship said he wants to take his meal in his study. Then he asked particularly for you."

A drop of black ink splattered across the white menu, ruining the careful writing on its surface. "For me?"

"Yes, ma'am. Said he wants a full board and for you to bring it to him."

She tried to speak past the painful lump in her throat. Instead, all she could do was nod and pray Jasper understood that he could now withdraw.

Clearly taking her meaning, he stepped back and closed the door behind him.

The instant he departed, Sebastianne slumped back into her chair, a fine tremor radiating over her skin.

Zut alors, she thought. *Drake remembers!*

Exactly what he remembered, however, remained to be seen.

Reaching the ground floor, Drake paused to rub his fingers over his eyes, massaging the faint headache that lingered just behind them. He ought to have taken breakfast in his rooms, he supposed, exactly as Waxman suggested. But he had matters to which he wished to attend, and, frankly, his valet's concerned hovering had been driving him mad.

"Good morning, your lordship," Stowe said, looking up from where he stood polishing the brass decoration on the front door. "I trust you had a good night?"

Good didn't begin to describe the night he'd just had, but he wasn't about to share all the unexpected details with his butler.

"It was . . . tolerable," Drake said, deciding that was an innocuous enough answer. His head throbbed briefly, reminding him of the first of the important issues to which he wished to attend. "Stowe, if you've a minute, would you come into my study?"

The older man paused, then set down his polishing cloth. "Of course, your lordship."

Without waiting a moment more, Drake strode into the room and went across to his desk. Feeling far wearier than he ought considering what time he'd gone to sleep last night, he sank into his desk chair. Stowe followed, coming to a halt on the opposite side of Drake's desk. Quietly, the servant waited.

"I had a glass of port last night. Where did you obtain the vintage?"

Stowe's brows rose upward. "Berry Brothers, as usual, my lord."

Berry Brothers was a highly reputable establishment with

an impeccable reputation. As wine and spirits purveyors to the Regent himself, they were above reproach. Still, there had been an odd flavor to the wine last night. Perhaps it had simply gone off, then again . . .

"Have you noticed any problems with the wine lately?" Drake asked.

"No, my lord. Is there is a problem? If so, I shall certainly say as much to Mr. Berry himself."

"No no, don't trouble him over it. I'm sure I am just being particular."

But even as he said the words, Drake felt certain there had been something wrong with the wine. Was that why he'd grown so extraordinarily sleepy. Had someone tampered with the bottle? He remembered the break-in a few weeks ago. What if the two events were associated somehow? What if the French were trying a new set of tactics? Even so, it made little sense since no one had tried to burgle the house. Mayhap he was merely suffering from a case of paranoia.

Glancing to his side, he looked at the painting on the wall that hid his concealed safe. Everything appeared to be in order. Nevertheless, he would have to check again to make sure, paranoia or no paranoia.

"And the delivery?" Drake continued. "Were there any new men on the route?"

Stowe frowned. "Well, it's generally the same fellows who do the deliveries, but every once in a while there's a different man. I'd have to check the date to be certain when those bottles of port were put into the cellar, but even then I couldn't be certain. Maybe Lyles or Jasper might recall. Shall I inquire?"

"Yes, if you would. We don't happen to still have last night's bottle by any chance?" Drake asked.

"No, my lord, I decanted the wine as usual and as I recall

that was the last of it. I washed the decanter out myself only last night. Shall I check to see if we have another bottle of the same in the cellar?"

"All right, yes," Drake agreed slowly. Still, he knew that the other bottles of port would taste exactly as they were supposed to taste—like good-quality wine and nothing else.

Stowe departed soon after.

Once he'd gone, Drake relaxed back in his chair and closed his eyes, the slight ache in his head making itself known once again. Rubbing the bridge of his nose, he wondered if he ought to have stayed in bed.

Memories of silken arms and sultry kisses flooded over him, his pulse speeding faster while his shaft hardened with abrupt longing.

And this, he thought wryly, *is the reason I could not remain abed.* There wouldn't have been any point, since he wouldn't have gotten a minute's sleep—not with Anne on his mind.

Suddenly, he caught a faint hint of violets drifting on the air, and his eyes sprang open.

And there she stood, framed in a warm pool of sunlight that made the red and gold in her hair burn like fire and the fine strands of grey gleam as if they were polished silver. She didn't meet his eyes, he noticed, her concentration apparently centered on the heavy tray in her hands.

"I've come with your breakfast, my lord," she stated in a businesslike tone, her voice holding none of the passion he'd heard as she'd lain in his arms.

Had it only been last night? Had it really happened as he thought it had? Yes, he was sure of it, despite her calm, efficient demeanor. Still, pieces were missing here and there. At one point he thought they'd had a conversation in his bathing chamber of all places. He couldn't recall what had been said. And had they started kissing there? He rather thought they had.

She set the tray down on a nearby table, her back turned toward him. "Shall I pour you a cup of tea, your lordship?"

His eyes lowered to her hips and the rounded curve of her bottom. He had a sudden, vivid memory of stroking his hands over that particular span of creamy flesh as he pressed her near.

Clearing his throat, he shifted in his chair. "Yes. That would be most welcome."

Steam drifted into the air as she prepared his cup, the clink of silver on porcelain as she laid a teaspoon on his saucer cutting across the silence that had fallen in the room.

Tea in hand, she crossed to him. She still did not meet his eyes.

Her grasp remained steady as she placed the cup and saucer on his desk. He waited only long enough for her to draw clear of the hot beverage before he reached out and caught her wrist inside his fingers.

Her gaze flew to his, her eyes a gleaming, burnished gold. Her hand trembled inside his grasp.

"Aren't you going to say anything?" he asked in a curiously composed voice.

"About what, my lord?"

Using the force of his will, he compelled her not to look away. "You know what. Or did I imagine doing a great deal more than touching your wrist last night?"

She trembled again.

"Why were you in my room?" he shot in a near whisper. "How did you come to be in my bed?"

For a long moment she said nothing, then she tugged her hand free.

He let her go, watching as she cradled her wrist in her other hand.

"I-I came to . . . look in on you. You seemed unwell, and I thought I might offer to make you a posset or some such."

"*A posset!* In the middle of the night?" He paused, mulling over her words. Abruptly, he frowned. "I didn't . . . force you?"

Her gaze flew to his again and she shook her head. "No, my lord. You were . . . insistent, but you never did anything I did not wish."

He relaxed slightly, only then aware of the tension that had been riding him since he'd realized exactly how he'd spent the night. "Still, I suspect I owe you an apology of sorts since I've never before taken advantage of a woman in my life, especially a woman in my employ."

Her shoulders drew straight. "No apologies are required, my lord. Now, you really ought to eat your breakfast before it gets cold. Mrs. Tremble will be most put out if you send back her food untouched."

She moved to turn away again, but he caught her wrist once more, holding her in place. "Don't be distressed," he said. "I didn't mean to upset you. Hell, I barely know what I mean this morning, everything is so mixed up. As you said, I wasn't exactly myself last night."

She tugged against his grasp, but this time he held firm.

Softly, he stroked his thumb over the tender skin inside her wrist in a way that elicited another quiver. "I liked what we did together in my bed. Rather more than liked. I find myself wanting to do it again. Badly."

Then, before his next words had even fully formed in his brain, he was blurting them out. "Let me take care of you. I'll give you carte blanche. A house and a carriage, clothes and jewelry, everything you could possibly desire. You'll have a full staff to command as well, but not as housekeeper this time. Instead, you'll be mistress, able to come and go as you please."

He raised her hand to his mouth and pressed a kiss onto the warm, fragrant silk of her palm. "And you'll have me to show you the Town as you've only dreamed of seeing it. I'll take you everywhere, balls and parties and on holiday to a host of magnificent climes. I promise you nothing but pleasure, both in bed and out."

Sebastianne swayed, heart pounding in her chest, as a sharp longing pierced her like an arrow. He spun tales of a fantastical idyll, promising a life of luxury and excitement. She could almost imagine how it would be, spending her days as a pampered lady and her nights taking wanton pleasure in his arms. In such a fantasy world, she would be free to give her love, and if she were very lucky, find it returned as well.

How wonderful it would be.

"Say yes, Anne," he whispered. "Tell me you'll be mine."

The sound of her false name on his lips shattered her reverie, returning her to reality with the same abrupt shock she would have felt if he'd tossed her into a wintry lake. Her heartbeat slowed to a dull rhythm, the weight of her duty and allegiances rushing back.

She pulled her hand away for a second time. "I may have shared your bed last night, Lord Drake, but that doesn't mean I wish to become your whore. Besides, I believe you already have a mistress here in Town to see to your needs. I would prefer to keep house for you as your housekeeper, not as your light o'love."

He said nothing, a new frown creating lines across his handsome forehead. She almost reached out to smooth them away but curled her hand against her skirt instead.

Suddenly, a fresh thought occurred. "Unless you want me to give notice?" she said, a frown gathering on her own brow. "Are you dismissing me?"

What if he demanded that she did leave? Without the cipher, she couldn't afford to lose her position in his household now. What if sleeping with him had not only cost her

her heart but her chance to finish the job that had brought her so far from home as well?

"Of course you are not dismissed," he said gruffly. "Do you think I would turn you out simply because you refused my carte blanche? What kind of blackguard do you take me for?"

"Drake, I never meant—" she whispered.

"Your employment with me is secure so long as you wish it. And should you harbor any fears concerning a repetition of my advances, you may rest easy. You have made your sentiments plain, in spite of sharing my bed last night. I do not importune women who don't reciprocate my interest. Now, I believe I will take my breakfast."

She hesitated, wanting to explain her refusal but knowing she could not. How could she when doing so might expose the real reason for being in his bedchamber last night? She was fortunate he truly had been asleep when she'd copied the key and that he'd accepted her explanation at face value rather than questioning her further.

If he only knew he would be furious.

If he only realized, he would have no qualms about giving her the sack.

Instead, he would likely see her clapped in irons and led off to Newgate. No, it was better she had wounded his pride by her rejection. Better he would stay away.

So why did a wistful part of her wish it were otherwise?

Turning, she crossed to the breakfast tray, preparing to carry the plates to him. Before she could so much as remove the covers, he forestalled her with a wave of one hand.

"Do not trouble yourself over serving me, Mrs. Greenway. I shall see to matters on my own."

She hesitated again, then linked her hands against her skirts. "As you wish, my lord."

He didn't acknowledge her further, her dismissal clear.

Chest aching again, she walked to the door.

Chapter 15

"*D*id your dog die or something?" Cade asked Drake three evenings later as he and his brother stood together on the balcony at the Pettigrews' annual ball, each of them puffing idly on cheroots. "You're as morose as an undertaker."

Drake tapped a bit of greyish ash, watching the flakes scatter over the hydrangea bushes underneath. "My humor is fine. And as you're well aware, I do not have a dog."

"An omission Esme would be only too happy to correct. She believes everyone needs canine and feline companionship," Cade observed, referring to their little sister, who was a great animal lover and kept a menagerie of beloved creatures at Braebourne. "Yet somehow I don't think it's a lack of furry friends that's troubling you. A female have you in knots?" he added with uncanny perception.

Drake took a long pull on his cigar, the end flaring brilliantly red. "No," he lied. "Just don't know why Mama insisted on my attendance tonight when it's clear I have no interest in any of the eligible misses. I'd much rather be working than dancing a cotillion."

"At least you *can* dance," Cade stated. "Every time I watch Meg stand up with some fellow, I wish she were dancing with me."

Drake waved off the remark. "She loves you just as you are and doesn't care a whit that your bad leg keeps you from standing up with her at balls. The men who partner her on the dance floor mean nothing, you know that."

Cade's eyes flashed. "I do know. If I thought otherwise, I'd forbid her from leaving the house and run all those would-be cicisbei through with my sword."

"I'd love to see you forbid Meg from doing anything," Drake said with a low chuckle. "She has the countenance of an angel and the heart of a Titan."

"She is magnificent," Cade said with obvious love and pride. "But we're not talking about my wife, we're talking about you."

"Are we? I thought we were talking about dogs—Meg's admirers included."

Cade gave a snort, then took a puff on his cigar. With elaborate style, he blew a curling stream of smoke high into the night air. "Enough with the diversions. Tell me why you're so blue deviled."

Drake scowled.

Although he knew he could tell his brother anything—for Cade was a supremely trustworthy confidant—Drake wasn't in the mood to share. Over the past three days, he'd done his best to forget his midnight tryst with his housekeeper and her rejection of him the next morning. *What's done is done,* he told himself, and he was determined to put her aside once and for all.

Unfortunately, her presence in his house made the effort all but impossible. Every time he thought he'd mastered his emotions, the lilting strains of her voice would carry along the hallway. Or else he would catch the faintest hint of her scent, magnified by his senses, as if violets were bursting to life through the floors.

He tried his best of avoid her, and when he couldn't avoid her, to ignore her instead. But it was as though his brain was connected directly to his bollocks these days, leaving him with a persistent arousal that turned him irascible as a baited bear.

He ought to pay a call on Vanessa, he supposed, and slake his pent-up lust on her. She was his mistress, after all. By damn, though, he didn't want Vanessa. And the thought of visiting one of the myriad bawdy houses that populated London's less seemly addresses held even less appeal. Which left him in his present state—blue deviled and in a near agony of lust as well.

Because no matter his resolve to forget what had happened between him and Anne, he wanted her still. Knew he would take her to his bed again with the slightest show of interest on her part. But she'd denied him, and so he would abide by her wishes, even if it ended up turning him into a sexual cripple from lack of carnal satisfaction.

Torture, that's what it was. Pure and simple torture. Lord above, save him. But in this regard, he didn't think the Lord had anything to share.

"As I said before, it's obviously a woman," Cade declared, intruding into Drake's thoughts. "Has it anything to do with Miss Manning?"

"Who?" Drake mumbled, his mind still full of lustrous autumn-hued hair and satiny white female flesh.

Cade shot him a quizzical glance. "Apparently not. Miss Manning will be vastly disappointed to know your visits were of no moment."

"Well, yes, I was only being polite."

"Is it Vanessa then? Has your affair come to an end?"

Drake's brows drew even tighter. Vanessa, he realized,

provided him with the perfect excuse. And Cade was right about one thing, Drake realized, his affair with her was over—at least for him. He would have to find a considerate way to break it off with her.

"Yes," he stated. "Vanessa and I are through."

Cade studied him again as if he weren't quite satisfied by the answer. "In that case, then, it sounds as if you're in need of a gentleman's night out with your brothers and a few male friends. Drinking, gaming and wenching."

"None of which your wife or the other wives will allow although I'm sure Leo and Lawrence know the best spots for such activities."

"From the reports I've heard, they know *all* the spots, the best and worst alike." Cade paused, tapping the ash off his now-cold cheroot. "How about an evening in then? A nice dinner, a few rounds of billiards and good conversation. None of the ladies can complain about that. Of course, my town house won't do," he mused aloud, "nor will Clybourne House. And I'm sure none of us wants to risk squeezing into the twin's new digs . . ." He trailed off, leaving a significant silence.

Drake raised a brow and ruefully shook his head. "I suppose I'm to volunteer my own town house then?"

Cade smiled as if Drake had just had the most brilliant idea in the world, clapping him on the back. "Excellent notion. I'll contact the guests, you arrange the supper."

Restraining a sigh, Drake agreed.

The key will be ready in two days more, Sebastianne thought the following morning as she stood in the upstairs hallway, counting the linens and inspecting them for stains and worn spots. Finding one with a small tear along one corner, she pulled it free and set it into a large wicker basket she'd carried upstairs for just such a purpose.

With her schedule, though, she knew there would be no opportunity to collect the key until Friday next, when she had her regular full day off. She'd taken a big enough risk concocting an excuse that had allowed her to visit the key maker across Town. Coming up with another "urgently" required item for the stillroom might raise curiosity, or worse, suspicion. So she would have to bide her time, waiting for her day off and the freedom it gave her to travel through the city unaccompanied and unnoticed.

The month Vacheau had allotted her was slipping rapidly past, but she still had nearly two weeks remaining, enough time for her to secure the duplicate key and copy the cipher.

If only I had both of them now and could leave, everything would be so much easier, she reasoned, ignoring the painful lurch her heart gave at the idea of her inevitable departure from the house and, most especially, its master. But the break would have to be made whether she liked it or not, just as she'd done what was necessary when she'd refused Drake's offer to become his mistress. Not that she would ever truly have entertained the idea of being any man's mistress. Yet, in Drake's case, she had been tempted.

Lord Drake, she scolded herself. *He's not Drake to you. He's your employer, not your lover, even if you did spend one astonishingly beautiful night together.*

As for Drake . . . *Lord Drake* . . . he certainly seemed to have recovered after being summarily turned down. Whenever she saw him—which wasn't all that often—he was pleasant and polite if a bit reserved. But that was only to be expected, she supposed, given the situation and the fact that she was just a servant.

His servant. To command in any manner he chose.

But true to his word, he'd made no further overtures of an amorous nature toward her; it was almost as if the night hadn't happened. In fact, if she hadn't had the wax case in her possession and wasn't having a key cast from it, she might have thought their passionate interlude nothing but a dream.

Suddenly glancing down, she found her knuckles squeezed white, her fingers clutched around one of the sheets. Instantly releasing it, she took a moment to collect her emotions, then went back to her inspection.

She was nearly finished when she heard footsteps coming toward her in the hall. Half-hoping it was Drake, she turned toward the sound.

"Mr. Stowe," she greeted, lowering her lashes in case disappointment showed in her gaze. "What brings you this way?"

"Good morning, Mrs. Greenway," the butler replied. "I have news that I thought required your immediate attention and decided not to wait until you returned belowstairs."

"Oh? And what might that be?"

The older man gave her a faint, almost apologetic smile. "His lordship has decided to host a dinner this evening. Twelve guests, all male, in need of supper and refreshments. I shall leave the menu planning to you and Mrs. Tremble. And, of course, I shall see to the table service myself with Jasper and Lyles assistance."

A dinner! Tonight!

Mince alors, what did she know about arranging a dinner for a bunch of aristocratic gentlemen? The biggest table she'd ever set had been at home for Christmas with her father, brothers and a few neighbors, all come to share the holiday together. When her mother had been alive, they'd had an English plum pudding as well, full of fruit and nuts and whiskey. In Drake's case, however, she didn't think *pot au feu* and a king cake would be in keeping with either the summer season or the company.

At least, there wouldn't be any ladies in attendance or the

need to provide an array of after-dinner delicacies and tea in the drawing room while the gentlemen relaxed separately over their brandy. Nevertheless, what was Drake thinking to give her and the rest of the staff so little time to prepare?

Obviously, he believed that, as a lord, his servants ought to be more than capable of readying the house for guests and know how to lay a satisfying meal before them. Even more to the point, he clearly assumed that his housekeeper was up to the task of overseeing every detail of the preparations.

Which, she thought with a fluttery jiggle in her stomach, *remains to be seen.*

Allowing none of her inner turmoil to show, she gave Mr. Stowe a look of easy confidence. "Thank you for bringing the matter to my early attention. I shall finish here with my linen inspection, then be along to consult with maids and kitchen staff."

The butler nodded with obvious satisfaction. "Excellent. Mrs. Tremble already has a list of their lordships' preferred dishes and His Grace's as well."

"His Grace?"

"Lord Drake's brother, the Duke of Clybourne. He will likely be in attendance tonight."

Mon Dieu, she thought, forcing her eyes not to widen. *That's right, one of Drake's older brothers is a duke.* She hoped he hadn't invited the Prince Regent along as well. She didn't think her nerves would be able to take such a revelation. But Stowe made no further alarming remarks about the guest list, giving her another brief smile before turning away.

She waited until she heard his footsteps recede in the distance; only then did she let her shoulders sag.

Today is going to be a very long day.

Chapter 16

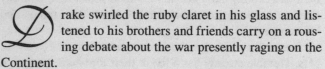rake swirled the ruby claret in his glass and listened to his brothers and friends carry on a rousing debate about the war presently raging on the Continent.

"Wellington will win the day," Adam Gresham declared, gesturing with the tines of his dinner fork. "He's on the verge of driving the French out of Madrid, and soon they'll be out of Spain entirely."

"That is the hope," Edward agreed, taking a swallow from his own glass of wine before setting it back down on the table. "But I wouldn't count Boney's forces out yet."

"Not even after the beating they took in Russia last year?" Leo challenged. "Field Marshal Ney limped out with fewer than twenty thousand men."

"And that's after beginning the campaign with nearly half a million," Lawrence added, his square jaw set at an identical angle to his twin's.

"And yet they still limped out," Cade observed with the cool calm of an experienced soldier. "So long as the will remains strong, the battle continues."

"True as that may be, I have no doubt we'll drive Boney from power eventually," Edward stated in a resolute tone. "The only question is when and at what further cost."

Murmurs of agreement issued from around the table.

Drake sipped his wine, then signaled for the empty dinner plates to be removed. The footmen sprang to attention with sublime efficiency, their actions barely noticed by the gentlemen gathered around the long dining table, the men continuing to talk at a relaxed pace.

Normally, Drake might have interjected a comment or two himself, but try as he might, he couldn't quite get into the spirit of the evening despite his brothers' and friends' best efforts to provide him with an amusing diversion. He supposed they presumed his silence meant he was lost in another one of his mathematical reveries. He was known for "drifting off," so that was nothing unusual. But his mind was focused on things he'd be better off not dwelling on—or rather a certain someone who shouldn't be on his mind.

I am not thinking about her tonight! he told himself as he tossed back the last of the claret in his glass.

This was a celebration, and, by God, he ought to be celebrating, whether or not she was somewhere in the house.

Belowstairs, most likely, working in her office, or the stillroom perhaps. Bah, he cursed inwardly, shoving the thought away.

Across the room, Stowe stood pouring glasses of brandy. Drake had told him to forgo serving the port since there had been no resolution as of yet concerning the suspect bottle from which Drake had drunk a few days ago.

The night he'd been drugged.

The night he'd made love to Anne.

Drake stared, noticing Niall Faversham wave a hand in the air to highlight whatever it was he was saying. Drake forced himself to listen, wishing he were enjoying himself as much as his companions.

There'd been talk earlier of playing a few hands of cards. Perhaps that would divert him. Cards were his brother Jack's area of expertise, but he could count them as well as his talented brother when he wished to go to the bother. He had no interest in winning money from anyone; but maybe he would dust off his old skills tonight if for no other reason than to occupy his mind. Surely, if he was busy calculating odds and remembering clubs from spades, he wouldn't have time to dwell on her.

Then suddenly she was there, entering the dining room for the first time that evening. In her hands she held an elegant glass bowl containing what appeared to be a beautifully made trifle—cake, custard and liquor-soaked fruit layered into a heavenly confection.

No one else seemed aware of her arrival as she glided on silent feet toward the sideboard on the far side of the room, where the footmen had stacked dessert plates for service. Setting down her burden without so much as a glance his way, she picked up a large silver spoon and began carefully dividing out portions.

Drake reached for the brandy Stowe had just set before him and took a hearty swallow.

"Incredible that she had the entire Ton duped," Faversham said. "Philipa Stockton was a calculating vixen, I'll grant you that, but who would have thought she was in league with the French?"

Across the room, one of the plates rattled.

"Have they set a date for her trial?" Cade asked in a serious tone.

Edward shook his head. "Not yet, but soon I hear. She's been quite forthcoming with information of late, no doubt in hopes of gaining leniency. Prison has a way of loosening stubborn tongues."

"And will they give her leniency?" Adam inquired.

"Considering how attractive she is, I wouldn't be surprised if she manages to gain the judges' sympathy," Faversham remarked.

"Unless she slept with one of them, then cast him off," Leo said with a smile.

"Or cast all of them off!" Lawrence quipped.

Chuckles filled the air.

Lord Howland, however, gave a derisive sniff. "Well, if you ask me, she deserves everything she gets for being a damned spy. Woman or not, they ought to put her on the gallows and let her hang."

A clatter rent the air, as the big silver spoon Anne Greenway had been using to serve dessert, slipped from her hand and crashed to the floor—cake, cream and fruit splattering over the boards.

She bent down quickly and reached for the utensil, clutching it in a white-knuckled grasp as she whirled to face the assembled company, her face flushed and golden eyes wide.

"My most sincere apology for the interruption, gentlemen," she said in a rush. "Pray forgive my clumsiness and continue on with your discussion as if I am not even here. I shall have your dessert served and this mess cleaned up in a trice."

"And how could we pretend not to notice such loveliness in our midst?" Leo piped, displaying an engaging, white-toothed smile. "Forgive us for not taking note of your presence immediately, ma'am. We were obviously suffering from temporary blindness."

Lawrence gave an identical smile. "Just so. To my way of thinking, your interruption is exactly what this sorry lot of males needs to break up all the serious talk of politics and war. This is supposed to be a party, after all."

Anne said nothing as the footmen, Jasper and Lyles, appeared. She stepped slightly aside as they began wiping the floor clean with pair of cloths. Mr. Stowe took the opportunity to walk to the silver chest at the far end of the room to retrieve a new spoon.

"See?" Leo observed. "There's no harm done. Just a tad of pudding and cake that's easily mopped away. Is that not right, Drake?"

For his part, all Drake could do was stare, his heart beating in a vicious thrum as he took in the light dusting of pink across her cheeks and the soft strawberry tint of moist lips that were parted with clear embarrassment. "No," he murmured. "No harm done at all."

On his left, he saw Cade give him a long, speculative look, one chestnut eyebrow raised high.

Ignoring him, Drake lowered his own gaze and reached again for his glass of brandy, hoping the liquor might help his pulse to slow to its normal rhythm.

"Clearly, the twins have the advantage of the rest of us, presumably having already met you . . . Mrs. Greenway, is it?" Edward said with a curious expression in his own blue eyes.

"Yes, my lord, how do you do," Anne replied before sinking into a surprisingly elegant curtsey.

Edward smiled.

Only then did Drake realize how strangely loath he was to introduce her to the others. Not because he was embarrassed by her but because he didn't want to share. Until now, in its own way, she had been all his. Except for the twins, of course. Odd they hadn't gone blabbing to everyone else in the family, but apparently not. Still, it would seem that matters had gone too far not to make introductions.

"Gentlemen," Drake announced gruffly, "this is my housekeeper, Anne Greenway. Mrs. Greenway has been in my employ for the past several weeks now and has been a fine addition to my staff."

"I'm sure she has," Howland remarked.

"Wish I had a housekeeper like her," Faversham shot back in an undertone that still managed to carry.

Drake's jaw tightened, wanting to tell them to keep their rude comments to themselves. "Allow me to make you known to the company, Mrs. Greenway," he continued.

She linked her hands together, burying them in her skirts. "Oh, that isn't necessary, my lord."

"I believe it is."

And suddenly, oddly, he wanted her to know his family—the male half anyway. As for his friends . . .

"I'll start around the table, left to right. My brother, Cade."

Cade inclined his head, the speculative expression still on his face.

"You know Leopold and Lawrence, of course."

The twins sent her a pair of identical grins.

"Next to them is my brother-in-law, Adam, Earl of Gresham."

Adam sent her a pleasant smile and nod.

"Friends, Lord Howland and Mr. Faversham."

Drake didn't give either of them a chance to reply.

"And my eldest brother, Edward, Duke of Clybourne. I've one additional brother, Jack, but he is presently in the country with his wife and children. I've two sisters as well."

Why he'd decided to volunteer that last bit of information, he didn't quite know.

"Your Grace," she murmured, turning her attention once again to Edward. "Forgive my error from before. I did not realize whom I was addressing."

Edward sent her a friendly look. "No harm. It's rather nice sometimes not being known straightaway as a duke."

She dipped her chin in gracious reply.

A moment later, she straightened her shoulders, her normal color returning to her cheeks as her gaze roved over all the men at the dining table. "It is a pleasure to make your acquaintances, my lords and gentlemen," she said with all the aplomb of an educated, well-mannered lady. "And I thank you for the kind introduction, Lord Drake. However, if you will permit me, I believe Mr. Stowe has retrieved a fresh spoon, and dessert still awaits. Shall I serve now?"

Rousing murmurs of agreements went around the table. She turned away then and resumed service.

Cade leaned close, and whispered, "I see the trouble now. She's very pretty."

Drake sipped his brandy. "She is my housekeeper. Nothing more."

Cade didn't remark further, reaching for his fork as a plate laden with a delectable-looking trifle was set before him.

Moments after, Drake followed his lead and did the same.

Sebastianne smothered a yawn as she climbed the servants' staircase to the main floor several hours later, the clock having struck two in the morning some minutes past. Despite Mr. Stowe's being in charge of the dining room and its guests, she'd been up and down the stairs numerous times that evening, attending to one matter or another during Lord Drake's dinner party.

But now, thankfully, the evening was over, and the last of the gentlemen had gone home, leaving her and the other servants free to end their duties and seek the comfort of their beds. As for herself, she planned to do one final check of the house to make sure everything had been properly cleared, cleaned and put away, then she would continue on to her bedchamber.

The moment she entered the dining room, however, the debacle with the dessert service came rushing back, dual sensations of embarrassment and panic flaring back to life within her.

As housekeeper, it had been her job to make the fancy dessert. If only Mr. Stowe and Mrs. Tremble hadn't insisted she carry the trifle into the dining room as a show of her talent for baking, none of the subsequent events would have occurred. She would never have been in the room; never have overheard the men's conversation about that woman, whoever she was, who had been sent to prison for being caught as a spy; and never made a spectacle of herself.

Her stomach clenched at the memory, a fresh chill running through her veins at the remembered words.

She deserves everything she gets for being a damned spy. Woman or not, they ought to put her on the gallows and let her hang.

Her fingers had gone nerveless in that moment, the spoon tumbling top over end to the floor. Somehow, she'd managed to recover quickly before anyone in the room had a chance to realize she was distressed over more than the mess. But what if they had realized the truth? Rather than cajoling and reassuring her, would they have turned cruel? If any of the gentlemen at dinner knew who she really was and what she planned to do, would they want to put her on the gallows as well?

Would Drake?

The idea made her sick, not only with worry and fear but with sorrow. For try as she might to put him from her heart, she loved Drake Byron. Loved him, even knowing how much he would surely despise her were he ever to learn the truth about her true identity.

Sebastianne Dumont.

Widow of an Imperial cavalry officer.

Daughter of a near-penniless French mathematician, who'd started life as a gentleman's son, fled France to escape the Terror, then returned home from England years later only to fall prey to Napoleon's calculating schemes.

Eldest child of a British squire's daughter, who'd risked her family's censure and been disowned in order to marry the man she loved.

Sister to a pair of boys who would grow to be fine young men if only their youth and their lives weren't stolen first in this hateful war.

And now, just like her mother, she too loved imprudently. But where there had been hope for Maman, there would be none for her. For unlike her mother, she was a liar and a spy, and given that, Drake Byron could never be hers.

Forcing herself to attend to the matter at hand, she inspected the dining room, then blew out a last few remaining candles. Out in the corridor, she made her way toward the stairs. She was just about to ascend when she noticed a patch of light shining out of the library.

Had one of the footmen forgotten to snuff the candles? Deciding to make sure, she walked down the hall, pushed open the door and walked inside.

The room appeared empty, a large branch of candles illuminating only a narrow portion of the spacious, book-lined interior. The scents of leather, parchment and ink perfumed the air, along with the unmistakably sharp tang of brandy. And there was another scent as well—clean, sultry, spicy and wholly male.

"My lord," she said, whirling to find Drake lounging in a wide leather armchair, a glass of spirits dangling idly between his fingers. "Your pardon. I did not realize you were here."

For a long moment he said nothing, just sat regarding her

out of heavily lidded eyes. Languidly, he took a sip from the glass. "Up late again, I see," he drawled. "Always the last to bed, aren't you?"

Her forehead drew tight. "No, not always. I was simply checking to make sure the house is secure for the evening."

"Isn't that the butler's and footmen's job?" he challenged.

She clasped her hands together, willing herself not to rise to his bait. Clearly, he was in a foul humor despite the visit from his brothers and friends. Actually, she realized she'd never seen Drake—*Lord Drake*—in a true temper before since he was generally a very coolheaded and logical sort of man. But . . . there was a light in his clear green eyes that warned of trouble.

"Mr. Stowe and the footmen make certain the doors and windows are locked and the house secure," she explained calmly. "I was merely verifying that the rooms are neat and well-ordered for the morrow. I only came in here because of the light. I was worried a branch of candles might have been forgotten."

"Well, as you can see, they were not." He swirled the amber liquid in his goblet, then took another drink.

Definitely foul-tempered, she thought.

"If there is nothing further then, I shall bid you a good night, my lord." She turned to walk to the door, but his words stopped her.

"*My lord,*" he repeated in a scornful tone. "So formal. But then I suppose the two of us need to be formal in order to maintain the proprieties. Of course, you weren't so reserved the other night when you were lying beneath me in bed, moaning my name."

She pulled in a sharp breath, her shoulders suddenly taut. A long moment passed before she could form a reply. "In deference to your present impairment, I shall overlook that remark."

"What *impairment*?" he growled sardonically.

"The fact that you are drunk, my lord. Now, if you will excuse me—"

"I don't believe I shall." He set down his glass with a thump before rising to his feet. "But you're right. I am drunk. A vice in which I rarely indulge since drink has a way of addling a man's mind."

Crossing the distance between them in a few quick strides, he reached out and pulled her into his arms. "Just as you addle my mind. Try as I might, I cannot get you out of my head, cannot forget the feel of you against me, or the taste of your sweet lips on mine."

She flattened her hands against his chest, her pulse beating in erratic strokes, even as she made the feeble attempt to keep a bit of space between them. "Drake, we can't."

"Why can't we?" he asked, tugging her closer. "We did the other night, and you liked it. I know you did, even if you refused me afterward. No woman could respond the way you did and have it all be a lie."

"It wasn't a lie," she admitted on a whisper. "It's only that it cannot be again."

"I refuse to believe that," he said. "I refuse to let you end whatever this is between us, however insane it may be."

Then his mouth was on hers, plundering her lips with a raw sensuality that demanded her response as well as her surrender. She knew she should resist, realized that she ought to push him away as her conscience warned she must. But it felt so good, so right to be with him like this, the brandy-flavored taste of his tongue intoxicating as it glided over her own, the heady warmth of his strong, masculine body making her want to twine herself around him and cling like a vine.

But she couldn't.

She shouldn't.

Not when fate decreed she must soon leave him behind.

Yet even as she struggled to resist, her desire flared higher, his kiss too wonderful to deny. What did her conscience matter when she wanted him so desperately? Why should they remain apart when his slightest touch made her dizzy, and his darkest passions left her aching for more?

Would surrender really be so terrible?

Suddenly, he took the choice from her, wrenching his mouth away, breath panting from his lips as though he'd just run for miles. His arms loosened, yet he did not release her, as though he couldn't quite bring himself to end their embrace.

"Forgive me, I'm a brute," he said, the words seemingly torn from his heaving lungs. "I'm drunk and half out of my mind, doing only as I wish with no concern for your own desires. You refused me, and I haven't the right to force you. You told me no, and I promised we would go on as before, master and servant only, however much I may wish it otherwise." His face drawn in lines of remorse, he met her gaze. "Forgive me. I'm sorry."

His hold loosened more, his shoulders tightening as he prepared to step away. But she stopped him, reaching up to lay a palm against his cheek.

He shuddered beneath her touch.

"I'm not," she murmured, her heart thundering in her chest with the violence of a summer storm. He was giving her permission to end their affair once and for all. He was willing to put his desires aside and let her go.

But she couldn't do the same.

Nor could she stop herself from acting the fool. Not when she wanted him so much. Not when she loved him as if her heart would swell until it burst.

In that instant, she threw the last of her caution aside. What did it matter if they had so little time together? How could their parting possibly hurt more since, regardless of the path she chose, he would still curse and hate her when this charade of hers was finally done? Why deny herself— and him—this small place out of time? This fleeting, unforgettable span of happiness?

"What did you say?" he asked, choking out the words.

"I said I'm not," she repeated, her voice strong and sure, "sorry, that is. I want you, Drake Byron, and I'm using my prerogative as a woman to change my mind. Now are you going to kiss me again, or will you make me beg?"

For a moment he looked incredulous, then abruptly he smiled, his mouth curving into a wide, irrepressible grin. His arms tightened around her again as he drew her flush against him. "Who am I to deny a woman her dearest wish? As for your begging, I'll have to take that under further consideration."

Before she had time to contemplate the full import of his statement, he lifted her high against him and crushed her mouth to his.

Chapter 17

At first, Drake wasn't sure that he'd heard her correctly or if he was just too bloody foxed to tell the difference between reality and wishes.

Yet here she was in his arms again.

Here she was kissing him with a fiery passion that sizzled all the way down to his toes.

Under the circumstances, who was he to quibble over a little thing like reality when he had exactly what he wanted?

Who was he to question anything when she was standing in his arms, her lips and tongue doing things to him that even the most seductive temptress couldn't have done better?

He shuddered, his arousal growing swift and hard. Cupping her bottom, he pressed her willing body even more firmly against his to let her feel his response. Rather than demure, she twined her arms tighter around him and glided her hands in widening circles over his shoulders and back.

Still it wasn't enough.

There were too many layers of clothes in the way, too much space keeping his flesh from joining hers.

Without breaking their rapacious kiss, he swept her off her feet and crossed the room in three bounding strides. Reaching the brown silk-upholstered divan, he laid her on it carefully, glad for once of the prevailing furniture style that dictated the piece have only half a back.

Sinking down beside her, he speared his fingers into her hair, pins springing away in wild arcs and pops as he freed her long, autumn-hued tresses from their bonds. Taking up a fistful of her hair, he buried his face in her satiny locks to breathe in their luxurious scent. Loath to let go, he wrapped a few thick skeins around his wrist, using it to gently arch her head back, so he had full access to the most tender parts of her throat.

Smiling, he pressed his mouth to the underside of her jaw, teasing there with his lips and tongue before scattering kisses against her cheek and temple and around to her ear. He blew softly, eliciting an answering shiver. He groaned as her small palms slid beneath the material of his coat and waistcoat.

In response, he bit her earlobe, working the small nub of flesh between his teeth in a way that made her gasp and writhe beneath him. Abandoning her ear, he used the edge of his tongue to paint a wet line along her exposed neck before pursing his lips to blow on that too, making her shudder violently. Nuzzling her delicate nape, he opened his mouth to give her a long, drawing kiss.

Apparently unwilling to be outdone, however, she collected herself enough to ease her fingers under the waistband of his trousers. He arched as she found bare skin, then again as she caressed him along the base of his spine and lower across the top of his buttocks. His shaft throbbed, as hard as if she'd just taken it in her hand.

Holy hell, he cursed in his head, *she's driving me mad.*

But then he was already half-crazed with lust for her, so what was a little more insanity?

Leaning up suddenly, he shucked off his coat, flinging the garment to the floor. His waistcoat and cravat came next, sailing through the air, already forgotten. She watched, her whiskey gold eyes hungry, as he pulled at his shirt and peeled that away too.

His body turned hot as she laid her palms against his naked chest, his eyelids sliding closed as he reveled in the sensation of her caressing hands moving over him.

Exploring him.

Inflaming him.

Tormenting him.

Definitely tormenting him, he realized, drawing in a sharp breath as she flicked her nails over his flat male nipples. His eyes sprang open, a groan leaving his lips.

"You'll have to pay for that," he said warningly.

She gave a feline smile. "I certainly hope so, my lord."

"Drake," he ordered. "When you're in my arms, I'm Drake and you're Anne."

Her expression sobered for a moment, making him wish he knew what she was thinking. Then the look disappeared, her palms making wider forays across his chest and arms and shoulders as though she were trying to memorize him.

"You have far too many clothes on, madam. Far more than I," he observed, his fingers going to the buttons that ran the length of her sensible, dark blue bodice. "Let's remedy that and get you naked."

Suddenly, the bold temptress in her fell away, an expression of vulnerability crossing her face. "Maybe we should go upstairs," she whispered.

He shook his head, his body instantly rebelling against the idea. Even the short trip to his bedroom would be too long to wait. Besides, what if he agreed, and she changed her mind along the way?

"No," he said roughly, "I want you here. Now." To emphasize his point, he kissed her, leaving her lips rosy and damp.

Her eyelids drooped, and she trembled against him. "Can we at least lock the door?"

Only then did he realize she was right and that the door was standing half-open. He'd been so caught up in making love to her that he'd completely forgotten any notion of discretion.

In a flash, he was up and back, the room securely barred from any chance of discovery despite the fact that the house seemed quiet and all the servants presumably asleep.

"We're alone now," he said on his return. "Stand up."

Her eyes widened, but after a brief hesitation, she obediently she did as he commanded.

His hands went to work, stripping her of her garments with an efficiency that demonstrated his confident familiarity with feminine attire. Left only in her shift, she trembled visibly, all of her earlier bravado gone. Stepping close, he caught her to him and kissed her—long, slow and with a thoroughness that urged a helpless moan from her throat.

Untying the little bow just above her breasts, he eased the cotton open to reveal her charms. A small push against the straps had the cloth tumbling lower to sag around her hips. Skimming his hands over her, he inched the cloth the rest of the way off, where it fell into a pool at her feet. Taking a single step back, he stared at the beauty revealed before him.

"So pretty," he murmured, as he cupped one of her breasts inside his palm. "So perfect."

And then he had to taste her, his mouth literally aching to have her warm, womanly flesh moving against his tongue. Sinking to his knees, he pulled her to him and began suckling, using long, leisurely draws that had her sagging in helpless desire within his grasp.

* * *

Sebastianne didn't know how it was possible for her to still be standing upright. If not for the iron strength of Drake's hold, she knew her knees would have buckled already and she'd be sprawled in an insensible heap on the floor. Instead, she swayed within his grasp, trembling as he lavished her with such sweet sensation she could barely recall her own name.

Dieu. It was so good.

Everything he did.

Everywhere he touched.

It was as though her body was no longer her own to control, as if he'd stolen her will and made her forget everyone and everything but him and this moment together.

Dizzy with longing, she combed her fingers through the thick, chestnut silk of his hair. Caressing his head, she silently urged him on as he played his tongue and lips and teeth over her aching peaks, moving from one breast to the other until she wasn't sure she could bear the pleasure any longer. Her legs quivered, the last of her strength seeming to give way as a keening moan escaped her lips.

In the next moment, she found herself lying once more on the divan, its feathered softness cushioning her body. But she didn't have time to consider her new position; he didn't give her any time as he raked his teeth over one highly sensitive nipple before drawing so forcefully upon her that she shook from hair to toes.

She cried out, blood pounding in violent beats in her throat and wrists and temples. She cried out again moments later as he parted her legs and slid a pair of fingers deep inside where she was already wet and aching with need. Her thighs tightened involuntarily against his hand, unintentionally driving him deeper. His lips curved against her breast, giving her a mind-numbing little nip before he began stroking her tender inner flesh with devilish intent. Her legs fell wide of their own accord, giving him as much latitude as he wished.

And oh, did he wish, his fingers sliding in and out and around with a finesse that was nothing short of heaven.

Or hell perhaps.

She wasn't sure which, the pleasure was so intense, so decadently sexual that she wondered one moment how she could live through it, and the next how she could ever live without it.

Then he rubbed a spot that sent her straight over the edge, his other hand and clever tongue simultaneously caressing her breasts in a way that turned her world upside down and sideways. She heard a thin wail and only half realized that she was responsible for the sound, pleasure rippling through her in a nearly overwhelming wave.

Blackness curled at the edges of her vision, rapture flowing though her veins with the heat of white-hot ash. Dazed, she lay limp and replete, eyes closed as she drifted in a sea of blissful delight.

But Drake wasn't done with her, far from it, she realized as he traced his wide, capable palms over her body from cheekbones to throat, breasts to stomach, thighs to calves to feet. He stood, the air between them rippling with an almost electric anticipation. In some vague part of her brain, she heard the sibilant rustle of clothes as Drake divested himself of the remainder of his garments.

She opened her eyes in time to find him silhouetted in the candlelight, his tall, lithe physique one of the most beautiful things she'd ever seen in her life. Needing to touch despite her pleasurable exhaustion, she reached out.

Her fingers tingled as she glided her palm along the firm muscled length of his hair-roughened thigh and upward over the narrow jut of his hipbone and the lean, flat plane of his stomach. Quite visibly, the heavy erection between his legs jerked, his shaft powerfully hard and clearly eager to receive the same intimate attention she was lavishing elsewhere. Rather than appease him, though, she slid her hand sideways to retrace the same wandering path over his other hip and thigh.

He groaned, his fingers turning to fists at his sides.

Yet he made no move to stop her teasing caresses, apparently willing to let her enjoy a bit of silent retribution for all the delicious torment he'd put her through this night. He withstood far more of her sensual provocation than she expected, his gaze burning fierce and green with raging hunger as he met her eyes.

Her own blood warmed, desire creeping back to life as her breath came faster, and her mouth grew dry.

Finally, she put him out of his misery by wrapping her fingers around his thick shaft, holding him as he pulsed velvety-hot and strong inside her hand. Her own lips parted as she touched him, using long, slow strokes that made him groan aloud.

"Enough," he said roughly, abruptly taking hold of her hand to pull her away.

In a move so swift and sudden it completely stole her breath, he parted her legs with his hands and knees, then thrust himself fully and powerfully inside her. Despite her readiness, her body rebelled for the slightest instant, but just as quickly, took him in. Enthralled and utterly seduced, she accepted everything he was, welcomed everything he had to give.

Her body shivered violently against the staggering beats of pleasure, his penetration deep and sure as he set up a relentless rhythm that she did her best to match. Wrapping her arms and legs around him, she held on, a keening cry rising inside her throat. He kissed her, muffling the sound as he ravished her mouth in a joining that mirrored the frenzied movements of their bodies and hearts.

Eyes squeezed tight, she gave herself over to the rapture, each stroke, every movement, better than the last. Her skin grew slick and her mind dull as he drove her higher and harder toward her peak until she thought she might die of the bliss. Suddenly, ecstasy exploded inside her, her nerve endings alive with heat and life and a sizzling joy that flung her straight into the heavens. She shook, her body barely her own, her mind awhirl.

Drake shook as well, claiming his own satisfaction moments after hers as he poured himself fiercely inside her.

Falling and floating through the aftermath, she clung, needing him, loving him, knowing there was no place else she would ever long to be more. He kissed her, slowly, dreamily, the pair of them cocooned in a place of absolute happiness and peace which, for that instant, nothing could disturb.

Chapter 18

*S*ebastianne came awake with a start.

It took her a few seconds to realize that she was still in the library, lying on the divan. It took her no time at all to realize that she was lying on top of Drake, her bare limbs entwined with his longer, equally naked ones. Apparently he'd rolled over onto his back after they'd made love, then arranged her on top of him so she could use him as a bed while she slept.

And a very comfortable bed he is too, she mused, *firm and smooth and blissfully warm.*

Lifting her head, she met his watchful green gaze, wondering if he'd slept at all.

"What time is it?" she whispered.

"A little after three," he said, low and throaty.

She bit back a sigh, supposing that she ought to make herself get up and get dressed. Servants rose at dawn, and she needed to make her way to her room while she still had a chance to do so unobserved. "I should go."

His arm tightened across her back. "Relax. There's still time."

She shook her head. "The hour is far too advanced already. If I wait much longer, someone may awaken and discover me out of my room, clearly having never been to bed."

"They won't. I've given everyone leave to sleep late this morning because of the party, remember?"

A frown marred the smooth expanse of her brow. Now that he mentioned it, she did remember. Mr. Stowe had come into the servants' hall just as everyone was finishing up their party duties last night and made the announcement, much to the staff's delight. "Even so, I need to sleep—"

"You were doing a fine job of it here until a minute ago." He stroked a hand over her hair, causing delicious tingles to ripple over her skin. Then he glided his fingers over her bottom.

She tried to shift away. "You know very well that if I stay, neither of us will be getting any more sleep."

A slow grin spread over his face. "Do you think not?" Gathering her closer, he took her lips in a leisurely kiss that left her mouth wet and aching, not to mention other parts of her body.

Beneath her, she felt him stir, his intent plain.

Inserting an elbow between them, she levered herself away, or tried to at least. "I cannot stay."

"All right. Then come to my room instead," he said, punctuating his words with kisses. "We can continue this in my bed."

"We most certainly cannot. If Waxman discovered me there—"

"He didn't the last time."

"No, but I was lucky. I doubt I will be again. Now let me up, my lord."

"Drake," he reminded.

"*Drake* then. Be reasonable."

"I am," he said, gliding his hand under her hair this time.

"And I don't see why you're making such a fuss. They're all bound to find out about us soon enough, especially once you leave."

Her heart missed a beat. He knew she planned to leave? *How?*

"—I thought a house on Half Moon Street might do well for you," he continued, "although mayhap even that is too many streets away."

She relaxed, relieved to discover he hadn't meant leaving in the same way she did.

"I want you close, you know," he intoned. "Very close."

"I am close now. Drake, you aren't talking again about my becoming your mistress, are you?"

His hand stilled, coming to rest this time in the dip at the base of her spine. "You already *are*," he said. "After tonight, I should think that much is obvious. Or are you going to claim you don't want to again."

She pulled away.

This time he let her go.

Climbing to her feet, she reached for her shift and pulled it over her head. When she met his gaze, he was wearing a scowl as black as the night outside. "I want to be with you again," she said in a clear voice, "but not as your kept woman."

"Why not?" He scowled harder. "Is this because of Vanessa?"

Ah, so that is her name, Sebastianne mused, fighting the rush of jealousy that burned like tar in her stomach at mention of his actual mistress.

"Because if it is," he went on, "you've nothing to worry about. I told her that it's over, and she and I are officially at an end. Actually, it's been over between us for some time now. I haven't been with her in weeks, not since I met you."

She couldn't help but lift a knowing eyebrow.

"All right, I was with her once since I met you, but only once, and that was because I wanted you and wasn't supposed to touch. Actually, I've wanted you from the moment you came to interview in my office that very first day."

Her lips parted at the revelation. "And you hired me anyway?"

He shrugged. "I needed a housekeeper, and I told myself I could get past my inappropriate longings." Reaching out, he caught hold of her hand and brought it to his lips. "I can't."

She swallowed, her heart thundering so hard it hurt.

"So if not my mistress, then what?" Turning over her hand, he pressed it against his cheek, his skin slightly abrasive now from an evening's growth of whiskers.

"Your lover," she murmured. "But only in secret. I need to keep my job."

Lines gathered on his forehead. "Why, when I could give you so much more? When I want to give you a life of pleasure and luxury?"

"Because a servant has dignity and the right to leave with a sound character intact, whereas a mistress—" She let the sentence trail off, realizing there was far more to her decision than the simple expediency of remaining in the house in order to complete her mission. Her hateful mission that forced her to lie and deceive the man she loved.

Yet, in this moment, she knew she would have refused him again in any case. For as tempting as his offer might be—and it held a certain decadent appeal—she was no man's property and would never allow herself to be bought. What she chose to give, including her favors, was hers alone to decide. Hers alone to share, exactly like her love.

"Lovers only," she said. "Will that be enough for you?"

He looked for a moment as if he might like to argue further, but then he nodded. "I'd still prefer to pamper you, but since you insist otherwise, then I accept your terms."

Catching her around the waist with both hands, he tugged her close. "So, lover, give me a kiss."

Breath suddenly shallow in her lungs, she bent down and touched her lips to his, tunneling her fingers into his hair to cradle his head as she met his ardent demand with a simmering desire of her own.

Time spun away, so that she didn't know how many minutes passed before she found the will to pull away, her knees alarmingly weak and unsteady as she did. "I need to go upstairs to bed," she declared, clearly trying to convince not only him but herself.

"You're right," he said, leaning over to retrieve his trousers from where they lay on the floor. "We do need to go to bed." Slipping on the garment, he fastened the buttons of his falls. "I presume you would rather come to my bed than have me make my way up another flight to yours."

Her hands, which had been busy shaking out her gown, fell still. "I can't do either as I told you already. Not tonight."

"Yes you can. There're a couple hours left before anyone in the house will be awake, and I want you with me."

"But—"

"No buts. It's my bed or yours, *lover.*"

Her fingers tightened against the material of her dress. "I need to sleep."

"Then that's what we'll do."

She shot him a skeptical look. "Even if I believe that, what if I oversleep?"

"I'll make sure you don't. I'm generally very good at rousing myself at specific hours. Plus, I have a clock that gives a tiny chime of alarm that I can set if you are worried."

She stared at him, wavering despite her better judgment. "You are most unfair, you know."

One side of his mouth quirked upward. "Who ever said I was fair?"

"And stubborn."

"Guilty as charged. Now come along, you're wasting precious time."

And he was right, she was delaying. But why, when being with him was what she wanted too? Giving in to both their desires, she reached for her stays.

"Don't bother with those," he said, stopping her from donning the garment. "Just slip into your dress and bring your corset with you."

"But what if someone sees?"

"They won't. Everyone is long since abed." Pulling his shirt over his head, he picked up his waistcoat and draped it over his shoulder. Meeting her eyes with a direct and open gaze, he held out a hand.

Knowing the reward was more than worth the risk, she laid her palm inside.

Good as his word, Drake let her sleep.

After reaching the privacy of his bedchamber unobserved, the two of them had slipped out of their clothes again and between the soft sheets on his bed. In spite of an erection that he made no effort to hide, he'd tucked her close against him, pulled the sheets high and gone to sleep. Quickly, she'd followed suit.

Trusting that he would keep his other promise and wake her at dawn, she slumbered deeply. She was lost in a world of dreams when sensations that had nothing to do with nocturnal wanderings began to intrude upon her slumber.

Shifting restlessly, she rolled onto her side. That was when she became aware of his hands, gliding over her body from breast to stomach to leg and back again. And of his mouth, as he scattered warm, wandering kisses along her neck and shoulders and back.

Her body arched of its own accord, need throbbing wet and desperate between her aching thighs.

He isn't supposed to be doing this to me, she thought, her mind muddled by waves of unrelenting pleasure. *Not now when surely I have to leave soon.*

"W-what time is it?" she sighed, her words coming out on a low moan.

"Nearly dawn," he said on a gravelly rasp. "I couldn't let you leave without being properly awakened."

But there was nothing *proper* about his methods, a breathless gasp escaping her lungs as he slid a leg between her thighs and opened her wide for his possession.

With her fists buried in the bedclothes, she hung on as he stroked within her, their position allowing him to go powerfully, devastatingly deep. He brought her to completion twice, her cries of helpless ecstasy muffled against her pillow. Only then did he claim his own satisfaction.

Lying spent in the aftermath, she wondered how she was ever going to be able to move again.

"Good morning, my dear Anne," he said, dropping a kiss on her cheek and another on her neck before rolling over onto his back. "I must confess, I like waking up with you. Are you certain you need to depart?"

At the reminder, her eyes opened wide.

Depart?

She groaned, thinking suddenly of the day ahead. The long day ahead that he'd totally driven from her mind with his ardent and thoroughly blissful lovemaking.

Blinking against her weariness, she forced herself to sit upright. "Oh, what have you done?" she wailed.

And how had she allowed him to do it? Then again, he'd caught her in a vulnerable state while she was asleep, so what else was she to have done? Still, wasn't she always in a vulnerable state when it came to Drake and his undeniable talents in *l'art d'amour,* whether she happened to be asleep or awake at the time?

"I believe these many minutes past speak for themselves," he observed, his mouth turning up at the corners, rather like a cat who'd consumed a particularly tasty mouse. Reaching over, he stroked his fingers over her bare knee and thigh with an idle caress.

She batted his hand away. "They certainly do speak for themselves. You were supposed to wake me up, my lord, not . . . not—"

"Tup you to within an inch of your life?" His smile widened. "You liked it, did you not?"

Her forehead drew tight, a slight flush spreading over her skin. "Yes, but that's beside the point."

"I don't see why? You're awake, are you not?"

"Obviously, but—"

"Well, then, I did as you asked, so why are you upset?" Regarding her out of eyes that were as bright as new-mown grass, he tucked a clearly unrepentant arm beneath his head.

"I am upset because of the miserable, *tired* day I'm going to have." An eye-watering yawn caught her, as if to prove the truth of her statement. "Unlike you, Lord Drake, I don't have the luxury of remaining in bed all day."

His face grew serious. "Yes, you do. Inform one of the maids that you're not feeling well and sleep in. Take the entire day off, if you like. I shan't mind."

"But I shall," she said with a shake of her head. "I cannot very well tell them the truth, and they'll know I'm not really ill."

Sitting up, he gathered her into his arms. "Well, the choice is your own, and as much as I'm sorry to have left you weary, I cannot in all good conscience claim to feel any true remorse. When I awakened beside you this morning, I simply couldn't keep my hands off. As it is, I'm going to have a devil of a time waiting until nightfall to have you again."

Something fluttered inside her, and she softened. "So you think I'm coming back here this evening, do you?"

Catching her chin between his fingers, he gave her an uncompromising look. "You most assuredly are, and that's an order."

"Well, if it's an order," she said on a gentle tease, warmed by his words in spite of herself. "You know, for such a cerebral man, you certainly have powerful physical appetites."

His lips curved in a seductive smile. "Of course, I do. I'm a Byron, after all. It's in my blood."

Pulling her into his arms, he took her mouth with a leisurely thoroughness that made her toes curl and her limbs quiver like one of Mrs. Tremble's molded jellies.

Breath was soughing raggedly from her lips by the time he set her free. "You'd best run along," he murmured roughly, "before I tumble you back in this bed and ruin all your well-laid plans to keep our affair secret."

"Is that what we're having? An *affaire*?" she asked, unable to keep the French pronunciation of the word from slipping out.

Luckily he hadn't seemed to notice her error, a curiously arrested expression settling on his face. "Yes, I suppose we are."

Aware she'd frittered away far too much time as it was, she nodded, then slipped off the bed to dress. To her surprise, Drake stood and came to aid her, lacing her stays but leaving them loose enough for her to slip easily out of them again once she reached her bedroom. Next, he helped her into her gown, brushing her hands aside when she moved to fasten the buttons that ranged along the length of her bodice. Finished, he took her hand and pressed a warm kiss against her palm. "Until tonight."

"Yes, tonight," she murmured.

Walking as silently as she could, she stole from the room.

Chapter 19

For the second time that morning, Sebastianne came awake with a start. Unlike before, she found herself alone in her own bed, inside her room on the third floor. Sunlight streamed through the dormer windows, filling the small chamber with a crisp, translucent yellow light. Too crisp and far too bright for early morning—or even midmorning. Sitting up abruptly, she wondered exactly how long she'd slept, or rather *overslept,* she thought with an inner cringe. A glance at the small timepiece on the fireplace mantel confirmed her worst fears.

Noon!

Oh, dear heavens, how could she have slept so late? When she'd lain down after returning from Drake's room, she'd promised herself she would only close her eyes for a few minutes, then awaken again in time to begin her duties along with the rest of the staff. Instead, she'd fallen asleep, deeply asleep, clearly worn-out from the night just past.

A tingling quiver of remembered pleasure chased over her skin, her pulse picking up speed as memories swept through her.

Of lying in Drake's arms.

Of sharing his kisses.

Of touching and being touched in ways that still burned in her blood and seemed branded into her bones.

She'd thought nothing could surpass her first time with him—it had been that good—but last night had been even better. She'd been his to take, his to command, and she'd reveled in his possession. The fact that she loved him only made their intimacy that much sweeter, that much more intense. Greedy in her need, she wanted more.

More time.

More lovemaking.

More Drake.

For in addition to loving him, she liked him as well. He was brilliant and inventive and astonishingly sharp-witted beneath the absentminded façade he frequently wore. Even more, he was kind and compassionate, gentle yet strong, the sort of man in whom a woman could put her unqualified trust and devotion. And then there was his sense of humor, a wry and irreverent turn of mind that he generally kept hidden from all but his closest companions. The fact that he'd chosen to share that side of himself with her spoke volumes. He hadn't said he cared for her and yet . . .

Do I want him to love me?

It would be easier if he didn't, better for him if he could turn his back and forget her and everything but the sting to his pride when she went away. As for that, she didn't know how she was going to bear it when the day arrived for her to depart. She'd lived with loss before, but she wasn't precisely sure know how she was going to live through this, live without him.

For the sake of her own sanity, though, she knew she had to put such thoughts from her mind. Until the inevitable break came, she promised she would enjoy each day with

Drake to its fullest—or rather each night since that was all they could truly have. Prudence dictated that she keep their affair a secret. She must, if her mission was to succeed. For in spite of the guilt that churned in her stomach like curdled milk, she had no choice but to proceed; her brothers and her father were depending on her.

If only she hadn't overslept. Despite the sanctioned late start for the household, she wasn't entirely certain how she was going to explain sleeping until noon as if she were the mistress of the house rather than the housekeeper. Mrs. Tremble would probably raise her eyebrows in silent disapproval while Mr. Stowe drew her quietly aside to ask for an explanation.

Well, I'd better quit woolgathering and get on with it, she decided, since delaying would do nothing but exacerbate the problem.

Tossing back the sheets, she leapt from the bed and flew across the room to the washstand. Pouring tepid water from the ewer, she made hasty work of washing her face and hands, and running a wet, soapy cloth beneath her arms and over her body. After rinsing and drying off with a soft towel, she changed the water for fresh, then brushed her teeth.

As clean now as the quick ablutions would allow, she hurried to the wardrobe and took out a neatly pressed, dark blue gown. Once dressed, she brushed her hair, then twisted it high onto the back of her head before thrusting in a sufficient number of pins to hold the heavy mass in place. With a quick glance in the small dresser mirror to make sure she looked presentable, she was ready. Drawing a reassuring breath, she turned and exited the room.

The servants' hall was hushed as she made her way along the corridor a couple of minutes later. Hearing the sound of voices drifting from the kitchen, she forced herself to walk on, even though she would much rather have gone directly to her office and thus avoid the looks and questions she was certain to receive. Reaching the threshold, she went inside.

The conversation ceased abruptly, Jasper, Parker, Finnegan, Polk and Mrs. Tremble's all turned their heads her way.

Do they know? she wondered with a lurching tug under her ribs. *Do they realize I spent the night with Drake and the real reason I slept so late?*

But then a warm smile creased Mrs. Tremble's thin face, the cook setting down a wooden spoon before striding forward with her usual brisk efficiency. "Here now, what are you doing up, Mrs. Greenway? Mr. Stowe told us you were feeling peaky and would be spending the day in bed. I'm making a pot of strong beef tea and was going to have Parker bring you up a cup after a while. Sit, sit while I make you something else. A bit of leftover quince jelly from last night's dinner should be light on your stomach and perhaps a dish of tea. Though if you're still feeling light-headed, mayhap you ought to return upstairs to bed."

The cook took hold of her elbow and steered her toward the nearest chair, hovering until Sebastianne did as instructed. "Won't do no good having you faint again," the older woman stated. "His lordship said you took a swoon last night, and he had to help you upstairs to bed."

That's one way to phrase it, she thought wryly, realizing that Drake must have told the staff, or rather told the butler, who'd then told the staff, that she'd fainted and he'd helped her upstairs. Although in actual fact, that was the truth. She *had* been rather faint after their lovemaking, and he *had* taken her upstairs to bed. He'd just apparently failed to mention that the bed was his own!

To her profound relief, she wasn't much given to blushing; otherwise, she knew her face would have revealed the guilty nature of her thoughts. "I was just overly tired. Up too late after the party."

"Well, it was a lot of excitement and hard work yesterday, and you up well before dawn," Mrs. Tremble said, giving her a motherly pat on the shoulder. The other servants nodded their agreement as well. "I just hope you're not coming down with the ague or something worse."

"Oh, I don't think so," Sebastianne said quickly. "I'm fine, really." Seeing skeptical looks on the others' faces, she amended her remark. "Then again, maybe a tincture would do me good. I'm sure I have something efficacious in the stillroom. I'll mix it up in a minute."

"You'll do no such thing," Mrs. Tremble declared. "Give the ingredients to Finnegan, and she'll do it for you. Won't you, Finnegan?"

"Of course," the maid agreed with alacrity. "It'll my pleasure, especially after the megrim draught you made me that time. Helped me headache like nothing else ever has."

Sebastianne's chest tightened as a fresh dose of guilt washed through her, not only for her current lie, but for all the lies she'd told since the day of her arrival. Gazing at the open, trusting, caring faces of her fellow servants, now her friends, she wondered how she could continue deceiving them. They'd accepted her and made her one of their own. They'd been kind to her when all the while she was dealing them false.

Bile swelled in a slick wave inside her stomach, making her feel suddenly as ill as they all imagined her to be. Still, she said nothing as she let them fuss and hover. Still, she held her counsel and continued to play her part, however repugnant she might find the role to be.

The next few days passed in steady succession. As they did, Sebastianne discovered that it was far easier to slip unnoticed into Drake's bedroom than she'd worried it might be. In her position as housekeeper, she knew that his valet was in the habit of retiring around eleven o'clock each evening, since Drake, with his erratic hours, had long ago ordered Waxman not to wait up for him.

Still determined to execute his duties to the best of his abilities, Waxman had developed an evening routine that included laying out Drake's robe as well as his garments for the following morning; making sure the copper reservoir in the bathing chamber was filled with fresh water, along with more for the pitcher on the washstand; setting out clean towels, shaving equipment and soap; and lastly preparing a small nightcap that he left in a handkerchief-covered snifter on the side table near Drake's reading chair.

One of the upstairs maids, generally Parker, came in next, to finish the last of her work before retiring to her attic room for the evening. She laid a fresh fire, drew the curtains, and turned down the sheets and coverlet on the bed. Drake's room was empty and the household tucked securely in their beds by midnight.

Everyone, that is, except Sebastianne.

Each evening, she too went upstairs to her bedchamber as the house quieted for the night. Once inside, she washed her face, brushed her hair and teeth, and changed into her nightgown and robe. Perched on her bed, she would wait for the clock to strike one, then, without the aid of a candle for fear of alerting a potentially sleepless housemaid, she would make her way in the darkness down the stairs to Drake's chamber.

Tonight was no different, she realized, as her slippered feet whispered over the plush Aubusson hall runner that led to his room, her heart crashing like cymbals between her ears with a mixture of anxiety and anticipation. Arriving at his door, she let herself inside without bothering to knock.

The instant the lock click closed, a pair of strong arms enfolded her, a warm masculine mouth fastening over her own to stifle the gasp of surprise that rose inside her throat. She squirmed for a moment but not to get away. Instead, she drew him closer, putting everything she had into the embrace.

"I thought you'd never arrive," Drake said between kisses, his nimble fingers working open the buttons on her robe. "I've been here waiting for nearly half an hour."

"You know I don't dare come any earlier . . ." she murmured, stroking her fingers across the angular plane of his smoothly shaven jaw. "One of the staff might still be awake."

"Even if they were," he pointed out, as he pushed the robe off her shoulders, "they wouldn't know you were on your way to see me."

"Is that what I'm doing? *Seeing* you?" She glided her fingers down his chest, pausing to slip them beneath the folds of his robe to caress his taut pectoral muscles with their swath of dark, curling hair. "It feels like something else to me."

He gave a low rumbling sound that was half laughter, half torment, and lifted her high against him. His hands cupped her bottom with a familiar intimacy, pressing her flush against him in a way that left her in no doubt as to the extent of his readiness.

"Oh, it's something else," he agreed, "and I'll show you exactly what in a moment."

He kissed her again, circling his tongue against hers in a satiny, sophisticated glide that made wet heat pool between her thighs. Trailing his mouth along her neck, he found her earlobe and caught it between his teeth for a teasing nip. "You're a deuced distraction, madam, do you know that? Try as I might, I haven't been able to focus on my work for days. Instead of experiments, all I can think of is new ways to touch you. Rather than numbers and theorems, the only thing I can calculate is the minutes and hours until I can be here like this with you again."

Spearing her fingers into the short silk of his hair, she bent her head to dust slow, sultry kisses across his temple and cheeks, chin and jaw and throat. "It's hard for me too. My mind has a way of wandering these days when I'm supposed to be inspecting linens and measuring spices. I added cayenne instead of cinnamon to the sweet bread I was making this morning. Aren't you glad I caught my mistake in time?"

He met her gaze, his eyes smoldering like green fire. "It would have been a spicy surprise, but I'm finding lately that I like your surprises, spicy and otherwise. What do you have in store for me tonight?"

"Take me to bed, my lord, and I'll show you."

Smiling with clear promise, he did exactly as she asked.

A long while later, Sebastianne lay relaxed and replete, her head pillowed against Drake's shoulder, the sheets and counterpane kicked to the foot of the bed. A delicious glow suffused her, pleasurable pings and twinges dancing all over her body in the aftermath of their lovemaking. She smiled as he ran a broad palm over her hair, smoothing the tousled strands back into some semblance of order.

"I love your hair," he said, gently combing his fingers through its length.

She angled her head meet his gaze. "Truly? I find it a dreadful burden most days."

"But it's glorious," he proclaimed. "Like autumn leaves at their peak on a sunny October day."

"How lovely, my lord, and most poetic, particularly for a man with your mathematical and scientific gifts," she said, warmth spreading through her at the compliment. "But then you haven't the care of my coiffure, have you? It's thick and heavy and a terrible bother to wash and arrange, to say nothing of the grey in it, of which you must surely have taken note." She paused for a moment before continuing. "I worry that all my color will have faded by the time I'm middle-aged, and that I'll be left completely grey."

"Silver, you mean," he observed, taking a few of the strands between his fingers. Reverently, he stroked them. "If that should happen, your hair will look just as lovely then as it does now in all its burnished glory."

She couldn't help but send a skeptical look toward the ceiling.

Seeing it, he caught her chin between his fingers. "Don't scoff. There are certain people who age gracefully, and I know you shall be one of them. No matter your age, my sweet, your beauty will never diminish."

The glowing inner warmth expanded inside her once more, his words making her believe, at least for this moment, that his predictions really would come true.

If only he could be there with me when that day arrives, she thought. *If only we could have more time, and there wasn't any need to part.*

Clearly sensing her wistful mood, he touched his lips lightly to her own, then tunneled his long, aristocratic fingers deep into her tresses. "Besides, I rather fancy the silver bits. They're like strands of some precious metal woven into a tapestry of gold and red and brown. Lends you a rather regal aspect, I think."

She couldn't help but give a fresh snort. "Regal? Turning prematurely grey is called many things, but regal isn't one of them. I shall have to remember to share that with Papa. He'll find it highly entertaining. He grows weary of being told he looks 'distinguished' for his age."

"Does he now? So your father's hair greyed early as well?"

"Oh yes, he was already losing his original brown by the time I was born. He's as grey as a pewter tankard now. I suppose the boys will follow suit as well, as they mature."

His hand slowed. "The boys being your brothers, I presume. Are they younger than you, then?"

Somehow, she managed not to stiffen, knowing he would have felt her alarm. Inwardly, she cursed, realizing she'd done it again. And here, she'd been so sure she could keep her promise not to discuss her family, especially after the last time she'd slipped up.

But she was so comfortable with Drake, too comfortable. Yet how could she be anything else when she was lying here in his arms with nothing, not even a piece of clothing, between them? That rationale wasn't strictly true though, for as naked and vulnerable as she allowed herself to become when they were intimate, a world of differences still remained between them. A world of ulterior motives and lies that forced her to conceal her real self though she wished she had no need to dissemble.

She glanced away for fear of what might show in her eyes. "Yes, they're younger. Still just boys."

"You must miss them a great deal. I presume they reside in your home territory in the Lake District?"

That's right, he knows—or rather he'd guessed, she reminded herself, thinking back to the first day they'd met when she'd come to the town house to interview for the housekeeper's position. She knew that any hint of a regional British accent was slight due to her mother's upper-class background. Yet somehow, Drake had picked up on the faint inflections left over from her time living in the lake country when she'd been a child. In fact, she'd spent the first eight years of her life in England, until Papa, who could no longer stand the exile from his native land, had decided to move her and her mother to France.

Ironically, her little brothers hadn't even been born until their arrival back in France, and consequently, they spoke no

English at all. The boys were both late babies—miracles, as her mother had called them—born unexpectedly after years of miscarriages and barrenness. When Maman died, not in childbed, but from a severe lung infection, Sebastianne had taken over her adult role, acting as both mother and sister to her young brothers, who'd been little more than toddlers at the time.

So when Drake asked if she missed them, he didn't realize what he was saying. After all, it was for them that she now risked everything, for them that she would forfeit her love for Drake, her very heart.

Sitting up slowly, she reached for the sheet. "Yes," she said in a dull voice. "I miss them."

Clearly sensing her pain, he rubbed a soothing hand over her back. "Perhaps you might like to visit them. If you would permit me to accompany you, maybe we could go there together in a few weeks. I could take you. Where do they live?"

In France, in Montsoreau, came her answer.

But those were two places Drake could not take her. Two places of which she must never speak.

But, of course, he thought her brothers lived in England, in the Lake District, where none of her family resided any longer. Even her maternal grandparents were dead, and any distant cousins had scattered to the four winds long since.

She should make something up, she knew, think of a likely lie. But she was so sick of lying, so tired of having to prevaricate and dissemble and watch over every word that rolled off her tongue. In a few days more, she would be gone from this house, from his life, so what could it hurt if she told him the truth? How could it matter now?

"Ambleside," she answered honestly. "It's a pretty place. Lush and green, with deep blue lakes and rolling hills that look as if they could go on forever." Even now, all these years later, she could still recall the land, the lakes, vivid even in her childhood memories.

"Then we shall go," he stated, as if the matter were already decided.

Turning her head, she forced herself to start lying again. "Yes, we shall go."

Unable to bear another moment apart, she leaned down and kissed him, letting her love flow with a kind of near desperation. Despite his murmur of surprise over her sudden amorous zeal, Drake made no objection, his arms wrapping around her back to pull her tight.

Not long before dawn, Drake awakened to the slight movement of the mattress as Anne slipped from the bed. Rolling over, he lighted a candle on the night table, then lay back against the sheets to watch as she donned her nightgown and robe. After combing her fingers through her long hair, she extracted a ribbon from her pocket to tie back the heavy tresses. Padding barefoot across the carpet, she located her abandoned slippers and tucked her feet into them one by one.

"I suppose you have to go," he remarked on a rumble.

She nodded, her eyes the dusky color of ancient gold coins in the low light. "Everyone will be rising soon."

With an absolute lack of modesty, he directed a glance toward the unmistakable peak tenting the sheet that covered him. "It would seem I am risen already."

Her mouth curved into a slow smile, a twinkling light in her gaze. "Sadly, I shall have to leave you to deflate on your own."

He stretched out a hand. "You could at least console me with a farewell kiss."

A soft laugh rippled from her throat, her smile widening as she shook her head. "Oh no, there'll be none of that. I've far too little time left to return to my room as it is. If I let you kiss me, you'll only muddle my senses and confound my resolve."

"Is that what I shall do? I had no idea I held so much sway over you."

The smile slid from her mouth, a kind of curious introspection stealing into her gaze. For a moment she looked vulnerable, almost fragile, her lips parting as if she wanted to reveal some deeply held confidence. Then her eyelashes swept downward, her gaze moving away. "Go back to sleep, my lord," she told him quietly. "I shall see you after you wake."

Rather than press her further, he let her go, silent as she walked from the room on a soundless glide.

What secrets are you hiding, my lovely Anne? he thought as the lock clicked closed behind her. *Why do you keep a wall between us that you will not let me breach?*

And there was a wall, invisible but formidably solid nonetheless. He'd sensed it for some while now, and knew instinctively that she kept bits and pieces of herself hidden and inviolate. When she was in his arms she was so open and giving, so utterly without pretense. In those moments it was easy to forget that anything stood between them. There were no differences. Only pleasure, only mutual delight.

But afterward, when their passion was spent and the pressures and responsibilities of the real world began to assert themselves once more, her barriers slid back in place, clanking shut like a set of iron bars.

What was it she didn't want him to know? What was it she was so determined to protect?

Last night had been unusual since she rarely spoke of her family. Come to think, he could recall only one other occasion in which she'd revealed anything about them, and even then he'd received the distinct impression that she'd regretted allowing the confidence. That she loved her family was clear, so it seemed reasonable to assume that her reluctance to discuss them didn't stem from a case of familial discord. Mayhap it was simply that she missed them and was too deeply pained by their continued separation to dwell on thoughts of loved ones who were so far away. Then, of course, there was her dead husband, of whom he knew even less.

His fingers tightened into fists against the sheets, his mind shying away from the subject. Even so, he couldn't help but wonder about the man she'd married and about her relationship with him before his death.

Had she loved him? Did she still?

Is that the reason she keeps her emotional distance? Is that why she won't let me in?

And he did want in, he realized with no small measure of surprise. He didn't just want her body, though, he wanted *her*. Everything there was to learn and understand about Anne Greenway. Her hopes and aspirations. Her likes and dislikes. Her fears and regrets. Her mind and heart—yes, even her soul—he wanted them all to belong to him.

And should he find a way to win them, to win her, what then?

His heart pounded inside his chest with a heavy, almost painful beat as the truth came upon him.

Because, for the first time in his life, and quite without any plan or wish to find himself in such a state, Drake knew he was in love.

Now the difficulty was, what was he going to do about it?

Chapter 20

*J*ust before ten o'clock on Friday, Sebastianne took a seat in one of the two carriages brought around from the mews for the servants. She remained quiet as the others settled themselves, content to let them chatter excitedly about this afternoon's excursion to Green Park.

A couple of days before, Drake had surprised the staff with a generous invitation to join him for a balloon ascension. Apparently, he'd agreed to assist a friend in the launch of his airship and said he thought the servants might enjoy witnessing the event. Everyone from Mr. Stowe to Polk, the scullery maid, had cheered with excitement.

Everyone, that is, but Sebastianne.

The news had come as a shock, panic twisting through her with all the subtlety of a rusty knife. Not only was Friday her day off, it was the day she'd planned to travel across town to the locksmith's shop and retrieve the copy of the key to Drake's safe. More importantly, it might very well be her final opportunity to obtain the key, and thus the cipher, before the month Vacheau had allotted her expired in a few more rapidly dwindling days.

But hurrying off that morning on some essential errand would have required explanations, and begging off from the outing to Green Park was entirely out of the question. She had no choice but to attend, particularly since Drake so obviously wished her to be there.

"I'll make sure you have a prime view of the ascent," he'd promised when she brought him his tea later that afternoon. Closing the door of his workshop, he'd drawn her into his arms. "Have you ever attended a balloon ascension before?"

"Yes, actually, I have," she said truthfully.

One of his dark eyebrows winged upward. "Really? When? Where?"

In Paris with my father, she thought, realizing too late that she ought to have kept her mouth shut, particularly since balloon ascensions weren't all that common an event. How should she answer?

"Oh, it was ages ago when I was a child," she said as casually as she could. "I scarcely recall the details. Seeing it again now with you will seem like the first time all over again." She fiddled with one of her cuff buttons, lowering her gaze so he couldn't read the deceit in her eyes. "I'm quite looking forward to the outing."

She waited, wondering if he would question her further and praying he would not.

"Well, I wanted to do something special that you would enjoy." Catching her hand inside his own, he carried it upward and pressed a kiss against the tender skin of her wrist.

She trembled with undeniable pleasure at the caress.

"I hoped this might be just the thing," he continued, "as you won't let me take you out on your own."

Her gaze flew to his as a new thought occurred. "Have you invited the entire household then, just so I could attend?"

"Am I so transparent?" He bent his head at a sheepish angle, then sent her a boyish grin that made her heart squeeze with love and longing.

"Yes, just a bit," she murmured, silently marveling at his efforts. He desired her, she knew, but was there more? Did she want there to be more when nothing but heartache could come of it?

"I'd take you in my carriage," he went on, clearly unaware of her musings, "but I suppose it would look odd if you didn't travel with the others. So I shall see you as soon as you arrive, and afterward ply you with all the sweetmeats and lemonade you can consume."

She couldn't help but smile at his promise. "I thought you were supposed to help your friend launch his balloon, not worry over keeping me laden with treats."

"Oh, I'm a man of many talents. I'll assist him *and* find time to attend to you as well."

How lovely it all sounds, she thought, as the coachman put the horses in motion to drive her and the others to the park. Or at least it would sound lovely if only there were time for her to visit the locksmith and collect the key as well. Though while she was wishing, what she'd really like was to have no need for the key at all. In her wished-for world, there would be no Vacheau, and her brothers and father would be safe and sound instead of living in fear for their lives. If only there was some other way out of this dangerous tangle. If only she had no need to lie to anyone, most especially Drake, whom she grew to trust more and more each day. Yet was that trust enough to overcome her fears and allow her to reveal her secrets.

So many times, she'd imagined how he would revile her if he knew the truth. But what if he didn't? What if she confessed and he understood her dilemma? What if she confided in him, and he found some means to help her?

But no, such a thing would be too much to hope.
Or would it?

Striving to calm her nerves, she forced herself to listen to the excited chatter going on between Parker and Cobbs, who were busy speculating aloud on what they might see in the park.

Not long after, the coach arrived at Green Park, the grounds thronged with spectators, some who'd come on foot, others who'd arrived as she and the other servants had, by horse and conveyance. As she climbed down onto the soft grass, the sunny June day wrapped around her like a warm embrace, causing a measure of her anxiety to fall away. Jasper, who'd been one of the servants to set out earlier with Drake, loped across the field with a glad wave. After a brief greeting, he turned to lead them back through the crowd to the balloon.

Then, suddenly, Drake came into view before her, his chestnut hair glinting with honeyed hues in the crisp, late-morning sunlight. He'd stripped off his jacket, she noticed, having obviously decided to ignore propriety in favor of the freedom of movement his dishabille provided. As she watched, he reached over to adjust one of the mechanisms that was feeding hot gas into the huge balloon atop the airship, heat shimmering in the visible waves directly above him. Pausing, he called something out to a thin, rawboned man with a head of the brightest red hair she'd ever seen. The man nodded in clear agreement with whatever Drake had said, then went to pull on one of the ropes tethering the flying machine to the ground.

She drew to a halt, her pulse hammering in sudden alarm at the sight of Drake so close to such a clearly dangerous contraption. What if he moved incautiously and burned himself? What if he became tangled in the lines that coiled like snakes at the base of the gondola and caused himself an injury?

But in observing him, she couldn't help but admire the

confident manner in which he moved, as well as the obvious expertise and careful precision with which he worked. Clearly, Drake knew exactly what he was doing, his actions skillful and practiced in a way that allayed her fears—the worst of them anyway. The fact that he was enjoying himself was plain as well, a smile making tiny lines fan out around his eyes.

Suddenly, as though aware he was being observed, he turned his head and looked straight at her. His smile widened, a pleased recognition that was disturbingly intimate, turning his eyes greener than the grass beneath their feet.

With her pulse thrumming in swift beats, she smiled back, then dipped her bonneted head lest anyone else see.

After calling again to the red-haired man, Drake strode forward.

"You've arrived," he declared in happy tones. "All of you," he added to the other members of his household, who had also come to a halt nearby. "Welcome! Go ahead, if you'd like, and take a closer look at the balloon. Carter won't mind so long as you don't touch anything."

Carter, Sebastianne surmised, must be Drake's friend— the redheaded companion he'd been assisting with the balloon.

Emboldened by the invitation, the others walked toward the airship. She remained behind.

"So? What do you think?" He gestured a hand toward the balloon that rose behemoth-like behind him.

Her gaze moved up, then up again. "It's big."

He laughed. "It had better be big, or it will never manage to carry anyone aloft."

Abruptly, her smile disappeared. "You're not going to be that someone, are you?"

He laughed again, a serious light coming into his eyes. "And if I were, would you care?"

"Yes."

His eyes darkened with emotion.

"After all, if you were killed," she continued, needing to lighten the mood once more, "just think of the bother I'd be put to, having to find another employer."

He chuckled at her teasing before lowering his voice so that it was deep and silky and for her ears alone. "Not to mention finding another lover."

Her gaze locked with his, her breathing no longer steady. "Hmm, that too."

His grin deepened, and he took a step forward.

Aware they were in a public park where anyone might see them, she held up a warning hand. "Perhaps you ought to go help your friend. He looks as if he could use the assistance."

Idly, Drake cast a quick glance over his shoulder toward the balloon and the thickening crowd gathered around the gondola. Carter wore a harried expression, as he tried to work on the balloon while also keeping an eye on the people surrounding him. A burst of ruddy color suffused his cheeks a moment later as one man in the crowd made a move toward the gondola with the clear intention of climbing inside. Carter let out an angry warning, and a shouting match ensued.

Drake rolled his eyes heavenward. "Looks as though you're right. I'd better go rescue him before a riot starts. Meanwhile, there're some refreshment vendors just across the way." Digging a pair of fingers into his waistcoat pocket, he pulled out a coin, then pressed it into her palm. "Buy yourself a lemonade and anything else you fancy."

Glancing down, she saw that he'd given her a gold guinea. "But this is far too much," she protested, aware she could buy lemonades for half the assembled crowd with the amount of money he'd given her.

Drake didn't hear her though, already out of earshot as he

strode across the field at a rapid pace and hurled himself into the fray. Any concern she harbored for his safety vanished as she watched him wield a firm grip and use several well-chosen words that quickly put an end to the altercation.

With calm and order restored, her worry for Drake faded. As for her own worry about retrieving the key, there was nothing she could do about it at the moment. So for now, she reasoned, she might as well enjoy the balloon launch and have that refreshing glass of lemonade while she was at it.

As for the guinea he'd given her, she would buy her own beverage and return the coin to him tonight. She knew him well enough by now to realize he would protest its return, but she wanted no favors, no special gifts based on their intimate relationship. She came to him freely, out of love, and wanted nothing else between them.

Except for my lies, of course, she thought, with an inward cringe. *And my deception.*

As for telling him the truth . . .

Frowning, she turned away, deciding to put such weighty topics aside for now and focus instead on lemonade.

Several minutes later, Sebastianne stood with a cool glass in hand, chatting with Mrs. Tremble, who'd decided to sample "the competition," as she called it.

"Not near as good as mine," the cook remarked, smacking her lips after drinking another long swallow. "Too much sugar and not enough juice. Watered, I suspect."

Sebastianne refrained from commenting, finding the citrus flavor quite tart enough for her liking. Although to Mrs. Tremble's credit, her lemonade was indeed superior. Still, the vendor's beverage was refreshing, particularly given the increasing heat of the day as the sun rose steadily toward its zenith.

"I think I'll sample one of them meat pies to get this taste out of me mouth," the cook declared. "Will you be coming along then?"

Sebastianne shook her head and took a step backward into a wide band of shade cast by the leafy canvas of a nearby oak. "You go on. I'm content to remain here."

"As ye will. I expect that contraption will be sailing up to its doom before long," Mrs. Tremble stated with a nod toward the now-fully-inflated balloon. "You'll have a prime view of the catastrophe when it happens."

Sebastianne smothered a laugh, well aware of the cook's dire views concerning manned flight. Mrs. Tremble was convinced that poor Mr. Carter wouldn't make it through the day alive. Sebastianne certainly hoped the other woman was mistaken.

Once the cook departed, Sebastianne moved deeper beneath the sheltering canopy of the great tree, free to observe the comings and goings of the meandering crowd. As she watched, a familiar face came into view several yards distant. She couldn't recall his name . . . Lord something or other that started with G . . . but she knew that the dark, broad-shouldered man had been one of Drake's guests the night of his dinner party.

On Lord G's arm strolled a strikingly beautiful, fashionably dressed young woman with eyes so blue, Sebastianne could discern their color even from a distance. The woman had silky, evening-dark hair that was pinned upward in an elegant sweep beneath her sailor-style straw Victoria hat whose yellow satin lining matched her glorious, primrose-and-white-striped walking dress. With clear, creamy white skin, she presented a perfect foil for her handsome, swarthy-skinned companion, the two of them making an extraordinarily appealing couple.

Accompanying the pair was a girl who looked to be around her own brother Julien's age, twelve or perhaps thirteen. She was a pleasant-looking child, but judging by her bone structure and the overall shape of her face, Sebastianne knew the girl would one day be as heartbreakingly lovely as her older sister was already.

The fact that she and the young woman were sisters was obvious. The fact that they both bore an unmistakable resemblance to Drake was plain as well.

Heavens, those must be his sisters, she realized.

And the man, whose name she abruptly recalled as Lord Gresham, was his brother-in-law.

She hadn't realized Drake's family would be in attendance. Were his brothers and their wives there as well? Perhaps his mother, the Dowager Duchess of Clybourne?

A quick scan of the crowd didn't reveal any other familiar faces. Then again, with so many people milling around, it was easy to be swallowed by the mass.

Just then, Lord Gresham bent his head toward his wife and murmured something into her ear. Whatever it was must have been amusing, since she gave a deeply appreciative laugh that rang out as harmoniously as church bells. She gazed into his eyes, her face alight with clear happiness and love. As for Lord Gresham, his expression of adoration made Sebastianne look away, feeling that what she'd witnessed was far too intimate for another's eyes to have seen.

She'd known a girl's love with Thierry. She knew a woman's ardor now with Drake, and yet she found herself wondering what it must be like to share that kind of intense, unwavering mutual devotion? To live in a world where she was free to let herself love without fear of its being taken away. To know there was a future with years and years of joy ahead, where there would be children and family and the certainty of being able to build a life.

She turned away, not wanting to see any more, not wishing to dwell on what she knew she could not have. Her chest ached as she stepped deeper beneath the tree's sheltering embrace, the rough bark of the wide trunk pressing up against her back.

She stood there in the cooling shade, fighting her emotions, finding herself wishing and wondering once again if she dared trust Drake with the truth? Could she, should she, risk everything on the chance that he would help her rather than turn away? Dare she throw herself and her family's lives on his mercy and pray he could find a way to bring them all to safety? His family was powerful, influential, with deep ties to the government. Perhaps there might be some way.

As for her love, had she the right to hope he felt affection for her too? That he might care enough that he could find a way to forgive her? She sensed he felt strong emotions for her, but was it love? And even if it was, would it be enough?

Sighing, she drank the last of her lemonade and supposed she ought to venture forth to watch the festivities. She was about to step away from the tree when a cold voice whispered from behind her shoulder. "Be quiet and stay where you are. It wouldn't do for us to attract unwanted attention."

A shudder chased over her skin, leaving her arms peppered in gooseflesh despite the warmth of the day. Her fingers twitched nervelessly, the empty glass sliding from her grasp into the soft grass below.

Vacheau.

Like the devil, he had a knack for being able to appear out of nowhere.

Chapter 21

"What are you doing here?" Sebastianne asked in a calm tone that in no way revealed the true state of her emotions. "I thought we weren't to be seen together."

"And I thought you were supposed to be working to acquire the cipher, not traipsing around London attending showy amusements," he remarked from where he stood in the deepest shadows behind the wide tree trunk.

She resisted the urge to turn around despite the awkward nature of their conversation. "His lordship invited the entire household staff. I couldn't very well say I did not wish to come. My absence would have caused talk."

"Talk among the servants? Or talk from Lord Drake? You seem rather cozy with your employer these days. Is there anything you'd like to share?"

Her blood turned to ice at his question, a shiver raising fresh goose pimples on her skin. Had he been watching earlier when she'd been talking to Drake? Had he noticed their relaxed, casual rapport and read through their friendly regard? Did he know they were lovers? Her stomach gave a nauseated turn at the thought.

"No, I have nothing to share," she said, unable to keep the sour taste of disgust from her tone.

He laughed, cruel and without humor. "Not to worry, *ma petite*. I don't mind if you're working your wiles on his lordship. All the better if it aids you in retrieving the item we seek."

She heard a faint rustling at her back and sensed him step closer. "Speaking of retrieving things," he continued in an unctuous drawl, "I have something I believe you were supposed to acquire today."

Before she could react, he caught her wrist in his grip and forced something solid into her palm, closing her fingers over it.

The key!

"How did you—" she gasped.

"—You don't think I haven't been keeping an eye on your progress, do you?" He released her wrist but leaned closer, his serpentine breath wafting against her neck.

Exactly how much does he know? she wondered. *Too much,* she acknowledged with a sinking heart.

"I was quite pleased when I learned from the locksmith what you'd brought for him to copy," he went on. "When I realized you weren't going to be able to keep your appointment this morning, I took the liberty of retrieving the key myself. I assume you will be putting it to good use soon, otherwise—"

He didn't need to say anything further. Sebastianne knew precisely what was at stake and that he held even more of the cards than she'd originally assumed. He'd laid his trap far too well, making sure there were no flaws or possible avenues of escape.

As for her foolish notion of confiding in Drake, the idea

was absurd. Even if he were inclined to aid her, which was highly doubtful, he could no more help her out of her dilemma than he could wave his hand and end the war. He couldn't save her or her family. She was alone, trapped with no way out. As much as she hated the realization, she knew she would have to go through with her original plan.

Just as Vacheau had intended from the very beginning.

She squeezed the key tightly in her hand, letting the bite of the tiny metal teeth mirror her inner agony.

"Two days," he said, "and I expect to have the cipher in my possession."

Her heart gave a desperate beat. *Only two more days!* "But that may not be enough time," she said hurriedly. "I have to get into the safe, then have a chance to copy—"

"Two." The word was a command, absolutely nonnegotiable. "I grow weary of waiting. We will meet in Covent Garden again. Do not bother to look for me. I shall find you, *comprenez-vous?*"

She nodded with a kind of deadened resignation.

And then, as if he'd been no more substantial than a breeze, he was gone.

Sebastianne sagged, her entire body shaking and cold.

Dieu, help me.

"Oh, lordy, 'tis astonishing, ain't it?" Parker exclaimed in clear delight as the balloon sailed higher and higher into the sky. "Just look at it go. A right marvel, 'tis, that flyin' machine."

Agreement rang out among the servants, who'd gathered into a small group to watch the ascent. Cobbs and Polk applauded, while Jasper and Lyles let out whistles and whoops. Morton, the coachman, puffed ruminatingly on his pipe as Mr. Stowe and Waxman traded remarks about the marvels of the modern age.

Mrs. Tremble, for her part, tsked loudly about the dangerous display, making more dire predictions that the craft would come crashing back to earth at any moment. "If God meant man to fly," she stated tartly, "he'd have dressed us all in feathers." But even she couldn't help but gaze upward with an expression of wonder on her aging face, a hint of an amazed smile teasing the corners of her mouth.

Sebastianne listened with a curious detachment, as if she were watching everything from a distance, even herself. For in spite of the half hour that had passed since her unexpected encounter with Vacheau, her mind and emotions were still reeling.

Her first instinct after he'd gone had been to leave the park, to flee to a place of safety where she could hide from her pain and fear. But even as she turned to go, she'd realized there was no place of safety, nowhere in the world she could find refuge from the path she was being forced to walk. Her fate was set, and her only choice was to accept it. Besides, if her deception was to continue successfully, she couldn't make a mad dash back to the town house on her own. The other servants would want to know what was wrong. As for Drake, he would demand a better explanation than a headache, and she worried that in her present humor she might end up making a fatal mistake by saying more than she should.

And so she'd rejoined the others, pinning a happy expression on her face as though she were enjoying the festivities as much as everyone else. Thank heaven, Drake hadn't come in search of her to ply her with sweets as he'd promised. Instead, he'd remained across the way, occupied with his family and a few aristocratic acquaintances, their group looking like a bevy of elegant swans amidst flocks of ducks, geese and pigeons.

Now that Mr. Carter and his balloon were aloft and on

its way to Dover, where he planned to set down again, she hoped the event would conclude and she would be able to return home again. She wanted to hide the key, which burned inside her pocket like some evil talisman, a portent of the misery and betrayal that soon awaited her. For now, though, she must continue to pretend, to act as though she were carefree and happy and wasn't about to rip out her heart and stain her soul in treachery.

"Well, that were something, I must say," Finnegan piped dreamily. "And ever so kind of his lordship to bring us all here today to see."

A fresh round of agreement went through their small group, all the servants heaping effusive praise on their employer.

Mrs. Tremble folded her hands at her waist and nodded. "We're lucky to work for such a fine and generous gentlemen. Not many have it as good as us, even if his lordship doesn't keep a regular household, as some might say. It's regular enough fer me."

"Hear, hear," Waxman said with his usual steadfast loyalty.

"Seems as though it might be regular enough fer someone else soon too," the cook continued, directing her gaze across the field to where Drake and his companions stood. "I'm friendly with the cook at Clybourne House, you know."

"Mrs. Mays," Waxman put in again, plainly eager to share his knowledge.

"Just so," Mrs. Tremble said. "I were talking to her not long ago and she says his lordship's been driving out with a certain young lady who's in London for the Season."

The fog around Sebastianne abruptly melted away, her attention coming into sharp focus.

"I happen to know," Mrs. Tremble continued, "that the young lady in question is here today and is talking at this very moment with his lordship. See her just there, the one in the peach frock. Her name is Miss Verity Manning. I know because she was pointed out to me one day while I was visiting at His Grace's house."

Sebastianne's gaze swung across the field, her eyes going immediately to the woman dressed in an exquisite gown of peach silk. She looked hardly more than a girl, seventeen or eighteen, with a pretty heart-shaped face and blond hair. Sebastianne had thought nothing of her before, but now . . .

"The rumor is," Mrs. Tremble offered in notes of barely contained excitement, "that Lord Drake may finally have found himself a bride."

For several long seconds, Sebastianne forgot how to breathe.

Marry that child? Non! C'est impossible!

But as she watched, she realized she had no right to protest.

Miss Manning was precisely the sort of girl Drake should court. Refined and graceful, she was a blooded aristocrat who'd been tutored over a lifetime to be the wife of a nobleman. And from the look of it, the girl idolized Drake, her face glowing with undisguised pleasure as he bent his head to address a comment to her.

Does she love him?

Sebastianne suddenly hoped so. Drake deserved a wife who adored him. Anything less would be a crime.

Praying the agony in her heart didn't show, she turned away.

Drake had made no promises to her, she reminded herself, nor she to him. Truly, it was better if he found someone else. After all, in two days, she would be gone. In two days, Drake would hate the very sound of her name and would have no trouble turning to another. Perhaps Miss Manning would be exactly the comfort he needed.

She swayed and fought back tears. A brief touch on her arm moments later forced her to blink them away.

"Are you all right, Mrs. Greenway?" Jasper asked quietly.

"Of course," she said, turning to him with a false smile. "Too much sun, I think. And excitement. Yes, far, far too much excitement for one day."

"—do you not agree, my lord?" Miss Manning said, her soft words coming to him like the ebb and flow of a tide.

"Hmm," he murmured, as whatever she said next faded out of his consciousness. He knew he ought to be listening, but his thoughts were on Anne as he surreptitiously observed her where she stood among his household staff several yards distant.

Ever since he'd left to help Carter finish the last of the calibrations and preparations for the balloon launch, he'd been trying to find a way to rejoin her. The few words they'd exchanged earlier in the day had been nothing more than a tease. He'd invited her here today in the hopes of sharing a few pleasant hours together, but circumstances kept interfering.

After he'd broken up the minor scuffle with the onlooker who'd wanted to climb into the gondola, he'd gone back to work helping to prepare the balloon for flight.

Once done, he'd been reaching for his coat when Carter called him over to consult on a new problem. The wind speed had apparently increased, and he needed Drake to verify his calculations and trajectory so that he didn't overshoot his landing. "Wouldn't do to put down in the Channel," Carter had quipped with a toothy smile. "Or worse, in France!"

Nodding, Drake had returned to do what was needed to reassure his friend.

He'd just shrugged into his coat of tan summerweight wool when he'd been hailed by a pair of acquaintances who had a fascination with aeronautical science. Without intending to, he'd found himself pulled into a lengthy debate on the potential of air travel and that day's impending flight.

Then various members of his family had arrived, beginning with Adam, Mallory and Esme, the youngest of his siblings at thirteen. Sketch pad in hand, Esme had settled herself on the grass to capture the highlights of the day in pencil and pastels. Drake noticed after a glimpse at one of her drawings that she seemed to be paying particular attention to the dogs and birds in the park rather than the people. Typical, he thought with a smile, given her love of animals.

Cade, Meg, their toddler son and infant daughter had appeared next, with Edward, Claire and their own fifteen-month-old daughter not far behind. Claire's sister, Ella, had accompanied them as well, clearly happy as she divided her time between two of her most devoted suitors.

In addition to a trio of nursemaids who'd come with their party to attend to the children, one of the Clybourne House footmen had accompanied them as well. As Drake saw to his amusement and amazement, it was the servant's job to carry around a chair for the heavily pregnant young duchess. When she noticed Drake's expression, Claire, who everyone knew ought to have been in confinement by now, declared that she wasn't going to be held prisoner inside her own home simply because she was increasing. Nor, she stated as a clearly concerned and exasperated Edward helped lower her into the chair, was she going to miss out on such an entertaining event as a balloon ascension.

"I am not due to give birth for ten more days," she stated, linking her hands stubbornly over her huge belly. "So I fail to see why I should have to miss out on all the fun."

"No one expects you to pine away at home, love," Edward said, bending down to kiss her cheek. "We just don't want you giving birth in a public park."

As the assembled company laughed, Claire playfully swatted Edward's hand away. Then she laughed too.

Drake might still have been able to slip away at that moment had it not been for the arrival of another trio of people—Miss Manning; her father, Lord Saxon; and on his arm looking almost girlish, Drake's mother, Ava.

He'd frowned at the sight of them, unable to help but stare at the middle-aged pair as they talked and flirted, Ava's frequent laughter skipping lightly on the air at Saxon's throaty remarks. Just what was the man playing at? Drake wondered. If Drake didn't know better, he would think Lord Saxon was courting his mother!

He'd been mulling over that astonishing idea when Miss Manning stepped shyly to his side and began asking about balloon flight. Unable to find a polite means of excusing himself, the minutes ticked past. But as he watched the airship rise into the clouds, his head and heart had been with Anne rather than the pleasant yet uninspiring Miss Manning.

But now, manners be damned, I've had enough, he thought.

"—So you'll join Papa and me at the fête on Wednesday next," she was saying, a happy smile on her pink lips.

"Yes . . . I mean no . . . *what?*"

Her smile dimmed slightly. "The fête. You know, the one I was telling you about. You said you'd be there."

"No, I didn't."

Or had he? Hell and damnation, given my preoccupation, I might have agreed to nearly anything.

"My pardon, Miss Manning," he said, "but I am afraid I must not have been attending properly to the conversation."

"Oh." Her smile disappeared completely. "You have other things on your mind."

"Yes," he told her honestly.

"Mathematics, then? A new theorem?"

"No, but other matters of import. I pray you'll forgive my lapse."

For a moment, she looked as if she didn't think she would, but then gave a resigned nod and a forced, half smile. "Of course, my lord. You are known for your brilliance, as well as your distractions."

Yes, he thought, *but not over women. Certainly not over one woman in particular.*

Seeing Miss Manning's downcast expression, however, his conscience twitched with guilt. Just because he wasn't attracted to her in a romantic way, didn't mean he had the right to wound her.

Devil take it, this just isn't my day.

"I can't promise I will be at the fête," he said, "but I expect we shall see each other again soon at another entertainment. In the meantime, you shall not lack for partners, I am certain. Your dance card must always be full."

She appeared to rally again at his remark, squaring her small shoulders with a healthy measure of pride. "Yes, it is, my lord. I am sought after by a great number of gentlemen."

Just not you, came the unspoken conclusion to her rejoinder.

"Then I wish them good fortune in winning your affections. The gentleman who secures your hand will be a lucky fellow indeed."

She gave a small, nearly silent sigh, linking her fingers in front of her before she looked up. "Lord Drake?"

"Yes?"

"Is it . . . is it me?" she asked in a quiet voice. "Or is there someone else?"

His features softened, deciding he owed her nothing less than the truth. "You may rest assured, Miss Manning, that it most definitely is not you."

Her lips rounded in an O of clear curiosity.

Before she could question him further, however, he bowed and stepped away. Perhaps there was still time to buy that sweetmeat for Anne after all.

He'd taken no more than five steps away when a sudden cry made him swing back around.

Claire stood next to her chair, gripping the back, a peculiar expression on her face as if she'd just received a rather unexpected shock. "Well, good heavens," she said in wonder.

Edward moved quickly to her side and slipped an arm around her back. "What is it?"

"Nothing to fear. But I believe in all the excitement, your son has decided to arrive early."

Edward blanched. "You're in labor?"

Claire nodded. "Yes. And if you don't want the next Marquis of Hartsfield to be born in a park, you had best get me home straightaway."

Chapter 22

The servants returned home abuzz at the news about the duchess. Imagine Lord Drake's sister-in-law going into labor in Green Park? By nightfall, they all agreed, the tale would be the talk of the town.

Luckily for Sebastianne, no one seemed to notice her distraction. What with all the hullabaloo, her unusual quiet went just as unremarked as it had earlier that morning. As for Drake, she assumed he'd gone with his family after the duke had scooped his pregnant wife into his arms and strode hurriedly toward the waiting carriage.

Not long after she entered the town house, however, she realized that Drake had returned home instead. Without intending to, she found him in his workroom, busy gathering a few items together, including a thick journal and a handful of pencils.

"Anne . . . Mrs. Greenway," he corrected, looking up from where he stood behind his desk. "Come inside and close the door."

Aware that both footmen and Mr. Stowe were in the hallway and might have heard his familiar use of her first name, she hesitated. But what did it matter now if any of them guessed the true nature of her relationship with Drake? She would be gone soon and would never see any of them again. And once she disappeared, they would have a great deal more to discuss than their speculation that she'd shared a bed with Drake. They would have her betrayal to gnash over and her character to shred and trample like so much hay in the stables. Spirits low, she stepped inside the room and shut the door at her back.

Sending her welcoming smile, Drake placed the items he'd gathered into a neat stack at the edge of his desk, then came around to her. Reaching out, he captured her hands in his own. "Sorry about today," he said. "You wouldn't believe how many times I tried to get away and join you, but events kept conspiring against me."

She gave a little shrug. "It doesn't matter. I understand."

"Do you?" Raising her hand, he kissed her palm. "Then you're an angel."

He won't think so in two days' time, but for now I'll let him keep believing what he will.

"I wanted to see you for a few minutes before I have to rush off," he said. "With a new Byron on the way, the whole brood will be gathering at Clybourne House, and I'm expected to join them."

"Of course, you are. Naturally, you must be with your family."

"Yes, but I didn't want to leave without seeing you first, to tell you that I won't be home tonight."

Her heart lurched in her chest. "Not home?" she said, vaguely aware of the quaver in her voice.

"It's just for tonight," he reassured. "The whole family will sleep over, either to wait for the birth or to celebrate once it's happened. I wanted you to know."

Agony sliced through her like a blade. Despite what she'd

seen in the park and the possibility that he was considering marriage to another woman, she'd been counting on making love with him tonight. One last time together before she had to flee. One last chance to create memories that would have to last her for a lifetime.

But he wouldn't be there. Worse, with him out of the house, she knew that tonight was the perfect time to copy the cipher, the sensible move. Once she'd done that, she would have to leave. Instead of two days, she would have none.

Mon Dieu, this is the last time I shall see him.

She clenched her fingers until her nails bit deep into her flesh, using the pain to keep herself from weeping. For heaven knows she would have plenty of time later for tears, years in which to mourn Drake's loss.

And mourn him she would.

His loss would be like another death to her, only worse in a way than Thierry's because this time she was the one killing their union. She was the one willing to let him go.

A dreadful pressure built in her chest, a swelling ache that threatened to pull her under as if she were caught in a fatal current. But she couldn't afford to break down, she knew, couldn't possibly allow him see that she was falling apart inside.

With a fortitude she hadn't realized she possessed, she forced her lips into a smile. "I shall miss you, but as you say, it's only for one night."

Some hint of her desolation must have shown in spite of her brave façade, since he slipped a finger beneath her chin a moment later and lifted her face so she was forced to meet his gaze.

"Don't be sad, sweetheart," he said. "I'll be back soon, and when I return, I promise I'll more than make up my absence to you."

Lifting her hand, she caressed his face from temple to

jaw, tracing the shape, memorizing each contour and plane. "Kiss me, Drake," she said.

He smiled, then pressed his mouth lightly against her own.

"No, not like that," she told him, a bit of her desperation creeping through. "Really kiss me, like you'll never kiss me again."

His eyes widened in momentary surprise, then darkened with passion. "With pleasure."

This time when his lips met hers, there was no restraint, no hesitation as he claimed her mouth with a wild, ravenous ardor.

Closing her eyes, Sebastianne gave herself over to the intensity of the sensations, savoring each glide and stroke of lips and tongue as she tunneled her fingers into his thick hair to draw him nearer. His healthy male scent swam in her head, a combination of fresh air, warm wool, and clean perspiration. He tasted even better, of sweet wine and fragrant spices, the flavors saturating her tongue as he played over the delicate inner flesh of her mouth. Shuddering, she kissed him with a feverish longing, giving free rein to her need and desperation, aware that each passing second led her closer to the end.

Stepping more fully into his embrace, she held him tight, wanting nothing between them, not even her fear of the parting to come. Dark and fierce, the tempo of their kisses deepened, growing slower and richer in a way that mirrored the heavy slamming beats of her heart.

From this time forward, these moments would be seared into her memory. Even more, they would be imprinted on her flesh like a brand that could never be scrubbed free. Forever after, Drake would be the one to whom she would compare all others. The man who would cast all other men into the shade and make them seem weak and wanting.

She was ruined for anyone else, she knew.

She was his now.

Always.

Kissing him harder, she gave herself utterly to the embrace, trying not to think of anything but the majesty of his touch and the beauty of being in his arms.

Drake, she whispered in her head. *Je t'aime.*

Toujours, mon coeur. Mon amour.

And then slowly, as both of them labored to catch their next breaths, he set her aside.

"*Sweet Jesu,*" he swore, "that was one hell of a kiss. Remind me to go away more often." He smiled, still straining to regulate his breathing.

She didn't answer, afraid of what she might say, of what she might reveal.

Giving his head a shake, he sent her a smile, then crossed back to his desk. "I'd better be on my way. If I don't leave now, I never will. I won't have the strength. I'll have you upstairs in my bed instead and plague take the family."

Gathering up his belongings, he walked to the door. "Don't look so downcast, sweet. I'll be home again before you know it."

But I won't, she thought. *I shall be gone.*

"Good-bye, Drake," she said softly, drinking in the sight of his beloved face one final time.

With another smile, he opened the door and stepped through.

Quite suddenly, she couldn't breathe again, a pain unlike any she'd ever known before threatening to cleave her chest in two. For a moment she wondered at the agonizing sensation, then realized what it must be.

It was the feeling of her heart breaking, the sensation of its dying.

She didn't know how long she stood there, alone and motionless. Luckily, no one entered. No one came to see how she was and what she might be doing inside Drake's workroom.

At length, she steadied herself, an icy sensation of cold sweeping through her body to leave her numb.

This was the end, the day she had been both dreading and anticipating since her arrival in England. Tonight she would copy the cipher. This evening, after everyone else was abed, she would betray the man she loved in order to save her family across the Channel—two little boys and an old man who needed her more.

Could any woman be more wretched than she?

Wondering how she was going to make it through the next several hours without anyone's noticing her distress, she did the only thing she could think of.

Waiting until the hallway was empty, she walked to the library where she knew Drake kept a small store of liquor for guests. Opening the cabinet with her housekeeper's key, she poured herself a hearty draught of whiskey. She tossed it back quickly, the alcohol burning her throat and nearly making her gag. The spirits did nothing to erase the chill that had settled like winter into her bones, but at least it steadied her nerves enough that she could force a smile and form a coherent sentence.

Cleaning and drying the glass, she put the cabinet to rights again, then locked it. Drawing a deep breath, she turned and strode from the room, as ready as she ever would to do what must be done.

Chapter 23

"It's a boy!" Edward announced from the doorway of the morning room not long after sunrise the following day. A huge grin of happy exhaustion creased his stubble-darkened face, his usually impeccable attire stripped down to shirtsleeves, waistcoat and trousers, his cravat long since discarded and forgotten in some distant part of the house.

Drake returned his eldest brother's exuberant smile from his place at the dining table, where he, Cade, Leo, Lawrence, Adam and Quentin, their cousin by marriage, had gathered to have tea and eggs while they awaited news of the birth. As for the women, they'd kept vigil with Claire, taking light repasts at odd hours of the night when the opportunity allowed.

Sometime around three in the morning, Drake had tried to catch a few hours' sleep, but like everyone else in the house, hadn't managed more than one or two amid the waiting and worrying, and the distant, disturbing echoes of Claire's cries of pain. But all was well now, a jubilant calm having descended over the town house with the arrival of the new baby.

Leo stood, since he was closest to the door, and offered his seat to Edward. Gratefully, Edward accepted, another wide, spontaneous grin spreading across his face as the rest of them offered a hearty round of backslaps and congratulations.

Drinking from a cup of hot coffee one of the footmen set before him, Edward told of his part in the birth. He was glad, he said, that he'd decided to ignore the convention of fathers staying out of the birthing room, so that he could be there to support Claire as their new son came into the world.

Cade and Quentin, who were fathers themselves, stood in complete agreement, while Adam stated he wouldn't miss being at Mallory's side when her time came a few months from now.

Leo and Lawrence rolled their gold-and-green eyes and traded identical looks of horror, while Drake kept his silence and reapplied himself to his breakfast.

What must it be like watching the woman you love give birth? he wondered. *What would it be like with Anne?*

Disconcerted by the notion and even more by the fact that he somehow didn't mind the idea of Anne Greenway having his child, Drake frowned and bit into a slice of buttered toast.

"Claire is getting some badly needed sleep at the moment," Edward told them, his own eyelids drooping ever so slightly as he drank another cup of dark brew and started in on a plateful of ham, toast and eggs. "The baby will have her awake again soon enough for a feeding, since she insists on doing it herself. I suggested a wet nurse, but Claire says Robert's first meal won't be from a stranger."

Drake glanced up from own plate. "Are you naming him after Father then?"

The others looked on with interest.

Edward nodded. "Yes, and Claire's father as well. Robert

Henry. We thought it fitting somehow given the fact that they're the ones who arranged our match in the first place."

Everyone fell silent for a moment as they considered the remark and all that had happened since that childhood betrothal.

Some of the ladies appeared soon after.

Meg sauntered in to perch on the arm of Cade's chair and eat the bacon off his plate, while she reported that mother and child were still asleep and doing beautifully. Quentin's wife, India, slipped into the seat next to her husband and sipped a cup of tea; Mallory followed, taking a place between Adam and Drake.

Looking decidedly owl-eyed, she yawned numerous times over the piece of jam-coated toast her husband placed in her hand. Adam waited until she'd eaten it, along with half a coddled egg, before gathering her up to lead her from the room with plans to seek their bed.

Edward drank the last of his coffee, then bid them all a hasty adieu as well, excusing himself so he could return to Claire and their new son. He also planned a visit to the nursery to see their young daughter, Hannah, who would be waking soon and undoubtedly wanting her mama.

Once he'd gone, the others found themselves slightly at loose ends.

"I suppose we ought to get a bit of rest as well," Lawrence said at length, covering a yawn with a curled fist. "Lord knows none of us slept much last night. A couple of hours abed wouldn't go amiss, then we can celebrate properly. Cook is busy preparing a special supper tonight that we dare not miss. Mama would have our heads, after all, if we skipped out on it in favor of a Ton party or to visit a gaming hell."

"So we'll stay and eat here, *then* skip out," Leo said with a grin. "Plenty of amusement to be had in Town after midnight."

The twins chuckled with clear and premeditated devilment.

Amusements after midnight, Drake mused. He could certainly think of a few of those himself. Already he was missing Anne and looking forward to returning home to her. *Home to Anne,* he repeated, liking not only the sound of it but the rightness of the idea.

Gazing across the table at the two couples still seated, he considered the obvious happiness of their unions. Cade had returned from war a man broken in both body and spirit. Then Meg had come into his life and exorcised all of his demons. Love had quite literally brought him back from the brink.

As for his cousin India, she'd charmed Quentin Marlowe, a cynical rake with a hardened veneer that had cracked open to reveal a loyal and loving heart, which now beat only for her.

Once, not long ago, Drake would have scoffed at such maudlin, sentimental fancy. But now that he'd met Anne . . .

What had begun as a lusty, passionate affair had turned to something far more intimate, far more meaningful. She was no longer just his bed partner. She was the woman he missed when he was away. The woman he thought about during the day and wanted to sleep with at night. The woman who he wanted to talk with and laugh with and make happy. Plainly put, she was the woman he loved, of that he had not an ounce of doubt.

She was in his employ and not of his class, but such matters scarcely signified to him. She was intelligent, well-spoken and had far finer manners than many aristocratic ladies of his acquaintance. She was a credit not only to herself but to her gender. And if she had secrets she was reluctant to reveal, well, with time, the necessary trust would come. With time, she would come to love him as much as he did her.

So what came next?

More stolen nights and clandestine encounters that never seemed to be enough?

More dissembling and denying the real nature of their relationship?

More pretending she meant nothing to him when actually she meant the world?

He'd offered to make her his mistress, to shower her with leisure and luxury and love. But she refused. So if she wouldn't be his ladylove, would she be his lady instead?

Would she consent to be my wife?

He froze, inwardly stunned by the idea.

Me? Married? No, he thought, as all the old reasons came to mind.

He didn't want to get married.

He had no time for a wife, or children for that matter.

His life was too erratic, too complicated and complex.

A wife would never understand him or tolerate his habits and distractions. A wife would nag and complain and want to change him. A wife would interfere with the well-ordered chaos of his life.

But Anne wouldn't, came a resounding voice. *Anne understands me already. She knows who I am, good and bad alike, so there wouldn't be any unpleasant surprises in store. Anne Greenway suits me right down to the ground.*

"Drake. I say, Drake. Are you in there?"

Drake blinked and looked across the table at Leo, who was waving a hand back and forth, not far from his eyes. "What?" he said, scowling and pulling his head away.

"Sorry to intrude on the wheels turning in your head, but I just wanted to make sure you're all right before we leave," his brother said. "You looked kind of odd, you know, even for you."

A glance around the table confirmed Leo's remark, since

everyone else still seated was regarding him with a combination of interested concern and resigned amusement.

"I'm fine," he snapped. "Just thinking. I do that sometimes, you know."

Cade laughed. "Had an epiphany, have you? For a minute, you looked as if you'd gone a round with Gentleman Jackson and lost."

Had he? He supposed that perhaps he had. It wasn't every day a man changed his mind about something as fundamental as marriage and his willingness to enter into the state.

Drake cleared his throat and pushed back his chair. "Hmm, something like that. Now, if you're all done amusing yourselves at my expense, I'm taking myself off to my old bedroom for a couple of hours' sleep."

Meg yawned delicately, her silvery blue eyes watering at the edges. "Sleep sounds delightful. I believe I shall follow your lead. Cade, are you ready?"

"Always, darling. Ready and able."

She flashed him a look of teasing reprimand. "Behave yourself, my lord."

"But if I did that, love," he said as he followed her from the room with his halting stride, "just think how bored you would be."

Meg's lilting laugh trailed them out into the hallway, making Drake suspect it would be a while before the pair settled down to rest. India and Quentin, who exchanged secret smiles of their own, departed as well. The twins walked out next, heads bent together as they debated the variety of entertainments they could pursue later that night.

Alone, and rather glad of it, Drake followed. But even as he turned toward his bedchamber, he hesitated. He wasn't all that tired, at least not anymore. What he really wanted to do was go to Anne and propose. But first, he needed a ring.

Making an about-face, he headed for the staircase and took them down two at a time.

Drake entered his town house a few minutes before eleven that evening, the ring he'd purchased from Rundell, Bridge and Rundell warm in his pocket. With the assistance of old Mr. Rundell, he'd selected a bloodred ruby with an elegant circlet of diamonds that he thought suited the passionate streak in Anne's personality. He hoped she liked it. Even more, he hoped she accepted, both the ring and his proposal of marriage.

A ripple of nervous anticipation ran under his skin, making his stomach rebel slightly against the elaborate dinner he'd consumed at Clybourne House a couple of hours earlier.

The family-only party had been festive, especially when Claire, looking far too young to be a mother, with her long blond hair tied back in a ribbon and attired in a flowered silk dressing gown, joined them for dessert. Smiling serenely, she'd informed them that being brought to childbed that morning seemed to have left her with a sweet tooth. Forty-five minutes later, her eyelids drooping, Edward had carried her back to bed.

Drake had departed not long after, promising to visit again soon.

Next time he stopped at Clybourne House he hoped to bring news of his impending nuptials, and shortly after that, the bride-to-be herself. He wanted the family to meet Anne and to like her. Most of his brothers had made her acquaintance already though not in a social context; they knew her instead as his housekeeper. But they would accept the reversal of roles without a great deal of bother, he suspected. As for the Byron women, they would come around as well, he felt sure, even if it might take them a little while longer.

Although to give Mama credit, she had welcomed the rest of her daughters-in-law with open arms regardless of their wealth or lineage, so perhaps she would do the same for Anne.

The Ton, on the other hand, might prove tricky. Society matrons in particular could be a pack of narrow-minded old bats when they wished. Knowing Anne as he did, however, he guessed she would stare down each and every one of them and win their favor in spite of themselves.

First, however, he had to secure her hand. After that, everything else would seem easy.

"Good evening, Stowe," Drake said as he strode into the house.

"Welcome back, my lord. It is good to have you home. And may I offer congratulations on the arrival of the new Clybourne heir."

Drake smiled. "You may indeed. Mother and son are doing splendidly." Sliding a hand into his pocket, he touched the small jeweler's box containing the ring. "Is Mrs. Greenway still about? If so, would you ask her to come to my study."

Stowe's normally placid brow drew taut, his gaze fixed. "I am afraid Mrs. Greenway is not here."

It was Drake's turn to stare. "What do you mean, *not here?*"

"With you absent, my lord, she informed me this morning that she would be taking her usual day off today. I thought it a prudent decision under the circumstances and bid her good day around ten o'clock. We expected her for dinner, but she has not yet returned. The moment she does, I will send her to you."

Drake's fingers tightened around the ring box, tracing its edges. She usually took Friday off, but owing to the sojourn to the park, she had missed her free day this week. She had every right to leave the house for a few hours, of course, but where could she be at this hour of the evening? It wasn't like her to be out late, and she had known he planned to return home this evening. Surely nothing untoward had happened to her.

His stomach pitched at the thought.

No, he assured himself, *she must be fine.*

With the warm weather and late sunset, perhaps she'd decided to attend the theater and take a bite of supper afterward. Still, it didn't seem likely, as she was alone. At least he assumed she was alone. Mayhap she had gone with a friend.

His scowl deepened, a slow ache starting in his chest.

"There is one other matter, my lord," Stowe said, breaking into his reverie.

Drake met the butler's gaze. "Yes?"

Stowe's upper lip curled slightly. "A man is here to see you . . . a Mr. Aggies, or so he says. His evening call is most irregular, but he insisted on remaining until he had spoken to you."

Aggies? Here tonight? He was one of Edward's men, an ex-Bow Street Runner who'd been set to watch the house and the man they'd seen spying. They'd agreed that he would report on any further suspicious activity. The fact that Aggies had seen fit to arrive on his doorstep an hour shy of midnight did not bode well.

"Why didn't you tell me he was here?" Drake said, worry adding a clipped edge to his voice. "Where have you put him?"

"In the tradesman's parlor, my lord. I didn't know where else to have him wait."

The tradesman's parlor was little more than a closet with a pair of chairs inside. But Aggies wasn't the fussy sort, so Drake supposed he'd been comfortable enough waiting there.

"Send him to my workroom," Drake ordered. "And advise me the moment Mrs. Greenway returns. She ought to have been back by now."

The ache in his chest spread another inch.

"Yes, my lord," Stowe replied, striding quickly away.

Drake squeezed the ring box in his hand again and strode down the hall.

Aggies arrived less than five minutes later, his hat clutched in his grasp. A small, wiry man with a narrow face, he always reminded Drake of a hunting terrier, albeit a hairless one, the man's bald pate gleaming dully in the candlelight.

"You have news?" Drake said without preamble as he took a seat behind his desk. Waving a hand, he indicated that Aggies should take one as well.

But Aggies remained standing, pacing a few steps before drawing to a halt again. "That I do, yer lordship. The kind what couldn't wait."

"Is it the man you and your team have been tracking? Have you located him again?"

"That we have, and he's a right nasty customer, 'e is. Goes by the name of Jones, but I don't believe that's 'is real name fer an instant. Got that much from one o' the girls what works the Garden. He left her in a bad way, he did, beat her senseless and more besides."

Aggies's face puckered with disgust, his mouth screwing up as if he wanted to spit, then thought better of it given his present surroundings.

"But that's not the worst of it," he continued, swallowing his gall. "One of me best snitches, good man even if he 'as been known to work the lightfinger trade on occasion, well, I set him on ter Jones. Wished I hadn't now, since he's gone missin.' Ain't seen 'im this last week entire. He might 'ave gone ter ground, Smiley'll do that sometimes. But he's left a fair lot 'o his possessions behind, and I gots a bad feelin' about it. Awful thing is, if he does turn up in the Thames, might not be enough left ter recognize. Plenty 'o unidentified corpses fished regular-like out 'o that river."

Drake frowned and slowly drummed his fingers against his desk. "What a dreadful commentary on our society. Let us sincerely hope your friend is not among such unfortunate souls."

Aggies nodded in sorrowful agreement.

The other man's gruesome tale made Drake think about all the possible dangers in the city, especially at night, and the fact that Anne still had not come home. Stowe would have alerted him if she had.

Where in the deuce is she? It will be coming on midnight soon.

Forcing the unsettling thoughts away, he refocused his attention on Aggies, who was speaking again.

"Afore Smiley disappeared," Aggies said, "he had word 'o some exchange supposed to take place and the address of an 'ouse in Cheapside. Decent middling sort of place, not the kind you'd think to suspect. I put a man on it to watch. Ordinary couple lives there, husband, wife, pair o' kids. There weren't nothing unusual until today."

Drake met Aggies's gaze with interest. "Did Jones show up?"

Aggies shook his head. "No, but someone else did."

Drake waited, taking note of the way the older man was absently turning his hat brim between his fingers in a nervous sideways motion.

"Well?" Drake prompted, wanting to get this interview over, so he could go out and look for Anne. "Who was it?"

Aggies swallowed and stopped turning the hat. "It were someone ye know, my lord. Someone none of us would ever have suspected. It was your housekeeper, Mrs. Greenway."

rake stared for a long, incomprehensible moment, his fingers grown abruptly still atop his desk. "*What?*" he said dumbly.

"Yer housekeeper. Who would 'ave thought someone so close to ye, someone from yer own household staff, would turn out ter be in league with the other side?"

Drake's ears began to buzz with an odd sort of hum, his heart contracting in shallow draughts as if it couldn't quite pump enough blood.

No, he thought, *there must be some kind of error. Aggies could not have seen Anne doing what he said he had.*

"Perhaps you are mistaken and it wasn't Mrs. Greenway at all," Drake countered.

Aggies shook his bald head. "Nah, it were her all right. Can't miss a woman with so many shades o' color in 'er 'air, an' such a pretty Nancy besides."

Drake's heart gave another thick beat. "Maybe she was at that house for a different reason then. You said yourself the family seems harmless. Her presence could just be a coincidence, and she is nothing more than a friendly acquaintance of theirs."

Aggies sent him a pitying look. "Might have thought that meself except one of the boys what lives in the house went running with a note as soon as she showed up. He came back near two hours later with another. She left not five minutes after his return, looking grim around the mouth."

"Go on," Drake said, forcing himself to take a breath.

"We followed her, of course, to see where she was off to and she led us to St. Paul's Church in Covent Garden, then straight inside. She slid into a pew and waited. That's when *he* showed up, Jones. Sat right next to her, and it were clear she knew who 'e was though to her credit she didn't seem to like 'im much. You could tell from her face that she weren't happy."

Drake gripped the arm of his chair, Anne's lovely face swimming in his mind's eye as he imagined the scene. "Then what," he said in a dead voice.

"They talked for minute, Jones lookin' none too 'appy hisself, as if she'd done somethin' she weren't supposed to. Then she handed him a piece 'o paper, and his face cleared up right quick. Bastard smiled this nasty, toothy grin, he did, as if she'd just given 'im the crown jewels."

Drake's forehead drew tight as he considered the information. Anne had handed Jones a piece of parchment that visibly pleased him. Drake could think of only one item that fit such a description, and that the French—who he was sure Jones must work for—would give their firstborn to possess.

The cipher.

But it wasn't possible. Even if Anne had somehow discovered his hidden safe, she wouldn't have had access to the key. He kept it around his neck four-and-twenty hours a day. Except that lately, he reminded himself, she'd been spending a portion of those hours in his bed, including that first night together when he was sure he'd been drugged.

His scowl deepened at the implications.

"Where is she then?" he demanded, low and strained. "You have her in custody, I presume? And Jones as well?"

Aggies crushed his hat inside his hands. "Well now about that . . . we had 'em cornered right 'n' tight, but Jones is no rube when it comes to such matters and must have caught wind we were there. Before we realized, he had her up and out through one of the doors behind the altar and into a nearby alley. Disappeared like a pair 'o black cats at midnight." Pausing, he ran a palm over his smooth pate, eyes averted. "We searched for 'em for hours, which is why I didn't show up here at yer town house afore now. Plain truth is, the pair 'o 'em could be anywhere by now. Even France."

Even France?

But Anne was English, or at least he'd thought so until to-night. Now he didn't know for certain who or what she was. For all he knew, her name wasn't even Anne Greenway. She could be anyone since clearly she had lied about her reasons for being employed in his house. And in his life. Had she lied about that as well? Had she come to his bed to steal the key, uncaring that she had stolen his heart as well?

His hands turned to fists, sudden anger burning away the sick sensation in his belly, leaving a raw scalding heat in its wake.

And to think I was worried about her when she knew precisely what she was doing. What else had she known?

"Mr. Aggies, would you step out of the room for a moment? Tell Stowe to serve you a libation while you wait. I may have further questions."

"O' course, yer lordship. And that's right generous 'o ye about the drink. I could use a dram after the night I done 'ad."

Drake waited until Aggies had let himself out of the room and closed the door behind him. The instant he had, Drake sprang to his feet and crossed to the painting that concealed his safe. The chances were infinitesimal that she'd gotten inside and taken the cipher, but he had to know. Taking hold of the chain, he pulled the key from under his neckcloth and off over his head. Fitting it into the lock, he opened the safe with a gentle click.

The cipher was kept inside a small leather sheath that he habitually kept on the right side of the interior. Removing it, the burn in his chest increasing, he untied the fastener.

And there it was, the cipher folded and tucked away exactly as he'd left it. For a moment, he stood unblinking, wondering if Aggies had been wrong after all. Perhaps Anne—or whatever her real name might be—had met with Jones for an entirely different reason; although what that reason might be, he couldn't fathom. Reaching in, he withdrew the page and opened it to reveal the numbers and symbols of the code, formed in his own distinctive black handwriting. He read it through, just to be sure the mathematical formula was the same, and found that it was. Puzzled but satisfied of its authenticity, he began to put the parchment away.

And that's when it came to him, drifting upward like a taunt, a silent slap that made his blood run hot and cold at the same time.

The scent of violets.

And Anne.

Night darkness lay like a shroud over Sebastianne, the odors of sea brine, sweat and rotting fish permeating the hold of the small sailing vessel that was taking her home to France. The plan was to smuggle her in through Le Havre, since it had been deemed far too likely that the English would be suspicious of any ship making the shorter crossing to Calais.

Weary to the bone and numb with cold, she forced herself not to think of what—or rather whom—she had left behind. Ever since she'd left the town house on Audley Street late yesterday morning with Drake's cipher burning like a brand in her pocket, she'd been surviving on sheer nerve alone.

Traitor, thief, betrayer had run like a litany through her brain as she'd walked to the rendezvous point in Cheapside. She hadn't cared if Vacheau might be angry with her for not waiting until the next day to keep their scheduled appointment; she'd just wanted out. The protective house, which was not to be accessed except in an emergency, was the only way she could think of to get a message to him. But as far as she was concerned, the situation constituted an emergency. She didn't dare remain at Drake's town house, and who knows what might occur if she stayed in a hotel.

As Lord Drake's housekeeper—former housekeeper—it was unlikely, but still possible that someone might recognize her, particularly if she stayed in a reputable lodging. As for the disreputable ones, she wasn't going to risk her personal safety to satisfy Vacheau.

And so she'd gone to the contact house in Cheapside and sent her note.

Just as she'd expected, Vacheau had been furious.

"Didn't I say I would find you *tomorrow*?" he'd hissed as he slid like a serpent onto the church pew beside her. "Your stupidity might have compromised us."

But he'd seemed well enough pleased when she'd handed him the cipher. She'd shivered at the soulless smile that had crossed his lips when he'd received his prize.

Soon after, her heart had pounded with fear when he'd told her he believed someone had indeed followed them to the church and was watching. Fearing capture more than Vacheau, now that she'd stolen the cipher, she let him whisk her out of the church and down a series of narrow alleyways until he'd deemed it safe to stop. His concern had nothing to do with her welfare, she knew, but with the plan instead. Her arrest would have instantly alerted the War Office and made

Vacheau's work in England impossible and any chance of escape back to France extremely difficult indeed.

Setting events in motion, he'd put her in a coach bound for Southampton, where a fishing vessel flying a Dutch flag would smuggle her into France. The transfer had gone surprisingly well although she'd been compelled to bribe the ship's crew for a blanket and something to eat. The bread, cheese and wine she'd been given had proven plain but filling. As for the blanket, it left much to be desired, the wool moth-eaten and musty-smelling.

She was so cold at the moment, though, she didn't much care, huddling beneath the cover as if it were all that was keeping her from turning to ice. Listening to the chilly waters of the Channel slap rhythmically against the ship's hull didn't help matters either, nor did the misery that had settled upon her, thick and impenetrable as a fog.

Ever since Drake had kissed her good-bye, she'd been unable to shake her sorrow. Her heart still beat, but some vital part of her spirit seemed to have died, snuffed out like a guttering candle. Perhaps that was the real reason she couldn't get warm because there was nothing but ice left inside her.

She wondered where Drake was and what he was doing. He must have returned to the town house by now, the new baby long since born. She wondered if the duchess had given birth to a boy or a girl, and realized she would likely never know. Just as she would know nothing more of Drake unless one of his mathematical exploits made its way into the newspapers or a scientific journal.

What had he thought of her disappearance? The original plan had called for her to hand in her notice in person and depart. But she'd known Drake would ask too many questions if she suddenly announced her decision to leave, and more if she abruptly tried to end their affair.

So she'd done the cowardly thing and left a note in her room, resigning her post. In it, she said only that she'd had a change of heart about the job and living in the city and that she had taken a new post in the countryside. In a way, it had not been a lie. She would be living in countryside, she simply hadn't mentioned that it would be the French countryside and that her new post consisted of caring for her young brothers and elderly father.

As for her belongings, the few things she truly cared about—a silver-backed hairbrush and comb, a bottle of violet water, and a small brooch she'd brought with her from home—had fit easily inside her reticule. As for the rest—clothes, shoes and other essentials, she'd left behind. They'd been made for her as part of the role she'd played, and she had no use for them anymore. Besides, she would never have been able to carry a portmanteau from the house without notice, or drag it around London as she was fleeing from unknown watchers.

She wished she could have said more in her note. Told him she was sorry. Explained that she'd never meant to cause hurt to him, or any of the others for that matter.

She'd had no choice.

She'd done what she had to do.

But he would care naught for that, particularly if he had any idea what she'd done. Would he realize her true intentions? Would he discover she'd taken the code from his safe?

She'd tried to be careful, copying the cipher in precise detail before returning the original to its proper place. She didn't believe she'd left any clues, and yet there was always room for error.

Had she made one?

Then again, did it matter any longer? Even if he found out that she'd taken the cipher, he could do nothing to stop its passing into French hands. It was already in their possession since she'd given it to Vacheau the day before, or at least that was what Drake would think.

Because the truth wasn't always what it seemed.

Aware that Vacheau was both devious and cruel, she knew she couldn't trust him for an instant. He'd used threats and coercion to force her into his scheme, promising that she and her family would be left alone once the mission succeeded. But she didn't believe his assurances and feared he would try to double-deal her. Once she returned home, she suspected he might renege on his promises and come up with another "little job" she could do for him. After all, with the cipher in hand, what sway did she have should he and his masters decide they wanted more? She'd been used once, badly, and she had no intention of ever being used again.

And so, unbeknownst to Vacheau, she'd given him only the first part of the formula. The other part, the section of the equation needed to unlock the code, she'd kept for herself. Of course, once Vacheau realized what she'd done, her safety and that of her family, would once again be in jeopardy. Even her life might be in danger.

But by the time he figured it out, her part of the cipher would be hidden somewhere safe, a place Vacheau would never find and that she would die to protect. It was her insurance, her bargaining chip, which she would play in order to win her family's freedom for good.

And her price for a true exchange?

No less than a letter of free passage and personal autonomy, signed and sworn by Napoleon himself. No one would dare to trouble her with the Emperor's pledge in hand, and should matters progress so that she was again in fear for her loved ones' safety, they would flee the country if need be.

Go to Italy, perhaps, or Greece.

She thought she would like that, like the heat. Maybe the

Aegean's sun-kissed shores would be enough to melt the ice that had crystallized deep in her bones and solidified around her heart.

She wondered again what Drake was doing and if he was sorry she was gone, or if he was even now cursing her very name.

She'd left him a bloody note of resignation!

After once more scanning the formal statement she'd written in her neat, flowing hand, Drake crushed the foolscap into a ball and flung it toward the unlighted fireplace grate inside her third-floor bedchamber. The paper bounced away and rolled beneath the washstand.

Stalking toward the wardrobe, he wrenched open the doors and yanked out the clothes she'd left behind, tossing them onto her neatly made bed. Shoes came next, which he chucked in a clatter onto the floor.

Nothing.

Crossing to the small chest where she kept nightgowns, petticoats and shifts, he rifled through them, flinging each atop her discarded gowns.

Nothing again.

Not so much as a receipt or a hint of anything important left behind, just her servant's attire and the lingering fragrance of her scent.

His jaw tightened, a muscle bulging in his cheek at the reminder of violets and the cipher she'd stolen from under his nose. She was a thief and a traitor and when he caught her—and catch her he *would*—he'd see to it she was tossed into the deepest, darkest gaol they could find.

For a moment he relished the thought of her behind bars, tears streaming down her face as she told him how sorry she was, begging his forgiveness and confessing her love.

Sinking abruptly onto the bed, he fought the shallow ache

in his chest. Picking up one of her shifts, he buried his face in the thin cotton and breathed her in.

Ah God, how could she have left me without a single word of good-bye? Of regret? Did I mean anything to her, or was I nothing more than a mark?

Stomach twisting, he looked out the dormer window at the growing dawnlight. He hadn't slept. How could he when she had played him so false? When she had duped him with the skill of a consummate actress, a heartless charlatan.

Clearly, that was exactly what she was.

He would have to tell Ned, of course, and he, in turn, the War Office. The breach was serious but not irreparable. He'd already been working on an advanced code to replace the one she'd stolen. He would have to work harder, faster to get it finished. Even so, the loss would prove costly in the short term, a setback that England and her allies could ill afford to suffer.

No, he'd lost the cipher, and it was his responsibility to get it back, or at least do his utmost to mitigate the damage. His first duty, therefore, was to track and locate Anne Greenway.

Assuming that was even her name.

Bitter gall rose inside him at the realization. He thought he'd known her, thought he understood her and that she felt the same for him. To think he'd been on the verge of offering her marriage. Him, the confirmed bachelor brought to his knees. Well, thank God for her timing before he'd made a complete fool of himself, before he'd shown her exactly how vulnerable he'd become to her practiced wiles.

So where had she gone?

To the north, possibly to Scotland, Aggies had speculated. On her character, she'd listed her last place of employment as the Isle of Skye. Given all the lies she'd undoubtedly told, however, that was probably one as well.

Another strong possibility was France. With the cipher

her goal, it was clear she had been planted in his household by the French. Now that the code was in her possession, had they smuggled her out of the country? After all, it would be nigh impossible to find her inside the war-torn country, especially without getting caught.

But it would be his pleasure to try, and worth every ounce of risk.

As he turned over the options as to her possible whereabouts, a conversation he and "Anne," for want of a better name, had had. Their words played inside his mind.

Where does your family live?

Ambleside, she'd answered in her lilting, musical voice. *It's a pretty place. Lush and green with deep blue lakes and rolling hills that look as if they could go on forever.*

Ambleside.

In that unguarded moment, could she have possibly been telling the truth? Such vivid descriptions as the one she'd provided didn't generally accompany falsehoods, particularly the sort conjured up on the spur of the moment. Had she revealed something real about herself in among all the lies and deceits she must have told?

The journey to the Lake District was two, maybe three days, hard riding from London. It would be a good place to start, and maybe he would get lucky. If he didn't, he would continue on to Skye and see what turned up there as well. In the meantime, Aggies and his men could continue to scout the docks and shipyards along the southern coast, hoping to find someone who'd seen a woman fitting his former housekeeper's description.

His lover as well.

He was glad of a sudden that she'd insisted on keeping their affair a secret. At the time, he hadn't cared, but now, he was relieved. He was even more relieved that he'd had no opportunity to tell his family of his plans to wed her.

Aware of the ring that sat like a curse inside his pocket, he withdrew the box and flicked open the lid. For a long moment, he stared, studying the stone, mourning his love for her, his loss, her betrayal.

She'd made him want things he'd never thought to want. She'd made him wish for a life with her that would last them all their days. She'd shown him the possibility of a future he'd never imagined he would ever desire.

Then she'd left and taken his heart with her.

But he was done wallowing in his misery. He wouldn't give her the satisfaction of caring anymore. He was a logical man, and as such, knew he would recover. He just prayed it didn't take him the rest of his life to do it.

Staring a moment longer at the bloodred stone that now left him cold, he snapped the lid shut and closed the door on his dreams.

Weary from the hair on the top of her head to the soles of her feet, Sebastianne trudged the last few yards to her father's cottage near the village of Montsoreau. Her heart gave an extra beat when she rounded a bend and saw the small, greyish white stone dwelling come into view. The last rays of afternoon sun rained over the house, splintering off the small glass panes into a thousand golden starbursts of light. The aging oak front door, with its faded white paint, looked no better than when she'd left. In fact, the house hadn't changed at all.

But I have, she thought, with a desolate sigh. *Will I ever stop thinking about Drake? Will I ever quit missing him?*

She frowned, not liking the answer.

But she was home at last, she told herself, and her family would welcome her with open arms. She needed their comfort now more than ever.

She walked past rows of wild pink rosebushes, which

turned the air sugary-sweet, then along the short, pebbled path. Reaching the front door, she stopped, hesitating to turn the knob.

Should she go in and surprise them, or knock? She'd had no way of sending a message ahead to let them know of her return, so they would not be expecting her. Still, knocking on the door of her family's home would feel odd, so she reached again and pushed it open.

Instead of the raucous cries and vociferous greetings she expected, she encountered only silence. The wide main room that served as both kitchen and living space stood empty. The deep stone fireplace was cold, the scarred pine-trestle table bare of its usual assortment of foodstuffs and dishes. The copper pots and pans that hung from the gnarled wooden rafters above the fireplace held an even deeper patina of green than she remembered. And the bundles of fresh herbs and lavender she'd gathered just before she had left still dangled upside down along the wide, main beam, looking dusty and unused.

Where are they? she wondered, as her stomach gave a queasy flip. Had Vacheau realized what she'd done and somehow gotten here before her? Surely that was impossible, since she'd traveled ceaselessly all the way from London four days ago. Or had one of his henchmen come for them? In England and unable to write, she had no way of knowing whether they were here or not. Perhaps Vacheau had deceived her and taken them away from the beginning.

Stop it, she told herself, gulping against the fist-sized lump lodged inside her throat. *You're assuming the worst before you even know if you have reason.*

She would walk to the village, she decided, and see if her brothers and father were there. It was quite likely they were. And if not, the villagers knew her. They would know the truth and relate it to her, whatever it might be.

Spinning on her heels she started toward the door. A rough scraping noise sounded outside. She froze dead in the center of the room as the handle began to turn.

The door opened, revealing a thin sprig of a boy with reddish brown hair that was in serious need of cutting and a pair of deep-set caramel-hued eyes. They widened in clear astonishment, his mouth dropping wide at the sight of her.

"Sebastianne!" he shouted, barreling across the room toward her.

She nearly lost her balance as he careened into her, his wiry arms locking like steel bands around her waist. *"Tu-es ici!"*

"Oui, I am here, Luc," she said, her words thick with the tears that sprang to her eyes. Enfolding him in her arms, she hugged him to her.

After a moment, she looked up and into the gaze of Julien, the older of her two brothers at twelve years—thirteen actually, since he'd had a birthday while she had been away. He remained unmoving, staring at her with far too much seriousness for a boy his age.

She held out an arm to him and smiled, still hugging Luc against her side. The battle Julien waged showed on his face; the man in him angry that she'd left, the boy happy at her return and ready to forgive. He took a single, jerky step forward, even his body uncertain and struggling.

Suddenly, as if something broke free inside him, he raced toward her with every bit as much speed as his sibling and threw himself into her arms.

Tears slid over her cheeks as she clutched him near, cradling them both. For a long moment, she stood in the three-way embrace, savoring the joy of reunion and the relief that no harm had come to her brothers as she'd feared.

"When you weren't here, I grew worried," she said in rapid French, the words sounding odd and strangely rusty on her tongue. "I thought perhaps you had gone. The kitchen doesn't look as if it's been used in some time."

"It hasn't," Julien volunteered, the old smile she remembered back on his face. "You know Papa cannot cook, and Luc and I burn everything. We almost caught the cottage on fire trying to make soup, and that's not an easy thing to do."

She laughed. "I am relieved the house and both of you are well. So where is Papa?"

"He will be here soon. We were at Madame Breton's for a meal. She says since her husband died in the war, the dishes she makes are too much for her to eat on her own. So she lets us share her table. I think she is just lonely and likes the company, Papa's in particular."

Sebastianne digested that nugget as she loosened her arms from around her brothers and let them step back. Luc, obviously unwilling yet to be parted, slipped his hand into hers.

She gave it a squeeze.

"Well, I am back and shall cook for you all again," she declared, deciding as she cast another glance around the room that the house needed a good cleaning as well.

Julien peered at her with his too-serious eyes. "So you're here to stay? You won't leave again?"

"No, never again," she said, determined that her promise would not be a lie.

After a moment, Julien relaxed, his lanky muscles visibly unwinding in a way that left him looking younger and more like the boy he still was.

There was a scraping noise on the threshold just then that drew her attention toward the door once again. Poised in the entrance stood a slender man of middling years, a pair of round wire glasses on his nose that gave him an owlish expression. He had a shock of long, thick grey hair that he kept tied back in a queue, an affectation that belonged to a bygone era, a way of life that had all but been swept aside by years of blood and violence.

"*Ma fille,*" he said gruffly. "You have come home."

"*Oui, Papa.*"

"And your cousin in Paris? She is well?"

Sebastianne lowered her gaze, thinking of the lie she had told him before her departure—the lie she had been forced to tell them all. She wished she could unburden herself, wished she could tell them everything—except perhaps of her love for Drake. Of that she would tell no one; some losses simply cut too deep to be shared.

"Cousin Paulette is as well as can be expected," she said, hating the necessity of her continued deception. *Dieu, but I am so weary of lying.*

Some glimmer of her anguish must have shown despite her attempt to hide it since her father sent her a look of concerned understanding. "It is never easy nursing the sick. I have missed you, child. We all have," he said, opening his arms wide.

And this time, it was her turn to run.

Releasing Luc's hand, she sped across the room and into the warmth and comfort of her father's strong arms.

And finally, she was home.

Chapter 25

Three days following his departure from London, Drake took to the village streets of Ambleside. A market town, whose origins traced all the way back to Roman and Viking times, it held flavors of both rural quaintness and burgeoning industrialism.

Drake began his search in the center of town, deciding to focus on the older generation of townsfolk who might have some memory of Anne's family, assuming she hadn't been lying about having once lived in the village. Spotting a grizzled old man seated outside one of the town's public houses, he approached.

"Pardon me," Drake said, "but I'm wondering if you can assist me. I am looking for a woman."

The man shot him a look out of curious grey eyes, the stem of a long-handled pipe tucked tight inside one withered cheek. "A woman, eh? Well, ain't we all lookin', at one time o' another." He cackled at his own remark, shifting the pipe to his other cheek as he coughed out a laugh.

Drake restrained his impatience. "No, not that sort of woman. A specific one in particular." Flipping open his notebook, he located the sketch he'd done of Anne all those weeks ago at the theater. An uncomfortable pang twisted like a blade in his chest as he gazed at the pencil rendering. He'd captured her likeness remarkably well, too well perhaps. Sternly, he pushed the sensation away and turned his attention back to the old man.

He held out the notebook. "Do you recall ever seeing her? Might you know her family? I am given to understand she is from this area. Her surname is Greenway."

The old man peered at the drawing. "Can't says as I do. Ne'er seen 'er and don't know no nobody by that name in these parts."

"You are certain?" Reaching into his pocket, Drake withdrew a pair of shillings and held them pointedly between his fingers.

Rather than reaching for them, the codger just stared. "Ye can put away yer coin. Won't get ye what yer looking for. Like I says, don't know 'er or 'ers. Wot she done anyway? Wot ye want 'er fer?"

Drake considered how best to answer. "She was in my employ and departed unexpectedly. I am trying to locate her."

A pair of thick white eyebrows went high although Drake couldn't tell if the other man was surprised or amused, or maybe both. "Nicked the silver, did she?"

"Not exactly."

"Weel, she's naught to me," the man declared, clicking his tobacco-stained teeth against his pipe stem. "Ye might try the magistrate, fancy gent like you, but he won't know naught either. He's only ever 'ome when it suits 'im and it don't suit 'im much."

Drake flipped the notebook closed, realizing he would get no further. "Yes, well, thank you for your help." *Or lack thereof,* he thought irritably.

"My pleasure," the old man called as Drake moved away. Grinning, the codger leaned over and spit, cackling as he put the pipe back in his mouth.

Determined to proceed, Drake walked on.

There were a large number of people gathered in the town center, all come to buy or sell the market wares. Walking among them with patient deliberation, he continued his search for information about Anne.

Her father and brothers, he quickly learned, were not members of the local community, and no one seemed to recognize his drawing of Anne. Obviously, she'd lied to him again, he realized, and this journey north amounted to nothing more than a wild-goose chase. He'd guessed as much, but he supposed it had been worth the attempt.

He finished questioning one last woman, a kindly-faced fruit seller, who'd beamed when he bought a pennyweight of her sweet cherries. Deciding he might as well admit defeat for now, he tucked his notebook back inside his coat pocket. He would start for Skye in the morning and see if that produced more satisfactory results.

"I hear ye've been askin' about the Greenways," said a quiet, feminine voice not far behind his right shoulder. Turning, he glanced down at a small, round-hipped woman attired in a well-made but faded brown cotton dress, who had a basket of vegetables hooked over one arm. She regarded him out of sharp, pale blue eyes that looked as if they never missed a trick.

"That's right," he told her. "Do you know them?"

She nodded, the lace edges of her cap fluttering around her face. "I did, but the last of the family moved away a good long while ago, near fifteen years ago, if I remember right."

Fifteen years!

He was still absorbing that sliver of information, when she continued on. "The squire died years afore that, of course, and his wife not long after. Terrible tragedy, them both going so soon after each other. The house and land passed to some distant cousin. Skinflint of a man, who sold it off before his relations were barely cold in their graves. That's why folks don't much think of the name now. Been more than twenty years since it all began."

Her information wasn't exactly to the point, but he would ask about the drawing just in case.

"I have a picture," Drake began, reaching into his coat pocket again for his notebook, "perhaps you might take a look—"

Her eyes twinkled with lively anticipation. "Certainly, yes, I'd be pleased to look. But first, why do we not continue our conversation over a spot of tea? So much more enjoyable than talking in a public square. I'm sure a fine gentleman such as yourself must be growing parched on a warm day like this, and I could do with a sit down about now. My joints, you understand, they plague me something terrible, and the marketing only makes them worse. My house is just along the way, not far at all."

Drake only barely kept his eyebrows from narrowing into a frown. "Thank you, ma'am, for your very kind offer, but I'm afraid my time here is limited. If you could just take a look—" Flipping open the cover, he displayed the drawing for her inspection.

She ignored it and gave him another cheery smile. "Pete at the hotel tells me you've taken a room for the night . . . Lord Byron is it?"

His brows drew down this time. This "Pete," whoever he might be, obviously had a wagging tongue. "No, I am Lord Drake. Byron is my family name."

Her cheeks pinked with excitement. "Byron. Like the poet? Are you a relation of his?"

"No. None at all."

"More to the better, I suppose." She sighed with a note of disappointment. "He does have such a dreadfully shocking and scandalous reputation."

So does my own family on occasion, Drake thought in silent amusement, deciding not to enlighten her despite the obvious delight it would bring her.

"Mr. Wordsworth is a far more respectable sort," she continued. "He's a resident here, did you realize? The family took up lodgings at Rydal Mount only this spring. Perhaps you are acquainted with him?"

"No, I fear I have not had the pleasure," Drake said, forcing himself to be patient. Although considering the indiscreet staff at the less-than-elegant hotel, perhaps he should apply to Mr. Wordsworth and his wife for a night's lodging. "Now, about the picture. I really must ask if you would take a look."

"Yes, yes, I shall. But tea first. Come along, my lord." Turning, she trundled off on legs that showed no apparent sign of the rheumatism from which she claimed to suffer. Aware that he wouldn't get any more information out of her unless he accepted her hospitality, however, he followed.

Twenty minutes later, he sat perched on a low, horsehair settee in her best parlor, watching as she fussed over the tea. If he didn't miss his guess, Miss Pruitt, as she'd introduced herself, was the town gossip, and he, her latest prize. Quite likely his visit would keep her telling stories about her brush with the nobility for a full year of Sundays. Nevertheless, as town gossip, she clearly knew everyone, and everything that had ever happened in this town.

Now, the trick was to get her to tell him if she recognized Anne.

With a smile, he accepted a china cup, took a polite sip. "Delicious."

She beamed and nudged the plate of cookies she'd offered twice before in his direction.

He took one and set it on his saucer untouched. "Back in the market square, you were telling me about the Greenways, and there was the drawing I mentioned that I hoped you might review." Placing his teacup and saucer to one side, he withdrew his notebook again. With firm deliberation, he opened it to the page that bore Anne's likeness. "Have you ever seen this woman?"

Clearly aware her stalling tactics were finally at an end, Miss Pruitt gave a tiny sigh and leaned forward. For a long moment, she studied the drawing. "No, my lord, I am afraid I have not."

Drake held back a growl, wondering if she'd made up the story about the Greenways in order to get him into her parlor.

"She is oddly familiar though," Miss Pruitt said after a moment, as she tapped a contemplative finger against her lips. "She reminds me rather strongly of Clara."

He stopped. "Clara? Clara who?"

"Clara Greenway. She was the squire's only child and caused quite the stir when she refused to accept the troth of her cousin. The sour-faced one I told you about, if you recall?"

He nodded, his interest suddenly riveted. "Yes, of course. Pray continue."

At his encouragement, she drew breath and eagerly went on. "Well, the cousin arrived right after the squire's untimely death, swooping in rather like a vulture to pick over the bones, some remarked at the time. He offered to let her remain in the family home if she would but marry him. Any sensible girl would have accepted, but not Miss Clara."

Miss Pruitt clacked her tongue with a mixture of admiration and disapproval. "She had fallen madly in love with some Frenchman, you see. An émigré of noble birth, who was sadly penniless, as so many of them were after the horriblc goings-on over there in that heathenish country. Imagine chopping off people's heads like that!" she added with horror-struck relish, her blue eyes popping wide.

Drake decided not to point out that France had once been viewed as the center of all civilized culture. Neither did he make mention of the fact that English history was littered with examples of Englishmen—and women who had lost their heads to the axman, although admittedly not for several decades.

"So Miss Greenway made an imprudent alliance," he stated.

"Precisely so!" Miss Pruitt told him with a vigorous nod, clearly delighted to have so attentive an audience. "More tea, my lord?"

Drake shook his head. "Thank you, but no. I am interested to hear the connection between Miss Greenway and the woman in this picture."

"Is it recent? The drawing, I mean."

"Yes," he confirmed. "Quite recent."

The spinster cast another accessing glance at the image. "I cannot say for certain, but based on the resemblance, particularly around the eyes, I wonder if she might be her daughter. Clara and her Frenchman had a little girl after their marriage, you know. The family lived here in Ambleside for several years before they left. Children change so much though as they age, it's hard to tell if this is her."

His heart pumped faster. "What was the child's name? Do you recall?"

"Mmm, let me see. It was something unusual. French, wouldn't you know." Picking up her teacup, she took a thoughtful sip. "It started with S but had a very English-sounding end. Let me see, what was that now."

Drake squeezed one hand into a fist.

"It was Sabatine," she said. "No, no wait, *Sebastianne*.

Yes, that's it, Sebastianne! Oh, I remember now. I used to call her little Miss Annie."

Sebastianne . . . Annie . . . could it be her? Could the child Miss Pruitt described be my Anne?

But not my Anne anymore, he reminded himself harshly. She'd lied to him, betrayed him, deserted him. Without knowing or caring, she'd taken his heart and twisted it like so much clay. But it had hardened since then, grown tough and resilient. She was nothing more to him now than a thief, a stranger, whom he'd sworn to track down and from whom he would demand restitution.

What kind he hadn't yet decided.

He forced his fingers to relax. "Can you recall her surname? You said Clara Greenway married and lived here for a time. How was she addressed?"

"Ah, it's all coming back." Miss Pruitt smiled and waggled a finger. "Miss Clara's married name was Calvière. Mrs. Clara Calvière. Vastly elegant, do you not think?"

"Vastly," he agreed in a somber tone.

So then, it would seem he was looking for a Sebastianne Calvière. Although if she had been telling the truth about being married, she would now bear another man's name.

Good God, what if the husband isn't really dead? What if she lied about that too?

His insides recoiled at the idea, both hands turning into fists this time. Force of will alone enabled him to relax his body again so that the spinster across from him wouldn't detect his inner turmoil.

He smiled. "You said the last of the Greenways left this area fifteen years ago. Where did Madame Calvière and her family go?"

"Madame Calvière? . . . oh, you mean Miss Clara. Yes, she and her family packed up and went to France. We all warned them not to go, that the trouble there wasn't done.

But her husband would insist. Said Napoleon was welcoming back the old émigrés, and he missed his home. Said he wanted to show them the beauty of France and raise his family there. Clara adored him, so she agreed."

Miss Pruitt broke off, a row of tiny lines forming between her brows. "I received a letter from her every now and then over the years. She was a kindly, polite young woman, who always respected her elders, even foolish spinsters like me. Had her letters for nearly six years, then all of a sudden they stopped. I haven't heard a word since then. Do you think she might have died?"

He met her sad blue eyes. "I do not know. Let us hope that is not the case."

Miss Pruitt's lower lip quivered briefly, her gaze sliding away. "Yes, let us hope."

"In her letters, did she say where they lived?"

She glanced up again. "Paris, for a time, I remember that quite plainly. She said their apartment in the city was burned, and they lost a great many of their possessions. She had two more children, sons."

Brothers? Drake thought. Anne . . . *Sebastianne*, he corrected, had mentioned having two younger siblings, both boys. The more he heard, the more the puzzle pieces fit together.

"Did they remain in Paris?"

He hoped not. Entering Paris undetected might prove extraordinarily difficult though not impossible.

She shook her head, the lace on her cap fluttered again. "No, she wrote in her last letter that they moved into the countryside. I am sorry, but I cannot remember the village."

Damn. Without the name of a town, there was a good chance his search would be hopeless, particularly as an Englishman skulking around inside an enemy nation. His French was good, but still, he was far from a native, and his

Parisian dialect would make him standout among the country folk. Still, there had to be a way to find her. He would just have to put his mind to the problem.

"If it would help, I still have the letter," Miss Pruitt offered in a helpful voice."

He stared at her. "What?"

"The letter. Her last one to me. Would you like to see it?"

A smile moved over his lips. "Yes, thank you. I most definitely would."

Chapter 26

*E*ight days after her return to France, Sebastianne had settled back into her old life—or nearly so, since nothing felt quite the same to her anymore. During the day, she smiled and laughed and tried to be the warm, loving daughter and sister she'd always been. But at night, when she was in her bedroom with no one there to see, a hollow emptiness stole through her. Sometimes the pain was so fierce it left her gasping, and she would press a fist to her mouth so no one else could hear.

She didn't cry, or at least not much; some wounds were simply too deep for tears. But she ached, and in her dreams she did cry, reaching out for Drake, who turned away from her with angry words and hate-filled eyes.

Then there was her constant worry about Vacheau. When would he realize what she'd done? When would he appear to demand the rest of the code?

On the morning after her return, she'd left the house to go shopping in the village. But she'd taken a detour first, making her way into one of the many troglodyte caves scattered throughout the area. There was one long-abandoned cave inside a high cliff face not far from the house that she'd explored quite often when she was younger. Its entrance lay concealed behind a thicket of wild rosebushes and trailing vines that discouraged most people from venturing inside. Beyond, however, lay a fascinating arrangement of ancient tunnels carved of fossil-laden tuffeau stone that provided any number of clever places in which one could conceal an object. It was into one of these hidey-holes that she'd placed the cipher, wrapped safely inside a protective length of oil-cloth.

Then she'd begun to wait.

And wait.

But so far he had not come, and in her heart of hearts she wished he never would. Having decided it was safer for her family to remain in ignorance about what she'd done, she said nothing to them, not even her father. Instead, she left him to his books and his ideas, sending him off with a smile to the small outbuilding that served as his workshop and library. Which left her with her brothers inside the house most of the day, particularly now when there were no lessons at the small village school.

"I am finished," Julien declared, as he laid his fork across his empty breakfast plate. "May I go visit Marc for a while?"

Marc Rancour was a nearby farmer's son and Julien's closest friend.

"Me too!" piped Luc, not wishing to be left out of any excitement.

Julien groaned aloud and rolled his eyes.

She gave Julien a quelling look that told him to be kind to his brother, or else. As for his request, what she wanted was to keep them locked inside the house and never let them out of her sight. But they were growing, energetic boys, and she couldn't keep them prisoner no matter how much she wished she might. Besides, if she refused, she would be compelled to give an explanation, and that she did not wish to do. Vacheau had never harmed them in the past, she told herself, so surely they would be safe enough in her neighbor's care for the day.

"*Oui*, you and Luc may visit," she said, "but promise you'll go straight there, no detours, and stay close to the Rancours' house. I don't want you boys wandering off or getting into trouble. And don't speak to strangers."

"What strangers?" Julien piped. "No one new ever comes here."

Sebastianne scowled, wishing that were always true. "Be that as it may, should you encounter anyone you don't know, you are to say nothing to him and go find Madame Rancour. Is that understood?"

Julien gave her an appraising look, then shrugged. "We'll be careful. No strangers. May we leave now?"

Despite her concern, she smiled and gave him a nod.

Shoving back his chair, he sprang to his feet. Luc followed his older brother's example, and as if a wind had risen under their feet, they sailed across the room and out the door.

She stood, arms crossed for a long moment before leaning over to pick up their plates.

Finished washing the last of the breakfast dishes some minutes later and setting them aside to dry, she wiped her damp hands on her apron. Crossing to the small larder next to the kitchen, she gathered the onions, carrots and potatoes that would form the basis for that night's soup.

Yesterday, the village butcher had offered her a prime cut of beef and some bones that would add flavor and substance to the soup. He'd also asked her to walk out with him after church on Sunday. She had accepted the bones, paid for the beef, and uncategorically refused his attempt at courting. The last thing she needed just then was to give even a hint of encouragement to any would-be suitors. She wasn't interested in a husband and wanted to make that quite plain.

Of course, if Drake had asked me . . . she thought with a wistful ache. But she would never see Drake again, and he would never ask her to be his wife.

In need of herbs and a few of the tomatoes growing fresh in the small garden at the back of the cottage, she slipped a small knife into her apron pocket. Fitting a simple straw bonnet onto her head, she hooked a shallow woven basket over one arm and left the house. Papa, should he decide to emerge from his workshop, would know where to look for her.

The July sun beat down—hot, fat and yellow. Glad for the shade that her hat provided, she reached the herb bed and knelt to cut what she would need for the cook pot. The delicate sweetness of thyme sent forth a succulent perfume as she laid the stems with their tiny green leaves into her basket. Next, she cut fragrant springs of marjoram and tender tufted branches of parsley.

She moved on to check the ripeness of the tomatoes, plucking two that weighed down their stems like a pair of fist-sized rubies. Deciding to inspect the progress of her *haricot vert* vines in hopes of picking a mouthful of tender beans to go with that night's beef dish, she walked farther along the rows.

Suddenly, a shadow loomed over the tilled earth like an eclipse that blocked out the sun. Peering upward from beneath her bonnet brim, she gave a shudder as she met the cold, brutal gaze of the man whose arrival she'd been both expecting and dreading.

Her hand tightened instinctively around the knife. Her day of reckoning had finally arrived.

"Where is it?" Vacheau demanded without preamble. Grabbing her upper arm, he gave her a rough, little shake. "Did you really imagine I wouldn't find out what you'd done? You ought to have run, you know. You ought to have had the sense to hide while you still had the chance. By the time I'm through with you, you'll wish you'd found a hole somewhere and buried yourself in it too deep to find."

Unflinchingly, she met his gaze. "I had no wish to run. Or to hide. I knew you would find me. In fact, I was counting on it."

His eyes widened in clear surprise. "Really? Then apparently you aren't as intelligent as I assumed."

"Are your threats supposed to frighten me? If so, I'm afraid you'll have to do far better. Now, take your hands off me, *coquin,* or it will be more than herbs and tomatoes I slice open with this knife." To emphasize her statement, she lifted the blade in her hand a few significant inches higher.

He glared for another long moment, then abruptly let her go. A laugh rippled from his throat, his lips pulled back from his teeth in a smile that didn't reach his flat, dark eyes.

Shark's eyes.

She suppressed the need to shiver again, determined to let none of her inner emotions show.

"You've certainly grown brave since last we met," he mused. "Stealing seems to have made you bold, or don't you care about your family's welfare anymore?"

"I care about them more than ever, which is why you would do well to stay as far away from those I love as possible."

Her words drew a fresh laugh from him.

"Oh, I wouldn't be so amused if I were you," she stated with apparent calm. "I'm the only one now who can give you what you want, and if you put so much as a scratch on my brothers or my father, you'll never get it. Your superiors won't like your returning empty-handed, now will they?"

His jaw tightened. Plainly, his superiors were displeased with him already.

"You see," she continued, "I did take the time to hide something. I've put the solution to the cipher in a place you'll never find. There are a million and one spots around here where a person can conceal a prized object. What are the chances of your locating that particular place all on your own?"

"Not bad if I torture the location out of you."

She shrugged as if his threat didn't made her insides twist with horror. "You're welcome to try, but it will do you no good. You see, I realize that once you've got the entire code in hand, you'll slaughter all of us anyway, so I have nothing to gain from confessing to you."

"What of your brothers? Your father? They might not have your . . . fortitude."

"No, they don't. Which is the reason why I've told them nothing of what I've done. They don't know anything about my keeping the solution to the cipher, so brutalizing them will gain you nothing."

"You might be lying," he said through his teeth.

"I might." She met his serpentine gaze, her own absolutely unwavering. "But I'm not."

He glared, frustration rolling off him in almost palpable waves. "Then what is it you want? What do you hope to gain with this foray into blackmail?"

My freedom, she thought. *My family's freedom. For now and forever.*

"I want a writ of safe passage, signed and sealed by the Emperor himself. I want Napoleon's hand-sworn assurance that I and my family are free to live in peace, or should we wish to do so, to leave the country with no restrictions or conditions set upon us."

Vacheau laughed again, this time with genuine amusement. "A letter of safe passage from Napoleon? You don't ask for much."

"I ask for a very great deal," she said with complete seriousness. "Those are my terms. Bring me the Emperor's writ, and I will give you the working cipher. Otherwise, you can try to obtain it again on your own. I have to warn you, though, that I doubt you'll be able to insert a spy into Lord Drake's household again. Fool him once . . . but I assume you know the rest of the saying."

His fingers clenched, flexing at his sides as if he were imagining her neck between them. "I should kill you for this."

"You could, but it still won't get you the cipher."

He shook, his rage so great she could see veins pop out on his forehead. "I shall return."

"I shall be here."

His gaze black as death, he spun on his heel and stalked away.

She stood motionless, watching long after he had disappeared from view. Only then did she make her way to the small wooden bench tucked against the side of the house. Sinking down, the basket forgotten in her numb fingers, she let herself shake.

Four days later, Drake arrived on the outskirts of Montsoreau. He took care to avoid the village center, just as he'd taken care to steer clear of any large enclaves of people on his long journey through France. Not that he hadn't encountered the occasional farmer or innkeeper on his way, but in spite of his more-than-passable French, he saw no reason to invite undue scrutiny. He'd already deflected more than one query about his "Parisian" accent and where and why it was he was traveling. To satisfy the curious ones, he'd concocted a tale about being on his way to visit a sick aunt, a story which explained both his "foreign" manners and obvious lack of familiarity with the countryside.

So far he'd been lucky to avoid encounters with any authorities, except for one afternoon at a coaching inn where a band of soldiers had taken seats in the tavern where he'd been having a meal. Slipping quickly outside to the stables, he'd waited for his horse before riding away without inviting their notice.

Now finally, he was in Montsoreau, where Clara Greenway's letter said she and her family had settled. He hoped they still lived there. He hoped her daughter Sebastianne was *his* Anne.

And if she was? What then?

He would decide when he saw her. He would decide, when she once again stood before him, exactly how he would claim his retribution.

For her lies.

For her thievery.

For her betrayals.

Walking along a path on the outskirts near the village, he surveyed the tree-lined fields, his boots crunching quietly against the gravel. A bird warbled out a jaunty tune, a pair of bees buzz-buzzing in syncopated harmony as they droned lazily from one flower to the next. In other circumstances, he would have found it a pleasant scene and taken enjoyment in the clear July day, but his reasons for being here in France, secretly and in a time of war, made it rather difficult to relax. He hadn't let down his guard once since leaving England, not even when he slept. He would need to keep up his vigilance here as well, particularly since he would have to approach one of the houses soon to ask for directions.

He'd walked only a couple more yards when an odd rustling noise drew his attention to a nearby stand of bushes. In their depths roamed a boy of nine, or perhaps ten, years of age, his golden brown hair glinting in the sun as he beat the foliage with a stick. Clearly unaware he had company, he grumbled something under his breath and gave the bush another savage swipe.

"*Bonjour,*" Drake said in his most casual-sounding French. "Are you hunting for something in that bush or simply annoyed with it?"

The boy stopped and stared at him, the stick motionless in his hand. He looked Drake up and down appraisingly. "*Non,* the bush has done nothing. I'm just angry, that's all."

"Ah. Bad day," Drake said sympathetically.

The child nodded, his lower lip thrusting forward in a pout. "Julien and Marc wouldn't let me go with them to climb the cliffs. I'll get hurt, they said, and land them in trouble. But I wouldn't! I'm a good climber." Raising the stick high, he brought it down again on the bushes. "They aren't even allowed, you know," he confided mulishly. "They're not supposed to climb the cliffs either."

"Your brothers?" Drake asked, tucking his thumbs into his pockets.

"Julien is. Marc's his best friend. They don't want me around 'cause they say I'm a pest and spoil all their fun. I'm not a pest or a tattle."

Drake concealed a smile. "That's the trouble with older brothers and their friends. They can be mean and unfair sometimes. I should know, since I have three older brothers."

The boy's stick fell quiet again. "Three? Wow." He scuffed a foot against a clod of turned earth, then mashed it down with the sole of his shoe. "I wish I could go to the village and see my friends, but I'm not allowed right now."

"Oh? Why not?"

"My sister says it's not safe, that there are bad men around because of the war."

"It sounds like your sister is a very wise woman," Drake stated, his interest piqued. Could this boy be one of Anne's young brothers? She'd told him she had two. Could luck have led Drake directly to her doorstep?

The child nodded. "She says I'm supposed to stay close to home and not talk to strangers." With those words, his eyes bulged, and he clapped a hand over his mouth, clearly realizing his error.

"I wouldn't worry," Drake said soothingly. "I'm sure she can't have meant me since your sister and I are acquainted."

"You are?" the boy said, lowering his hand to his side.

Drake nodded. *At least I believe we are,* he thought, deciding suddenly to put his hypothesis to the test. "Her name is Sebastianne, is it not?"

The boy nodded again, confirming Drake's suspicions.

So I have found her. But is Sebastianne the woman I know as Anne Greenway or not?

"And you must be Monsieur Calvière," he said, taking another calculated risk.

A giggle rippled from the child. "I'm Luc!"

"I'm Drake." Leaning forward, he extended a hand. "It is a pleasure to meet you, Luc."

An irrepressible smile moved over the boy's lips, clearly flattered to be treated in such an adult fashion. "You too, sir," he said as he took Drake's hand to shake.

"Now that we've been properly introduced, we are no longer strangers."

Luc thought that bit of logic over for a minute, then relaxed as if they'd known each other for a lifetime. "The house isn't far. Do you want to come and see Sebastianne now?"

"Yes," Drake said darkly. "I would like that."

Leading the way, the boy began to chatter with great animation about his family. Listening attentively, Drake followed.

Chapter 27

Turning away from the outdoor well, Sebastianne picked up the rope handle of the wet wooden bucket and made her way into the house, taking care not to spill the freshly drawn water inside. Part of it she would use to prepare that evening's meal, the other portion for cleaning up as she went.

She had the house to herself for the afternoon. The boys were outside playing until dinner since it was impossible to keep them cooped up inside, as much as she wished she might. As for Papa, he was in his workroom as usual, poring over stacks of books and journals as he contemplated his next theorem.

She was glad her family was content and blissfully unaware of the latest devil's bargain she'd struck and the danger hanging over them all. There was nothing they could do, and worrying Papa and the boys would gain them nothing but anxious days, and nights of lost sleep. The gamble had been hers to take and the fear a burden she rightly carried on her own.

As for her own worry, she did her best to push it aside,

especially around the others. In the days since her encounter with Vacheau, she'd heard nothing. Then again, she supposed his silence was only to be expected considering the magnitude of her demands.

He must still be seething, she mused with a pinch of inner satisfaction.

Nevertheless, she could take no real pleasure from the knowledge nor find solace, not even in sleep. When it was done, and her family was safe and free, only then would she be able to let down her barriers, only then would she have time to mourn for all she'd been through, for all she had lost.

And who.

I shall not think of him, she told herself sternly, ignoring the ironic fact that she thought of him every day, every hour, and often every minute too.

Setting down the water bucket, she went to check the loaves of bread dough she'd tucked into a draftless corner to rise. Satisfied with their progress, she took up the linen towel full of unshelled green peas that had been a gift that morning from Madame Breton. Sebastianne had returned her neighbor's generosity with an invitation to join the family for supper this Sunday, which Madame had happily accepted.

The rare treat of fresh peas, however, would be just for her and the boys and Papa. A boiled chicken, potatoes, and freshly baked bread with butter would complete the meal. Taking a seat at the wide kitchen table, she began shelling peas into an earthenware bowl.

One minute slid into two, then three, as she worked with quiet efficiency. Her head was bent over her task, her mind wandering to places it shouldn't go, when the drumming of running feet broke the stillness.

"Wipe your shoes on the mat," she called without looking up, recognizing her brother's footfalls. The boys were forever tracking all manner of dirt and debris into the house, particularly when they returned from playing outside. She waged a constant battle to keep the house clean and neat.

"Do I need to wipe my shoes as well?" a deep, hauntingly familiar voice inquired.

Her head came up, peas flying out of their shell to scatter wildly across the floor. Heat rushed through her veins, and her heart gave a single, painful thump.

It cannot be, she thought, not believing her eyes as she drank in the sight of him.

Drake.

He was everything she remembered and more, his presence filling the small room with an energy that made all the rest seem insignificant. He looked as if he'd been traveling hard, his plain tan jacket, white shirt and trousers far from aristocratic. He was less precisely groomed than she was used to seeing him, his chestnut hair tousled around his head, a day's growth of beard darkening the angular line of his jaw. Yet he was unbearably handsome in a way that made her ache, his face so dear she longed to rush up and into his arms.

Instead, she sat frozen, unable to move or speak.

He met her stunned gaze, his own eyes burning like emerald fire. "Hello, Anne," he said in perfect, mellifluous French. "Or should I say *Sebastianne.*"

Blood drained from her face, her skin turning cold, her fingers numb.

Mon Dieu, he knows. And he's found me. But how?

Luc chose that moment to dive down to collect the wayward peas, scooping up a handful to toss back into the bowl. With a kind of absurd distraction, she decided there was no harm done since the vegetables would be washed before being cooked.

"Look who I met on the path," her brother chimed in

happy, innocent tones. "Your friend, Monsieur Drake, has come to visit us."

She forced a smile. "Yes, so I see."

How had he come to meet her brother and what had he been saying to the boy? Monsieur Drake indeed!

"Luc, I haven't had a chance to check the coop for eggs this afternoon. Would you take the basket and collect what the hens have laid?"

Luc appeared momentarily mutinous, as if he knew he'd miss some interesting bits of conversation if he departed. But he was a kind, generous child at heart and never liked to gainsay her, even when it went against his wishes.

"*Mais oui, bien sûr*," he said before crossing to pick up the egg basket. As he headed for the door, he paused, turning toward Drake. "You will still be here when I return, *n'est-ce pas*?"

"Yes," Drake said.

"We shall see," Sebastianne said at the same moment.

Drake arched a brow at her remark.

Apparently satisfied by Drake's response, Luc hurried from the house. The instant he was gone, Sebastianne wished she hadn't asked him to go, suddenly aware just how alone she was with Drake. At least she was seated, since she didn't think her legs would have held her upright.

"Why are you here?" she whispered. "H-How did you find me?"

Drake crossed his arms. "I believe we both know the answer to your first question, but we'll leave that for the moment. As for finding you, I had your mother's help."

Her lips parted. "*Ma mère*, but she's . . . how?"

"You oughtn't to have told me your family was from Ambleside. I paid a visit and had a most illuminating conversation with one of the residents there, a Miss Pruitt."

Sebastianne frowned and shook her head.

"Don't remember her? Well, she remembers you and your family. Apparently she and your mother exchanged a few letters, one of which mentioned the name of this village. After that, it was simply a matter of following the trail."

Mon Dieu, undone by Maman from beyond the grave.

Then what he'd said truly sank in, along with the knowledge that he was in France, where he shouldn't be, where his very presence put him in jeopardy.

Abruptly, she came to her feet, wringing her hands together. "You ought not to have come, Drake. Our countries are at war, in case you haven't noticed. What if you're caught?"

"Oh, I won't be caught," he said roughly. "As for my presence, I've come to take you back."

Her pulse leapt, and for one crazy instant she imagined him braving capture as he crossed France because he missed her and wanted her, because he couldn't stand the loss of their being apart.

But those were her emotions. That was how she felt, not he.

Drake had come here for one reason and one reason alone.

Revenge.

Reaching out, he grabbed her arms and drew her near, his voice lowering to a harsh murmur. "How could you have done it? How could you have stolen from me? Lied and betrayed me? Did you think I'd do nothing after what you did? Did you imagine I'd just let you go. If you knew me at all, you'd have realized that I'd never rest. That I would hunt you to the ends of the earth and back."

But that was exactly what she'd thought. That he would let her go, that he would have no choice because he wouldn't be able to find her, would have no clue as to her real identity. So why had she been so foolish as to give him that clue? On some subconscious level had she given him the knowledge he needed in order to track her down on purpose? Had some secret part of her wanted him to find her no matter where it might lead.

"You don't understand, Drake. I had no choice but to betray you," she pleaded.

"No choice? That's rich. You're a liar and a spy, and I'm going to see to it that justice is served."

"Please, let me explain."

"Explain what? That you used and deceived me? That everything about you is a lie, even your name. *Mrs. Greenway*," he sneered.

"I couldn't tell you who I really was. I wasn't allowed."

"Not allowed? By whom? Your husband? Are you even a widow or was that a lie too?"

She blanched again. "Yes, I'm a widow and don't bring him into this."

"Why not, when you had no difficulty putting his name aside when it was convenient? What is your real name anyway, since Greenway came from your mother?"

"Dumont," she murmured. "I am Madame Dumont."

"Well, *Madame Dumont*, the time of reckoning is upon you."

Her ribs squeezed with a pain that was both sorrow and regret. "That day has been upon me from the moment I left this cottage last spring. My fate was written from that time on. Now, please let me go, Drake. There are things I need to tell you."

"What things? More lies? More manipulations?" He pulled her closer, crushing her breasts against the hard warmth of his chest. "I've had enough of those." Reaching up, he laid a palm against her face and locked his gaze on hers. "Was any of it real? Or was your seduction strictly for your cause and nothing more?"

"No," she said, trembling in his grasp. "I never meant for us to become lovers. It just . . . happened."

His eyelids grew heavy, his gaze moving to her mouth as if he wanted to kiss her. Her blood beat faster, love and longing rising inside her in spite of all the lies and enmity between them.

He bent his head.

"Who the hell are you and what are you doing with my sister?" demanded an angry voice.

Sebastianne startled and looked across the room to find Julien standing just inside the doorway, his hands clenched at this sides. Drake loosened his hold but did not release her as he too turned to gaze at her brother.

"I asked you a question, *monsieur,*" Julien stated in a voice that was far more adult than his thirteen years. "I demand to know why you are in our home and what you are about, molesting my sister."

Sebastianne leaned closer to Drake. "Please say nothing," she whispered. "He isn't involved and doesn't know where I've been or what I've done. I beg you not to tell him or Luc. They're only boys."

Their gazes met again, Sebastianne pleading silently for his forbearance. Perceptible only to her, Drake gave a faint nod of agreement. Slowly he loosened his grip.

Exhaling in relief, she stepped away, then forced a smile. "Julien, what are you thinking to say such things? You have misread the situation entirely. This gentleman is a friend, and he and I were merely exchanging a greeting."

Julien stared, looking less than convinced.

"Come and say hello," she encouraged. "And put away that cross look since it is far from welcoming. Julien, let me introduce you to my friend, Lor—that is . . . I mean—"

"Byron's the name," Drake interrupted, easily covering up her near use of his title. "Drake Byron."

While it was true that aristocrats weren't hunted or as reviled as they had been during the years of the Terror, they were still unusual in France. Even their father, who had come from noble blood, no longer used his title, going by plain Monsieur Calvière now.

Walking forward, Drake held out a hand. "It is good to meet you. Sebastianne has spoken often of you and your family."

Julien did not take his hand. "She hasn't spoken of you. Who are you? Where did you meet my sister?"

"Paris," Sebastianne said quickly. "Monsieur Byron was in the city this spring while I was there helping poor Cousin Paulette. He was most kind to us. We even went to a balloon ascension one afternoon."

She glanced at Drake and caught the trace of amusement in his eyes at her embellishment of the truth.

Julien's fists relaxed slightly, an expression of begrudging interest on his face. "You didn't tell me you'd seen balloons," he said half-accusingly to Sebastianne. "I should love to see one fly."

"A friend of mine owns a balloon," Drake said. "Perhaps someday you will have a chance to take a ride."

Julien's features turned rhapsodic, as if such an experience would be a dream come true.

"Well, that will be a while since trips to Paris don't grow on trees," Sebastianne said. "In the meantime, why do you not wash up, and I shall make you some tea and a snack."

"I'm back with the eggs," Luc announced, entering the house like a small burst of wind. "Did I hear you say something about a snack? I'd like one too. I'm starving."

"Wash up too then, and I'll make you something light that won't ruin supper," she told him.

"Jam sandwiches?" he asked hopefully.

She smiled and took the basket of eggs from his grasp. "That might be arranged."

"Make some for Monsieur Drake as well," Luc declared with a smile. "Are you not famished from your travels, sir?"

Suddenly Drake did look a bit road weary. "I could do with a repast, if your sister would be so kind."

"Did I hear you mention food?" a new voice said, her father coming through the rear door that led to his workshop in the backyard. "It's been ages since breakfast."

Sebastianne turned in time to watch him register Drake's presence.

"And who might you be, *monsieur*?" her father said, tipping his iron grey head to one side in curious inquiry. "I do not believe we have been introduced."

"This is Monsieur Drake," Luc piped helpfully.

"Not Drake," Julien corrected in a superior tone. "Monsieur Byron. Drake is his first name."

Luc shot him a nasty look and opened his mouth to argue.

But their father spoke first, his gaze fixed on the other man. "Byron? Drake Byron?"

"Yes, sir," Drake said.

"The mathematician and inventor?" Her father shot out his hands, clasping one of Drake's in his own for a resounding shake. "I am Auguste Calvière, and it is an honor to have such an esteemed mind in my home."

"Calvière?" Drake said. "The theorist? My God, I should have realized as soon as I saw the name. Of course, it all makes sense now."

Her father smiled again. "Does it? Well, good, good. But come, we must talk. Sebastianne, that tea, if you please." Taking Drake by the elbow, he steered him toward the table. "So tell me, sir, whatever are you doing here? There's a war on, or have you not heard?"

Chapter 28

Nearly an a hour later, with their light repast finished, Sebastianne sent the boys off to do a few chores, while her father drifted back to his workshop with promises from Drake that he would join him there soon. Clearing a forgotten plate and cup from the table, Drake joined Sebastianne where she stood across the room washing dishes in a bucket of hot, soap water.

He handed her the china. "How long has he been this way?" he asked in quiet English.

She rubbed a cloth over a plate, not pretending to misunderstand. "Since Maman passed," she replied, also in English. "Although it's been a gradual change. In most respects Papa is quite lucid, in others he's . . . well, he likes to live in his own world. The real one, I think, is simply too hard for him to face, especially this past year."

Drake took a moment to consider her words. "He was brilliant in his day. I remember reading his work at university."

She shot him a look, then turned to dunk the plate in clean water. "He's still brilliant, just not as focused as he used to be. He's working on prime-number theory at the moment. It would be a great kindness if you would consult with him a bit. It would . . . it would make him happy."

"Prime-number theory? It sounds as if you speak with some familiarity."

She shrugged and washed a cup. "Papa taught me what he could, and I understand a fair amount of mathematics. But I'm no theoretical mathematician. I haven't the patience for it or the singular turn of mind."

He couldn't help but laugh. "Is that what it is? My family calls it drifting off and not paying attention."

"But you are paying attention, just not to them."

She smiled, and he smiled back.

His chest tightened, nerve endings humming with sudden awareness. She looked so lovely, even in a faded, brown cotton dress with her hair pinned haphazardly around her face. If he let himself, he could drown in her whiskey-colored eyes, die for a taste of her sweet, strawberry pink lips.

His brows drew into a scowl, and he glanced away. How could he still want her after everything she'd done? How could he stand here laughing and talking as though everything were fine? As though she hadn't lied and betrayed him and ripped out his heart?

"I wondered how you knew," he said gruffly.

Her hands paused in the water. "Knew?"

"How you knew exactly what to look for, that you chose the right equation among all the other equations in the safe."

Slowly, as if she were taking particular care, she scrubbed and rinsed a cup and set it aside to dry. "I told you, I know enough to understand what I'm looking at. I just can't originate it." She washed another dish. "Now it's my turn. How did you know?"

"Know what?"

"That I'd made a copy of the cipher? I was very careful to

make sure I replaced the original exactly where I'd found it."

His smile returned, wry this time. "You did, and very likely I would never have known it had been copied if not for one thing."

Her hands fell still and she met his gaze. "Yes?"

"Violets. The paper smelled like violets. Like you."

Her lips parted in silent astonishment, then slowly curved upward. "Well, I guess I'm not so clever at this spying game after all. Or maybe part of me wanted to be caught, considering how much I hated doing it."

An aching sensation burned in his chest. "Did you? If that's true, then why did you do it?" he demanded harshly. "Was it for the money?"

She gave a hollow laugh and set the last dish aside to drain. Picking up a towel, she dried her hands. "What money? Does it look as if we live in fine style here? Believe me, if there were any money, I wouldn't be washing dishes out of a bucket."

His jaw tightened. "Then why did you do it? Or are you a true believer in Napoleon's cause?"

She flung the towel aside with a disdainful toss. "I don't care a jot for his cause, whatever it may be. All I can see is that he's brought war and destruction to France—men, women and children whose lives have been torn apart by hardship and loss and misery. I hate the Emperor as much as you do, even if I still love my country."

"England is your country as well, at least on your mother's side."

"*D'accord,* but Maman is gone, and Papa's life is here. My brothers have never known anything else. This is their home. You want to know why I did it? For them. I did it all for them. Now, if you're done with your interrogation, I have supper to prepare."

"Anne—" He reached out and took hold of her arm.

She tugged herself away. "*Sebastianne.* I'll thank you to call me by my proper name."

"Very well, Sebastianne."

"Now, go visit Papa. He, at least, will enjoy your company. As for tonight, you can bed down in the stable since it's too much of a risk for you to stay in the village. There would be talk, even if you weren't a foreigner. In the morning, you can leave."

He stepped nearer, her sweet, clean scent coming to his nostrils. "I have no intention of leaving, not without you."

"Then you're doomed to be disappointed since I'm not going anywhere with you. Nor can you compel me. All I need do is tell them in the village that an English spy is in my house, and you'd be hauled off in an instant."

"You could reveal my presence, it's true," he mused aloud. "But you won't."

Her chin tilted upward. "How can you be so sure? After all, I betrayed you once, why not again?"

He met her gaze, searching for the truth in her golden brown eyes. After all, she was right. How could he trust a word she said?

"Because if you wanted to turn me in," he observed, "you'd have done it already." Reaching up, he curved a hand around the back of her neck, his thumb stroking under her hair.

Her eyelids notched lower. "I just haven't had time. Once you're with Papa, I'll be away to the village to tell them you're here."

If he were smart, he would take her statement at face value. He was a fool to believe she would do anything but use and deceive him, and yet he sensed there was more to her actions than he yet knew. She said she'd taken the cipher for her family. But at whose behest? Someone had planted her in his home, he knew that much. Someone influential had gone to a great deal of trouble to arrange her employment. What else had they done to get their way? Suddenly he wanted answers more than revenge.

He carefully tightened his fingers, holding her in place. "You won't tell a soul about me."

A shiver ran through her, air soughing breathlessly from her lips. "No, I won't."

And he believed her.

"As for my sleeping arrangements," he said, smiling, "I can think of far more appealing accommodations."

A flush rose on her face, and she tugged against his grip. "You are not sharing my bed."

He brushed his thumb against her nape. "Shall I not?"

"No," she stated firmly. The effect was ruined, however, when another tremor ran through her body. "Go away, Drake."

His smile widened. "For now. Be warned that our conversation isn't over. We have a great deal more to discuss."

"In that, you are right. Now release me. The boys will be back anytime."

At the reminder, he lowered his hand and stepped away.

He would go see her father, and while he was there, take a few minutes to contemplate everything he'd just learned, including the fact that, fool that he was, he still wanted Sebastianne.

"*Vous êtes brilliant,* Lord Drake!" Auguste Calvière declared from where he sat behind the desk in his workshop. "That was precisely the suggestion I've been needing."

Drake inclined his head, glad he had been able to help the older man, whose work was still impressive despite his mental retreat from the world.

"What luck that you could visit now." Calvière stood and crossed to a cabinet on the far side of the room. Opening a door on the cabinet, he withdrew a bottle and a pair of small glasses. "I have so little opportunity these days to consult with colleagues," Calvière continued as he bustled back to his desk, bounty in hand. "It's all but impossible to keep up a reliable correspondence with one's peers. They read everything, you know, *la militaire*. Like a pack of ferrets, nosing in everyone's business. Have you not found that to be true, *monsieur,* even on your side of the sea?"

Actually, Drake supposed he had, aware that it had been slow and frustrating trying to maintain relationships with fellow mathematicians and scientists in countries other than England. As for the military reading his letters, he doubted they had the time or the nerve, especially considering his connections to the War Office. Then again, if some junior clerk wanted to snoop into his professional correspondence, Drake could only pity him since he doubted that the man would have enough knowledge to understand more than every third word.

Calvière pulled the cork from the bottle and poured two glasses of what gave every indication of being brandy. He slid one glass across the desk to Drake. "Glad my girl's back safe and sound," he said. "I worried about her while she was away, alone in Paris with only her sick cousin." His thin grey eyebrows drew together on his forehead like a pair of diagonal lines. "Funny that I don't recall having a cousin Paulette, but Sebastianne swears we do, so it must be true."

He smiled, displaying teeth that were straight but faintly yellowed with age. "My pride and joy, Sebastianne. Never was there a better girl. Smart, you know, with a head for numbers. Sad she wasn't born male. Oh, the wonders she might have wrought. Alas, neither Julien nor Luc has the gift. No talent for mathematics beyond the ordinary, though not many do, I suppose."

Calvière shook his head with regretful introspection

while Drake found himself thinking that despite Sebastianne's intelligence and abilities, he was very glad she had not been born a boy. He liked her exactly the way she was.

"Drink, drink," the older man encouraged, pointing to the glass sitting untouched before Drake. "I've been keeping this for a special occasion."

Drake hadn't realized this was a special occasion. Then again, perhaps Calvière was right, since it wasn't every day he secretly crossed into enemy territory and spent time with a man who had once been an idol of his. Lifting the brandy glass, he took a swallow, finding it to be an excellent vintage.

"So you met my girl in Paris, correct?"

Drake paused, considering the truth of where and how he and Sebastianne had met. "In the city, yes."

"I'm glad she had a man such as you around, not like that other one." Calvière's lips curled into a sneer. "He's a bad sort. Came sniffing around here just before she left to take care of her cousin."

Drake's fingers tightened against the glass in his hand. "What man is this?" he asked, careful to keep his voice calm.

"Same one that was here a few days ago." Calvière frowned. "Sebastianne was in the garden gathering vegetables, and the boys were off playing. Everything was quiet, then I heard voices, hers and his, arguing. I only caught bits and pieces of what they said, but enough."

"What were they saying?"

"He wanted something, something she was supposed to have given him. She told him she'd hidden it, and that she wouldn't hand it over unless he gave her something else in return."

"What kind of something?"

"Don't know," Calvière said, glancing at Drake for a moment before furtively looking away. "I couldn't hear that part. I just know that he threatened her and said he'd be back. I don't want him back. I don't want him anywhere near my family. He's a vile, evil man. He must go away. He must stay away." Calvière shook, his entire body suddenly trembling so that he was in danger of tipping over his drink.

Reaching out, Drake slid the glass out of harm's way.

Calvière continued to shake, opening and closing his fingers against his thighs, muttering to himself under his breath.

Drake understood now why Sebastianne had made up her tale about caring for an invalid cousin rather than telling her father the truth. Whatever her motivations for going to England, her father clearly would not have been able to deal with the truth. Obviously, something had broken in Calvière. Whether from the death of his wife or from too many years living under the darkness of upheaval and war, he could no longer cope with reality. Instead, he dwelled behind a shield of rosy delusions and professional abstractions, which Sebastianne was wise enough to maintain.

As for her brothers, Drake reasoned, they were too young to be confidants, although he suspected Julien understood far more than the boy let on. Did he know that Sebastianne had not spent the spring in Paris? Was he also aware of the man who threatened her with harm? Julien had immediately come to Sebastianne's defense when he'd found her with Drake, protective and willing to fight. What other responsibilities had he shouldered while she was away, as a boy who was on the verge of becoming a man.

"You are not to fret, *monsieur*," Drake said soothingly to the older man. "You have my word that I shall take care of your daughter and your family."

Calvière glanced up, his eyes filled with a mixture of hope and relief. "You would do that? You would see to their safety?"

"Yes, I would do that." And Drake realized in that moment that regardless of his original reasons for tracking Sebastianne here to her home village, none of that mattered anymore. She was in trouble, and in spite of what she had done, he would come to her aid.

Sebastianne's father blinked, his eyes slightly pink around the edges. "You are good, my lord, a true and noble gentleman. It is a pity you were not born French."

At the remark, Drake couldn't help but laugh.

Seemingly recovered, Calvière picked up his brandy and tossed it back, sighing with pleasure at the excellent libation.

Drake hesitated, not wishing to upset the older man again. Yet he had to know. "One last question, *monsieur,* before we return to our adventures in prime numbers."

At the reminder of mathematics, Calvière's eyes gleamed with excitement. Drake hoped he hadn't made a mistake by mentioning Calvière's favorite topic and thus losing the other man's focus entirely.

"Did you happen to hear his name?"

Calvière stood and crossed the room, leaning down to root through a stack of papers. "Whose name?" he asked distractedly.

"The one who came to the garden. Do you know how he is called?"

Calvière's fingers slowed, the frown returning to his face. For a long moment, Drake didn't think he would answer.

"Vacheau," Calvière whispered with a quiet shudder. "The villain's name is Vacheau."

Chapter 29

ebastianne went about her usual routine for the remainder of the afternoon—if anything could be considered "usual" under the circumstances. She cleaned and tidied the house, gathered herbs in the garden and put the bread in the oven to bake and the chicken on the stove to boil, as she'd originally planned. The boys returned from finishing their chores, then after washing their hands and faces, helped her set the table.

Just when she was about to call them for supper, her father and Drake emerged from his workroom, both men still deep in discussion over number theory. Deciding Drake could be of help, she thrust a bottle of red wine and a corkscrew into his hands and left him to do the rest. With the food steaming fragrantly in bowls and platters on the table, they all sat down to eat.

She said little throughout the meal, content to let Drake tell the boys a few interesting tales that held them riveted. Even Julien relaxed the last of his guard, his eyes fixed with interest.

After the meal, she left them all at the table while she

went to wash up. To his credit, Drake did offer to help, but she refused, preferring to work alone while she considered the impact of Drake's presence in the house, and in France. The fact that he'd so easily charmed her family was both a blessing and a curse since she vowed that, come morning, she would have to kick him out.

And if he refused to leave?

She would think of a way to force him to go. It was dangerous enough having him in the cottage. But if Vacheau should arrive and discover Drake . . . a cold shiver raised gooseflesh on her skin at the thought of what might follow.

Non, she told herself, *Drake will stay the night, then go on his way.*

And once he was gone?

Her heart gave a sharp pang at the idea. Losing him once had been wrenching. Losing him again . . . she wasn't sure she'd be able to recover from the pain. But Drake wasn't here to woo her, he'd come for retribution, and she would do well to remind herself of that fact.

"You can sleep in Papa's workroom," she told Drake more than an hour later, as her father and brothers called good night and made their way to their rooms. "I've made up the sofa in there, and while it's not up to your usual lordly standards, it should suffice for one night."

She expected him to argue and renew his entreaties to sleep in her bed. Instead, he smiled and thanked her for the meal and the accommodations, dropping a kiss on her forehead before turning away.

Puzzled and strangely disappointed, she went to look in on the boys in the loft and say another good night before returning downstairs to her bedchamber at the rear of the house.

The night was too warm to sleep with the windows closed, so she left them open, allowing a faint breeze to bring the fragrant scents of grass and climbing roses into the room. Insects chirped out a soothing chorus beyond the drawn curtains, the occasional croak from a frog adding a punctuation to the harmony.

Easing out of her dress, she hung it in the wardrobe before pulling a thin cotton nightgown over her head. Crossing to the washbasin, she bathed her face, then scrubbed her teeth with a bristle toothbrush and a precious bit of tooth powder that she'd managed to bring back with her from London. Next, she took up her brush and gave her hair a hundred strokes that made the long strands crackle. Laying the brush down, she went to her bed and climbed in, then leaned over and blew out the candle.

She was nearly asleep when she felt a hand slide over her mouth. Panicked, she gave a muffled cry and began to struggle.

"It's only me," a deep, familiar voice said against her ear. "I didn't want you taking fright and waking up the entire house."

She stared at Drake in the darkness, her heart pounding in violent strokes beneath her breastbone. Glaring at him, she spoke again, but her words came out garbled and indistinguishable against his palm. Annoyed, she gave him a tiny nip with her teeth.

"Hey!" he complained, pulling back his hand. "There's no cause for that."

"Oh, isn't there?" She sat up in bed, the sheet falling away. "What are you doing here?"

"I came to talk. By the way, that sofa of your father's isn't very comfortable."

"Comfortable or not, you should return to it and go to sleep. We'll talk in the morning." When the sun would be shining and she would have the strength to send him away for good—she hoped.

"No," he said, soft but emphatic, as if he knew exactly what she planned. "We'll talk now."

"I'm tired, Drake," she said, realizing she was not only tired in body but in spirit as well. "Go away."

"Not until you've answered my questions." Walking to the window, he pulled back the curtains and let in enough moonlight for both of them to see. Nudging her over, he sat down on the bed. "Tell me about Vacheau."

She felt her eyes widen, her throat growing tight. "Where did you hear that name?"

"Your father. He notices far more than you might imagine."

She resisted the urge to groan.

"He heard the two of you arguing a few days ago. He says the man threatened you and that you have something that he wants rather badly. Is it the cipher, Sebastianne? I assumed you would already have handed it over. Is that not the case?"

She lifted her gaze to his, the rich green in his eyes visible even in the low light. Slowly, she shook her head. "I gave him only a portion."

"What do you mean, a portion?"

She raised her chin with a kind of defiant pride. "I made a few adjustments to the equation that left out some rather important bits and pieces. He is too poorly versed in mathematics to realize what I'd done and that I'd rendered the cipher essentially useless."

"So you duped him?" Drake barked out a quick laugh. "Good Lord." But his humor faded almost instantly. "But now he knows what you did."

She suppressed a shudder. "Yes, he knows, and he wants the real code."

Drake ran his fingers through his hair, a worried scowl on his forehead. "Why on earth did you cross him when you had to realize he'd figure it out eventually. What did you hope to gain, particularly after you went to so much trouble to acquire the cipher in the first place?"

"He promised to leave us alone if I went along with his scheme, but I knew he would never keep his word. So I decided to provide myself with a measure of insurance so he couldn't so easily betray me. Do you believe me, then? Do you see that I had no choice?"

"I'm starting to," he said. "Tell me everything and start at the beginning, then I'll decide what I do and do not believe."

Hugging a pillow to her chest, she unburdened herself to Drake, leaving nothing out from the moment Vacheau had shown up at the cottage last autumn to the hour she'd arrived back home in France. The only part she didn't include were her feelings for Drake. She knew what he must think of her, and she couldn't bring herself to admit that while she was carrying out her mission, she'd made the fatal error of falling in love with him.

By the time she was through, Drake was leaning against the footboard, his arms crossed over his chest, a half-incredulous, half-furious expression on his face. "So let me make sure I understand you clearly. You hid the genuine cipher in a cave around here and, in exchange for it, you're blackmailing Vacheau for a writ of safe passage signed by Napoleon himself?"

"Yes, that about sums it up."

He raked a hand through his hair again. "Either you're insane or far less intelligent than I gave you credit for being. My God, you can't seriously think he'll let you get away with this?"

"He won't have a choice," she defended. "If he wants the cipher, he'll have to give me the writ."

"And kill you the instant it's in his hand. A man like that has no morals, no conscience. He won't let you or your family go, Sebastianne. He'll never quit."

With a sinking heart, she knew he was right. After all, it took a miracle to save a soul from the devil. "But what else was I to do? I couldn't just hand the cipher over to him. I would have had nothing. He would simply have used me again."

A long silence fell, even the night creatures having gone quiet.

"You could have come to me," Drake said in a low voice. "You could have told me what you've just told me now and asked for my help."

She squeezed the pillow tighter against her chest. "I thought about it, those last few days in London. But what would you have done if I had come to you? If I had told you I had been deliberately placed in your household and that I was there to steal your code and hand it over to the French? You might have sympathized and offered to help me, but you might just as easily have had me clapped in chains and dragged off to Newgate."

Tossing the pillow aside, she leaned forward. "I couldn't take that risk, not with my family's well-being at stake. I couldn't take the chance that you would look at me with hate in your eyes like you did when you came here this morning. That you would turn me away, turn me in."

"I don't hate you," he said thickly. "I admit I've been very angry since I found out what you'd done, but I don't hate you."

"Are you sure? I've never seen you look at me the way you did today."

"And I never thought the woman I lo . . . the woman with whom I shared my bed and the most intimate details of my life could betray me the way you did. I was going to kidnap you, you know."

Her lips parted on a silent inhalation.

"I'd planned to find you and separate you from anyone

who might give you aid. Then I was going to cart you back to England with me."

She swallowed. "And afterward? Would you have seen me imprisoned? Punished? Humiliated?"

Glancing through the darkness, he met her gaze. "I honestly don't know. I told myself I wanted restitution, but now I'm no longer certain. Would I be taking you back to pay for stealing the cipher, or for lying and leaving me without so much as a word."

"I'm sorry, Drake. I never meant to hurt you, or any of the others. I did what I was forced to do, but I never liked it. I never wanted to deceive you. Please, after everything I've told you, you must believe that."

A long moment passed before he replied. "Strangely enough, I do."

An arrow of relief surged through her. "And I'm not lying now. I will never lie to you again."

"You swear?" he tested,

"Yes. On my family's honor."

He inclined his head. "Then I accept that promise and shall hold you to it."

"Since we're being honest," she said, idly studying the patterns of light and shadows playing against the walls. "I might as well tell you now that you cannot stay."

"What?"

Her gaze flew back to his. "Surely you must see how much danger you are in just by being here? You've got to go while you still can. Before someone sees you and realizes you do not belong."

He shot her a fearsome scowl. "Do you really think I'm just going to abandon you and your family to your fate? Do you imagine I'm going to turn tail and run and let that knave do worse than blackmail you? I'm not going anywhere, Sebastianne."

"But you must, you have to for everyone's safety."

"And let him double-deal you again? Let him have the cipher, then turn around and slit your throat?"

She put a hand up to her neck, shuddering at the image he painted, one she knew to be a very real possibility.

"No," Drake said, uncompromising. "I'm going to stay and help you, and you're going to let me."

Sebastianne stared at him. "But Drake—"

"No buts. Come morning, you're going to pack a few essentials for you and the boys and your father, then we're all going to leave."

"You mean flee? Abandon the house?"

He nodded. "That's precisely what I mean. It won't be easy traveling in such a large group without being noticed, but we'll find a way."

"A way to where?"

"England."

The air rushed out of her lungs, and, for a moment, she couldn't breathe. "But I can't go back to England. You must have told someone about the missing cipher and that I'm the one who took it. They'll want to make an example of me even if you say you no longer do." She gave her head an emphatic shake. "No, I'm not going anywhere. This is my home, my family's home, and I'm not deserting it."

Not again, she thought. She'd only just come back, she couldn't leave again so soon. The boys would be upset and devastated to leave their friends and the only home they'd ever known. As for her father, well, he'd fled to England once and missed France so much he'd returned in spite of the dangers. Asking him to go again . . . well, succeeding at that would take persuasive abilities of a Herculean proportion.

"Anne—Sebastianne, you must see that you don't have the luxury of staying here anymore, however much you might wish it," Drake said. "Vacheau is coming for that cipher, and once he has it, you'll have no leverage left. Your only option is to run while you can."

She pulled the sheet over herself again, suddenly chilled in spite of the warm night.

"I'll do everything in my power to help you," Drake went on, "but I cannot do it here in France. Once we're back in England on my home soil, I can protect you and your family. My brother Edward has a great deal of influence and can smooth your way."

"And if he can't? Or worse, if he won't? I've met the duke, and he strikes me as a man who follows his conscience, regardless of what others may wish him to do, even his brothers."

"Ned is fair. He'll hear you out and understand that you had your reasons for what you did."

"That still might not be enough." Then a new thought occurred that made her stomach ache. "Anyway, how do I know you aren't going to turn me in the moment we reach Britain? You said yourself you wanted revenge. How can I be sure you won't act on that and betray me yourself?"

His eyes glittered like emeralds in the low light. "You don't," he said bluntly. "You'll just have to trust me, as I've agreed to trust you. And don't forget about Vacheau and what he'll do if you stay here. Better a refugee in England than dead here in France."

Yes, better alive and possibly in prison than used and murdered. Still, there had to be a way out. There were always options, even in the darkest of times—though at present she couldn't think of a single one.

"If I agree," she said quietly, "will you give me your word that you'll look after my family no matter what may happen to me? My brothers are innocent boys, and you know the state of my father's mind. He is of no harm to anyone."

Leaning forward, Drake took her hand. "Matters may yet work out better than you imagine, but yes, I give you my word. I swear to you upon my honor as a gentleman that I shall care for your family."

At that, she relaxed, a strange calm sliding through her. The decision was made, and it was now out of her hands. Whatever happened would happen and she would have to let destiny decide the outcome.

"Very well," she agreed. "As for leaving tomorrow, I don't see how it can be done. We'll need at least a full day to prepare. The boys will want to say good-bye to their friends, and my father will insist on taking some of his books."

Drake shook his head. "We can't afford to travel with books, but if it will satisfy him, I'll promise to replace your father's library once we're back in England. As for your brothers, they cannot be allowed to say good-bye to anyone. No one can know we are leaving."

She drew in a breath. "Yes, you're right. I suppose I was thinking of their feelings and not the dangers involved. But what shall we tell them? They don't know anything about Vacheau."

"In Julien's case, I wouldn't be too sure of that."

Her stomach gave a flip.

"If it allays your worries, however," Drake hurried on, "we can say we've decided to take a trip. We'll tell them the destination once we're out of harm's way."

"I'm not sure that will work, but we can make the attempt. Still, I'll need the day. Morning isn't enough time."

"It'll have to suffice though I suppose we can depart in the afternoon if that will make things easier for everyone."

"It would, yes."

She tried to let the fatalistic calm roll through her again, but this time it didn't want to come. "If that is the case, then we should both get as much rest as we can. I'll need to pack some food and clothes and other essentials . . ."

Her voice trailed off at the prospect of what she and her family must do. They'd lost so much already, but to lose their home and virtually everything they held dear, why, it was unthinkable.

How could she ask them to go?

Yet how could she not?

Still, people were of infinitely more worth than possessions, and the lives of those she loved was the only thing that really mattered.

Raising her gaze to Drake, she traced her eyes over his face, and knew she included him in that equation. For better or worse, she loved Drake Byron and knew she always would.

"Yes, it is late," he said. "I suppose I should return to that rack you call a sofa." But even as he said the words, he made no effort to leave. Instead, he leaned forward and slowly extended his hand.

She could have stopped him, she supposed, but she didn't. Holding still, she let him stroke a length of her hair, twining it around his fingers before he let go again. Using only his fingertips this time, he glided them over her cheek and along her throat in a way that made her shudder. Her eyelids slid low, her lips parting as he moved his palm so that he cradled her head, his thumb pressed against the pulse point just under her skin so there was no hiding the maddened drumming of her heart.

"Did you mean it?" he murmured with raw seduction.

"Mean what?"

"About being sorry? Are you really?"

"Yes," she swallowed convulsively. "I truly am sorry."

"Good. Then perhaps you'll give me a chance to change your mind about the sleeping arrangements."

Her eyes flashed back open.

"Don't send me away, Sebastianne," he whispered. Bending closer, he brushed his mouth over hers, warm, slow and easy. "Just say yes. That's all you have to do. Say yes."

Chapter 30

A firestorm of longing swept through Sebastianne the instant Drake's mouth met hers, memories burning in her brain and blood as she thought about the last time they had kissed, the last night they'd made love.

Mon Dieu, how she'd missed this.

Missed him.

The taste of his mouth, the scent and touch of his skin, were like nothing else she'd ever known. Being in his arms was sweet heaven—although perhaps hell might be a better description, since there was nothing the least bit saintly about the way he made her feel.

Giving free license to her hunger and to the power of her love, she matched each slide of his mouth, every sultry, devastating stroke of his tongue. Yet she knew they could not go on, however much she might wish it to be. He wasn't hers to keep, and she would be a fool to forget it.

"Drake, we can't," she said breathlessly, wrenching her mouth away from his.

"Why not?" he murmured darkly, kissing a path along

her throat as he reached up a hand to cover one of her breasts through the thin material of her nightgown.

Flames rippled over her skin. "B-because the cottage is small, and Papa and the boys might awaken."

He reached an arm around and shifted her so he could unfasten the short placket of buttons along the front of her bodice. "Your brothers are upstairs in the loft and won't hear anything. As for your father, he was snoring so loudly when I made my way here to your room, I doubt anything less than an earthquake could wake him."

Papa did sleep soundly, it was true. Still . . .

"B-but I'll know. Besides, we have to awaken early to-morrow and have much to do before we depart. We need to sleep."

"Oh, we'll sleep," he drawled thickly. "Later."

Slipping open the front of her nightgown, he exposed her naked breasts to the warm night air. She trembled, damp heat collecting between her thighs. But when he lifted his hand to touch her again, she wrapped her fingers around the width of his wrist to prevent him.

"No, Drake," she said. "Don't."

His head came up, his verdant, spring-colored eyes flash-ing warningly as they locked with her own. "No? Why not? Or was your former desire for me equal only to your need for information? Have I outlived my usefulness in that regard?"

"*No!* That's not it at all. I just . . ."

"Just what?"

And her real hesitation, one she hadn't been able to fully reason out, not even in her thoughts, came surging to the surface. "Are you marrying her? Are you engaged? When we go back to London, will she be waiting for you?"

An expression of utter confusion moved over his face. "Who? What are you talking about?"

She swallowed, forcing herself to continue. "That young

woman, the lady in the park who had you hanging on her every word. Are you going to make her your wife? Mrs. Tremble said—"

"Oh?" One of his brows arched high. "And what did Mrs. Tremble say?"

"She told me it was quite the expected thing that you were going to propose to that girl . . . Miss Manning, I believe she was called."

"Manning? You mean Verity Manning?"

"If that is her name, then yes." Sebastianne tried to shrug away from him, but Drake held her in place.

He stared for a moment before tossing his head back on a laugh.

"Do be quiet," she admonished, "or you really will wake all the others."

With obvious effort, he stifled his mirth, his lips continuing to twitch. "So you're worried I'm going to marry Miss Manning, are you?"

She shot him a fulminating glare. How dare he taunt her, his callous attitude slicing an even bigger hole in her heart. Perhaps this was how he planned to take his revenge. Maybe he wanted her to know she was nothing more than a plaything and how little she truly meant to him.

"I had no idea you could be so jealous," he remarked cheerfully. "I must confess I rather fancy seeing you like this."

This time she genuinely struggled to free herself from his hold.

"Calm down," he said, fitting her more tightly inside his arms. "I'm not engaged."

As soon as his words penetrated, she fell still. "You're not?"

"No. Although considering everything that's happened, I probably should have tortured you a bit longer over the possibility that I was. A little more spark and fire on your part might have been amusing to see."

"So you're not planning to marry her?"

He shook his head. "No, I'm not. Despite my cook's often excellent judgment, she is grievously mistaken in this instance. Verity Manning is most assuredly not my style."

"But you seemed so attentive to her that day, and she is an eligible English debutante."

"I am often attentive to eligible English debutantes. Such overtures are what is known in Society as 'being polite.' That doesn't mean, however, that I have any interest in marrying one of them, since I most emphatically do not."

"Oh," Sebastianne said.

"Oh, indeed." He caressed the side of her face before slipping a bent knuckle beneath her chin. "There is only one woman I want, and she happens to be you."

"Oh," she said again, slightly breathless. And yet, she was unable to help but notice that he'd said want rather than love. But she supposed she was tilting at windmills if she expected to hear that she'd won his undying devotion. Knowing he wasn't engaged and that he desired her above any other woman was more than she had dared let herself hope.

It is enough, she told herself. *For tonight. For as long as he wants me.*

For propriety's sake, she supposed she ought to resist and send him back to his solitary bed. But why, when their time together might end at any moment? Why, when she loved him so dearly that it pained her not to always be in his arms? With her mind at ease, tension flowed from her body.

"So, may we continue where we left off?" he asked softly, brushing kisses over her forehead and temple and cheek.

Her eyelids slipped to half-staff. "*Oui,* though we must still take care not to be heard."

A slow smile moved across his face. "I can be quiet as

a mouse if need be." Peeling back the edges of her bodice again, he took one of her breasts in his hand, circling the tip with his thumb. "Let's find out if you can be too."

She bit her lip to hold back a moan, her eyelids sliding shut again as a fiery rush of sensation burst through her. He kissed her, claiming her mouth with a dark possession that demanded no less than her full and unrestrained cooperation.

They'd been lovers when she'd left England, and now that they were together again it seemed as if no time had passed at all, as if they'd never truly been apart. Wrapping her arms around him, she held tight, her palms roaming at will as she explored the hard, tensile shape of his shoulders and the long, lean curve of his back. Reaching lower, already in search of skin, she tugged at the fine linen material of his shirt to free it from the waistband of his trousers.

He drank in her sounds of satisfaction as her fingers stole beneath the garment to retrace all the places she'd already touched, already knew. His own growl of pleasure rumbled against her lips, his fingers playing like a sorcerer against the most sensitive places on her body as he wove his magic around her.

Urging her to lie back across the sheets, he replaced his hands with his lips, the wet, raw heat of his mouth and tongue suffusing her core with a wet, raw heat of its own. Limbs trembling, spine arching, she only barely remembered that she had to keep quiet, that she couldn't let herself cry aloud from the shuddering wash of delight. Laying her forearm across her mouth, she muffled the long, lush moan that crested inside her throat.

Ah, it is so good, so right. How had she survived without him? How would she ever be able to survive again?

Stripping off her nightgown, he laid her bare, and in the moonlight she saw the expression in his eyes, as if he were a starving man looking at a feast, as though she were a priceless treasure with a worth beyond rubies or pearls.

He leaned up a moment later and tore off his own clothes, then just as quickly came back down beside her. Parting her thighs, he cradled himself in between. But he didn't enter her, not quite yet, despite the rampant evidence of his desire.

Instead, he kissed her again, first her mouth, then across her cheeks and chin and throat before gliding lower in a series of caresses that left her trembling, restless and very near the brink. Only then did he take her, sliding deep, in a single, heavy thrust that lodged him as far as he could possibly go.

Dieu merci! she thought with hazy gratitude, relieved to know he'd had the presence of mind to cover her mouth with his own, since she'd given a cry that would surely have awakened every soul in the house. Maybe even in the neighborhood. Ecstasy poured through her, a honeyed spiral of pleasure that wound itself into her skin and bones and blood. Her mind ceased to function, her body seeming to take on a ravenous will of its own.

Then, suddenly, she was flying, soaring to places only he could take her, as the crisis lifted her in its grip and tossed her like a piece of driftwood caught inside a storm. She quaked, Drake smothering another helpless wail of rapture, as he pushed her toward the final and fullest reaches of her completion.

Only when she had fully claimed her own satisfaction did he claim his.

She held him, her arms and legs locked tightly around his back and hips as he gently eased them both back down to earth. Lying amid the tangled sheets in a haze of delight, she cradled him inside her, relishing the damp warmth of his flesh, the sensual fragrances of his body mingled with her own. She knew they should sleep, but somehow she wanted more.

As if aware of her thoughts, her needs, his body quite amazingly began to respond. "Again?" he said.

She nodded, unable to speak, and for the next while he gave her ample reason to be cautiously quiet once more.

At length, they settled, exhausted but replete next to each other, their limbs still entwined as if they couldn't bear even a hint of separation.

Brushing her hair away from her face, he kissed her again, soft and tender. "Sleep," he whispered. "Tomorrow will be a long day. Don't worry, I'll wake you come morning."

Trusting him, loving him, she closed her eyes and let the darkness sweep her away.

True to his word, Drake awakened her early the next morning, a few intrepid birds calling to each other in preparation for the sunrise that was only minutes away. With her thoughts still tangled in dreams, Sebastianne found herself momentarily disoriented, imagining for an instant that she was back in Drake's bed in the Audley Street town house, and that she needed to return to her attic room to prepare for the day.

But then she remembered that she'd left London, and it was Drake who had slept in *her* bed last night. Her eyes sprang open, as everything rushed at once upon her, the timber ceiling rafters of her cottage bedroom coming into view.

"Shh," Drake hushed, brushing his lips against her ear as he stroked a soothing hand along her arm. "I didn't mean to startle you. Go back to sleep for a few minutes more."

But she knew more sleep would be impossible, and that there was far too much to be done to indulge in more rest, particularly if the whole family were to leave today.

Her stomach sank at the thought and the knowledge that they might never return. How on earth, she wondered, was she supposed to explain her and Drake's decision to her father and brothers? How difficult was it going to be to convince them to flee?

After another quick kiss, Drake dressed and let himself out of the room. She hoped none of the others met him on the way back to her father's workroom and the sofa where he was supposed to have slept.

She bathed quickly, then began looking through her garments to decide what to wear and what to pack. They wouldn't be able to carry more than a single change of clothes. As for their other possessions, nearly all would have to be left behind.

Upon her mother's passing, Sebastianne had acquired a few fine pieces of jewelry—a diamond brooch, a strand of elegant pearls, and a pair of silver hair combs. There had been more pieces that she'd sold off long ago, but she had never been able to bring herself to part with these. She would sew them into the hem of her spare dress, she decided; that way, if they were unlucky enough to be searched on their way out of France, she might have some hope of retaining them. And if their situation proved dire, she could always use them as bribes.

There was one other piece of jewelry she'd kept, and that was her wedding ring, a plain gold circlet with her and Thierry's names engraved inside. Taking it out of the wooden box where she kept it, she stared at the jewelry for a long moment.

Once the ring had symbolized everything good—love, hope, and the prospect of a bright and happy future. Now it served as nothing more than a reminder of a lost life, of dreams whose time had come for putting away.

Thierry was dead, and although she would never forget him, or regret their time together, her future led in a new direction. No matter what might happen, she loved Drake. And even if he did not feel the same, even if her worst fears came true once they made it back to England—*if* they made it back—she must put her family's immediate needs first. If they had any hope of making it to one of the ports, they would require a horse and a conveyance large enough to carry the five of them. They didn't own a horse, but she knew someone who did.

Staring once more at the ring, she knew exactly what she must do.

Convincing her brothers to leave proved a far easier task than Sebastianne had ever expected. By the time she emerged dressed and prepared to face what must be done, she found Julien and Luc seated at the dining table, expressions of serious determination on the young faces.

In her absence, Drake had apparently taken the initiative to explain that their home was no longer safe and that all of them had to flee; exactly where they would be fleeing he hadn't yet said.

"Monsieur Drake says there is a very bad man who wishes to hurt you and that we need to go away for a while," Luc said, meeting her gaze for confirmation.

Reluctantly, she gave a nod.

"It's the one who came before, isn't it?" Julien stated in a voice that was far too mature for her comfort. "That man who stopped here at the house before you went away to see Cousin Paulette in Paris."

Suddenly Sebastianne wondered if Julien suspected she hadn't been to Paris at all. Suddenly she wondered just how much her brother really knew.

"Our leaving is only a precaution," she said, not wanting to frighten them. "We'll just be gone a few weeks until the danger is past, then we shall return."

She didn't meet Drake's gaze, not wanting the lie to show in her own.

"Luc and I don't need much," Julien said, having clearly accepted whatever it was Drake had told them. "We'll go pack." Standing up from the table, they raced upstairs to the loft, their shoes clattering against the narrow flight of steps.

Once they'd gone, she turned to Drake. "Have you told Papa as well?"

"I explained the situation to him first. He's in his work-room deciding which two books to take. I told him that was all he's allowed."

"And he accepted that?" she said in disbelief.

"I may have mentioned a private library that I could give him unlimited access to. He was surprisingly amenable after that."

She stared, unable to decide whether to laugh or cry.

"Well, if that's settled," she said a few moments later, "I suppose I should make all of us something to eat. There's not much point running off on an empty stomach."

Her own stomach jangled with nerves, however, as she prepared their meal; and once they sat down to eat, she had to force the food past her lips, feeling queasy and wishing she had the luxury of pushing it away.

After breakfast was finished, she sent Luc and Julien out to collect the chicken's eggs while she cleaned up the kitchen. That task done, likely for the last time, she went to find Drake.

"I'm going to visit Madame Breton," she announced. "We were supposed to have supper with her this Sunday, but that will have to be canceled now, of course."

Lines of concern creased Drake's forehead. "Is that wise? Can you trust her?"

Sebastianne threw up a hand in a very Gallic gesture. "I can't just abandon the house. The chickens will have to be cared for, and it would be a shame for the vegetables in the garden to go to waste. I'm planning to tell her that we have had a letter from my cousin in Paris and that she's asked us all to stay with her for a few months. Madame will care for the property while we're away, and when we don't return, she will do what is necessary. There is a war under way, after all. Our disappearance won't seem odd. Far less so than us leaving Montsoreau like a band of gypsies without a word to anyone."

Drake stood silent, clearly weighing his objections. "All right, go see her and tell her your story. You make a good point about raising suspicion if we sneak away. Meanwhile, I'll pay a call on the local blacksmith about acquiring some means of transportation."

She shook her head. "No, you stay here. It's foolish for you to risk exposure by going into the village."

"But we need a horse, and you don't have one."

"Madame Breton does." Tucking a hand into one of her pockets, she touched the ring she'd earlier slipped inside, finding the gold warm against her skin. "She owns one of the few horses and carriages left in the village. I'll persuade her to let us use them."

He studied her. "Are you sure she'll agree? Perhaps I should accompany you, after all. I brought gold and a few gemstones to use as tender."

Which meant she could keep her ring. Yet was she not already beholden enough to Drake without adding another debt onto the tally? She hated to part with the wedding band, but still . . .

"No," she said, resolved to act on her earlier decision. "We don't know how difficult it will be to reach the coast and secure safe passage back to England. We may have need of every coin and gem you brought. I shall convince Madame, do not worry. You stay here and make sure Papa and the boys finish their packing."

His lips parted as if he were about to argue further, then he closed them again. "Very well, but be careful."

She smiled. "I always am."

Nearly an hour and a half later, Sebastianne departed Madame Breton's small yet comfortably appointed house.

Over tea and sweet biscuits made with Madame's treasured store of sugar, Sebastianne had spun her tale. Madame had been instantly sympathetic, agreeing that, of course, they must go to the Paris if their cousin had such need of them. She was equally amenable to looking after the house and livestock for as long as they were away.

Sebastianne left the matter of the horse and carriage for last, knowing how much pride and enjoyment Madame took in riding to church in the rig each Sunday morning. The carriage had been a gift from her husband, one of the last purchases he had made before his death. Being widows was a commonality she and the older woman shared, a link that had long since made them far more than neighbors. Withdrawing the ring from her pocket, Sebastianne had pleaded her case, one widow to another.

At first Madame had said she couldn't possibly take Sebastianne's wedding band. But Sebastianne had persisted, persuading the other woman that, under the circumstances, it was a fair trade.

"I shall consider this collateral and keep it for when you return," Madame said, accepting the ring and wrapping it carefully in a handkerchief. "The horse and carriage are merely a loan that you shall send back to me as soon as you no longer have need."

"Yes, I shall send them back," Sebastianne promised, knowing she would do everything in her power to have the horse and vehicle returned to Madame. Since Drake said he'd brought funds, with luck, there would be enough remaining to hire an honest man to drive the team back here to Montsoreau.

"*Adieu, madame*," Sebastianne called amid cheek kisses, tears and heartfelt farewells. Madame did not realize, but there was a very great chance they would never see one another again.

More melancholy than she had expected herself to be, Sebastianne set off again for the cottage, she and Madame having agreed that Julien and her father would return in a couple of hours to collect the carriage. Dabbing at her eyes with her sleeve, she walked the familiar path, her footsteps silent against the packed earth. Her thoughts turned inward, she didn't notice the soft rustling of the bushes a few yards ahead.

Suddenly, someone stepped onto the path.

Raising a hand to shield her eyes from the sun, she felt the blood drain from her cheeks.

"*Bonjour, Madame Dumont*," Vacheau said. "As you can see, I have returned." Reaching into his coat, he withdrew a thick, folded document and held it up, waggling the heavy paper between his fingers. "I've brought what you demand, signed by the Emperor himself."

Her chest tightened with a mixture of fear and excitement. Was it truly the writ? Had he actually succeeded in obtaining the document? If so, and the writ was indeed genuine, then it meant their freedom—even Drake's.

But to use the writ, she had to take possession of it, and that meant dealing with Vacheau and not ending up dead first.

"Now," he said, his voice hard and silky, "I've held up my side of the bargain. Time for you to uphold yours."

Chapter 31

She's been gone too long, Drake thought, as he twisted the blackened metal lever that closed the fireplace flue. Straightening from the chimney, he withdrew a handkerchief from his pocket.

She ought to have returned by now, he mused as he wiped soot smudges from his fingers. Maybe she and her neighbor were simply having a long last visit. Then again, maybe not. His muscles were knotted with a sensation he always equated with his gut instinct, and his instinct was telling him that something wasn't right.

I'll give her five more minutes, then I'm going after her.

He only lasted two before he decided to start his search.

"Luc," he called up to the loft where he knew the boy was sorting through his belongings one final time.

Moments later, a golden head appeared over the railing. *"Oui, monsieur?"*

"If your father asks," Drake said in French, "tell him I've gone to escort your sister home. We shall return in a short while. In the meantime, don't leave the house."

"*Oui, monsieur*," the boy agreed again. "Shall I tell Julien?"

"No, I'll find him."

But Julien found him first, pelting down the path at a dead run less than a minute after Drake stepped out of the house. The boy skidded to a halt, pebbles scattering beneath his heels.

"Where have you been?" Drake demanded, knowing Sebastianne had told her brother not to stray from the grounds. "You know you weren't supposed to leave."

For a second, Julien had the grace to look guilty, breath coming rapidly from his still heaving lungs. "You should be glad I did," he panted. "I went to visit Marc, and on the way back, I saw him."

The instinct inside Drake came wide-awake. "Him? Who do you mean?"

"The man," Julien said. "The one who was here last autumn before Sebastianne went away. The one who scares her. I followed him and . . ."

"And—" Drake encouraged, his heart pounding with sick dread.

"He stopped her as she was walking home. I couldn't hear everything they said, but he wants something from her and said it was time for her to honor her side of the bargain."

Which could mean only one thing—Vacheau had returned and wanted the cipher.

Plague take it, Drake cursed, as he took a couple of pacing steps. He knew they ought to have left first thing that morning rather than delaying their departure. Why had he given in to Sebastianne's need to wrap up loose ends and bid farewell to her neighbor? Instead, he ought to have insisted each of them pack a bag and start out at first light.

"Where is she now?" Drake said urgently. "With him?"

Julien nodded. "They went toward the caves. I followed long enough to see where they were headed, then I ran straight here."

"Good thinking. Can you find them again? There are a lot of caves around here."

"I've climbed all the cliffs and caves a hundred times and I—" He broke off, realizing what he'd just admitted. "That is—you won't tell Sebastianne, will you?"

"If I find her unharmed, I'll never say a word. Right now, it wouldn't matter to me if you'd climbed a thousand cliffs, I just want to find Sebastianne and get her away from that bast—"

"*Bastard?*" Julien supplied helpfully.

Drake narrowed his eyes. "Are you sure you're only thirteen?"

Julien grinned, the pair of them suddenly in complete accord.

"Come on," Drake said. "Let's go. We haven't a moment to waste. When we arrive, though, I want your word you'll come straight back here to the cottage. It won't do any good having all of us at the caves while your brother and father are alone at home. I want you there to look after them."

A frown creased Julien's forehead, as if he might argue over being cut out of the action. Still, he straightened to his full height, clearly proud to be given the adult responsibility of looking after his family's welfare. "Very well, I shall return home. What about the man with Sebastianne? It will just be you and him, and I think he has a gun."

"So do I," Drake reassured, patting the small weapon tucked inside his coat pocket. "Not to worry, I'll make sure your sister is safe and that he has cause never to bother her again."

After many long minutes of walking, Sebastianne came to a halt at the base of a long, high cliff. Perspiration dampened the back of her dress, but she knew it had nothing to do with exertion. She'd traveled this path many times over the years and had never shown effects from the effort—until today.

"This is it," she stated. "This is the place."

Vacheau glanced around, then up, his lip curling as he surveyed a series of openings hewn high into the sides of the rock. "Here, hmm? All I see is a lot of vegetation and stone."

"The cipher is hidden in one of these caves. I'll tell you which one and where to find the code. But first, we have a trade to conduct."

His eyes narrowed rather like a snake observing a mouse, as a soft chuckle escaped his mouth. "You are a marvel, Madame Dumont, and never fail to amuse and amaze me. You must imagine I'm an idiot if you think I am going to give you anything before I have the cipher in my possession. The *real* cipher."

Brandishing a pistol, he waved it toward her. "Go on. You show me which cave you've tucked it inside, and I shall follow."

Ignoring the slick churn in her middle, she shook her head and held out her palm, forcing her fingers not to tremble. "The writ first, then we'll go. I want a chance to see what it is I'm trading the cipher for. After all, how do I know the writ is real?"

His face darkened, a muscle twitching near his jaw. "It's real, all right. My superiors were very displeased to be put to the bother of producing it."

"Landed you in an awkward position, did I?"

"Why, you little bitch—"

"Insulting me won't get you what you want," she stated with far more bravado than she felt.

"Shooting you might."

"I'm afraid that won't do either. As I said once before, if

you harm me or mine, I'll never tell. I will go to my grave with the secret."

Which is where I'm likely to end up no matter how I may attempt to outwit him, she knew.

Her only hope was to delay him long enough for Drake to come. But Drake had no idea where she was, she realized with a sinking heart. By the time he found her, it might well be too late. She could only hope that if the worst happened, and she died, he would keep his promise to care for her father and brothers.

"The writ, if you please," she said, extending her hand. "Then I shall tell you the location of the cipher."

His finger tightened on the gun, and, for an instant, she thought he was actually going to shoot her. Instead, he growled out a vivid curse and reached inside his coat. With another curse, he tossed the paper on the ground at her feet.

Deciding not to give him an opportunity to change his mind, she bent and scooped up the document. Unfolding it, she took a moment to study the darkly elaborate script with *Ministère de Guerre* written large at the top. At the bottom, beneath a great deal of official-looking text, lay a nearly indistinguishable scrawl. Peering closer, she saw what appeared to be the signature of Napoleon himself.

"Enough delaying," Vacheau said in a harsh voice. "You've got the writ, now give me that damned cipher. And it had better work this time, or so help me God I'll track you down no matter where you may go. There'll be no place on the face of the earth you can hide."

"It will work," she said, wishing there was some way to avoid giving him the complete code. Once she put it in his hands, she truly would be a traitor to both her mother's country and to Drake. But what choice did she have? For, in spite of her brave words, she wasn't ready yet to die.

"It's up there in a cave behind that thicket of wild roses

and vines," she told him truthfully. "Climb up along the cliff path, and you'll see the opening."

Vacheau gestured with the gun. "*You* climb up and show me. I'll follow. Go on, before I change my mind about putting a bullet in you."

Unable to control the full-body shiver that moved through her, she drew a breath and walked forward.

Drake reached the cliffs and had just sent Julien back home when he caught sight of Sebastianne and a man he could only assume was Vacheau, standing many feet above on the cliff path. As he watched, the two of them disappeared behind a screen of foliage into what must be a concealed cave.

The hiding spot, he realized. The one Sebastianne had told him about. His gut clenched at the thought of her alone with Vacheau, and what the other man might do once he had the code in his possession.

Leaving his own place of concealment, Drake ran to the cliff path. Taking care to hug the rock face as much as possible to escape notice, he made his way up.

Roses sweetened the air on the ledge not far from the cave entrance, the scent seeming oddly incongruous to both the place and the occasion. Silently withdrawing the pistol from his coat pocket, he crept closer, wondering how best to go in after Sebastianne without revealing his presence. Making a rescue attempt wouldn't do her any good if he went charging in only to find Vacheau armed and waiting for him.

The decision was taken out of his hands moments later, however, when Vacheau emerged from the cave, the man pausing to tear at a few pieces of vine that clung to his hair and around his shoulders.

Sebastianne did not follow after him.

A hard kick of dread caught Drake just beneath his breastbone. Forcing aside the sensation, he stepped forward and pointed his gun at the center of the other man's chest. "Where is she?" he demanded. "Where is Sebastianne?"

Vacheau's eyes widened in obvious surprise as he turned to face Drake. "Byron? Is that you?" he said in precise English. "How unexpected. I must say this is an honor since I feel as if you and I are old and dear acquaintances. I know so much about you, you see."

"I know almost nothing about you, other than the fact that you are a liar, a spy and a murderer."

A slow smile curled over Vacheau's lips, rather like a cat who'd just chanced upon unanticipated prey. "Then you *do* know me, much better than you think. I'm flattered."

"Don't be."

"I have to admit I am surprised to see you here," Vacheau continued. "I hadn't realized you'd managed to slip into the country. Obviously, our intelligence measures aren't as infallible as the government would like to imagine."

"I would have to agree with you about a lack of intelligence," Drake said. "If you French had any brains, you wouldn't have had to resort to stealing my work in the first place."

Vacheau's dark eyes hardened, but his smile didn't waver.

"What have you done with Madame Dumont?" Drake continued. "Did you force her to give the code to you?"

Vacheau made a tsking noise. " 'Force' is such a harsh word. 'Suggested' might be a more apt description. I used my gun to *suggest* she turn it over to me."

Drake's heart stopped, missing a full beat. For a moment, he couldn't breathe, his hand tightening reflexively against the gun. *Dear God, is she dead?* he thought. *Has the blackguard killed her?*

If he had, Drake vowed, then Vacheau was about to die too.

"Frankly, I'm surprised you have such a care for Madame

Dumont, or should I say Mrs. Greenway, since that is how you knew her in London, did you not?" Vacheau remarked. "Were the two of you lovers? I must confess I have wondered about that, and just how far she went to gain your confidence."

Drake didn't answer, refusing to take part in the other man's game.

Vacheau continued to smile. "Considering how falsely she played you, I would think you would be more interested in exacting revenge rather than providing her aid."

"It would seem she played you false too from what I understand. She was supposed to have given you the cipher, but she didn't. At least not a version that worked."

"Yes, but I have it now."

"Do you? Are you certain?" Drake questioned, deciding to play his own game. If he could shake Vacheau's focus, he might have a chance of disarming him. Only then would he be able to go after Sebastianne.

"You're right about wanting revenge against my former housekeeper—and lover. But that's not the only reason I went to the bother of following her all the way to France. I came to retrieve the code, and it would seem I beat you to it. She told me where she hid the cipher, and I took care of the rest. Whatever she gave you just now, it's useless."

Vacheau's eyes narrowed, flashing with fury and disbelief. "You lie. She wouldn't have told you about this cave or where she put the code."

"Wouldn't she? She's not the only one who can use an intimate relationship to suit their own purposes. I told her what she wanted to hear, and in turn she told me about the cipher, and about you. By the way, she says you're a fool when it comes to mathematics and that you barely know the difference between an equals sign and a minus. Given how she duped you with the first copy of the code, I confess I must agree."

A growl rumbled in Vacheau's throat, the gun trembling in his hand. Abruptly, he glanced sideways, back toward the cave.

Knowing it might be the only chance he got, Drake sprang forward and reached for the other man's gun. But quick as a cobra, Vacheau deflected his advance, sending Drake's own gun skidding away out of reach.

Straightening, Vacheau raised his weapon and prepared to shoot.

A woman's scream split the air, jarring them both and causing Vacheau's shot to go wide.

Drake glanced toward the sound and saw Sebastianne, standing just beyond the cave entrance, clinging to its side.

His heart leapt with joy to know she was alive, but sank again when he noticed the thin, wet lines of blood staining her temple and cheek. She was hurt, how seriously he couldn't tell.

He realized that his moment of distraction had cost him when he saw Vacheau recover and raise his gun again to fire. Acting purely on instinct, Drake ducked and ran.

The second shot whizzed past his head, so close he actually heard the humming speed of the bullet and felt its heat. Above his head, bits of rock splintered wildly, pulverized rock raining down onto his head and hair.

A breeze rose up just then, taking fragments of rock dust with it as it blew straight into Vacheau's face. Frantically, the Frenchman wiped at his eyes to clear his vision, stumbling backward as he did.

Instinctively, Drake called out a warning, as Vacheau's feet came perilously close to the path's outer edge, pebbles flying off into the void to make the fifty-foot drop to the earth below.

His eyes streaming, Vacheau sneered at Drake, showing his teeth in a jeering grin. "Nice try, Byron. Do you think you can trick me again, you and that conniving bitch? I should have killed her back in the cave when I had the chance."

He shifted slightly, seemingly oblivious to his position along the ledge. "I thought it would be a more fitting punishment to do what I'd originally planned and send her dotty old father off to prison and her brothers to serve and die in the Army. Seeing them go would have been worse than death to her.

"Did she tell you that was how I convinced her to steal the cipher in the first place? If she didn't have such a soft heart, that was so easy to exploit, we'd never have gotten close to you. But as I warned my superiors, never send a woman to do a man's job."

Vacheau's expression turned merciless. "Now, I want that code, the *real* code, since I can't go back without it. One more error, and *my* life will be the one in jeopardy."

Reaching into his coat, Vacheau withdrew another gun. "Did I fail to mention that I always travel with a spare? One never knows when an extra weapon will come in handy." Smiling, he raised the pistol. As he did, the earth crumbled away from his feet, rock sliding from beneath him as the edge of the path gave way.

With a scream, Vacheau fell and disappeared from sight.

Drake raced forward, and to his astonishment discovered the other man still alive and dangling one-handed from what remained of the cliff edge, his spare weapon no longer in his grasp.

By rights, Drake knew he ought to let the man die, he deserved no less. But, unlike Vacheau, he was no murderer. Dropping onto his stomach, he inched forward and stretched out a hand. "Grab hold," he called.

Vacheau stared up, his dark gaze locking with Drake's. He hesitated for what seemed an eternity, then finally extended his hand. Catching hold, Drake began to pull him up.

But rather than aiding him, Vacheau let his weight drop, so that Drake was the one being pulled down.

"There's nothing left for me if I fail," Vacheau called. "If I've got to die, the least I can do for my country is take you with me."

"Don't be a fool, man," Drake told him. "I lied about the cipher. It *is* real. Let me pull you up."

Vacheau's eyes blazed. "I don't believe you. It's just another trick."

But even if he had believed him, it was too late, Vacheau's grip was too precarious now for him to recover. Desperately, he clutched at Drake, but Vacheau's weight kept pulling Drake closer to the edge. Drake's heart pumped violently in his ears, time slowing as he fought to keep his balance on the ledge, digging in with every ounce of strength he possessed to stop the inexorable slide forward.

Suddenly, a pair of arms came around him, locking at his waist and chest to pull him back. Sebastianne's arms, clutching him, holding him, as she too strained to keep him from going over the edge—to keep him alive, even at the cost of her own safety, her own life.

With a fierce bellow, he felt Vacheau's hand begin to slip as pain radiated through the bone and muscle of his arm and up into his shoulder. His skin grew slick, Vacheau's fingers slipping another inch against his own. Their eyes met one last time, then suddenly he was gone, Vacheau falling untethered through the air.

Drake closed his eyes.

With a great, shuddering heave, he flung himself and Sebastianne away from the edge, rolling the two of them back from the precipice.

Chapter 32

*S*he and Drake clung together, her face pressed into the vital, breathing warmth of his chest. He was alive, and by some miracle, so was she.

When she'd seen Drake being pulled over the cliff, she'd done the only thing she could think of to save him. For several long, terrifying moments, while they teetered together on the brink, she'd thought Vacheau would win. She'd feared that he would have his final revenge by sending all three of them to their deaths.

But somehow she and Drake had won, somehow they'd survived.

Exercising great care, Drake slowly eased them both into a sitting position, moving them a safe distance away from the ledge. She wasn't entirely sure how he managed, but he did it all without once loosening his hold on her.

"Are you all right?" he murmured as he cradled her against him.

She nodded, then winced as the movement sent a stab of pain through her head. She must have moaned as well since deep lines of concern gathered on Drake's forehead.

"How badly did he hurt you? You're covered in blood." Gently, he smoothed the hair away from her face, seeking the wound.

"Am I? I didn't realize," she said, letting him dab at her injury with a handkerchief. "Once I gave him the cipher, he hit me in the head with his pistol, and I lost consciousness. When I woke, it was dark; he'd taken the candle with him. Thank heavens I'm familiar with the inside of that cave or else I might have wandered around in there forever."

She shivered at the thought, remembering her terror and pain and confusion. "I heard your voice, and I followed. I saw the light through the vines and heard you and Vacheau and . . ." Her words tapered off as a new memory awakened.

"You're badly bruised and have a gash on your temple," Drake said, tenderly pressing the cloth against the wound to staunch the last of the bleeding. "I don't think it's too serious, but we should get you home."

"Did you mean it?" she asked dully.

"Mean what?"

"You said you'd come for the cipher and for revenge against me. You told him you'd cozened the information out of me, used me to gain your own objectives. That all you really cared about was keeping the code out of French hands."

His hand grew still. "Is that what you think?"

Gazing up, she met his eyes. "I don't know what to think anymore."

"Why did you save me then if you believe that? Why not let Vacheau and me go to our graves? You'd have been free. You could have taken the writ and the cipher and gone anywhere you pleased."

A tear slid down her face. "Because I couldn't let you die, not when I—"

"Not when you what?" he asked softly.

"Not when I love you. And I do, no matter how you may feel about me or what punishment you may have planned. You're more important to me than my life. You're the most important thing on this earth to me."

She didn't have a chance to say more as Drake's mouth came down on her own. He kissed her with a lush ardor that was both tender and tantalizing, careful not to jar her injury as he cradled her face on his shoulder to deepen their embrace even more.

Her eyes slid closed. Trembling, she sank into a heady sea of pleasure. She wondered if she were still back inside the cave and dreaming, or if she really had plunged over the cliff ledge after all and found her way up to heaven. Never wanting their joining to end, she kissed him back, showing her love in all its depth and splendor.

Finally, he eased away but kept her tucked close, stroking his fingers over her cheek in wandering, idle caresses. "I love you too," he said in a thick voice. "I've loved you for a while now and nothing you do, not even stealing my bloody secret code and nearly getting both of us killed, can change how I feel. There is nothing that could make me stop loving you."

"Drake," she gasped in wonder, not quite sure how it was possible he was saying such words.

"So you're stuck with me, you see, whether you want to be or not. This Englishman loves you, and he isn't leaving France without you by his side. You and your whole family are coming with me, and I won't take no for an answer."

An incredulous laugh escaped her lips. "As you command, my lord, since I wouldn't dream of objecting."

"I should think not," he said with all the hauteur of a born aristocrat before he ruined the effect with a smile.

She paused, a tiny bit of the blissful fog in which she'd been drifting, melting away. "What about your government?

Might they not object to letting me go without exacting some kind of retribution for my spying?"

"The cipher is in our possession so there's no harm done. Besides, they need my testimony to proceed against you, and they won't have it."

"They could compel it, could they not?" she asked, still concerned.

He shook his head. "Not if I'm your husband, or aren't you aware that spouses cannot be forced to testify against one another?"

Her heart thudded like a hammer beneath her ribs. "Spouses? As in married? To each other? But—"

"But what?" He gave her a penetrating look. "What did you think I meant when I said come back to England with me?"

"I just assumed . . . that is . . . since you asked before . . . I thought that . . . that—"

"That?" he prompted.

"I assumed you wanted me for your mistress."

His eyes darkened to the color of a forest. "And you would have said yes this time?"

She nodded. "A part of me wanted to say yes before, but I couldn't, not with everything going on—"

He kissed her again, long and deep, so that she could barely catch her breath when he finally let her come up for air again.

"You'll be my wife," he told her. "I already bought the ring. It's waiting back in Audley Street."

Her heart startled with another shock. "You mean you wanted to marry me before I left England?"

"I did." His expression grew deeply serious, as if he were already taking a vow. "I do."

She tightened her arms around him. "Oh, Drake. *Je t'aime.*"

"Don't 'oh, Drake' me. Just say yes."

She laughed, holding back a groan at the ache it caused in her head. "Yes! *Oui!* I will be your wife if you're certain you want me."

"Didn't I already say you're the only woman I want?"

She nodded, remembering.

"Now," he said with clear satisfaction, "I think we should get off this damned cliff and go back home."

Nodding again, she let him help her to her feet.

Nearly an hour later they arrived at the cottage, Sebastianne grateful for the supporting comfort of Drake's arm around her waist. He'd offered to carry her since her head and bruised face still ached from the blow she'd suffered, but she'd refused.

"Papa and the boys will be alarmed enough seeing me like this," she'd told him. "Only imagine what they'll think if you carry me inside like an invalid. I can walk."

Sebastianne could tell he'd wanted to argue, and although he made no complaint, she knew he was hurting too from the struggle at the top of the cliff. She knew it would be better for Drake if she returned on her own two feet.

Before beginning their journey back, however, they had stopped at the base of the cliff where Vacheau's broken body lay a few yards distant. Not wanting to see him up close, Sebastianne had perched on a conveniently located rock while Drake went on alone. They needed the cipher, and the writ, and unfortunately both were inside Vacheau's coat pocket.

"Should I bury him?" Drake had asked her, as she settled on the rock. "I could come back tonight with a shovel and do the job."

Sebastianne shook her head. "No, I think it would be better if we just leave him. Someone will find the body soon, and they'll assume it was an accident. They'll think he was climbing the cliffs and slipped, which in a way is exactly what happened."

After a bit more discussion, Drake agreed. Why risk suspicion regarding the true circumstances of Vacheau's death? Why take the chance that someone would know they had been involved?

Once Drake had retrieved the papers and the pistols Vacheau had dropped, he rejoined her, and with his arm looped supportively around her waist, they walked home.

They were still coming up the path when Julien raced toward them. "What happened? Are you all right?" he said in quick, voluble French. "Sebastianne, you're hurt. Was it that man? Where is he?"

Drake shared a look with Julien that struck Sebastianne as being very adult. "Your sister has been through a terrible ordeal today, but she will heal and be well. As for the man, let us just say that he won't be bothering us again, any of us."

Julien nodded, an expression of relief crossing his face that made Sebastianne wonder once again just how much he knew about Vacheau and the cipher.

Before she had time to ask, he went on, "There's something you should know, Monsieur Drake. Two men are here. They . . . um . . . they are waiting in the house. I tried, but I couldn't convince them to go away." Julien's jaw grew stiff with irritation.

As for Sebastianne, her chest tightened, her nerves stretching tight again.

Drake scowled. "What men?"

"I don't know. They said they know you though. Told me they would wait."

Instinctively, Drake withdrew his gun from his pocket, then exchanged a pointed glance with her. "You and Julien wait here," he said quietly. "I'll go ahead."

"No, I'm not letting you go in there alone," she argued.

"Yes, you will," he stated in a tone that forbade further discussion. "Julien, look after your sister. Where are Luc and your father by the way?"

He made a face. "Having wine and cheese in the kitchen with those men as if we always entertain uninvited guests. Papa is telling them stories!"

"Good. Then they'll be relaxed and distracted when I go inside."

"Be careful," Sebastianne said.

"I will," he told her, leaning down to kiss her firmly on the lips, in spite of her brother's wide-eyed interest.

Stealthfully, Drake approached the house.

"Whoever you are, turn around slowly," Drake ordered as he burst through the door, pistol at the ready.

One dark golden head twisted around, followed by another, two sets of hazel eyes fixing on him in surprise. "Well, hallo, Drake," drawled the first man. "I certainly hope you're not planning on using that on one of us."

"No," remarked the second. "Shabby way to greet one's brothers, I dare say."

With an owl-eyed Luc and a surprised Monsieur Calvière looking on, Drake lowered the pistol to his side. "*Leo? Lawrence?* What in the bloody hell are you doing here?"

Identical grins broke out on his brothers' faces.

"Came to help, of course," Leo said.

"Thought you might need a hand," Lawrence offered. "We overheard Ned and Cade talking about how you'd raced off to France on some secret mission and that they planned to follow you."

"So we offered to go in their stead," Leo continued.

"And they let you?" Drake asked skeptically.

The twins traded looks. "Yes, once they realized we were the most logical choice."

Drake crossed his arms. "And what made them decide that?"

Lawrence smirked. "I believe it had something to do with maintaining domestic harmony and their complete inability to figure out how to sneak off without Claire and Meg finding out what they were up to."

"Being murdered in their beds by our sisters-in-law was mentioned a time or two, as I recall." Leo rose from his chair. "So, we volunteered."

Drake put his gun away. "You needn't have bothered. I have matters well in hand."

"Do you?" they said together. "We thought perhaps you could use a bit of help getting back out of the country."

"I suppose I could at that since our party seems to keep increasing." He sent them a pointed glance. "But we can work that out later. What I want to know is how you found me? I took great care not to leave a trail."

The twins shared another smile. "You may have been careful, but we're good at chatting up the right people."

"The right people?" Drake asked. "Who are those?"

"Barmaids," Lawrence proffered.

Leo nodded. "They notice everything and everyone. Pass them a bit of coin and few other choice favors, and they'll tell a man anything."

"At least us, anyway," Lawrence concluded.

Luc stared between the two, clearly intrigued by the advice. Drake knew he would have to separate the boy from the twins in the future. *Bad influences. Very bad.*

"Just a minute, and I'll be back," Drake said, striding to the door and back out the way he'd come.

By the time he returned with Sebastianne and Julien, the twins and Monsieur Calvière were laughing, while young Luc sat happily eating his way through a plate of cheese.

Everyone stared the moment they saw Sebastianne.

"I'm fine," she said, holding up a hand to forestall their exclamations of alarm at her battered appearance. "Just a little mishap." Glancing across the room, she nodded at the twins. "Bonjour, my lords. How good to see you again."

The twins stood up from their chairs, mouths hanging open. "Mrs. Greenway, what are *you* doing here?" Leo said first.

"It's Dumont, actually," she told him in a tired voice, a sudden wave of exhaustion washing over her. "If you'll forgive me, I need to lie down. Your older brother can explain everything. He's a marvel, you know, and not just at math," she said, letting all the love she felt shine in her eyes.

Epilogue

London, England
August 1813

"*D*o I look all right?" Sebastianne asked as she ran a hand over her carefully coiffured hair, then down the skirt of the elegant new afternoon dress of sky blue sarcenet that Drake had insisted on buying her.

"You look exquisite," Drake said soothingly. Taking up her hand, he pressed a kiss against her trembling palm. "You know, for a woman who successfully infiltrated my household, stole a secret code, and outwitted a dangerous spy, you're remarkably nervous."

"Of course I'm nervous," she hissed, trying her best not to be further intimidated by the elegant surroundings of the Clybourne House drawing room, with its golden silk-lined walls, delicate Chippendale furnishing, or hand-painted ceiling that that looked as if it had been rendered by one of the old masters. "I'm meeting your mother today, aren't I? Why wouldn't I be nervous?"

"But you needn't be. She'll love you."

"And what if she doesn't? What if she abhors me and refuses to let us wed? I was your housekeeper, after all. She can't be terribly overjoyed at the thought of her aristocratic son marrying a servant."

"Which you never really were. Besides, you come from a fine lineage, even if your father has been dispossessed of his lands and title. And your maternal grandfather was an English squire, a very respectable heritage."

"For ordinary people, perhaps, not for a duchess." She smoothed her gown again, then clasped her hands together in a death grip. "I may not be completely ignorant of proper manners, but I wasn't raised to be the wife of a lord. I just don't want to be a disappointment, most especially to you."

Drake took her in his arms, ignoring her hushed concern about wrinkling her finery. "You could never disappoint me," he said with complete sincerity. "I love you exactly as you are, and by some miracle, you love me too. You know all my foibles and idiosyncrasies, yet somehow you want me regardless."

She met his clear green gaze. "Of course I want you. How could I not?"

"There are a great many other women who wouldn't, particularly when I bury myself in my work and drift off into my own thoughts at odd moments of the day and night." Pulling her closer, he kissed her. "What other woman would willingly volunteer for a lifetime of that?"

"I can think of several, but I suppose I am well versed in the habits of mathematicians."

"Yourself included. I look forward to formulating some very interesting theorems with you."

She couldn't help but smile. "Ah, so is that what we shall be doing together once we are wed—formulating theorems?"

"Among other things," he said in a husky voice as he stroked a hand across her hip.

"None of that, my lord," she murmured. "Only think if your mother should walk in and catch us."

"I suspect she would take it in stride. After all, she is a mother of eight, so I think she knows a bit about what goes on between a man and a woman."

"Drake!" she scolded, trying to be outraged and failing.

He chuckled. "My mother may be a dowager duchess, but you'll find that she's very liberal in her views and not at all puffed-up like some of the nobility. My sister-in-law Grace's father, for example, is a complete commoner, without so much as a drop of blue blood in the whole family. Mama welcomed Grace with open arms. Frankly, I think she was simply relieved to see Jack married at all. So don't fret, my love. You're going to dazzle her."

Dazzle her, hah! Sebastianne thought.

"Mrs. Tremble wasn't dazzled," she said sourly, remembering the cook's reaction to her return.

Drake's staff wasn't privy to all the details of Sebastianne's life or her real reason for having worked as Drake's housekeeper, so they were shocked when she arrived back in Audley Street with an elderly father and two young brothers in tow—all of whom spoke rapid French and were clearly not of English origin.

Nor had the servants forgotten or forgiven Sebastianne for her unexpected disappearance from the house—a slight they took personally since they had been frantic with worry at the time. To make matters worse, Sebastianne had had no choice but to reveal that she was not "Mrs. Greenway" after all, and that she hadn't been strictly truthful with them about certain other details.

"Just how old are you then?" Mrs. Tremble had demanded on the day Sebastianne and Drake assembled the servants in the drawing room to explain as much of the truth to them as seemed prudent.

"I am two-and-twenty years of age, soon to be three-and-twenty," Sebastianne said honestly.

"Hah! Well, if I didn't have the right of it all along," the older woman said, slapping a hand against her thigh.

Drake had stared at Sebastianne in astonishment, clearly as unaware of that particular revelation as all the others. Recovering quickly, and giving her a look that said they'd discuss it in more depth later, he'd continued smoothing over Sebastianne's return by announcing that they were engaged to be married.

The servants exclaimed with surprise, then delight, their affront rapidly dissipating. Even Mrs. Tremble was on the verge of forgiving her—or at least she had been until she found out that Sebastianne would be living in Drake's town house until the wedding.

"It ain't proper," the cook protested. "Ye're marrying Quality now, and ye ought to behave as such. And I don't care if yer brothers and father are staying here too. We've all met the lot of them. They're hardly fit chaperones, even if they're sweet as a picnic hamper full of jam tarts."

"She'll come around," Drake told Sebastianne, as her attention returned to the present. "Mrs. Tremble is just set in her ways, but she'll adjust. You won her over once; you'll do it again."

"I hope so. Surely she must see that Papa and the boys and I cannot remove to a hotel." And the notion of living at Clybourne House, or worse Braebourne, was out of the question, she added silently. She was nervous enough meeting his mother, but living alone with his family . . . no, she would just have to bear a bit of disapproval. Besides, her reputation was ruined already, she rationalized, so what did it matter where she resided for the next month?

He turned her slightly in his arms. "Speaking of accommodations, it has come to my attention that the town house is rather cramped now that we are a family of five. I was looking at some land west of the city. I wondered what you might think of building a house there?"

"A house? For us all?" she said, faintly amazed. "But I just assumed you would want Papa and the boys to take up residence elsewhere, you know, after we are married."

"No, love. You would be lost without them, and curious as it is to say, I'm coming to enjoy my daily discussions with your father. He's fascinating. As for Julien and Luc—"

"Yes?"

"They're wonderful young men, and they'll be excellent uncles when the time arrives for us to start our family."

Something inside her melted, her love growing deeper if that was possible. Leaning forward, she crushed her mouth to his for a thorough and highly satisfying kiss.

"A house in the west sounds grand," she murmured. "We'll make it big, so there is plenty of room."

He nodded, brushing his lips across hers again. "Yes, very big. After all, I am excellent at addition."

She was leaning forward for another kiss when the sound of whispering skirts broke the quiet.

"*Ahem,*" a gentle feminine voice said. "Forgive the intrusion. I can always come back."

Sebastianne tried to whirl away from Drake, but he caught her hand and drew her arm through his. "Not at all," he said, "I was just discussing residences with Sebastianne while we waited."

The dowager smiled. "So I see."

"Mama, allow me to present my future bride, Madame Sebastianne Dumont."

Ava Byron gazed at her out of soft green eyes—eyes that looked amazingly like Drake's. "How do you do, my dear?"

Sebastianne made a short curtsey. "A pleasure, Your Grace. Thank you for inviting me to your home."

The dowager glanced at Drake. "I can see why you chose her. She's lovely."

Stepping closer to Sebastianne, the dowager duchess stretched out a delicate hand. "You are obviously a very special woman to have captured my son's regard. I was afraid for a time that he was going to make good on his pledge to remain a bachelor. His head is so often in the clouds, you know."

"Yes, but he is so brilliant and interesting and so very kind that a little distraction now and then makes no matter," Sebastianne said. "At least not to me."

Warmth blossomed in the dowager's gaze, along with love. "Nor to me." Leaning near, she kissed Sebastianne's cheek and squeezed her hand. "Welcome to the family, my dear. You shall make a fine addition to this irrepressible brood of mine."

Drake sent Sebastianne a quick glance that said *I told you so.*

She began to relax.

"And now for *my* news," the dowager said, suddenly beaming like a giddy schoolgirl. "What would you two think of having a double wedding?"

"*Double* wedding?" Drake said, looking nonplussed. "Who else is getting married?"

"Me! Lord Saxon has asked me to be his wife, and I have said yes."

"Saxon!" Drake goggled. "Viscount Saxon, you mean?"

"The very one. Just because you didn't get on with his daughter doesn't mean I have to pass up the father."

Drake made a choking sound.

"Come," she told them, dragging Sebastianne toward one of the damask-covered sofas. "I shall tell you all about it over tea. Croft should be in any moment with the tray. Now, my dear"—she settled Sebastianne at her side—"you're a widow too, even if you're still quite young. How do you feel about white wedding gowns?"

Glancing across at Drake's shocked, pale face, Sebastianne began to laugh. Suddenly, she knew she was going to love being a Byron.

NEW YORK TIMES BESTSELLING AUTHOR

Tracy Anne Warren

Meet the Byrons of Braebourne!

Tempted by His Kiss
978-0-06-167340-5

When orphaned beauty Meg Amberley is stranded in a snow-
storm, she takes refuge at Lord Cade Byron's estate. To save
her compromised reputation, Cade proposes a pretend engagement and a London season where she can find a husband.

Seduced by His Touch
978-0-06-167341-2

Marry a young woman because he lost a bet? Unreformed rake
Lord Jack Byron would do anything to get out of it. But the
rich merchant who holds the debt insists he marry his on-the-
shelf daughter. Luckily the sensuous Grace Danvers isn't the
closed-in spinster he expected.

At the Duke's Pleasure
978-0-06-167341-9

Lady Claire Marsden has longed for Edward Byron, Duke
of Clybourne, since she was sixteen. But how can he expect
her to agree to an arranged marriage to him when he barely
knows her and doesn't love her?

Wicked Delights of a Bridal Bed
978-0-06-167344-3

To her surprise, Lady Mallory Byron finds herself walking
down the aisle with the Earl of Gresham. The charming rake-
hell is the last man she ever expected to ask for her hand.

At Avon Books, we know your passion for romance—once you finish one of our novels, you find yourself wanting more.

May we tempt you with . . .

- **Excerpts** from our upcoming releases.

- Entertaining **extras**, including authors' personal photo albums and book lists.

- Behind-the-scenes **scoop** on your favorite characters and series.

- **Sweepstakes** for the chance to win free books, romantic getaways, and other fun prizes.

- Writing **tips** from our authors and editors.

- **Blog** with our authors and find out why they love to write romance.

- **Exclusive content** that's not contained within the pages of our novels.

Join us at
www.avonbooks.com